PRESERVED
her reverse genus

ADELL RYAN

Published by Upside Down Red Umbrella
First Edition: April 2020

Cover Art by Upside Down Red Umbrella
Edited by G. Surley

DEDICATION

It's truly hard to believe I'm sitting here writing the final dedication for my first published series. Creating *Her Reverse Genus* has been... a whirlwind. You might recall that in the dedication for Expendable, I wrote a bit about adversity and how the production of my books often directly coincides with the challenges in my life. Today, oddly enough, I sit in isolation amid the COVID-19 pandemic, taking the final steps toward publishing the fifth — and final — book. This series is somewhat-contemporary, somewhat-science fiction with quite a lot of near-future, pre-dystopian speculation. The fact that Thessaly and her guys are in the throes of border closures and overall nationwide chaos is admittedly ironic considering the situation of the world today.

One thing is for certain, being in isolation has a way of making you realize just how much we need people in our lives, even for those of us who proudly wear the label "introvert." Should the act of publishing a book be likened to this government-prescribed isolation, I can only imagine just how lonely and devastating the process would be without human interaction — how important and vital people are to the process.

I can't imagine publishing a book without my incredible "social" circle: my friend and editor, G. Surley sticking with me throughout the entire series; my friend and Personal Assistant, Chaya Snipes, working hours upon hours behind the scenes to help me keep every facet of my business balanced; my Street Team members who go above and beyond the average reader and fan to make sure my name and my books stay visible in an ever-growing market; my Alpha Readers, who will absolutely give me hell if my books are lacking in any way whatsoever; the other authors in the amazing Reverse Harem community who push me to write more, check in on my wellbeing, and answer my many questions; and my husband and children, who are my biggest supporters.

What an even more harrowing situation it would be for Thessaly — and me — if she didn't have a social circle of her own. Not just the guys, their friends, and the UR, but the biggest, most dynamic social circle includes you... the reader. Without you, their troubles and their accomplishments (as well as mine) would be merely words on a page. With you, however, the cast of characters in *Her Reverse Genus* have been given the opportunity to come to life on those pages. Thank you for taking this journey with us. Most importantly, thank you for bringing Thessaly and the guys into your home and your heart over the course of this series.

PROLOGUE

Bauer scooped his arms under Roux's much larger ones and dragged him backward as fast as his much-slighter build could. With one glance at Roux's inanimate face, head slinging side to side from the less-than-delicate handling, Bauer quickly realized he was in a situation much too big for someone of his size and age.

This wasn't part of their plan. Roux should have never gone this far knowing his health was this big of a risk — not without a backup idea, at least. *Now what are we supposed to do?* Bauer internally mused, battling not only the strain of dragging a grown man through tight passages, but the mental dissonance due to the facility's blaring alarm too.

Bauer wasn't going to get an answer though. At least not before the wrong people were involved and it was too late.

Arms burning and sweat covering his forehead despite the chill in the air, he pulled on. He knew he had to get Roux away from the compound's boundary. In the distance, beyond the section they'd been passing, guards could be seen running to all sides of the property. They seldom used the hidden paths as passageways between sections. For that, he was grateful.

While most of them knew about the byways — because the more brutish guards took subjects there for unsanctioned one-on-one time — they were more often than not empty. As to how far back the paths led and how extensive the maze was, no one knew. No one cared — at least, no one who seemed to matter.

Because of that one major mistake in addition to the compound's cheap construction and poorly funded

5

security, Thessaly and her team were able to accomplish the seemingly impossible.

In a roundabout way, those overlooked measures may very well be the Resistance's saving grace and The Program's downfall.

With all the guards so focused on securing the perimeter, no one noticed a young boy and wounded man had literally slipped through the cracks. The gap between fencing sections provided a perfect space to sneak through, but not without a bit of extra push and pull to get past the tight fit.

As soon as they were back in the main part of the compound, Bauer pressed his com-device's button. Even though it wasn't the section Roux and Bauer were assigned to, protocol required he send out a call for assistance under such circumstances.

"Bauer here. This is a request for backup. I've got a man down."

"What's your location?" a guard responded.

Bauer looked around. "Uh... 7C, I think? These damn sections need signs."

"Ten-four. We're sending someone your way now."

Help didn't take long to arrive as most everyone was heading toward the source of the tripped alarm. What came as more of a surprise, though, were the backup guards and Zinna in attendance.

Zinna's eyes narrowed on the two of them, her glare a mix of wariness, concern, and rage rolled into one. Bauer couldn't make sense of her erratic facial expressions, but he did recognize his own dread as it quickly consumed him. When the man at her side began asking questions Bauer didn't know how to answer, he could do nothing more than open and close his mouth. Words and reactions failed him.

A series of thoughts flicked through his mind — the most prevalent being that of his introduction to Thessaly. Using what he learned from her that day, he opened his mind to the guards and Zinna, a skill Thessaly had helped him hone. He soon discovered that one of the people standing in front of him didn't project anything. Zinna, he assumed.

In his short time experiencing these empath connections, he had noticed some people could put up a barricade as protection, even if they were doing it unconsciously.

One of the guards, however, was an open read. Unfortunately, there was nothing more than the average guard's mental response to anything these days — cold detachedness. Nevertheless, he could at least tell this guy was not an ally.

"Take Roux." Zinna's sickening, grating voice finally pierced through Bauer's contemplative haze. "Have him seen to. He needs to be well enough to answer some questions." Zinna's teeth ground together and her chest rose and fell along with the command. "As for the boy, I'll handle him myself."

* * *

ROUX SQUEEZED HIS EYES SHUT TIGHT, the feel of the Underground Resistance's contact lens adding pressure and an uncomfortable dryness. Pain radiated in throbs and pulses from near his shoulder, something he didn't at all miss while blacked out. At this point, he'd be okay with staying that way: gone to the world… never again to deal with Zinna, the wound, nor the men that had been assigned to him.

After a while, he blinked a few times, giving in to the light. Once his vision was clear, the irony of his predicament slammed into him full-force. A dark room, a bright white light spotlighting him, the tink tink of metal on metal: he was going to be interrogated.

Zinna liked to play the role of villain, but Roux had worked with her long enough to know she really had no fucking clue what the hell she was doing most the time. All her efforts were always the result of some cartoonish episode in her mind of how something might go down.

Roux still found himself worried, despite how comical her behavior could be sometimes. He was scared... perhaps for the first time since he signed up under her rule.

Because, for the first time, he didn't have a plan or an alibi.

What's worse... because he *did* wake up, that meant the kid helped him. Which also meant they were likely interrogating him too. Just a fifteen-year-old boy, thrust into a situation he didn't ask to be in and without an alibi, because there hadn't been enough time to come up with something plausible.

If their two stories didn't line up, they would be screwed.

...and if Roux didn't get out of this mess, his daughter might be too.

CHAPTER ONE

"We've got a live feed!" a team member yells.

Several Tech members and I waited a long time for Roux's contact to transmit again. Too long. The feed has been cut since the moment we got Thessaly and Kait out of the facility and he'd passed out. Thanks to Jax passing off his contact to Roux, and Roux passing it off to Bauer, we'd at least had a visual from the boy's point of view.

Audio, on the other hand, was nonexistent. Now that Thessaly was back underground, we no longer had the audio feed from her tooth cap. Ironically enough, when we'd sent out a request to the Underground for someone who is deaf or can, in the least, read mouths, none other than Ruby — the head chef in the UR and my not-so-secret admirer — came to the rescue, much to Thessaly's chagrin... and my amusement.

Given the circumstances, at least something is funny.

"Keep your eyes on their mouths," I whisper to Ruby while focusing on the hazy scene. Despite a functioning feed, the visual still isn't clear. From what we can tell, Roux appears to be in an interrogation room. There's a bright light shining into the contact, but rather than that helping, it has the opposite effect; the spotlight on Roux is so bright, it blurs and hazes everything else around him.

One of our main concerns early on was that they would perform a full body search. Doing so would have called attention to the unusual contact and ruined our only way of receiving information. Thankfully, that was not the case.

Based on his constant blinking and fading vision I'd wager they fixed him up just enough to make him lucid so they could extract some information.

Bauer, on the other hand, got questioned right away — with very little brutality, thank goodness. From what we could tell without being able to read his lips, the boy did good. To our benefit, the interrogator often repeated what Bauer said. We hope this one does the same.

Now… we wait. If the two of them can somehow make their stories weave flawlessly, their chances of getting out of this mess will increase significantly.

"Too dark," Ruby says. "The man is talking… but there's too much shadow."

The screen blackens and brightens a few times in succession as Roux continues to regain consciousness.

"Do your best," I encourage, placing my hand on her shoulder. Ruby tilts her head way back and smiles up at me with a big, toothy grin.

I may or may not have bribed her with a dinner date.

The interrogator doesn't take it easy. It's evident that as soon as Roux is respondent, the man doesn't intend to keep him that way for long.

Round one: The man clenches his fist then swings, clocking Roux hard enough that the feed blackens for an instant and the side of the room comes into a blurry view. Something red and stringy appears on screen as Roux spits out a mix of blood and saliva.

I glance down to make sure Ruby is okay, and her wrinkled hand is over her mouth, her beady dark-blue eyes wide. But then she drops her hand and narrows a glare at the interrogator. "Eh," she says, waving a hand at the screen. "My first husband packed more than that. Your man'll be fine."

All I can do is shake my head and hold back the chuckle. The old adage, "*You should see the other guy*," comes to mind. Ruby is a small, but tough, package; I sure wouldn't have wanted to cross her. Still don't. Even so, whatever the situation, I'm glad she's out of it.

For over an hour the questioning and assault on Roux continues, and for over an hour, Ruby can't make sense of anything being said due to the poor lighting. Best we can do is assume that whatever information Roux is giving them must be working, because as time passes the hits and threats lessen.

When the lights come on, however, the group of us straighten and tense. Standing in the corner of the room is Zinna, her shoulder propped on the wall and spiky-heeled feet crossed. As usual, she is dressed to impress, but apparently she did not want to draw blood by her own hands… hence the henchman.

She steps away from the wall, walks up to Roux, and holds up a photograph. As soon as the image is visible on our screen, I cover Ruby's eyes. She instantly claws at my fingers and swats the back of my hands. But I wait until Zinna removes the image of the two dead men before letting Ruby pry my fingers free.

Warrick and Fen.

We'd been so busy dealing with the aftermath here and trying to take a step forward rather than two back, that other than making sure Thessaly, Jax, and Julian were being taken care of, we hadn't discussed anything else in detail. Plus, Robbie went radio-silent to spend extra time with Kait while the drug she'd been given wore off. So, needless to say, Fen and Warrick's deaths are news to me.

The screen moves side-to-side as Roux shakes his head in response to a question she'd asked. As to whether or not he truly knows anything about their deaths, that is yet to be determined.

"We need the screens back," one of the Tech guys states. "We can no longer afford to keep an eye on one person, when there's an entire community of people in there that need out."

"Yeah," I sigh. They're right. At this point, what we've got going on with Zinna and Roux is more personal than communal; the real problem goes so far beyond what's on the screen right now.

"Wait," Ruby whispers, stepping up closer to the screen. Her mouth starts moving in a silent mimicry of the words Zinna had been saying to Roux. She then turns to me. "Something about permissions? She's questioning him... asking if he had 'something to do with it.'"

"With what?" I ask.

Ruby squints and takes a deep breath. "Permissions?"

I return my attention back to the screen just in time to see Zinna leave and the henchman toss a towel at Roux before following.

12

"Guess he's off the hook." I shrug, continuing to watch as he stands — swaying and stumbling forward from the effort — balls the towel up, and throws it at the wall. "The screens are all yours!" I holler over my shoulder, taking Ruby's hand and scooping it into my elbow to lead her out of the room.

"Such a gentleman," she giggles and pats my hand.

"Yes, and this gentleman has a reunion planned with his girlfriend, so it's time for you to be on your merry way." I smile down at her and pinch her arm.

"Oh, what I would give to be fifty years younger." She sighs.

"Thanks for the help today, Ruby."

"There's something to that mention about permissions."

"I'll look into it, for sure — discuss it with the group and see if it rings a bell." Well, bring it up to Thessaly and Bram for starters; Jax and Julian are... a little out of pocket.

Ruby nods and lets go of my arm. "I can find my way from here. Stop by the dining hall before your... reunion. I have something I want to give you." She winks over her shoulder and shuffles away.

"Okay," I respond, but she's too far away and there are too many passersby for her to hear me. Reaching down, I pull the group pager out of my pocket and send a message requesting Thessaly meet me in the Combat room.

After our brief time together when they'd arrived, she'd insisted I go to the Tech room and check on Roux and Bauer. Being down there for the rest of the night and all the next morning wasn't exactly planned, but what

13

little information we did get was helpful. If for nothing more, it's been reassuring to know our two definite inside-allies are still in the game. Assuming, of course, Roux isn't still playing both sides... which has been questionable ever since he conveniently showed up on the UR's doorstep. Literally.

The guys and I collectively don't care much for him, but Thessaly does for some reason. When it comes to judging character, she hasn't been wrong... yet. Plus, his daughter cooed right into our lives and fucking ruined Bram and me. Jax and Julian are too high-risk with their radiation exposure to meet her yet. When they do, they'll be suckers too. Maybe not as much as me since I'm technically an exact opposite score to her. But they're only off by a fractional point, so the bond is almost as strong.

One thing we can definitely agree on, however, is that none of us are ready to be parents. Thank goodness Becky, Thessaly's old psychologist and current UR leader, made it clear that we won't have to be. She did mention that Roux explicitly insisted we're around the baby as much as possible though.

Also, he'd like us to give her a name because she doesn't have one yet. Which we all found quite... strange.

When we tried asking why she's nameless — and other details like where she's from and who her mother is — Becky just shook her head and said it wasn't her story to tell.

Thessaly explained that based on what she *did* get out of Roux, she learned the mother was no longer living.

I duck my head and enter the Combat room only to discover Thessaly is already there, curled up in the corner, her hands covering her face and shoulders shaking. Upon closer inspection as I approach, I notice blood is dripping down her hands.

In just a couple more strides, I'm at her side, scooping her small frame into my arms and pressing her tear-streaked face against my chest. My breathing jumps a notch, and I squeeze her tight, my fingers unintentionally digging into her arm as I battle the rage and fear that spike within me.

We stay like that — me dying to ask her what's wrong, her sobbing into my chest — until the sniffles begin to subside. Before breaking the silence, I lift one of her hands and turn it over in mine, inspecting her torn up knuckles. Then, I bring her palm to my mouth and place a careful kiss in the center. "Want to talk about it?" I ask.

Her shoulders shrug and she wiggles out of my arms to scoot back so she can look at me. For a moment, I analyze every inch of her face. Her blue eyes are even bluer with the glassy mix of tears and bright red rimming them. But she isn't sad. She's… angry. Her chest rises and falls and nostrils flare. Then comes an eye roll, a deep sigh, and the balling of her hands into fists.

"I'm fucking helpless, Tobias," she says through clenched teeth. "I can't…" Her tears spill again and she wipes them away, leaving bloody streaks across her face.

"I've yet to see you not be able to accomplish something you set your mind to," I respond honestly. "In fact… if you *can't* do something, you tend to find a way to make it so that you *can*."

15

"Case-in-point." I grasp her wrists, raising her hands to reveal the blood I presume came from several hits too many against one of the nearby punching bags. "So, what is it you supposedly *can't* do?" I'd felt the sting in my own knuckles. The bruising ache. But I was too consumed with trying to translate Roux's interrogation to come help.

"A lot," she deadpans.

I know where this is headed. Last thing I heard before going to the Tech room was Becky trying to convince her to become a UR leader.

"I'm just a normal person, Tobias! I'm not cut out to save people and shit. I can't fight." She waves her arms at the Combat room. "I'm not as techie as you. I don't know anything about botany, like Bram. I'm useless." Her voice drops. "I can't *lead*, Tobias."

I'm just a normal person, Tobias! I'm not cut out to save people and shit. She had made that exact comment when her parents were taken and she'd spiraled into a similar self-demeaning mindset. "But here's the thing," I say, "you're not a normal person. You *can* save people. You saved Kait. *You* did that. Also, you can learn to fight, and I'm sure Bram would be happy to teach you more about plants," I add with a wink.

She gives me a watery chuckle at that, but then her expression falls flat again. "I don't want to fight. I don't want to know about plants."

"Okay. What *do* you want?"

That question triggers a sluice of new tears to shed. Through frustrated hiccups, she explains, "I want Jax and Julian to be okay; I want Roux to be reunited with his daughter; I want The Program taken down. But... but

16

right now all those things are so out of reach that I fear they'll never happen."

"Jax and Julian will be up and at 'em soon. Can't keep those two down for long." I try to lighten the mood.

She shakes her head and looks away from me. "They put both of them into a medically induced coma today. Said they weren't healing."

The blood drains from my face, but I put on a soft smile, hoping it reassures her as well as myself. Maybe, through her blurred, teary vision she won't see the effect that news has on me. "I see... so you weren't down here bloodying your hands because of your conversation with Becky then?" Sure, I thought I knew; guess I didn't.

Thessaly shakes her head; she was beating the bags out of fear and anger for Jax and Julian... among everything else.

"It's my fault... you know it is," she states with confidence.

"Thessaly. No one helped you come up with the idea to go in... and no one helped you break the original plan when things changed and an impromptu decision needed to be made. You think and plan intuitively and intellectually." I tap my head for emphasis. "That's why they want you. Because no one can do what you do as well as you do it. Jax and Julian made the knee-jerk decision to enter the property for similar reasons. And in the end, thank god they did, because you wouldn't have gotten out of there in time otherwise."

She wants to believe me. She wants the mental and physical reprieve offered by what I'm saying, but her stubbornness prevents her from doing so. "Have you seen them yet?" I ask.

17

"No… they haven't let anyone back there because of contamination risks." Again her fists clench in her lap, splitting the cuts that are attempting to coagulate.

"Well, let's get you cleaned up, hm? And see about paying them a visit." I raise an eyebrow in suggestion, stand, and hold out my hands. She accepts, and I help her up. On the way out of the Combat room, when I know she's not looking, I slip my group pager out of my pocket, give it a quick glance, then curse the thing for broadcasting to our entire group every time instead of whom we selectively choose to message. Bram needs to be down here when she sees Jax and Julian for the first time, but I don't want her to know I've sent the message request.

CHAPTER TWO

Thessaly

What do I want? Tobias had asked. Gosh, it seems like a different lifetime ago when I was just asking myself that same question before deciding to return to the abandoned — now-turned death — facility.

More than anything? I want my independence back. Not just mine, but *ours*. Bram, Jax, Julian, Tobias… the entire *nation's*. When the DNA Networking Act went into play, our free agency drained away like our blood into the vials The Program collected. Our fate now held precariously in the circuits of a database… to the point of life or death.

Tobias and I sit in the electric-stone hybrid waiting room chairs, and I lean my head against his shoulder, taking in a deep breath and closing my eyes, remembering for a fleeting moment all the ways his woodsy-vanilla scent usually makes me feel good and happy.

"While we wait… why don't we take turns updating each other?" he suggests. "I know you want information on Bauer and Roux." My brief nostalgic reprieve poofs away, and I remove my head from his shoulder. "But you first," he insists, side-eyeing me. "What was Becky's leadership proposition?"

With a lead-filled sigh, I let my head fall back and stare at the stone ceiling for several seconds before speaking — news of Roux and Bauer motivating my every word.

"She explained that all the major leaders in history weren't just getting the popular vote solely because of their money, campaigning, or charisma like most would believe. While those things definitely helped, it was actually their low scores swaying the polls in the end. Their ability to empathically manipulate the nation via broadcasts, rallies, and so forth played a larger role in their election even if they didn't know that's why people liked them so much. She listed a few of the most controversial leaders across the globe over the course of history and how they won over their nation much to the confusion and dismay of a good portion of the population."

Tobias lets out a breathy chuckle. "Huh. Well... that explains things."

"Yeah... makes better sense than the reasons the media spins."

"What was she getting at?" Tobias asks.

"That I should be a leader. Not like a president or anything." I laugh for what feels like the first time in a long while. "But to rally the troops, you know?"

Tobias nods. "Presidents don't fight... and they don't specialize in botany. Everyone has a specialty. A role. You don't need to know how to do *all* the other things when you've got a support system to do it for you. That's really what leadership is about in the end — delegating."

"Yeah, but the good ones won't leave everyone to do all the dirty work, right? They'll get their hands dirty too. Lead by example. To me, that's the way a leader should be. And... well... I just don't feel qualified. Your turn." Ready to be done with my end of the bargain, I toss the ball in his court.

"Fair enough… but this conversation isn't over." He grins. "Both Bauer and Roux are alive." If I weren't already sitting, the news alone would have made me drop.

"That's… good," I say with caution, knowing my growing concern over Roux is a sensitive topic with my guys. I want to ask a billion questions: Did he get proper care? Is he healing? Will he be okay? Did he get caught helping us? But I don't. Instead, I let Tobias take the podium and lead the drip of information as he sees fit.

Tobias's mouth quirks up at the side. "It's okay if you have feelings for him," he states, no doubt reading my facial expressions; they had likely divulged everything I'd just struggled to refrain from verbalizing.

"Now, I wouldn't go as far as to say I have *feelings* for him…"

Tobias's eyebrows rise.

"Roux and I… we're the same in a way," I explain. Tobias lets out a chuckle of disbelief, to which a small smile reveals itself, morphing my otherwise dour expression. "The two of us have tunnel vision when it comes to the people we care about. As a result, we're both self-serving; we'll do stupid — oftentimes dangerous — things to get what we want, with little forethought for the people our behaviors might negatively impact. As long as it's not the very people we hope to protect."

Tobias doesn't push any more though. He just nods and squeezes my knee. "Do you know anything about *permissions* Zinna may have that Roux could've interfered with?" Tobias asks, his eyebrows knitting together.

With the drastic and alarming change in topic, my attention jerks toward him. "Maybe… A while back, when we were trying to access our database files to retrieve information, Robbie did something to her account permissions. Locked her out, I think." Gosh, I hadn't thought of that since it happened. "You had taken that trip to Michigan."

Tobias's head nods slowly, the far-off look in his eyes calculative. "Ah… right… that backdoor trojan Robbie embedded in the fake-score file on that chip we'd given Zinna. She's accessed the system since then though. I mean, I don't have proof that she has… but surely…"

"When I was in the Exam Center, my blood sample details and test results were definitely added to a file of some sort. Becky was looking at a tablet with my information on it when I first saw her." Ever since that horrible experience, bits and bobs of memory had returned little by little, and the entire ordeal is now clear as day in my mind.

Tobias's silver-blue eyes meet mine, and he smiles. "Thanks. Looks like I need to have a sit-down with Robbie and Becky and get to the bottom of this."

A buzz shocks my butt, and I jerk in the chair. "God I hate these things." I laugh breathlessly. The two of us stand and enter the saloon-style doors, watching for the doctor to peek his or her head around the opening.

As expected, Dr. Hughes's salt-and-pepper-colored head pops out. She smiles and waves us inside her assigned cubby.

"What have we here? I thought you hoped to never visit me again," she says, tsking.

With all the silliness stripped out of me due to recent circumstances, I can only manage to offer her a soft smile and shrug.

"That wild temper got the better of her this time," Tobias explains.

Dr. Hughes looks way up at Tobias and puts her hands on her hips. *That* makes me laugh. "These rooms are not cut out for giants like you. Now, if you will," she says, extending her hand toward the chair by the room's opening. Tobias chuckles, turns, and sits down.

She is quick to pat the table, gesturing for me to sit as well. I climb up, demurely placing my hands in my lap. "How are you doing?" she asks, lifting my hands and turning them to inspect the cuts.

"They sting a little is all. Not a big deal."

"No, I imagine not," she responds. "But that's not what I meant." She raises her eyebrows.

I dart a quick glance over her shoulder at Tobias, and he offers me a small, encouraging smile.

As if a special button was pressed, tears begin to well up, blurring my vision until I can no longer make out her appearance. I take a deep, shaky breath, blink away the tears, release a few stray ones, sniffle, and let out the breath slowly. "As best as I can. Can… can I see them?"

Dr. Hughes proceeds to clean and doctor my knuckles, shaking her head. "No… not yet." After a brief pause, she changes the subject from Jax and Julian back to me. "We have a mental health professional on hand if you need someone to talk to," she offers on a quiet breath.

"No. Thank you though. I'm afraid speaking to someone isn't going to solve all the problems."

"You're right. But doing so might help keep you stable in the meantime."

"I appreciate the offer. I really do. I'll tuck the suggestion away for the future should push come to shove."

She smiles up at me and pats my knee. "All mended up. The cuts were smaller than the amount of blood let on. Try not punching anything for a while, though, okay?" she instructs, nodding her head.

"Can't make any promises," I oppose her persuasive nod, shaking my head side-to-side.

She then turns to Tobias, hands returning to her hips. "See to it that she behaves, okay?"

"Sure will." He beams up at her before standing to his full height.

Her eyes follow as he does, and she shakes her head with an amused huff.

JUST BEFORE I LEAVE the Medical area, out of the corner of my vision, a tall blonde catches my attention, and my focus darts her direction. Celeste's red-rimmed eyes mimic my own as our gazes lock.

News of Jax's coma must've made its rounds to the Entertainment crew.

Tobias's arm wraps around my shoulders, and he draws me in close as we leave the Medical wing. "When was the last time you slept?" he asks, yawning.

My attention jerks away from Celeste, and I attempt calculating, but my synapses don't seem to want to fire properly. "I'm not entirely sure, but I think the last time was when—" The words get lodged in my throat upon realizing that I'm pretty sure it was when Jax and Julian had paid me a visit in my pod at the facility.

The reckless jerks.

But also, I'd never in a million years wish for them to not have been there that night. If only they hadn't fallen asleep. If only they'd left right after we'd been intimate together. Maybe then they would have been farther away when the pulse hit.

Tobias and Bram had been in communication with us via the tooth cap just prior to Jax removing it, so Tobias is able to piece the timeline together himself without any further elaborating on my part. He squeezes me harder, placing a soft kiss on the top of my head. "What do you say we go get some sleep?" he mumbles into my hair.

I let out a sigh. "Well... I can try... but I can't promise."

"Fair enough."

For a moment we're silent, but just before approaching the stairs to head up a level, he clears his throat and his free hand swipes through his sandy-blond hair. "Ruby wanted me to stop in before heading up."

"I know I give you a hard time about that old biddy, but I don't mind you talking to her." I laugh lightly. "She hates me though."

"Well, like you, she's a Low, so it's not a surprise that you two naturally butt heads. And it's not like the two of you have been around each other enough to learn to cope with it."

"Imagine if the entire population knew about this... how different things would be," I say.

"Imagine that," he agrees, leading us into the dining hall.

We dodge through the congregating groups of UR residents, walking straight back to the counter. As soon as word got out about the pulse and the extreme turn The Program took, the URs across the nation rallied to create

Search and Rescue teams. These teams serve two purposes: to collect food, medical stuff, and other supplies, and to search for people who are looking for asylum from The Program.

Now, though, it's no longer about running and hiding to avoid blood samples... it's about running and hiding to not be sent to a facility. In light of recent events, we have quickly learned apparently no one is exempt from that. Rumor has it, word of this unjust fate is starting to get around. If people weren't scared before, they are now... and if they *were* scared before, they're getting reckless.

The risk is higher, because the UR is no longer waiting for people to show up on their doorstep from word of mouth or mere happenstance. Now, teams are dispatched to find strays and bring them back here before the National Agglomeration Bureau, border patrols, or guards from The Program get ahold of them.

To be honest, obtaining blood samples wasn't all that difficult in most cases. Probably 90 percent of the national population already had turned in a blood sample at some point in their lives: DNA ancestry tests, blood donations, or even DNA testing for individualized meal and fitness plans.

Anyway, our numbers are growing larger than this underground cave system can handle. If something isn't done on a grander scale, we'll need to expand soon, which will mean a higher chance of visibility.

I'm snapped out of my thoughtful stupor with the wave of a hand across my field of vision. After a few blinks, Auden comes into view.

I tilt my head to the side and press my lips together, narrowing my eyes at him. He chuckles, shoves his hands into his pockets, and leans against the nearby wall. "Here to visit your favorite person?" he asks.

"Yep," Tobias answers, earning an eye roll from me and a laugh from Auden.

"Thessaly has enough on her plate right now, don't you think?" Auden asks Tobias with a smile. "And now she has to compete with two other females vying for your attention?"

"Exactly. What he said!" I tout, but my exasperation is replaced with a hint of laughter. "First Ruby... now the baby. However will I get you to myself again?"

"I'm wor—" Tobias starts but Auden cuts him off.

"You know, I often have plenty of free time on my hands. I'm happy to hang out with you." He shrugs, amusement and a budding confidence twinkling in his eyes.

Now it's Tobias's turn to huff in exasperation. "As I was saying... I'm working on that one-on-one time as we speak. But" — he crosses his arms and narrows a glare at Auden — "if you'd rather just 'hang out,' Auden is most definitely the right guy for that task."

Oh boy... is... Is that jealousy and concern I hear in Tobias's voice? I press my lips together to keep from smiling too broadly.

Auden goes back into his little shell under Tobias's intimidating glare, so I turn and smack Tobias on the arm playfully. He side-eyes me and gives me a wink before returning his narrowed glare on Auden again. The two continue their showdown with Auden shuffling from foot to foot, and Tobias trying hard not to grin.

"Okay, you two. That's enough." I laugh.

Auden lets out the breath he'd been holding, and Tobias claps him on the shoulder with a deep chuckle.

"Ruby said she had something for me?"

"Yeah," Auden says. "Let me go get her."

Apparently she, Auden, and a handful of other members live in a few of the small rooms nestled behind the dining area. I learned this tidbit of information upon our return from the facility when I insisted on making sure Robbie, Kait, and Auden got back to their rooms safely.

As soon as we all had returned, we split up — eager to get as much information as possible and tie up the loose ends of our infiltration while everything was still fresh. Tobias went to the Tech room to keep an eye out for news from Bauer and Roux. Bram had headed to the greenhouses to help aid in some sort of plant-based weapon breakthrough. And I walked with Auden to his room before ambling back to the Medical wing to support Kait, Jax, and Julian while they got poked and prodded.

But they wouldn't let me past the exam rooms. As an added precaution, the Medical team went through great lengths to quarantine the backmost portion of the Medical wing, putting on protective clothing and covering every opening and passage with thick white plastic.

Refusing to sit in the waiting room, I tested my boundaries by sitting on the ground just outside the containment area. With my knees up and head buried between them, I replayed the last couple days in my mind until the crinkle of plastic snapped my attention toward the opening. I'd hoped with all hope Kait, Jax, and Julian were coming out. But I knew that wasn't going to be the case no matter how much hoping I did.

Something had happened, however. The empath bonds I have with Jax and Julian had changed from vibrant and lively to steadily declining until they were radio silent.

Dr. Hughes went out of her way to retrieve the information I so desperately wanted. She'd come out to give me the news, and it was the exact opposite of what I'd wanted to hear: They were getting worse... not better.

The doctors decided to put Jax and Julian in a coma with the hope that their bodies would be more easily able to focus on healing rather than fighting.

The good news? Kait wasn't showing any signs or effects of radiation poisoning. Being in the pod when it happened saved her from that fate. And, thankfully, the road to recovery wouldn't be too difficult.

When I asked how long Jax and Julian would be out, she looked down at me, curved her eyebrows inward, and shook her head. That's where her breadth of information had ended.

With no one to talk to and nowhere else to go, I barged out of there and headed straight to the Combat room.

"Well, hello..." Yet again I am pulled from my inner turmoils in exchange for the here and now. As I blink away the memory, Ruby comes into focus, her beady eyes trained on mine. I dart a sideways glance, making sure Tobias is there and hadn't perhaps moved behind me — which would explain why she's looking in my direction. But he is still at my side, which means she did, indeed, address me directly.

"Oh... um... hello."

Ruby nods and takes something from behind her back, thrusting it forward into my hands. A small box, not too small, but not too big either; it's just big enough where I can't quite close my fingers around it as I accept the package.

I carefully pop open the flaps and peer inside. Several round balls... chocolate covered?... fill the box to the brim.

When I look at her, she clears her throat and darts a glance at Tobias before looking back at me.

"Chocolate. You take a bite, and the taste consumes you. Enough so, that for a moment you forget everything else. Even if only for a moment. Plus... it makes you horny. At least this kind does."

My eyes spring wide, and Tobias and Auden both cough to hide their amusement.

"Wh-why does this kind make you horny?"

"Because it's just that damn good. The only thing you can possibly equate it to is sex. So... naturally, after eating it, things tend to lead there."

I blink repeatedly at her, peer back into the box, and look at her again. "Umm...thank you," I whisper, completely conflicted as to how I'm supposed to feel about this — much less how to respond. When Tobias reaches his hand into the box, I give it a hard swat, my knee-jerk response speaking louder than any words I could have uttered at that moment.

We all laugh, Ruby's cackle the loudest of all.

"Thanks, Ruby." Tobias beams.

"Don't get any ideas," Ruby and I say at the same time. Her eyes twinkle in amusement, and she finishes: "They're for her... not you. Gotta keep you in shape." She pats Tobias's stomach. "Gotta fatten her up. She's too much of a competition with that petite frame of hers," she adds with a wry smirk.

My eyes narrow just as Tobias's hand scoops around my arm and he turns me around, dragging me away. "Thanks again," he says over his shoulder. Auden's laughter slowly quiets as we get farther.

Before we even exit the dining area, I bite into one of the chocolates and close my eyes, trusting Tobias won't let me run into anything.

Ruby wasn't wrong… they're delectable. Before I finish the first one, I pop another piece into my mouth, filling my other cheek.

"You look like a chipmunk." Tobias laughs.

"I feel like one," I mumble over the bite.

"So…" he pauses, gesturing for me to enter the stairway ahead of him. "Are they making you horny?"

CHAPTER THREE

"**S**he's something else," I say as the two of us plop onto my bed. I look around, taking in everything. The stone room is just as it was when we left: my Jax-made clothesline spanning from one end of the room to the other, the stone bed with mattress on top, and of course, the nook leading into my personal, somewhat primitive bathroom.

"She definitely is… something else," Tobias agrees. "So" — he lies back, arms beneath his head, his shirt lifting with the motion, showcasing the happy trail leading beneath his jeans — "you never answered my question."

I pause chewing to contemplate what he's talking about. Neither of us had spoken much en route to the room. "Possibly because I've been too busy stuffing these delicious balls in my mouth."

Tobias chuckles, and the movement of his abdomen causes my eyes to drift back to that happy trail. Removing my hand from the confines of the dessert box, I run a finger along the line. The skin-on-skin contact serves to remind me exactly what question he's referring to.

"Oh, right. Hmm… lets see…" I slip my fingers beneath his waistband. "All signs point to yes." Doesn't take long for me to reach my destination and wrap my fingers around him. Tobias groans. "Though I really don't think it has anything to do with the chocolate," I include, sliding up and back down, working him closer to his full size.

The jeans are too restrictive to get much more accomplished, so I remove my hand. Before my fingers break the barrier, however, Tobias has his thick fingers wrapped around my wrist, pausing the motion and pushing my hand back into his jeans. Once my fingertips graze his shaft, he lets go, freeing his hand so he can unbutton and unzip his pants.

With his jeans now situated just below his butt, his otherwise commando state is now obvious. Surprising? Nah. Not with Tobias.

Having still been preoccupied with the box of chocolates, it isn't until his shaft jerks beneath my touch that I finally ditch the chocolate and bring my full attention to Tobias.

During the moment of pause while adjusting, I'd apparently stopped using my other hand, and Tobias's hand wraps around mine again, helping to guide it in a way he wants.

Other than him forcing my hand to cup him — back before he'd left to take care of stuff with Amber — this is the first time I've touched him below the belt. Last time we'd been together intimately… every time we've been together intimately, in fact… there had always been specific parameters. As seems to be a pattern for him, I'd guess that's exactly why he suggested we come up here: So he could toss aside those parameters and finally connect with me in the way we'd been waiting far too long to do.

What's surprising, though, is that he's letting me initiate things. Then again… I'd tried to stop briefly, but he now squeezes and strokes himself, using my hand to do so — demonstrating he's still very much in control.

Surprise, surprise.

33

"I believe you'd made me a promise before I left…" I let the words trail, voice low, as I focus my attention on the way his hand holds mine and guides me effortlessly.

"Mmm… is that so?" he says over another yummy groan.

"Yes. If my mind serves me correctly, my hand's not supposed to be here right now. Only yours is…"

His hand squeezes mine, in turn causing mine to squeeze around his shaft. "But… I like your hand there," he grunts as I push all the way down to the base, tightening my finger and thumb around him like a ring. "Right… ah… damn…" The continued up and down motion seems to do something to his ability to speak.

"What ever happened to you having control over this thing?" I say with a lot of snark.

"You happened," he sighs. "But also" — Tobias pulls my hand away — "I do have control… see?" He flops my hand around, drawing out a laugh from deep in my belly.

Laughing feels great. Being here, with him, does too. In a quick motion, Tobias pulls me on top of him, his shaft standing at attention against the base of my tailbone, and he cups my face bringing my mouth down to his. As soon as our lips are interlocked, his fingers wrap around the back of my neck with one hand, and the other slips into the back of my pants.

Our tongues snake out synchronously, eager to toy and taste. His hand lowers farther until a finger can dip inside me. "Thessaly," he breathes against my mouth.

"Mmm," I moan in response.

"I don't want to wait any more." There's a rare vulnerability in his tone. A desperation. And it goes far beyond his need to simply get off. That's what he does…

wait. Tobias is all about that approval... that right moment. In all his dominance, in his own way he's both asking and telling — demanding — me that *right now* is our time.

"I don't either," I respond. Our kiss becomes desperate then, as if it's the one thing we've been waiting for since this entire ordeal began.

Every motion becomes desperate. One moment we're kissing, the next he's removing my shirt and my pants, and I'm ready to do the same to him. There's nothing smooth and sweet about it. We've waited this long, and we can't wait any longer.

Tobias grabs me around the waist and sits us up before I finish pinching the hem of his shirt to lift it off. When I try to move away so we can get his jeans, he wraps his arms around me again pressing our bodies together as he falls backward once more. "You stay," he breathes against my mouth. I nod slowly, dragging my lips over his as I do. He lets go and begins the difficult, and amusing, task of wiggling his jeans the rest of the way down while I'm still on top of him. When I intentionally dip my tongue between his lips to test his ability to multitask, he groans, and his efforts to remove the clothing pause for a moment, which in turn earns a chuckle from me. He then nibbles on my bottom lip and says, "Now, quit that... I'm trying to do something important here."

Our eyes lock and I do it again anyway, the sparkle of amusement no doubt clearly visible in my gaze. His eyebrows rise and the movement of his hands pauses as my kisses prove to distract him.

"You're not very good at this game," he says breathlessly, wiggling his butt side-to-side and scooting backward on the bed, using it as friction to help move the jeans down more.

"Didn't know we were playing a game. But now that I do, you better watch out because I'm quite competitive." My eyes drop to his mouth and back up to his eyes, and with a grin, I bite his lower lip. When he snakes his tongue out, I seize the opportunity to suck it into my mouth. With as much speed as someone of his size is capable of, he butterfly-kicks his legs in rapid succession until the jeans fall with a quiet *thoomp* onto the stone ground.

Legs now fully accessible, Tobias brings his hands up to the dip of my waist and he tosses me sideways with perfect control to swap our positions. His large build simultaneously blocks what little light the wall sconces provide.

Or at least I thought he was swapping our positions, until he stands, hovers over me, grabs my hips, and flips me onto my stomach. My chest heaves from the unexpected motion. Assuming he wants me on my hands and knees, I move to prop myself up, but his large hand comes to the middle of my back, and he presses me into the mattress. The air restricts around me and warms as his body comes closer to mine. The softness of his messy hair tickles my cheek as his mouth comes to my ear and his tongue draws a line around its shape. Goosebumps cover me from head to toe, and my entire body tenses in the best way.

"Stay, and don't move," he whispers just before the heat of his body leaves. The sound of retreating footsteps fills the quiet space followed by the echo of him rummaging through a bag. He's back quickly, and something lands with a quiet plop beside my head. In the

36

flicker of dim candlelight, the little spiky ball rolls beside my hand.

I pick it up, still trying to obey his order not to move other than to grasp the ball. I may have been teasing him moments ago, but the tone of his voice changed with his last demand, and I'm not yet willing to challenge something I know very little about.

A quiet crinkle echoes through the room followed by the tearing of something. My eyes widen, and I suddenly struggle not to look over my shoulder at what could possibly be making that noise.

The sound of it landing on the floor tells me the unidentified item was discarded. When I remember he never said I couldn't speak, I address him with a tremble of apprehension: "Talk to me."

Instead of talking, the bed depresses on either side of my body, and I squeeze that little spiky ball with all my might. Tobias's deep and low chuckle encases me as his hands move to either side of my head, bringing his head closer to mine.

"What was that noise?" I whisper.

"A condom," he whispers back, amusement in his tone.

Oh, right. Tobias doesn't have a contraceptive implant like the others do. "Oh," I whisper the same thought aloud. "Right…" I actually have never once slept with a guy who had to use a condom.

"Remember the rules?" he asks, moving my hair to the side and dragging his lips along the line of my neck to my shoulder.

"Yes," I whisper, rolling the ball between my fingers before closing it inside my palm. Then my mind repeats the rules: *Bunny fingers if I need something. Let go of the ball if I need him to stop.*

"Good." The heat of his body leaves mine again, and something cool and wide skims over my butt. My innate reaction is to look over my shoulder, but Tobias anticipates my curiosity, and his fingers slide into my hair near my ear, both caressing me and keeping my head still with a silent command.

The cool item meets my skin again, but this time he drags it up over the curve of my cheeks to my lower back and higher before bringing it back down and over my butt again.

The anticipation of what might come next, in addition to the gentle caress of the object, causes a pang of longing and need to rush through my body. With every touch, every motion, the mystery helps the gathering momentum morph into an unimaginable, torturous level of desire.

Tobias balances the toy, leaving it to rest while his hands come to each side of my head again. "I like it when you don't fight me," he confides. "That trust…" He hums in my ear. "Damn."

My eyes close as I revel in the feel of each word hitting my neck, my ear, and the fine hairs at the base of my head.

"It's a paddle." Tobias's voice changes from that liquid heat to his more informative tone — still low, still filled with sex… just more serious. "Can I use it on you?" he asks, drawing a finger down my spine. The weight of the paddle seems to triple at the comment, even though he's not wielding it.

I nod.

"Use your words," he instructs.

"Yes."

"Yes, what?"

I take in a shaky breath. "Yes, you can use the paddle on me."

His fingers trail back up to my neck, only to curve around the length of my hair and gather it into a low ponytail. With the hair in his grip, he pulls my head farther to the side, and takes my mouth against his, devouring me, tasting me with every swoop of his tongue.

When he releases the kiss, his lips peck my chin, down my throat, and over my shoulder before leaving me so he can return to the paddle.

His quiet and reassuring voice, the feel of his hand in my hair, and his gentle kisses soothed and calmed me, but with his absence, and the weight of the paddle being lifted off me, the situation returns with clarity, and my body naturally braces for impact. My eyes squeeze shut tight. My hands fist. Every muscle in my body tightens.

Using what must be the edge of the paddle, he places it gently between my shoulder blades and draws a long line down to the crease of my cheeks. "Relax your body, otherwise it'll hurt… in the way we *don't* want," he explains. "I won't start out hard. Promise. You'll like it."

With a few deep breaths, I do as he instructs, loosening each part of my body one muscle at a time.

Once he can tell I'm more relaxed — even if begrudgingly so — he rests the paddle against my butt again. A precursory warning. The paddle lifts and he lets it fall lightly, just enough to serve as an example — nothing even remotely painful. Again the unknowing and anticipation is too much. Every nerve vibrates with that simple, trial effort.

The paddle leaves my skin again, and this time it comes down harder. Tobias hits with just enough force to make it sting — and redden, no doubt. The sting, however, travels between my legs, and, in time with the pulses of pain from the swat, my insides pulse too.

Tobias chuckles and groans concurrently. "Well, that was different," he says.

"Wh—" I start to ask, but he hushes me.

"Never in my many years of pain play have I spanked someone and felt it on my own body."

Oh, that's right. A small smile curves up on my lips. I want to say something snarky, but I don't.

"I see you smiling over there," he calls me out. "Don't think for a second I'm afraid to feel a little pain myself." He then smacks my ass much harder and without warning. A squeak leaves my mouth, and I nearly drop the ball just out of pure surprise. Based on the lingering sting this time, I can tell he most certainly left a mark. My ass throbs just as surely as between my thighs.

Oh my god does it feel good.

Closing my eyes, I take in all the lingering sensations: The warm tingling. The aching throb between my legs. And, now, the coolness of his hand as he uses it, rather than the paddle, to rub lightly over my undoubtedly pink skin.

The light touch is soon replaced with the cupping of his palm as he squeezes playfully.

Waiting for the next thing to happen is agony. Before, my body was tense with an uncertain anticipation, but now it hums in pleasant anticipation… *everywhere.*

His slow remedying of the prior hit takes too long, and I find myself lifting against his palm for more. More something. More anything. His hand moves up to the dip of my lower back and higher to between my shoulder blades, and with it follows his mouth, kissing every inch along the line of my spine until he's at my ear and flicking my earlobe with his tongue.

"On a scale from one to ten, how much did you like that?" he asks. His tone and the heat emanating from him is so perfectly practiced that rather than pulling me out of this new daze I seem to be slipping into, it drags me in deeper.

"Seven." As punishment for stopping I decide to give him a solid seven.

"Seven?" He chuckles. "Okay... on a scale of one to ten, *ass*-uming that was a... three... with ten being the hardest I'm willing to hit, how hard should I hit next time?"

A three?! My eyes spring wide. *That... that was only a three?* Of course, I keep these thoughts all inside my head.

"Cat got your tongue?" Tobias asks, wrapping his hand beneath my hair to cup my neck.

"Five," I say, really hoping I don't regret that choice.

Tobias groans against my neck and nibbles the sensitive skin there. "Five it is."

First, he uses the paddle to warm up my skin, rubbing me with the smoothed wood before adding his fingers into the mix, tracing under the curve of each cheek before slipping between my thighs and inserting two. The in and out slide is slow and explorative, to match the slow and explorative movement of the paddle. Tobias strums me just enough to make me feel as though I'll burst prematurely if he doesn't stop soon.

And... he doesn't. Instead, he removes his fingers just as my walls tighten around him. Before I can come out of my lust-filled haze, the crack of the paddle echoes through the room.

In quick succession, he reinserts his fingers with one hand, while the other massages the sting. With heavy breaths my body trembles and jerks as I roll into an unexpected orgasm. Writhing and lifting my hips against the thrust of his fingers, I squeal into the pillow beneath my head. And when the orgasm ebbs, my lower half collapses back onto the bed, and he extracts his fingers while replacing the other hand, the one massaging, with the paddle. Once more warning and warming me all in one.

When the paddle leaves my skin, my fingers leave the ball. I dare a glance over my shoulder to find that Tobias had frozen mid-swing. He puts the paddle down and his hands return to my aching cheeks. "Talk to me," he says.

But I don't want to… not really. It… it just felt so good. But, I don't know if I can do it again so soon. Also, I can't move… my body, nor my mouth.

Tobias is flush against me in an instant. "You good?" he asks, brushing the hair out of my eyes. I give him a small nod. "Good," he reassures. "Can you tell me what made you drop the ball?"

I take in a deep breath and let it out, blowing away the remaining wisps of hair. "I need a break," I manage to mumble. "That… felt good. Too good almost. I think my body is in shock."

Tobias chuckles and changes his positioning, choosing to lie beside me instead. Knowing nothing's wrong, he props up on an elbow, cradling his head in his hand. He bites down on his bottom lip, and when he releases it a huge grin lights up his face.

Somewhat embarrassed he'd made me come so fast, I bury my head into the pillow, hiding the blush that spreads across my face.

"By the way, that shit hurt; I might need to reconsider my pain level categorizing," he admits.

That makes me chuckle, and I unbury my head to look at him. "Novice," I say, propping up on both my elbows and stretching my back a bit.

Tobias clasps his hand over his heart. "Oooh, ouch." He winks at me. My smile broadens.

Then his voice lowers, and he says through another grin, "I almost shot a load. Making you come like that? That was fucking hot."

"Yes… it was." Our eyes lock and he presses our foreheads together, lifting my chin with his finger and bringing my mouth to his.

The kiss is slow and sensual. I may have been the only one who finished just then, but there's a mutual post-intimate buzz humming between us. Our eyes fall closed, and we lose ourselves in the moment, alternating between small, sweet kisses and deep passionate ones. Tobias breaks first; his eyes open and lock with mine. Then his thumb traces over my chin and jawline, and his silver-blue eyes drop and follow the movement before they rise again and pierce mine.

"I love you," he whispers, dragging his thumb along my bottom lip.

I melt under his touch and words, nudging my cheek into his palm and closing my eyes. The tears I'd spent all day trying to fight off return. Anger, fear, and trepidation mix with the euphoric aftershock from my orgasm and the swelling of my heart, resulting in a display of emotions which showcase just how much it means to me that fate would bestow such a gift of love amidst the many hardships. A tear drips down my cheek, and I open my eyes as Tobias collects the tear with his thumb.

"I love you too."

He gives me a soft smile before consuming my mouth again with another kiss.

Heat fills me from head to toe once more, and that telltale ache returns to my center, knotting in a bunch before pulling tight, threatening to snap.

An unintentional, unexpected moan hums into the kiss, and Tobias dips in farther just to see what other noises he can pull from me.

Everything from there unravels slowly and delicately. He breaks away from the kiss, leaving me breathless. My shaky arms give way, and I lay my head back onto the pillow. Tobias takes the ball away from my hand, and tosses it toward our pile of clothing.

Then he pushes up and straddles me again. Just when I think he's likely reaching for the paddle, the weight of his body is flush against me, stomach pressed against my back. Now pinning me in place, his lips drag over my forehead, and down my jaw and neck before caressing my shoulder.

With my palms still flat against the mattress on either side of my head, Tobias's hands slide over the back of mine. He weaves our fingers together, closing his until they're curved into my palm and our hands are pressed deep into the mattress.

In this flat position, Tobias enters me, his length and girth filling and stretching me from behind. The weight of his body presses me into the mattress. When his mouth meets my ear and he thrusts deeper inside me, a gravelly grunt emanates from his chest and mingles with the increasing pants and moans coming from me. Every nerve inside me ignites.

Both of us now fully primed from the foreplay just a bit ago, it doesn't take long to find a rhythm. Tobias starts slow, teasing me with only a portion of what he has to offer, pulling out to the tip and reentering, until my body is angry with the need for him to penetrate me deeper, harder, faster. My hips lift the next time he moves inside, giving him better access. This time, he doesn't deny my body what it's so evidently begging for. Tobias's teeth graze my shoulder, his hands squeeze mine harder, and he fills me completely. The position stroking and teasing places inside me that have not yet been touched.

Every thrust grazes that special, erogenous spot inside me; each caress builds on the other until I reach the peak of pleasure and my body explodes. Lost to everything around me, even the bed seems to disappear. All I feel is the weight of Tobias's body, our combined heat, and a spiraling, all-consuming exhilaration.

CHAPTER FOUR

Tobias thrusts a few more times, pausing to encase himself as tightly and thoroughly as possible. He lets go of my hands and massages my shoulders as he pushes off me before disappearing for a short time.

Meanwhile, I can't move — my body is still lost in that euphoric haze and completely worn and used in the best way. In a way, I feel like if I don't orgasm again for another few months, I'll be just fine.

The longer I lie here, however, the weepier I get… which is unusual. There's no reason for tears, yet an odd moroseness overcomes me and I sniffle, trying to stop the tears that trickle down my cheeks.

Tobias is soon back at my side. Still naked, he lies beside me, propping up on an elbow as he had before. His hand runs in soothing motions up and down my back, his eyes following and thoughtful, but he remains quiet for a time. Hair had fallen into my face again, but I hadn't yet garnered the energy to move it. Dragging his fingers across my forehead, Tobias gently tucks the hair behind my ear.

Without a word, he lifts a corner of the sheet that's bunched between us and dries any lingering wetness from my face.

A few moments of silence pass before he speaks. "You know, it breaks my heart when you cry. I'd do anything to make sure it never happens — to never see you sad or upset." I want to apologize, since I really feel like I don't have a reason to cry, but he continues before I work up the energy to do so. "But I might have to reconsider, if crying is how you experience sub-drop." My eyebrows rise, and I blink up at him. "Sub-drop... that's when the experience puts you into something called subspace and your body gets a rush of higher than normal amounts of endorphins and dopamine, then they leave your system, and you drop."

I finally find my words. "So, the crying is normal?"

"For some, yes."

"Oh, good." I chuckle lightly. "Because I couldn't put a label on the reason I was crying this time. It just started happening."

Tobias smiles and slips his fingers under my hair to rest his cool hand on the back of my neck. "Is there anything I can do for you right now? Anything to help?"

This right here, just the two of us lying side-by-side and talking is nice. "No... just... maybe stay with me for a while?"

"You got it. I wasn't planning on leaving anyway." Tobias yawns and groans. "Not sure I could get out of this bed even if you pushed me off. Then again, if you did, I probably couldn't get off the floor either."

"Not sure I'd be able to push you at all right now, anyway; you're safe."

All the things I should be thinking about, planning, and doing choose the present moment to begin wiggling their way into the forefront of my mind, and I sigh.

Too soon, brain. Too soon.

Unfortunately, they don't relent. I'd gone too long without talking since we'd gotten back. If I don't form some of these thoughts into words, I fear the sleep my body so insistently demands won't come.

For the first time since we'd finished, I attempt movement. "You up for talking?" I ask as I grunt and roll myself over to plop onto my back. That's when I realize

47

that, unlike with my other partners, I don't have anything messy to take care of. Impressed, I turn the corner of my lips down and nod approvingly with a "Huh."

"Always," Tobias responds to my question. "What was that face all about though?" He laughs, scooting over a bit and stretching before grabbing my farthest wrist and pulling me to him.

I adjust my head to rest on one side of his chest, and he places my palm on the other before dragging his fingers along my forearm. "I must admit, I'm pretty thrilled that I don't need to go clean up right now." I glance down.

"Thrilled, hmm? Do people even use that word still?"

Hearing the word 'thrilled' in his deep, manly tone sounds ridiculous, and I burst into giggles. "Maybe not men. Definitely not you. You should refrain from saying that word ever again."

"Note taken." Tobias kisses the top of my head, a smile in his voice.

"Ugh." I let out a heavy sigh. "Tobias... I'm exhausted."

"Girl... same," he agrees.

"Oh goodness... yeah... don't say that either."

He laughs and wraps his arms around me, squeezing tight.

"I won't be able to fall asleep though," I say low. "Not until I talk through some stuff." I bite on the inside of my lip, worried he'd rather skip the talking part and just fall asleep.

"What's on your mind?" he asks instead of denying me.

"Everything." I breathe in deep and let it out slowly, watching in amusement as Tobias's nipple puckers and goosebumps cover his chest. His body does one of those sporadic shivers, and I can't help but smile.

"Well, where do you want to start?"

I mull it over for a bit and decide to try my chances on tapping into his wealth of knowledge. "Do you know anything about radiation poisoning and what possible consequences we're looking at with Jax and Julian?" I try to keep my voice even as I ask, but my current precarious emotions kick in, and my voice cracks at the end of the inquiry.

"I know the basics but nothing specific to their case," he answers. "Once they allow me to access their lab results, I might be able to tell you more. Right now, though, I'm in the dark too."

"What *can* you tell me?"

"Well... may I plead the fifth? I can give you a list of signs and symptoms, but they'll only serve to worry you more. And, just because I give you the list, doesn't mean Jax and Julian will have those problems." In response, I nod against his chest, trusting his judgement call. "This is one of those situations, though, where our scores come into play. Remember when I explained to you after we'd broken into that lab that your low score makes you less susceptible to things that people with higher scores are *more* susceptible to?"

"Yeah... I do." I remember feeling like it was absurd as well. Not the science behind it, just that my odds of getting sick were so significantly reduced — the whole "perfect" aspect. Subjective, I continue choosing to believe... but the label itself is still absurd in my opinion.

"I'm afraid their less-than-desirable scores are what ultimately landed them in this situation. They're at a greater risk for everything 'contagious.' Non-contagious things, too, really."

"No... Zinna is 'what ultimately landed them in this situation,'" I grind out.

Tobias's body softens beneath me, and his fingers draw comforting patterns on my hip. "You're right. But what I'm trying to explain is that say, for example, you had switched places with one of them. As odd as it seems, based on what we've seen of your rapid healing rate, the effects would have been minimal. Or, in the least, you would have healed faster and suffered less from chronic issues in the long run. Any closer to the pulse, though, no one can survive that... not even you."

"So, even if — *when* — Jax and Julian recover from this, they're looking at a lifetime of complications?"

Tobias is quiet for longer than I like as he contemplates either the answer, or how to present it. Still, his fingers continue their discovery of my skin, lessening the blow of the conversation, if only a little.

"Probably," is the response he chooses. "But everything is just speculation right now. Just like you, our numbers are extreme. Just like you, we don't fully know the consequences. Just like you, we take it one day at a time and do the best that we can with what knowledge we gain pertaining to our scores."

Even though Tobias isn't providing cut-and-dry answers, his logic and willingness to hash it out is comforting. It's better than what I had — the rampant, silent-suffering overreaction of my mind.

"Next." He pokes me in the side, trying to lift my spirits. It works for a heartbeat, but the topics that still need covering are anything but enjoyable.

"Roux and Bauer? We only spoke briefly about them. Are they okay, really?" Tobias had offered up information — enough to tell me they were both alive — but not much more beyond that.

"They each have a contact in, otherwise we would have no idea."

"Both? How'd Bauer get one?"

Tobias goes on to explain that when Roux checked on Jax and Julian at my behest, Jax had given him one to pass on to Bauer.

"Okay… Well, that's good."

"It is. No audio, though, so we're depending solely on visual. Ruby can read lips; she helped us as best as she could. From what we were able to decipher, Bauer is completely in the clear. His interrogation was simple. Roux, on the other hand… Zinna is officially uncertain about his loyalty. His interrogation was… a bit more brutal." I appreciate Tobias's honesty, but the news makes my heartbeat skip and stutter. "They must've doctored him beforehand… and loaded him up with drugs enough to make him able to answer their questions. By the end of the questioning, he was stumbling a bit but otherwise walking around, so for now he's good," he explains.

"But he has an infection…"

"It's evident Zinna's not ready to get rid of him. My guess is he'll be well taken care of in the meantime if for no other reason than to make sure he's fit to continue doing her bidding."

As much as I hate that vile woman, I believe Tobias is right in his assessment. "When can he come back to the UR, though? To do *our* bidding? To be with his daughter?" My voice is no longer calm and collected as my worry and uncertainty rise to the surface.

This time, not only does Tobias remain quiet, but his warm hand leaves its home on my hip and rises to swoop through his hair before an airy breath flutters through the hair at the top of my head.

"Tobias..."

"Thessaly..." Again he pauses, but for a shorter duration this time. "Are you really going to make me be the one to say it to you?"

Yes, yes I am... because I'm in a heavy case of denial, and for it to be true it needs to come from someone logical who has a far better head on their shoulders than I do at the present time.

"Okay... fine," he concedes. "It was never Roux's intention to come back. Not while his daughter is at risk."

Here come the tears again. God I'm so weepy. Why, I'm not entirely sure, because yeah... I knew he wasn't coming back. We need him there on the inside. He needs their medical services. His daughter needs the umbrella protection of the UR. Roux isn't stupid, that's for certain.

"How's she doing?" I ask.

"The baby?"

"Yeah."

Tobias shrugs, jostling my head. "Last I saw her was just before I went into the Tech room. She's staying with Becky... indefinitely."

"So... Roux and Becky?"

"Oh... umm... definitely not." Tobias laughs. "If you and Roux are selfish, add her to the list too. Having another extreme Low in her grip? She's in psych bliss. That, and she was never able to have children herself, so she's *thrilled* to take on the role of parent. She said it gives her something to do down here now that her hands are tied."

"Her hands are tied?" I laugh at his jesting use of the word *thrilled*. "So… she's disassociated herself from Zinna's team?"

"Yes, she had an easy out after the huge media debacle; she stole the opportunity and ran with it. Speaking of Becky… I told you earlier our conversation wasn't over about what the two of you discussed."

Yeah, I keep strategically avoiding that particular topic at all costs — masking it with other questions and problems. But in all actuality, that's the main topic keeping me wide awake.

I turn my head, propping my chin on his chest to look up into his blue eyes. "She wants me 'heavily involved' so to speak, leading the Central UR when the time comes to step out of hiding and take a stand." Tobias tucks his chin to look down at me. "Me… a twenty-two-year-old college student who doesn't even know what she wants to be when she grows up… but *does* know she doesn't want to lead a resistance."

Tobias kisses my forehead, lingering. "When you say she wants you 'heavily involved,' what do you picture? What scenario comes to mind?" he asks, his lips moving against my forehead.

"A sword-wielding badass, chopping heads, and kicking people in the gonads — existent or not."

"Really?" Tobias squeaks, then coughs to clear his throat.

"Are you laughing at me?"

"No…" Under my chin, his chest rumbles, but then he takes in a steadying breath. "You're not a fighter, Thessaly."

"Preaching to the choir, Tobias." I rest my cheek against his chest again. "Why the combat lessons then?"

"They're weeding people out. We'll need fighters... as many as we can get which is one of the many reasons why the Search and Rescue teams have been dispatched. But we'll need more than fighters. The UR needs leaders in other capacities too. Becky wants you tapping into your empath abilities to lead."

"I... I don't even know what that means though. She tried to explain her ideas, but my mind wasn't able to wrap around them yet. Perhaps not enough time has passed since the whole situation at the facility, and it was just too much for my mind to work through."

"That's understandable. But... maybe give it another chance, after you've gotten some sleep? Becky will be around. We all will. We'll come up with a plan together."

"You're right. I will..." My agreement is genuine, but my main concern is that the five of us will be separated because of our different talents.

Leader or not, justifiable reason or not, I don't want us to be separated again. Tobias's arms wrap around me once more, and he gives me a final squeeze before our conversation comes to a natural end, replaced by the beckoning of sleep.

CHAPTER FIVE

A recurring buzz pulls me out of heavy sleep. Neither Tobias nor I had moved — still naked and in each other's arms, having been too tired to adjust or separate. Tobias stirs, awakened by the same buzz. Once my brain catches up to my still-bleary eyes, I recognize the sound: our pagers.

Both of us jump into action at the same time, crawling to the bottom edge of the bed and reaching for the discarded devices buried in our pile of clothing.

The same message flashes across both screens: an emergency page from Tech.

Getting out of bed, I collect my clothes and pagers and rush to the bathroom to clean up a bit and get dressed. By the time I'm done and return to the room, Tobias is finished as well, and we head out.

Bram's fast asleep on his bed. The other one is empty — a painful reminder of recent events. I step to Bram's bedside, find his UR pager and check it, shooting Tobias a quick shake of my head before putting the pager back down.

They hadn't paged him. Likely because he'd been working nonstop in the greenhouses lately.

Not wanting to bother him, I tiptoe away. Tobias weaves our fingers together, and we leave for the Tech room.

With no windows and no knowledge of how long we'd been sleeping, I have no idea what time of day it is. Based on the amount of traffic in the intersections, I'd guess it must be past everyone else's bedtimes.

When we enter the Tech room, however, it's bustling with activity. Half of the Tech team is focused on the portion of the large wall display that spans one side of the room, while the rest of them scrutinize an interactive map on the remaining section. Robbie stands among those looking at the map, and I step beside him, letting go of Tobias's hand in exchange for Robbie's shoulder. After startling, Robbie turns to see who approached.

He looks horrible. Unlike Tobias and me, it's evident he hasn't slept a wink since we got back. There are deep, dark bags under his eyes, and his hands tremble slightly at his sides.

I run my palm down his arm before letting it drop and backing away. Tobias takes my place, looking down at me and giving me a soft smile first.

Reaching into my pocket and taking out my group pager, I separate myself from everyone for a heartbeat to send Auden a message requesting food. After his aid in our escape, he'd officially earned himself a connection to our group pagers and his own number.

Once that's taken care of, I return to the group and squeeze between Robbie and Tobias, feeling a need to be next to both of them. Tobias for his calming presence... Robbie because I'm afraid he's going to pass out.

"What are we looking at?" I ask the boss man.

Robbie peers sideways down at me before lifting his gaze back up to the screen. His jaw clenches and nostrils flare before he speaks. "Another pulse just showed up on our system."

Eyes wide, I push through the group of Tech people to get a better angle. Scanning the map, I find where a red dot pulses and radiates outward... in Northwest Florida.

Zinna had set another "clean-up" in the Central Region. My mind whirls with thoughts of Bauer and Roux... and of course the rest of the subjects — people — at the facility.

My finger grazes the red dot lightly. How many have we lost, all for the sake of science? I step back, taking in the entire image of the nation. "Is this only happening in Florida? There's a facility-type setup in each region, right?" I don't want the answer to be what I can only assume it is, but with as thorough as The Program seems to be, I can't imagine they'd only be doing this in one state.

Robbie answers. "Our tech is slightly more advanced than that of the other URs. As soon as the first pulse hit, though, the team was on it. They contacted the other UR's Tech leaders and started getting them set up. Right now, we're working on integrating our mapping systems, so we can all collectively see the pulses across the board. The other URs are reporting residual radiation in various areas across the United States but no actual pulses yet."

"Meaning... pulses have already hit, and they're only picking up the remnants?"

"That's what we're figuring, yes."

"Where?"

"In every region except Eastern so far."

"Do we know how many times they've pulsed the areas?"

"No."

With one last glance over the map, I rejoin Robbie and Tobias. My gaze travels to the other half of the room where the Tech team works frantically to finalize integrating the UR systems.

When my focus moves back to the map, my heart drops hard, my body finally reacting to the news. I place my hand over my stomach reflexively. "Everything okay?" Tobias asks.

"Yeah." I give him my best, reassuring smile.

Movement near the hidden entrance draws my attention, and Tobias's gaze tracks my line of sight. Auden enters, a large brown paper bag in hand. Tobias darts a glance at me and back at Auden before yanking his pager out of his pocket and tapping it frantically. Only then does it vibrate and deliver the page.

I shrug and turn to Robbie, placing my hand on his arm. Once again, not expecting my touch, he jerks before looking down at me. "Auden brought us food. I think the two of us could really benefit from some."

Robbie shakes his head and swallows hard. "Can't stomach anything right now."

"Give it a shot? I'll join you."

He considers for a moment but ends up nodding, and the two of us break away from the group. Robbie surprises me by walking over to the wall and swiping his finger along it to open the hidden door that leads to the cellar beneath the motel's bar.

Both Tobias and Auden follow. Robbie plops onto the couch, his head immediately falling back against the headrest. I get comfortable beside him, crossing my legs, while Tobias and Auden pull up chairs. Auden places the bag of food in my lap before taking his seat.

Robbie closes his eyes and bounces his knee. Keeping a cautious eye on him, I open the paper sack and dig through it, pulling out a couple sandwiches.

Robbie groans. "Even the smell would make an opossum puke."

Despite the comment being a bit comical, my eyes dart to Tobias, our gazes meeting, both of us confused and concerned as to Robbie's present state.

"Tell me about it," I say.

Robbie sits up, rests his elbows on his knees, and hangs his head. "Been like this ever since..." — he clears his throat — "since... killing those guys."

Auden sighs, and Tobias leans forward in his seat, ready to immerse himself in the details.

In all the hustle since returning, based on his response, I realize no one had a chance to tell Tobias about Fen and Warrick's timely end. Auden leans over and whispers in Tobias's ear.

Tobias nods and returns his attention to Robbie. "You're in shock, man. Probably dealing with early-onset PTSD."

Robbie's head falls into his hands. "I've never..."

Killed anyone? But he did it so easily. So nonchalantly... I'd assumed...

Instead of bringing up what's really on my mind, I pat his leg. "You know, Becky is a great ear. She was my psychologist when I was younger. Maybe you should take some time to talk with her. Might not hurt to have Kait talk to her while she's recovering too."

Robbie nods, not shunning my idea.

"So, how *is* Kait?" I inquire.

For the first time since I walked into the Tech room, Robbie fully looks at me and smiles a genuine smile. "She's doing great." The smile reaches his eyes but so does a collection of tears, threatening to spill over. Nothing comes out though; he takes in a shaky breath, blinks a couple times, and they're gone. "Thank you for getting her out of there for me."

I place my hand on his forearm. "Oh, I didn't do it for you." I wink at him, and he gives me an honest chuckle. But then he surprises me and scoops me into his arms, hugging me with so much force I can scarcely breathe.

My own arms mimic the motion, and I squeeze him back. The two of us embrace for a while, both so very grateful Kait is back with us and we all made it out of there… together.

The package of food smushes and crinkles between us, reminding us there's a much-needed meal to be had. When we part from our embrace, I open a sandwich, and hand it to him with a raised eyebrow.

He grabs it with a grimace but brings it to his mouth and takes a bite anyway. Motion for motion, I match him. Two more sandwiches are still in the bag, so I look up at Auden and Tobias.

"You two eat first," Auden says. "We'll take what's left." He brought extra just in case one didn't quite do the job for our famished bodies. However, both Robbie and I look at each other, back at the sandwiches, and at the bag with a groan.

"I think this'll do." I know I haven't eaten in a while, aside from that delicious chocolate, but like Robbie's, my stomach is also a bit sensitive due to the unfolding events.

I close the top of the bag then toss it in their direction. Tobias catches it easy, quickly reopening it and removing the two remaining sandwiches. Once the food is situated in their laps, he takes out four water bottles, twists off the caps one at a time, and slides the first two across the small table between us before placing the other two in front of Auden and him.

The four of us eat in silence, Robbie and I proceeding with caution while Auden and Tobias devour their sandwiches.

They're done in no time, balling up the garbage and tossing it back into the bag. Before Robbie and I can completely finish, though, a Tech member pops his head around the staircase. Robbie looks up, and once the man knows he has Robbie's full attention, he says, "We're live… and we've already got a hit."

We all shoot to our feet and rush back into the Tech room. Everyone is gathered around the giant interactive map looking at the bright red ping, in California this time.

"Well, on the bright side…" I give a morbid chuckle. "We know where the Pacific facility is now."

The entire Tech team turns to look at me at the same time.

"Holy fuck," Robbie whispers before saying it a second time, louder and with much more enthusiasm, while lifting me up in a tight hug and spinning me around. The team jumps into action — doing what, I haven't a clue, but whatever it is, they're excited too. A new, eager buzz fills the room.

There was such a to-do with finding the locations of the facilities. That's what got Roux and I into the facility predicament to begin with: He'd been part of a super-secretive team that stemmed from the Eastern Region UR called Group T led, in part, by Becky to infiltrate the necessary outfits — and in some cases the other URs — with the goal to find every lab and facility location across the nation.

Finding the Central Region's facility was a major breakthrough. Getting inside and having a first-hand look at what goes on within, even more so. Not only that, but by bringing audio and visual technology onto the property, Robbie was able to access a slew of other information including the ability to pick up that radiation pulse on the UR system.

Well... the Central Region's UR system at least.

Now that he knew what to look for, it was just a matter of tapping into satellites or some other related software in order to watch for other radiation pulses.

Apparently, what they hadn't considered is that finding the pulses also likely meant discovering the other facilities.

"Look at the brains on you! This is huge!" Robbie exclaims.

"But, wait, at what cost?" I continue my inner monologue aloud. "Before... the UR was at least being proactive. Group T was working in each region to find their facilities. Now... what... we wait until thousands upon thousands of people die before we do something about it?"

Robbie runs his hands down his face and shakes his head rapidly, trying to wake himself up. "We haven't called Group T off... yet," he says.

But the weight of what this might mean is so heavy it nearly brings me to my knees. Even so, I can't argue with him. I might be hopeful... but I'm not naive. Not any longer. Even if we were proactive — sending out Group T to continue the jobs they'd started — the pulses will likely hit before they find each location on foot. "And... when we find each? What then?"

"We scream in unison," Robbie answers. It takes me a minute, but the conversation we had the first time I ever stepped foot inside this Tech room floats to the forefront of my memories: *Screaming at deaf ears isn't necessarily the best approach. Sure, no one should be silenced; however, I do think whispering until it is possible to scream in unison might be more effective.*

"The Regional URs..." I whisper, thinking more to myself than anyone else. My attention jerks back up to him. "So, like... *what's the word...*" I bite at the inside of my lip, then my eyes widen. "A *multipronged attack* or something?"

Robbie's eyebrow rises, and he rubs the stubble on his chin. "There's a thought."

Tobias chuckles beside me. "Fucking love it when you use smart words."

I roll my eyes and laugh.

Robbie adds, "Those are the damn smartest words I've heard in a long time."

"Well, what the heck were you planning on doing before I gave you this genius — *obvious* — idea?"

"The Resistances have been in place for a few years, but they started out small. Plus, no one knew when, or why, we might be used or needed. Can't really plan for something when you don't know what you're planning for, right? Wouldn't want to prepare for a wedding only to show up at a funeral instead. Not sure the host would be much up for a housewarming gift."

I tame down the smile trying to break free. Gotta say, I love when Robbie starts using his weird — but oddly fitting — analogies. "In the least," he continues, "we set up the communications, combat, etc. The basics, you know? But beyond that, we've only just recently begun to scratch the surface of what we're planning for."

Can't say I fault them there — the story has been the same for us; we can't exactly take action when we don't know what we're taking action against.

As dour as the situation is — knowing the ramifications of that seemingly innocent little red dot —

I still can't help but feed on the energy in the room. With the start of a plan, I feel lighter than I have in weeks. Knowledge is power, and that knowledge is finally trickling down and into the right circles.

Looks like it's time to do something… helpful.

"I know Becky talked to you about joining us." Robbie dips his head and looks down at me, making sure I'm paying attention. By *us*, he means the other leaders. I take a deep breath and give him a sharp nod. "I'd like for you to come to the meeting right after the breakfast rush."

I blink rapidly. "Okay."

"Okay?"

"Yeah. I'll be there."

"Great." That affable smile so unique to Robbie appears, and I can't help but smile back.

* * *

AFTER MEETING WITH ROBBIE, Tobias goes on a mission to get the rest of the story regarding our escape from the facility. He avoids asking me directly at all costs though.

Just prior to Kait and me making it to the van, he and Bram had gone silent both on my tooth cap and along the com-line they had with Robbie and Auden in the vehicle. According to Tobias, Zinna had shown Roux a picture of two dead men — Fen and Warrick. The sight shocked Tobias… as well as Roux, neither having known about the murders until that moment. In the excitement of everything that has happened ever since, we hadn't really gotten a chance to detail what went down after the connection was lost.

With the combination of that picture and Robbie's bout of possible Post Traumatic Stress Disorder — that will likely continue to come and go for a long time to come — Tobias had quickly realized Robbie was the one who pulled the trigger.

In the process of getting all the details, though, he still tried to avoid talking to *me* about it. Which left Auden, of course. Thankfully, the scene didn't seem to bother Auden one bit. A result of his life on the streets for a while, perhaps? Or his first-hand experience watching and hiding from the initial, brutal attacks from the National Agglomeration Bureau?

How he, the youngest of us, is holding up so well, is astounding to witness. Auden was able to give both Tobias and Bram a quick play-by-play of everything. With the intel they needed now retrieved — and a better understanding of how to approach such a thing with the people you care about — Tobias ended his efforts by finally asking me how I was doing in light of that situation.

Numb. That's how I feel about it. But being inside the van separated me enough from the scene, that it almost felt more like I'd watched a movie rather than acted as an accomplice to murder. What is more concerning, however, is that I have no remorse for their deaths.

That is, I started coming to terms with it after asking Tobias to look up their backgrounds. Had Robbie taken them from children? Wives?

No.

No marriages.

No children.

In a way, I think learning those personal specifics aided in calming Robbie's high-strung anxiousness about it… even if only a little bit. For me, that knowledge was definitely helpful.

The hard truth, though, is that their deaths aren't the only ones we're going to see — nor the only ones that will likely happen by our hands before this ordeal is through.

It's an unfortunate truth that there are a lot of guards, employees, and citizens on the side of this so-called evolutionary change The Program provides.

Rather than resistant to the idea.

Like us.

CHAPTER SIX

"Thess!" Bram's voice travels through the hallway as we finally make our way back up to the rooms.

"Why is he yelling my name?" My eyebrows draw inward, and Tobias shrugs. There's something in his voice that's not there usually — fear.

My empath sensors spring open, and I verify the emotion. My casual walking turns into a sprint. "Bram!" I yell, Tobias and Auden following at my heels.

Bram and I almost collide as I round the corner that leads back into the intersection on the lower level. His hands grip my forearms, his chest heaving. "Jax..."

All the blood in my body rushes to my toes. Bram grabs my hand and starts pulling me toward the Medical wing. "What's... wrong?" I squeak, the words struggling to come out.

Bram doesn't answer me though. We all rush into the Medical area. Dr. Hughes is there, waiting for us. "Come here... hurry," she says. "You too." She points at Tobias and jerks her head. She requested him and me, but Auden and Bram follow as well. She's too focused to care or shoo them anyway.

"Sit," she directs, pointing at the available spots in the room. I take the exam table, climbing up with shaky arms and legs. Tobias and Bram stand, imposing, in the doorway. Auden takes the chair, leaving the stool for Dr. Hughes.

"Jaxon isn't doing well." She sits on the stool, pulling out her clipboard before turning her attention to

Tobias. "Rumor has it, you know a thing or two about medical-related subjects? And... the database?"

"A bit, yeah... but I'm not a doctor. Nowhere close."

"Hopefully that won't matter." She waves her hand. "Jaxon's white blood cell count is dangerously low. They're conditioning him now to prep for a bone marrow transplant. Julian's counts are showing the same declivity, just a bit slower. They're prepping him just in case, but a transplant for him is looking less likely."

"You need me to try to find them a match... out of the UR members?" Tobias asks, nodding.

"Yeah... we don't have access to the bone marrow resource databases down here. Not that they're up and running above ground anymore anyway."

I sit here, unable to speak — my tongue and mouth dry, mind numb, and body weak. *Please let it be me* is all I can think on repeat. When I finally find my voice again, I look at Tobias. "Check me first."

He gives me a sad face, but nods nonetheless. "The Tech room is pretty packed right now," Tobias warns.

Dr. Hughes taps her pen on her bottom lip. "How about the tablets? The ones Robbie uses to enter new members into our mock database?"

"Yeah... that might work. Even if I have to use it as a screen share. Minimizing the screen on the wall display..." Tobias's words trail as he considers the options.

"Why did you call us here?" I ask, still a bit muddled and stunned. She rolls over to me and places a hand on my knee. "You're his family... and I know how much you care for the boy. Plus... honestly? I think you and Tobias are his best chance for survival. I could be wrong, but if I were a gamblin' gal, I'd place a bet that you'll be a great donor match for him."

"Anything. I'll do anything." Even without knowing what "anything" implies.

She nods and looks over her shoulder at Tobias. "Go prove me right."

* * *

"BUT... OUR BLOOD IS SO DIFFERENT," I say. "Our DMIS opposite."

"Bone marrow has to do with markers on tissue. It's different than blood," Tobias reassures me as we all head back to the Tech room.

"But then how are you going to determine a match in the database?"

"Well, I'm not sure yet... but it's a DNA database, and bone marrow still has to do with DNA." We approach the hallway that leads to the hidden opening into the Tech room, and he turns to me. "Go with Bram and Auden, I'll let you know when I find something, okay?" he says, lifting my chin and giving me a small kiss.

After considering his suggestion for a moment, I decide he's right; staring at a screen filled with things I don't understand might only exacerbate my confusion and frustration. I give him another kiss and nod my acceptance before turning to Bram and taking his hand.

The next few hours are miserable. Bram and Auden's company is nice, but with the upcoming UR leaders' meeting and waiting on news of a bone marrow donor match from Tobias, my mind is completely occupied. No matter what topic Bram and Auden bring up in an attempt to take my mind off of things, I can't

69

focus. We walk around the Underground aimlessly for a while until our walking eventually leads to the Oracle Room.

Bram and I sit at the bar, and he orders a couple alcoholic drinks. I don't ask the reason, I just accept the offer. Auden, being underage, opts out, insisting he has work to do to help Ruby prep for breakfast anyway.

The bartender slides a glass to me. Out of habit, I look up in search of Kait's dimpled smile and blue eyes, only to be met with another blow to the gut.

It's not Kait, of course... just a bartender whom I don't know. She doesn't even smile; she just pours the drinks and moves on, busying herself with work-related tasks. Kait does that too, of course, but in a way where patrons seldom realize she's multitasking; most of the time it's amid friendly conversation.

I pick up the drink and take a sip, reveling in the feel of the heat moving down my throat and spreading over my chest. "Do you know how Kait is doing?" I ask Bram, staring into the liquid-filled glass.

"She's great," Bram answers. "They cleaned her up, watched her for about twenty-four hours, then released her. Robbie had only just left her side as I was headed up to our room after my shift. I ran into him en route. He said she'd fallen asleep, but that her short-term memory was already pretty steady."

"Meaning?" I take another sip.

"Meaning she remembers returning here and going to the doctors. But nothing before that."

"That's good. That's going to drive her crazy." I chuckle halfheartedly.

"Already is according to Robbie. Since she doesn't remember anything, she can't exactly experience shock or sadness over the ordeal, so she's just incredibly ornery about it instead. Robbie said something like 'she's behaving like a dog lapped her soup.'"

I snort laugh at that. "Robbie's such a classy guy."

Bram chuckles, taking a swig of his own drink. "Feeling better?" he asks, tilting the glass in my direction.

"It has relaxed me a bit already, I'll admit. I don't want to drink too much though — I need to be able to think."

"Nah... none of that." Bram smiles, placing his free hand on my back and gliding it up and down. "Pretty sure you've done enough thinking lately."

Scooting my stool closer, I rest my head against his shoulder. "I decided to consider Becky's proposition. I'll be meeting with the UR leaders here shortly."

"That's great, Thess," he says, leaning his cheek against the top of my head and moving his hand to around my waist.

"You really think so?" I ask before pulling a good bit more of my drink through the straw.

"Yeah, I do. You're a born leader, even if you hadn't realized it for yourself yet."

"Funny coming from the man who'd probably prefer I stay in a bubble."

"Yes, but only if the bubble includes me." He laughs, lifts his cheek off my head, and takes another gulp of his drink.

I sigh and push my glass to the opposite edge of the counter when the bartender approaches, I hold my finger and thumb about an inch apart and squint my eyes, indicating I'd like her to top it off. She pours a bit in and moves along, busying herself with more tasks.

When I look back at Bram, he's already looking at me. Watchful. "What?"

He shrugs. "You've changed."

My heart thuds harder. "Oh?"

Then he does that Bram thing where he doesn't say anything for a while, leaving my thoughts to bounce from one idea to another, wild with assumptions as to whether or not his comment is a good or bad thing.

He laughs and squeezes me tighter. "Damn, I missed you."

"More than words," I say, turning my head toward him so that our noses are almost touching.

"I didn't mean anything bad about what I said a second ago."

"A second ago? You left me hanging for like five minutes!"

Bram's gaze drifts to my mouth then back to my eyes, his brown eyes swimming with amusement. "We met as kids," he continues, pausing yet again. We did, and the thought always seems so surreal anytime I consider it. "Over the years both of us have changed, of course. Puberty, for one. Like, you know, when you got all that ass." His hand drops from my waist and cups the top of my butt.

"Right, like when you finally cut off that horrid mullet. And… when your voice changed…" Bram hasn't always had the sexy, deep, baritone voice he has now. Getting it was hilariously awkward though.

"You didn't like my mullet?" He gasps in a high-pitched voice, mocking my comment about his voice change. Returning his voice to normal, he says, "Yeah… like when every time I so much as looked at you, my dick would get hard and there was nothing I could do to make it *not* do that."

"You mean that eventually went away?" I give him a mock gasp and a wink.

"Nope, you're right. Still happens."

Even over ten years later, he can still make me blush. My cheeks burn red and I look down for a second, but he rubs his nose against mine and my gaze naturally rises again.

"Then you became a woman," he whispers, brushing his lips against mine. "Somewhere in the middle of all this chaos, a strong, smart, independent woman broke out of the still growing, still learning, still somewhat dependent one you were before. So, yeah… you've changed. I… I'm just glad I was able to continue watching it happen."

"Yeah, well… you'll be around for the next indefinite amount of life milestones too. At least you'd better be."

Bram brushes his lips against mine again until I can no longer refuse him entry. Our tongues meet; even our kisses have matured over time. Bram tastes like Bourbon and ice, his lips still cool from the last sip, but like always, he smells just like air and earth. Even down here in the Underground.

When we break away, our foreheads come together for a moment of quiet reflection before we separate fully and turn our attention back to the drinks.

It seems as though we're only in there for a few more minutes before the morning crowd begins coming in — the ones who start drinking at stupid-a.m. opposed to the ones who had been drinking since stupid-p.m.

In reality, Bram and I had probably been in there for a few hours sharing old memories, dancing — well, me dancing, and him… doing his *version* of dancing.

"That's my cue," I state, blowing a raspberry from my lips. "Time to level-up."

CHAPTER SEVEN

Here goes nothing.

I'd been here before — in the leadership area of the Underground — but under different circumstances. When we questioned Roux for the first time, for instance. Also, when we were meeting his daughter. Funny how that worked out.

When I arrive, everyone is sitting around the table, chatting about casual stuff as they wait for the meeting to start. In attendance is Ben, the Relay Director; Roark, Head of Combat; Becky Westley, my old psychologist, family friend, ex-member of Zinna's medical team, and one of the leaders of the UR's covert Group T; and Robbie, who is dubbed the Region's overall leader but also oversees the Weapon Division alongside a woman by the name of Sylvie and the Tech team, of course. Surprisingly, Ruby is here as well. I hadn't considered her a leader-type, but it makes sense seeing as someone needs to be in charge of the food situation.

A couple more men — ones I have not yet met — are at the table as well.

It isn't until I've taken in all these faces that I spot the most recognizable one of all. Kait and I catch each other's attention at the exact same time, and our faces light up.

Not wanting to disturb the chatter, we both hold back our squeals of delight. She pushes out of her chair in the corner of the room and rushes around the table, slinging her arms around my neck and rocking us back and forth. I match the motion and squeeze so tight she squeaks.

The two of us laugh, and I nudge her a short length away so I can get a better view. She looks great; no more dirt and streaks of who-knows-what on her face, arms, or hands. Her lips are still dry and cracked and her eyes are still a bit baggy and red, which is to be expected I suppose.

"Oh god," I breathe out and hug her again. "You have no idea how happy I am to see you're okay."

"Girl... yes I do. I was the hottest of messes when they took you. And... the things they di—" She cuts herself off, shaking her head, that adorable pissed-off look drawing in her eyebrows. We all know the horrid things they did to me in that Exam Center and the way Roux drugged me — using a drink Kait had served.

But she has no idea what she went through. Nor do we other than laboring in her assigned section, digging trenches. Like me, though, Robbie insisted she go through the *extensive* check-up process.

I grip her upper arms tighter and look into her eyes. "Are you okay? Those exams suck." I scrunch my nose up at her, hoping to get a smile. And I do.

"Aww, sweets." She waves her hand. "I've had a thing or two put up there before; ain't no big deal ta me." She at least has the courtesy to speak this overshare low enough so no one else can hear.

"Yeah... we're not going to elaborate on that." I chuckle.

"Ya mean not right now at least?"

"Yeah... not ever." We both laugh, but then my smile fades, and I find myself scrutinizing her again.

"Every test they ran on me had normal results." She gives me a soft smile and squeezes my cheeks together with her fingers and thumb. "Now quit biting that lip."

I hadn't even realized I was doing it. Some habits just can't be kicked it seems. "Yes, ma'am," I say with a grin. She slips her arm around mine, leads me to my assigned seat, and returns to hers, adding in a quick wink and her dimpled grin before the meeting commences.

Everyone is still chatting and remains doing so until the last member of the leadership team walks in — another person whom I haven't yet met — a pretty woman about ten years my senior. Behind her someone else enters, but I don't get a good look until the first woman moves to the side.

Celeste.

Robbie stands at the head of the table as the last two women enter and take the remaining seats. "We have new meat with us today! Starting to my right, we'll go around the table and share your name and responsibility."

"Ben — Relay Director."

"Harvey — Search and Rescue."

"Caleb — Guard Outfit."

Caleb is to my left, so that means I'm up next. "Thessaly — Um… Untitled."

The table chuckles, but the introductions move right on.

"Kole — Medical."

"Ruby — Food Service."

"Celeste — Entertainment Director."

Of fucking course.

"Milton — Human Resources."

"Becky — Special Teams."

"Liz — Botany."

While Celeste's presence certainly surprised me, her title didn't.

Liz's title, however, does — the leader of Bram's division.

"Roark — Combat."

"Perfect!" Robbie states, sitting back down. "This isn't a normal meeting as most of you know. Tech has information to share, and we want to discuss potential options. Put them out on the table. Without beating around the bush, I'll go ahead and say that we're looking at mass genocide," he says matter-of-factly, pausing after to let the weight of this news descend on the room. The news must not come as a surprise to some of the leaders — they don looks of apathy and numbness. Others, the women mostly, are more descriptive with their facial expressions.

Celeste, for example, turns an unbecoming shade of pale green.

Ruby clasps her hands on the table, and her beady bluish-black eyes unfocus.

Liz leans back in her chair, swallows hard, and tucks a lock of short hair behind her ear.

A couple of men show their unease with the rub of their hand over their face or the pressing together of their lips.

While all the reactions might be different, the collective buzz of fear isn't. Going into this meeting as a team member who is knowledgeable of empath stuff, I'd decided to start the meeting as an open book so to speak. Just like Roark had taught during my first Combat class, the leaders in this room vary in terms of how well I can connect to them on an empathic level.

Robbie is the farthest channel; I haven't been able to tune into him ever. Of the leaders I know, Celeste is the next most difficult to read. Ben follows. Then Ruby.

All their low scores prevent me from getting decent reads.

I probe around the room, trying to find the ones I can connect easiest with.

Liz falls among them — which honestly calms me a bit, because I'd be lying if I said that finding out Bram's leader is a pretty woman didn't trigger a bit of jealousy. Both Caleb and Harvey are very clearly Highs; their reads are the strongest. The remaining — Roark, Kole, and Milton — are all about equal; I can feel them but not as much or as little as the Highs and Lows respectively.

Neutrals.

For a few seconds, I feel like everything I've experienced since this all started led me to this moment. Confidence swims through me as I so easily read each leader in the room and am able to classify them by their scores. Nothing exact, of course, but a generalization at least.

In a way, I'm somewhat like a human exacentrifuge.

Huh.

Well, minus the database part.

But how can I use this talent to our benefit? That is the true question.

Robbie goes on to brief the table about the facilities and the radiation pulses. He'd used the information gathered from a compilation of my experience inside the facility, Jax's and Julian's experiences, feeds from the contacts and tooth cap, and the blueprints he'd been able to access.

Combined, we have quite the arsenal of knowledge. "What we don't know," he says, "is how many people they're expiring during each pulse. No

78

number is the best number, of course, and one is one too many."

The table murmurs agreements, including myself.

"But... why are they doin' this?" Celeste asks.

For one of the few times since my involvement in all this began, I finally feel like I have an answer to provide. Another pinnacle moment where everything we'd been through has led up to this. I raise my hand, just as a precaution since I don't know Robbie's rules on group discussion.

Not only does he allow me to speak, he segues my response with a more detailed introduction: "In case any of you are unaware, Thessaly is the reason why we have all this information. Every bit of it. Her word. Her... directive... is as good as mine from here forward." He then tilts his hand, passing the proverbial mic to me.

Oh... well, I sure wasn't expecting those kinds of accolades.

No pressure.

When my widened eyes meet Robbie's, he gives me a small nod of encouragement.

"For decades" — taking a deep breath, I begin — "scientists have been trying to find ways to cure disease. To prolong our life spans. To eradicate all the things that tend to cause us so much pain and loss. It's a commendable project, but they've bit off more than they can chew. New diseases, different strains of old viruses, more complex, incurable morbidities have begun to overpower even the best-funded, most intuitive research and testing. In short, these things can't be cured. We're overpopulated, and everyone knows that. But what everyone doesn't know, is that the life-death ratio has tipped toward the latter. After decades upon decades, due to rampant disease, illness, etc., we're starting to see a greater number of deaths than births on any given second of any given day.

"Amid these numbers is a portion of the population that's more immune, stronger. Out of desperation, a group of scientists and funders created a program designed to weed out the higher risk portion of the population... and breed those of us who are 'more ideal' by certain standards. To do this, they're using a new, advanced form of radiation to kill large groups of people at a time. All over the nation. In doing so, they're eliminating the carriers — the individuals who prove a higher risk to the population as a whole — and they're creating a new generation of citizens with low scores.

"Or trying to at least. However, what they didn't — and possibly still don't — know is that 'Lows and Lows' are not meant to breed, and therefore cannot bear healthy children. They don't know this because when two Lows come together, it's like flipping a magnet over and trying to get the similar poles to stick. They're naturally repellant. No matter how hard you try, the two similar poles will never attract. The same goes for 'Highs and Highs.' Basic science that even the smartest of scientists haven't taken into consideration. Maybe it's because we're human, and not a metal, that such a key factor in their plan slipped through the cracks. As a result, they're still trying. They've increased how often they're doing radiation pulses, and they're taking in more and more people as subjects daily in order to strengthen and speed up their efforts.

"That said, at some point, their hands must've been tied, and this plan — no matter how immoral — turned into something they had no choice but to follow through with. They're doing this... consequences or not.

Effective or not. And, as far as we know, the UR is the nation's only chance at stopping them."

When I finish, Robbie is grinning bigger than I've ever seen him grin before. But then he clears his throat and begrudgingly puts his leader face back on. "Right. Not only is she a wealth of information, she also presented a plan of action. Or at least the beginnings of one. A coordinated invasion. We gather UR troops from each region and hit the facilities in a multipronged attack."

"Multipronged? What does that even mean?" Celeste asks, her voice shaking.

"All troops converge on the facilities at the exact same time," Roark explains in short.

Ben pulls on his beard and nods. "Our com-system should be able to handle something like that with a little tweaking."

"We'll need to collect supplies to be able to feed that many mouths away from base," Ruby announces.

"Wait," I interrupt. "That's it? No one else has any ideas?" I twist my fingers in my lap under the table. A husky chuckle comes from behind me, and I sling my head around.

Tobias is standing in the doorway. "When you have a solid idea, there's no need to waste time trying to hash out lesser-quality ones."

"Tobias, my man... What's up?" Robbie asks, seeing as Tobias isn't supposed to be part of this meeting.

"Can I steal Thessaly?"

"Now? Can it wait?"

"It can... but now is better," Tobias responds, his tone no-nonsense.

Robbie looks around the table. "Becky," he directs his attention toward her. "You good with briefing us on your plans for Thessaly's involvement? Thessaly... you okay with that?"

Becky nods in agreement, and I follow suit. "Thessaly and I will speak when she's done talking to Tobias. But, yes, I'm happy to share my ideas in the meantime. Just know they're not set in stone until she agrees."

"Fair enough," Robbie says.

I push my chair back and leave with Tobias.

"HAVE A SEAT," Tobias says, holding his arm out toward the couch in the cellar. Apparently he'd been using a tablet, just as Dr. Hughes had suggested, and is now tapping into their system remotely from the comfort of the cellar's couch.

The two of us sit side by side. Before he begins talking, someone else enters from the Tech room, and I watch curiously, waiting for whomever it is to walk around the staircase.

Bram's tall, lean form steps out, his eyes a little glazed over, probably from having that one-more-drink when I'd left him at the bar not too terribly long ago.

"How ya feeling there, New Guy?" I jest, using the title Tobias, Jax, and Julian had given him in the beginning of this debacle. The humor helps tame the nervous energy fluttering in my belly.

"Warm." He winks at me, taking a high-backed chair across from the couch and sitting.

Tobias turns to me again then, placing a hand on my leg, squeezing just above my knee. "Our options for donor matches are slim," he starts. "I'm sure you can already guess that it'll be important we use someone on the lower end of the DMIS scale. Not only are they more likely to be a closer match, they're also generally healthier and more apt to be able to go through with the process without complications. So, honestly, I didn't even bother to look at Highs. Might as well save time."

I instantly think of all the Lows I know which aren't very many. Then again, I haven't exactly met everyone in the UR. In light of the new circumstances, though, I have a feeling that'll change soon.

I also have a feeling where this conversation with Tobias is headed…

He gives me a sympathetic look, and my assumption turns to conviction. Rather than make him be the bearer of bad news, I cut him off before he can even get her name out.

"Celeste is the match isn't she?"

Tobias's mouth shuts before reopening again. "Well, yes. But… you are too."

The puddle of dread that had begun to leak in my gut disappears, and hope takes its place.

Then my mind starts piecing other things together. I look over at a perceptive Bram and back to Tobias. Bram's here for a reason. Usually that reason is to pull the best friend card or to try convincing me of something the other guys might not have enough years of practice to pull off. I raise an eyebrow, alternating glances between the two of them.

Once Tobias has worked up the courage, he finally opens his mouth. "So, yeah, in a fun turn of events, Celeste is Jax's best donor match. But bone marrow matching facilities don't always go with the top pick. Sometimes, the donor can't do it, for example, in which case they go down the line to the next best."

"So, you're telling me I'm the second-best option for Jax? What about Julian?"

Bram takes the stage. "Julian has been cleared. Also, don't let your mind do that girlie thing where you overanalyze what Tobias meant by that." And Bram's purpose comes to light. "This has nothing to do with relationships. She's not his. You are. Not only do the scores prove it but how much you two care about each other does."

Receiving news that Julian is getting better lightens the tension of the moment. But only a bit right now. Ugh. Bram... almost always the logical one. I narrow my eyes at the two of them. "So why are you presenting me with this?"

Tobias clears his throat and swipes his hand through his hair. "Before presenting the information to the Medical team... or to Celeste... I wanted to give *you* the option to choose on Jax's behalf first. Dr. Hughes was right, we're the closest thing he has to a family here. So, you'll get to make the final judgement call. In this case, choose his donor. You can choose Celeste, knowing she's the closest donor match... or you can choose yourself. There's a third option, too. A man."

"Does gender make a difference?"

"Sometimes, yes... but in this case, Celeste is still the best choice."

Hearing that Celeste is a better match for Jax definitely does something to my psyche. Bram knows all too well. Selfishly, I want to raise my hand and take the responsibility of curing Jax — or at least getting him one step closer to a cure. But, internally — mentally — I battle with the rightness of it. If Celeste is the better match for him — his better chance of survival — then he needs her, not me.

So, also selfishly, I want to choose Celeste so I can have him back. For me. For us.

"There's always the chance Celeste might decline," Tobias includes, filling the silence.

"Heh... that's doubtful," I say with a sigh.

"Yeah."

"She's... healthy?" I ask. Knowing a little about her background, I can't help but worry if she's clean. As horrible of a conjecture as that sounds.

I don't have to elaborate, Tobias and Bram know exactly what I'm talking about. In fact, Bram speaks up. "I've seen her in the Medical wing a couple times," he explains, turning to Tobias.

"They'll do some additional testing and assessments on her before going through with anything," Tobias explains.

I nod, staring at my lap for a moment before looking up at Tobias, decision made. "She's the better choice here." The words are hard to say, I'll admit, but I don't stutter.

Tobias gives me a sharp nod. "Would you like to present her with the proposal?"

This question catches me off guard more than the news of their match. My eyes widen and I dart glances at Bram and Tobias interchangeably. "Why?"

Tobias shrugs.

"If nothing more, it might make you feel better about it? Give you a little sense of control in an otherwise helpless situation," Bram adds.

Celeste and I might be worlds different, but we do have one thing in common: we both care about Jax. "Yeah, I can do that."

Tobias's hand squeezes above my knee again, and he gives me a small smile. "Now?" He looks down at the tablet and back up. "I imagine the meeting should be about over. We can wait outside the room and intercept her as she's exiting."

I chuckle a little at the thought. "Poor thing wasn't handling news of the genocide well. She was also having a hard time understanding it at all." Not that anyone would handle that sort of news admirably. Celeste seemed a bit more erratic and emotional with her reactions though. "Add this to the mix, and she very well might pass out."

CHAPTER EIGHT

W hen we get back to the meeting area, leaders are filing out for a short recess. Ruby walks out first, and as soon as she sees Tobias, a big grin spreads across her face. Tobias squeezes her shoulder, but she keeps moving, no doubt ascertaining that Tobias has a reason for being here and it doesn't include chatting with her. Liz comes out next, and upon seeing Bram says, "Oh, hey! Glad you're here, I needed to run something by you."

Bram darts a look at me, back to her, and nods. The two of them move down the hallway a bit and step aside, immediately engaging in a conversation I can no longer hear.

Knowing I have a task at hand, I brush aside the impending flame of jealousy — a feeling I don't love to dwell on anyway. One that was never usually an issue with Bram. Upon further introspection, though, I determine it must have to do with the rockiness of everything going on right now. I'm somewhat emotionally unstable, having temporarily lost two of my loves. The idea of losing another comes easy.

When Becky comes out, Tobias tugs on her shirt and says, "Hey, stick around." She does so, beginning a discussion with the Combat leader to pass the time.

Celeste emerges next.

"Celeste, right?" Tobias asks, reaching out a hand to introduce himself. "I'm Tobias. I don't believe we've formally met."

That nerve-racking buzz I've noticed between close DMIS opposites vibrates slightly. Not as strongly as it did between Jax and Celeste, nor as strongly as it did between the baby and Tobias, but enough to serve as an added reminder of her empathic connection with my guys.

Celeste places her hand in Tobias's and the buzz grows stronger. "Nice ta meet ya," she says, darting a curious sideways glance at me. Tobias must feel something... different... because he clears his throat and lets go of her instantly before shoving his hands into his pockets and taking a step backward.

It takes every bit of effort not to press my lips together, clench my fists, and huff in annoyance. Instead, I cut through the angst and broach the topic we came down here to address. "Jax needs a bone marrow donor, and after some research, Tobias found that you... You're a match."

Tobias can sense I'm struggling a bit, probably due to the look of pure disgust on my face that I can't help when I'm around her, so he follows my comment with one of his own: "Would you be willing to donate your bone marrow? If not, we can go to the next potential donor."

He tries to be nonchalant with this mention, but she's apparently smart enough to piece together what that might mean. Her mouth curves up slightly at the corner, and she lifts her gaze to Tobias. "More than willing," she replies, her expression serious now though. Scared even. "When?"

"Now."

Her bright-blue eyes widen, and she blinks a couple times. She shakes her head side to side. "Has he gotten worse since... since the coma?"

Tobias nods slightly, and her eyes fill. This causes a chain reaction and my own eyes fill, but I turn my head to the side so no one will notice.

"Yeah... okay," she whispers. "Let me just make sure someone can take over for me for a few days."

I want to say something snarky like, "That shouldn't be hard to do," just out of immature jealousy and spite, but I don't. I might not be able to feel her empathically, but that ability isn't necessary to translate the worry and fear in her eyes.

Because that same worry and fear is reflected in my own.

"As soon as you're ready," Tobias continues, "go see Dr. Hughes. She's essentially the liaison between regular patients and the higher risk area. She'll help you get to where you need to be."

Free and clear of the tears that tried to spring up, I look at Celeste again in time to see her nod at Tobias and walk past him.

While still conversing with Liz, Bram catches the movement outside his peripheral vision and follows Celeste with his eyes as she walks down the hallway before flicking a glance at me.

To... what?

Make sure I'm still standing?

Make sure there isn't smoke coming out of my ears?

He then returns his attention to Liz, nods, interrupts her to say something, then breaks away.

"Well, I'd say that went well." Tobias beams, no doubt trying to assuage the billion negative ways I feel right now.

I turn to Bram. "Did you feel that buzz when Celeste was near Tobias just now? Or when Tobias was holding the baby?"

Bram looks at me dumbly. "Ah… nope."

Tobias finally takes his hands out of his pockets and crosses his arms over his chest, leaning back against the narrow hallway's stone wall. "Buzz?"

"Yeah… a fucking buzz."

Bram laughs at my cursing, considering even through all that we've experienced, I still tend to only swear when I'm super upset. He takes a spot against the wall, so I follow suit, since we apparently are waiting here for some reason. "We staying here?" I ask.

"Yeah, I wanted to talk to you, Bram, Robbie, and Becky about that permissions thing," Tobias explains. "While we wait, tell us more about this buzz."

Becky finishes talking to Roark but maintains her distance when she sees the three of us speaking to each other quietly.

"When compatible people are near each other, I sense a buzz," I explain. "Not quite a sound, nor a sensation… but an odd combination of the two."

"And you felt it just now between Celeste and me?" Tobias asks, raising his eyebrows.

"Mm hm."

His hands drop again and are swiftly shoved into his pockets. But then he looks up at me from his downward-tilted head, smiling. "If I tell you I felt something, will we have jealousy sex? You know, to secure my feelings for you and all?"

I narrow a glare at him. Beside me, Bram laughs. "Thess would totally do something like that."

"I… You two are horrible," I gasp, but I can't stop the smile and the blush that blooms on my cheeks. "Are you saying you still need to secure your feelings for me?" I ask, clasping my hands over my heart.

Tobias shakes his head, looks back down, and grins.

At that moment, Robbie and Kait come out, the last two people remaining. Kait doesn't skip a beat; she stands beside me and scoops our arms together. Robbie looks from one person to the next.

"What's up?" he asks, joining us on the wall.

"I have some questions, and I'm hoping you have some answers," Tobias states. "I would have walked in there, but I did a head count earlier and noticed that everyone but you and Kait had left. Didn't want to interrupt something."

Kait turns her face to me and waggles her brows.

Robbie waves everyone in, Becky included, and we all take seats around the meeting table. Tobias begins right away. "During Roux's interrogation, Ruby wasn't able to get much by the way of reading lips, but she did manage to get something about 'permissions'. The word *permissions* and something about Zinna thinking Roux had something to do with… it."

Robbie's eyes widen. "Oh yeah… I spoofed the account and locked her out completely. In order to get back in, she would've needed to make a trip to the company's administration office."

"*Will* need, future tense," Tobias says, staring at the wall and unfocusing his gaze.

"Huh." Robbie leans back in the chair, keeping his hands in front of him, strumming his fingers on the table. "That would indicate that she hasn't been using her account to track everything."

"She hasn't." Becky's eyebrows lift. "While at the Exam Center, she'd used mine. When we're mobile or

91

hopping, it's not unusual for someone to use another team member's open account. With her being in the position she's in, she can access our accounts no matter what, so no one bats an eye."

"How long do you believe she has known...?" Tobias thinks aloud.

We all wrack our memories. Both Bram and Becky have an answer to give at the same time: "The Exam Center.... When they got locked in..."

An image of her trying frantically to push buttons on the keypad while yelling through that window flashes through my mind. "Yeah... that's got to be when," I deduce.

"So... why is she still locked out then?" Tobias questions.

"Her interest is in Florida. The admin building is in New York," Becky answers.

"Weren't you up there after the media started leaking stuff? Dealing with the aftermath, I'm sure?" Robbie asks.

Becky laughs. "Oh no... the board met in North Florida. She was in the Central Region already, and they wanted to take a tour of the facility. It was a 'kill two birds with one stone' sort of deal."

"How likely is it she'll end up traveling back to New York to get her permissions reinstated?"

Becky is quiet for a moment. "Well, if she's asking, there must be a need for her to get in. Otherwise, she wouldn't bother. From what I understand, her permissions are pretty much the same as most of the board members."

"What are some reasons why she would want that reinstatement if her permissions are about the same?" I inquire.

Becky curves her finger and presses it against her mouth, resting her chin on her thumb. "Deeper access to the database perhaps?"

The room is quiet for an extended time while we all mull over the possibilities.

Becky's eyes lift hesitantly. "You all are aware she pretty much orchestrated The Program, yes?"

All eyes shift to her, heads shaking. Becky's hand drops and she props her elbows on the table, clasping her hands together. "A few years ago, a consortium meeting was held in which several attendees presented straw proposals for consideration in a top-secret project to be paired with the cataloging of DNA Mutation Immunity Scores. As Thessaly had so accurately explained in the meeting earlier, the purpose was to outline a system for cataloging certain genome constituents of all United States National Citizens with a long-term goal of designing a program that would use the gathered information to eliminate current genetic mutations that lessen the quality and longevity of life and to restrict the spread of future detrimental mutations. One of the specific goals was to merge all formerly cataloged DNA results from the Trial Study into the new, inclusive ExaIntel Database and initiate the nationwide mandatory sample submission process that came to be known as The DNA Networking Act.

"From there, the plan was to isolate human subjects with certain genotypes. As stated on the meeting report, 'The principal objective of the full project is the consummation of the working catalog system and commencement of a program to use the data collected therein to isolate and examine special DMIS candidates in order to sustain the next era of research relating to the eradication of genetic mutations on a national level. This includes both the verification of mutation counts — for instance, DMIS scores already cataloged — and a preliminary testing program in order to qualify subjects for subsequent, experimental project phases.'

"It's those 'experimental project phases' that required the straw proposals. Zinna's straw proposal won. She is the brains behind the pulses. She owns the concept but... nothing more. She's incredibly power hungry. Not to mention she's pissed off because she's not getting the 'air time' she thinks she deserves."

"But why so carelessly just... kill people?" I inquire.

"No one really knows if there's any motivation beyond recognition. We do know, though, that to her it's not 'careless.' For those who back her, for example, it very much comes from a place of caring, mostly about the future. With her plan, should it have been smarter than it is, the picture of longer life was painted: no life-threatening diseases and no pain, suffering, and loss of loved ones too soon — at least not from illness."

"No... from mass genocide instead." Tobias huffs.

Becky shrugs. "'Pain now for a painless future.'"

"Those are significant dreams. Both science and history dictate that diseases and viruses mutate into new strains all the time. They adapt in accordance to their environments. Her... this wild idea of a perfect species... a perfect future... is absurd," I announce.

Becky leans forward and whispers. "Newsflash: Zinna isn't a scientist nor a historian."

"Well, that sure as shit explains things," Robbie grinds out.

"She's a business woman. Driven. A speaker and a wordsmith. Plus, she has a low score. Science, as you have witnessed for yourself, dictates that with the power of persuasion, people will blindly follow her lead."

It all circles around back to the natural order of the empathic bonds people form — whether they realize it or not.

"She has the upper hand in a lot of things. But there's one important bit of knowledge she's still in the dark about — she doesn't know that the reason people follow her is because of this opposite score bond. That test we'd performed in the Exam Center between you and Julian was the closest she'd come to discovering that imperative piece of the puzzle. And that's only because you two were so tapped into the talent. We hadn't attached anyone to our equipment to verify such an assessment before then. I joined her team, I'll admit, for selfish reasons. I knew she had a low score, so I was intrigued by what I'd spent years researching regarding Highly Sensitive people. Plus, I wanted to carry on the research of a dear friend of mine.

"Anyway, my point is... she uses her empath abilities without even realizing she's doing it. You, my dear, have full control of the talent."

"So, do you think this is why she needs to get back into the system under her own permissions? Maybe she's on a path of discovery regarding the empath bonds?" I ask.

Becky shakes her head and leans back into her chair. "Honestly, I have no clue. That reason wouldn't be my first guess though."

"Well, what would your first guess be?" Kait asks, not really part of the conversation but thoroughly intrigued nonetheless.

In all this back and forth, the rest of the table had remained quiet, simply listening to the exchange. "Out of all that, one thing stood out among the rest…" Robbie leans forward, getting everyone's attention. "The fact that she's power hungry."

"Right…" I whisper, rolling the thought around in my mind. "And in the very least… without those permissions, she's at a disadvantage — her power is somewhat diminished."

"Her reasoning beyond that, though, is to be determined," Bram adds to the conversation.

"We've yet to take any action against her directly," Robbie points out. "Our aim is always higher. But I think in light of these informative revelations, she might be the one to target after all. At least in part."

"Yeah… these pulses need to stop. Above all else," I state with a sigh. "Then…"

"Then we take out the puppet master, and the puppets will fall," Tobias finishes my thought. The room becomes quiet, then a grin spreads over Tobias's face. "You know, I once likened *you* to a puppet master, in my thoughts," he says, directing his attention to me. "When it comes to Bram, Jax, Julian, and me… you very much control our strings at times, even unknowingly. And I don't mean it in a negative sense at all. But the empath connections between Highs and Lows are very much akin to a symbiotic relationship between master and puppet. While sometimes the puppets will be defunct or their strings tied up, it's usually the master that makes sure they're in proper working order.

"As much as I'm sure you won't like hearing this, Becky is right. In a way, you and Zinna are similar — at least when it comes to your influence over others."

My teeth go to that often-used innermost part of my bottom lip, and I gnaw on it contemplatively. But my mind seems to have reached a dead end for now. Hooray for the sluice of information; however, as to what to do with it, that needs a bit more time to marinate.

"How'd the rest of the meeting go?" I ask Robbie.

"We have the first stages of a solid plan, thanks to you."

I smile, still not sure I'm deserving of the appreciation. "That's great. Want to fill us in?"

"Sure thing. And while we're at it, Becky can go ahead and propose her suggestions as to your participation."

Becky nods.

Robbie nudges Kait in the arm. "Care to enlighten the class?"

Kait shoots a look of surprise at him but then beams wide. "Yes." She then turns her attention back to the table of rapt listeners. "So, here's the long and short of it: We wait for pulses to hit in every region. While we do that, the UR doubles up on trainin' and other preparations. As each location shows up on the radar, Group T will be dispatched and scope it out to verify what we're dealin' with in each area. Once we have every location locked and loaded, we dispatch troops to each, attackin' from both the inside and the outside. Tech teams from every UR will systematically shut down the radiation software, Combat will... well they'll fight the guards and extract as many people as possible." Kait smiles big again and looks at Robbie for approval.

"That's certainly the long and short of it." Robbie rubs his thumb along her jaw and gives her a kiss on the forehead before returning his attention to the table of attendees. "We'll be working hard in the meantime to fill in the gaps for things like where we're going to put all the extracted subjects, how we're going to transport them out of there, and a ton of other aspects that need refining."

"Well, they have all the transport vehicles they'd been using on site at the facility," I mention, a clear memory of the vehicles used to move subjects from the train station. "I'd say the trains and monorails too, but I assume you'd need someone who knows how to drive them."

Robbie nods, rubbing the stubble on his chin.

"I'm afraid I don't have any great suggestions on how to house them afterward. Unless, of course, you take over the facilities enough to use them for our purposes. At least then we'd have access to food and medical supplies until everyone has returned to good health and can go back to their homes."

Robbie belly laughs. "I love how you start out saying you don't have any suggestions only to follow it up with a suggestion."

"A very smart one, at that." Tobias grins.

"It's a confidence thing. She hasn't had any reason to believe her opinions are worth their weight until now," Bram explains.

"Right here, guys. I'm right here." We all chuckle. The situation does serve as quite the confidence booster though. My stomach flutters, but I push past the nervousness and turn toward Becky. "So, what role do I play in this puppet show?" I ask, darting a quick smile at Tobias.

"The role of puppet master, of course." She grins wide, pulling one from me as well. "We haven't actually determined where — as in which UR or purpose — you'll be most needed for the bigger picture plan, but for now, we're hoping you'll help assign teams. Make sure leaders are Low and their teams are most fitting to the empath bond situation. A recruiter of sorts. Matching up members with teams according to their strengths and weaknesses, and, of course, under the most fitting leaders. We're not talking about the individuals who currently lead, but new leaders. From there, the current leaders will train and prepare them remotely."

A heavy weight lifts off my shoulders. "Well, that doesn't sound so bad." I let out a quiet chuckle. "How do I handle the teams in the other URs though?"

"We don't like to push people too hard or too fast here." Robbie winks. "As for the other URs, you'll handle those via video transmission. Interviewing possible leaders and their team members."

Feeling much less terrified of the situation, I let out a sigh of relief, leaning forward and exchanging glances with everyone at the table. "So... when do I start?"

A vibration hums in the room, indicating a page. The pagers at my hip don't vibrate, though, so I know it's not for me. Both Tobias and Robbie look down, check their pagers, and look back up again.

"Well, if pulses are going to hit this short in between, we don't have much time at all," Robbie says. "It's safe to say you start immediately."

CHAPTER NINE

A high-pitched screech jolts me from a deep sleep — a much-needed sleep no less. Beside me, Tobias is passed out, not at all fazed by the banshee squeal that appears to be coming from the adjoining room.

Intermingled with the unnerving noise, Bram's unmistakable deep baritone mumbles and curses. Then comes a "holy shit," and his voice changes entirely; it drops lower, and he starts…. cooing?

Is… that…

The faintest of activity beside me pulls my attention from where I'd been staring at the small hallway trying to make sense of what I was hearing back to Tobias. Silver-blue eyes meet mine, sparkling in delight as Tobias bites down on his lip in an attempt not to laugh.

"What the hell did you do? Is… is that the baby?"

Tobias wedges his hands under his head. "Yep."

My eyebrows raise. Tobias moves onto his side, propping up on an elbow. "Becky needed a hand, and I like the little gal and all… but fuck I was tired."

"So… you left her next to Bram?"

Tobias nods, grinning broadly.

Bram's whispered, lyrical words travel down the hallway, getting louder by the second. Tobias plops back down and closes his eyes, feigning sleep. A huff of laughter escapes me briefly, and I turn my head to the side to hide my amusement. Once I have my expression under control, I return my attention back to the opening. Bram's holding the baby up near his shoulder, a baby bag slung over it as well, and he's attempting to put pants on one-handed at the same time. For a hot second I'm a little concerned at this unpracticed attempt at multitasking, but his balance and the hold he has on the baby seems secure enough, so I decide to leave him to his struggles.

He hops over to the bed, looking at me only briefly, his eyes still foggy with sleep... and with a lack of vision no doubt, considering he doesn't have on his glasses, nor his contacts if I had to guess.

Jeans now on, he returns his second hand to the baby, scooping her under the bum, and carefully places her, belly down, on Tobias's chest, letting the bag fall off his shoulder onto the ground. All the while the baby doesn't make a peep. As soon as Bram knows she's secure... and makes sure I'm watching and won't let her come to any harm, he gives me a sleepy wink and walks away.

Seeing the tiny baby lying so still on Tobias's big form is quite a vision. One that definitely suits him... and makes me feel all gooey inside.

My daydream perusal is short-lived, though, when a terrible stench makes me realize exactly why Bram deposited her where he did.

Tobias peeks an eye open, looking down his nose at her, and his mouth curves into a frown.

And... that's my cue to leave.

I'm out of that bed so fast, Tobias's fingers can only graze my side on the hasty retreat.

A groan comes from behind me as I rush through the hallway giggling.

As soon as I'm out, Bram's long arms are around me, and we're on the bed together, nose to nose.

"Good morning," he says.

"Morning," I respond. "Sleep well?"

"Was cut a little short, but otherwise, yes." His hand comes to my hair, and he tucks it behind my ear.

Over the course of a few days, the UR has been a flurry of activity. After the initial pulses appeared after integrating the systems, the map has since become radio silent. So much so we've begun to wonder if the connection was somehow compromised. If it weren't for the radar still picking up on the residual reads, we would have assumed that was the case. With each passing day of no news, though, we've all slept a little better.

Last night, dare I say, was the best sleep I've gotten in a long while. However, while one would think that no news is good news, in this case it's a double-edged sword. No news means we're nowhere closer to a solution. News means people are dying in mass quantities.

As a result, everyone walks around in a constant state of inner turmoil, jumping at every buzz of the pager. We're all equally upset and relieved regardless of the update.

Sleep is our only reprieve.

Tobias's baby-talk from the other room meets my ears, and I grin. "Well played," I say.

"I thought so." Bram gives me a proud smile. "Should teach Tobias not to screw with my sleep. Speaking of screwing..." His voice lowers and lips meet mine.

There's no question there. No curiosity. Bram is a man on a mission, and the kiss goes from light to insistent in a heartbeat. His hand scoops around the back of my thigh, and he draws my leg over his hip, moving his fingers up higher until the tips slide beneath my shirt and trace where the line of my underwear and skin meet.

In another heartbeat, he moves me onto my back and straddles me, using both hands to work my underwear down. I'd fallen asleep in just those and one of his plain white t-shirts. For that reason, this time he has no intention of taking off the latter.

With my panties now tossed aside, he leans down and reconnects our mouths, slipping his tongue in just enough to tease and make me lift my head for more. But then he pulls away, falls to his back, and whips out his readied length before tugging me on top of him again.

Both of his hands push through my hair, and he brings my mouth down to his as I adjust my knees to each side of his hips. From this position, I have full control, so I take my turn doing the teasing. First, I place a light kiss on his bottom lip then follow it with a gentle nip. One of those deep, chest-vibrating growls emits from him, and his hands move to my hips.

Bram lifts me up at the same time his head lifts to forcefully slip his tongue inside my mouth. In an instant, we're aligned, and he's fitting me over him, guiding me down until there's no farther to go.

His hands move from my hair to under the shirt and push upward until his fingers discover my breasts. Using my knees for support, I slowly raise and descend. When his touch meets my nipples, my head falls back, and I work myself into a faster, steadier grind. I continue riding him, milking him until the two of us can no longer focus on where our hands are or what they're doing because we're so consumed with the slapping of our bodies as they come together one convergence at a time.

A quiet sound — or perhaps movement out of the peripheral of my vision — draws my lust-filled attention to the hallway. Tobias stands there, baby free, fisting himself in harmony with my bouncing atop Bram. He sucks his bottom lip between his teeth, and his half-mast eyes meet mine, a slight grin pulling his mouth up to the side. With his free hand he lifts a finger to his mouth in a silent "shhh."

That's all it takes to push me over the edge. Eyes locked with Tobias, Bram deep inside, my orgasm rolls through me, and I let out a mix between a moan and squeal. Both men come at the same time — one inside me, the other in his own hand.

With a wink Tobias slips away as I continue to spasm and throb around Bram.

Bram cups my head again and brings our mouths together for one final kiss before guiding me onto my back and instructing me to stay still so he can get something to clean us up with. When I insist I can make it to the bathroom — even despite the trickiness of it after a moment like this — he still insists.

Bram closes the distance between the bed and the crawl space that leads to their bathroom, drops to his knees, and scurries through, not caring about my amusement this time. He's back in just a few short minutes, damp cloth in hand. I take it from him and clean myself up before standing.

When Bram goes back into the bathroom to finish cleaning himself up, I head toward mine. Half-naked, I rush past Tobias, who is cleaned up already and propped up on his side on the bed, rubbing the baby's back as if nothing happened. His eyes meet mine, a devious twinkle in them.

By now, I no longer stand there and stare at the shower to work up the courage to get in and put myself into hypothermic shock. Those tentative days have passed. I whip off my shirt, turn on the water, and jump in. What hasn't changed is the length of time I spend here. In and out. That's the best tactic.

When I'm done, I thoroughly rinse the cloth and hang it to dry, then I dry myself off, put on the shirt again, and head back into Bram, Jax, and Julian's room. The baby and Tobias are in there too. This time, though, Bram is holding her, belly down on his lap.

"You boys come up with a name for her yet?"

"Us?" Tobias asks. "No way… I'm not going to be responsible for naming her something Roux ends up hating when he gets back here." He gives me a soft smile. The gesture telling me he's trying to lift my spirits.

We all know now that's not Roux's intention. He made sure his daughter has a support system in case he won't survive through the rest of his dual-personality game. Zinna has raised the stakes; the chances of Roux making it out of her claws alive seem slim.

"…then we can see him." Tobias finishes whatever it was they had continued talking about, pulling me out of my thoughts about Roux entirely.

"See who?" I ask over the tearful whines of the baby.

Tobias's attention darts to me. "Where were you?" He smiles.

"Not here." I sigh, rubbing my face with my hand.

"Well listen this time, because you don't want to miss it," he insists, taking the crying baby from Bram and putting a bottle in her mouth.

"Okay, shoot."

"Jax's conditioning is finished. Celeste is going down today to do the transplant."

"That's… great!" All the thoughts swarming in my mind come to a screeching halt, replaced by a single-focused thought about Jax.

"Want to hear something even better?"

I nod, but say, "Not sure there's anything better than that, but hit me." Tobias's eyebrow raises and a smile quirks up. "You know what I mean." I roll my eyes at him.

"Sure do. Anyway… sorry, I got distracted. Julian's awake. He's been recovering well. They lifted the coma last night."

"Really?!" I jump out of the bed and rush to my room to get dressed, yelling over my shoulder, "Why didn't you tell me last night?"

"You were asleep," he yells back matter-of-factly.

"So! You guys have no trouble waking me up for… other reasons," I holler, pulling on some shorts, tucking in Bram's white shirt into the front of my waistband, and grabbing my pagers and clicking them to my pockets.

"Not to talk to you about one of the other guys though." There's humor in his tone.

"Jerk," I grumble, shoving my feet into the nearest slip-ons I can see.

"Yeah, I already made good on that promise," Tobias quips back as I rejoin them.

Oh my word.

"Get up… let's go." No longer caring about inner thoughts or conversation, I grab the baby's bag and motion at Bram and Tobias to stand.

Tobias adjusts her comfortably in his arms, balancing the bottle against his chest as he stands and reaches his hand out to take the diaper bag from me. Wanting to move them along, I don't question it. I just hand it over, grabbing Bram's hand in mine and tugging them toward the exit.

106

CHAPTER TEN

Much to my chagrin, Tobias insists on first eating and then stopping by to see Becky — to drop the baby off and touch base with her about psych and empath stuff and her involvement with Group T.

I can hardly stand still while the three of them discuss stuff, my mind now swirling with thoughts of both Jax and Julian. "When does Jax's transplant start?" I ask, completely unaware I'm cutting into a conversation until the three look at me, unblinking. "Sorry."

I'd spent the last few days busying myself to the point where I woke up, worked all day, and went to sleep, scarcely taking the time to eat in between. If it weren't for Auden, Bram, and Tobias making sure eating — along with other daily self-care tasks — happened, I'd likely be standing here a starving, stinky, hot mess.

I'm still a hot mess, though at least I'm fed and showered.

"In a couple hours," Tobias answers, placing a hand on my shoulder. His touch grounds me, and I blink away the thoughts of my bedridden men for a moment longer, shaking my head to focus on the conversation at hand.

"So... Group T?" Bram asks Becky, redirecting the conversation back to where it had been before I interrupted.

"We were able to get guys into the Pacific Region's facility and have a property check done where the other pulse hit in that region. Those two areas are good to go.

The best news is that they don't have a ton of guards at the supplementary facilities. We'll be able to take those over and get the Highs out of there easily."

"That's... excellent," Tobias says, surprised.

"Yes, it is." I finally join the conversation. "Our Combat numbers aren't the greatest. If we can send smaller teams to those areas, it will help increase our numbers at the main facilities."

"Exactly." Becky nods, saying it in a childish voice as she looks down at the baby and bounces her lightly in her arms.

"You all are in so much trouble as she starts getting older. Heck, you're already in trouble. Clearly." I gesture at the babe.

Becky looks up and smiles. "So, I was thinking... what do you all think about the name Leta?"

The guys look at the baby, and both step forward and start cooing the name Leta at her, testing it on their tongues. My eyes widen, and Becky catches my gaze, laughing at how that baby makes them stupid.

"I like it," Tobias says, clearing his throat and stepping back, trying to take back what just happened.

"Yeah, I think it fits her," Bram agrees.

"Perfect! Leta it is."

"What... I don't get to add my opinion on the matter?" I cross my arms playfully.

"Of course you do." Becky grins. "What do you think?"

"Why thank you for asking. I think... it's lovely."

"There we have it. It's officially a done deal. You know... when I started this hobby, I never in a million years would have pictured being here with two of the lowest Lows ever to walk the face of the Earth in front of me. It's the very definition of my studies. One was

108

brought to my office so many years ago, and the second was placed in my arms. Funny how fate has a way of weaving quite the web of coincidence."

It wasn't too long ago I learned of Becky's involvement in getting my parents to the safety of the UR once everything started crumbling on a national level. It was then I realized the circle of coincidence was way smaller than I could have imagined. "Yeah, no kidding," I say. "Like how you helped my parents."

"The history between Lena, Harris, and I goes back farther than you know."

Well... that's not surprising. My whole life is now filled with non-surprising surprises. Surprise, surprise. "Oh? How so?"

"Well, you see, we met through a mutual... friend..."

A mutual...

"Wait... the ever-elusive 'college friend' my parents had mentioned time and time again?"

No way...

"Yes. Well... at least probably." Her eyes water and smile fades. "He didn't live very long," she says, her voice dropping.

"That's the one." I try to offer her a small smile, but she adjusts to balance the baby in one cradled arm so she can push her fingers beneath her glasses and wipe the tears away.

"Richard was my husband. We were young college students but did the courthouse wedding thing before he died."

"Ritvo? That's the last name I knew you by."

"Yeah." She sniffles and sighs. "I kept the last name for a lot of years. It wasn't until just prior to making the decision to join in The Program's initiative that I dropped my married name for my maiden. I didn't want anyone on the board — or elsewhere — to connect my married name with the research Richard did. Not that his genius made it beyond his basement, but I didn't want to take any chances.

"Before he died, he asked me to keep an eye on you and your parents. The day they brought you into my office is a day I'll never forget. Right up there with the day you felt my heartbreak on the memorial of his death."

"I remember that day," I whisper. "You were in so much emotional pain I could scarcely breathe."

"That was also the day all his research and assumptions came to a peak — there in my office, in the eyes of a young girl. My sadness was heightened and served to cause a rush of memories — things he had said, sleepless nights of research, all of it sitting across from me, looking straight into my soul through innocent, clear-blue eyes." She takes a shaky breath. "We wanted children, so desperately. But our time together was cut far too short."

"And here you stand, another reminder of what he'd worked so hard to discover." I smile down at Leta.

Becky's eyes fill again. "Yeah… I can't help but think she's a gift from Richard, in a way, you know?"

"I can imagine."

"If Roux comes back, he's gonna have a hard time keeping her from me. Even if I have to take on the role of grandma, I'll take it." She straightens her shoulders and smiles. "As smart as Richard was, I can tell you he never would've imagined four partners to a Low primary. Several candidates, yes. Several close potentials." She glances briefly at Tobias, not meaning anything by it, but we still feel the weight of that look, and the air becomes a bit thicker. "But not more than one true match per person.

"You all are lucky to have each other. There's so much love and dedication between the five of you. It's… admirable… and sweet."

At that, I'm reminded of the two who are missing, and my anxiousness returns as though it had never left.

"Go," Becky insists with a chuckle.

BABY-FREE AND UPDATED on Becky's end, our schedule is finally open to visit Medical. Of course, I can't get there fast enough. At one point, I even stumble over one of those pesky stalagmites I've become good at avoiding under any other circumstance.

Bram, Tobias, and I don't even bother to sit in the waiting area. The three of us walk back into the higher-risk section until we reach that pesky plastic separating Jax and Julian from the rest of the patients.

I pop my head in, instantly earning a dirty look from a guard disguised as a lab tech in a white suit. "We're here to visit Julian Verratti." He nods, tells us to wait there, and waddles in that absurd suit toward the back. I shoot Tobias a glance, and he explains, "He must be a High, and therefore has an increased chance of contaminating the patients. Bram and I won't be permitted back there for this reason… unless we put on similar suits."

"Is he supposed to be able to fight people off while wearing that thing?"

Tobias shrugs. "I don't think there are many people to fight off to be honest."

"Fair enough."

111

Sooner than I expect, a male nurse peeks out of the plastic and waves me inside. The guys and I have become popular enough down here, that even though I don't know everyone's names, they generally know mine... and what we're all about.

After giving Bram and Tobias each a quick glance and smile and receiving ones in return, I slip through to the other side. The nurse brings me to a "clean room" where I'm instructed to thoroughly wash my hands up to my elbows while reciting the alphabet a few times. He then has me step into a chamber of some sort. After a quick ping and vibration, I'm let out — another step that likely helps to reduce the risk of carrying anything contagious on my clothing or skin.

Every nerve hums inside me as he leads me down the hallway. With the many distractions and how desperately I was trying to distance myself from the thought of Jax and Julian during the waiting process — if only to lessen the wait time until I no longer had control over the situation — I had turned off my empath connection. The emptiness with it open was maddening. Only now do I open again and seek out, mentally reaching for Julian.

My empath sensor absorbs his signature right away. In doing so, the tension that had been building in my muscles lessens with each step closer to where he's resting. Julian's eager mental poking meets mine in response, further assuaging my fears of what state I'll find him in.

His signature isn't as lively as usual, but it's there, and that's more than enough for now.

The nurse slows as we approach a room and then moves aside and tilts his head to indicate I can enter.

With a deep, shaky intake of breath, I step inside, my eyes immediately meeting Julian's olive-green ones. Only when I see him awake do I let out the breath I'd taken on entrance. I rush to his side, sitting in a chair that had no doubt been placed there just for me, and our fingers weave together. His head turns to the side, those amazing green eyes filled with life and a spark of... amusement. His curls fall over them, and I push them aside.

"*Cuore mio,*" he breathes, his accent thick. My eyes fill, and I let out the combination of a hiccup and a chuckle. "Rumor has it, I pulled through before Jax. Is that right?"

"Yes." A small frown tugs at my lips. But Julian grins wide. "We'd made a bet."

"Oh? What were the stakes?"

"He said, 'Like hell if yer gettin' in bed with her again before I do.' I begged to differ." Julian winks at me.

A real, complete laugh comes out of me then. "So, sick as dogs and the two of you arguing over who gets to sleep with me next. You both are impossible."

"Impossibly good in bed."

"Well... yeah... I can't deny that."

Julian's smile fades then, the weight of what winning truly means. "I wanted to win... but I didn't, you know?"

"Yeah." My voice drops low, but then I look up at him with an attempted smile. "He still has a chance... You're not exactly in the clear yet. Who knows, he may still recover before you do."

"*Uffa...* you're right. Guess I best keep working on getting better."

"Please..."

113

Julian's hand squeezes mine tight. "Doctor says I should be out in a few days."

"A few days? Really? That soon?"

"That soon?! *Sono pronto ad andarmene da qui!*"

His apparent cursing in his native language brings the smile back to my face. "You could curse in Italian and I'd still think it's sexy," I say, repeating what I'd said to him our first night spending real one-on-one time together.

"Good thing, *cuore mio*, because that's what I just did." His smile returns. "When Jax wakes, do me a favor will you?"

"Of course."

"Say, *maledizione, quanto mi sei mancato fratello, ma la ragazza è diventata mia.* Just… make sure it's the first thing you say to him. Promise?" There's a devious twinkle in his eye, but I agree. Hard to tell him no after all we've been through. Plus, what could it possibly hurt. "Let me hear you say it."

I repeat the words, them falling from my tongue easier now that I've been around Julian for a little bit.

"Ah, *perfetto!*" he says with a bit too much inflection in his tone. "Yes, that'll do."

His hand squeezes mine again, and he closes his eyes. "*Mio Dio,* I want out of here so bad."

"Same," I say, leaning over and placing a kiss on his cheek.

"Want to update me on everything I missed?"

I blow a raspberry from my lips. "Oh boy… there's been quite a lot. Where to start…"

Finding it difficult to pull on everything that has happened since we came back safely, I do my best to update him on Kait, Roux's daughter, the new pulses, the teams now forming, and the coordinated attack.

When I bring up the topic of the Search and Rescue crews, Julian's eyes light up. "That 'search crew' thing... sign me up. Before I landed myself in here, I was thinking about joining the Guard anyway."

I raise an eyebrow at this revelation.

"Before you laugh at me because I'm small... height-wise of course..." He winks, earning an amused eye roll in return. "I can hold my own. I know I'm not the same size as most guards, but I could still do it."

"There's no need to justify your... size." I smile at him. His rocky health, and the possibility that will be something that'll carry over for the remainder of his years, is what's more concerning. "You'd make a great member of the Guard. I've seen what you can do." A flashback of him beating the crap out of Roux flicks through my mind. Part of me selfishly wants to tell him to take that route... anything to keep him underground with me. Working with S&R means going to the surface and risking his life for others.

His eyes search mine, reading my emotions and my thoughts it seems. "I can't stay down here, *cuore mio*."

"I had a feeling you'd say that."

"You don't like it, hm?"

"No. But it'll take all of us to get through this. We're all so different in our talents. You're needed. Search and Rescue would benefit from having you aboard... as would the Guard." Combat would too, but I keep that one to myself, lest he get any grander ideas. "So... what do they serve you to eat down here?" I quickly change topics due to the loud rumbling of my stomach. We'd made a pit stop to eat before seeing Becky, but I couldn't stomach much. Not with everything going on.

Julian scrunches his nose, the picky chef in him coming out to play. "Nothing worth its salt," is his answer. "Stick around long enough, and I imagine you'll find out."

"Oh, I intend to. In fact, I'm not leaving until you get out. My responsibilities are taken care of... We're just waiting on more pulses to hit to finalize everything."

Julian's eyebrows disappear behind his curls. "Well... I'm sure not going to complain. How did I get so lucky?" His voice lowers, and the hand I'm not holding lifts, the IV and wires attached to his arms dangling. But he manages to reach for my head, and direct my face to his, pressing our foreheads together. He then brings my forehead to his mouth and places a light kiss there before resting his head back again.

"I'd kiss you, but I'm pretty sure the nurses didn't brush my teeth while I was sleeping." He grimaces and makes a smacking noise with his mouth. I lean forward and kiss his lips anyway, still respecting his personal disgust by not slipping in any tongue.

"Let's remedy that, okay? I'll let Tobias and Bram know that I will be staying here with you for a few days, and while I'm out there, I'll get some toiletries."

Julian nods. "While you do that, I think I'll take a nap."

The words remind me he's still not his best self, and my heart twists. I stand and kiss him once more, this time on top of his curls. In the least, they smell clean. No doubt the Medical team probably made them thoroughly scrub and wash on admittance — and several times since — in order to get off any lingering radiation.

With that, I leave the room and walk back to the plastic. As I approach, the blur of bodies moving on the other side catches my attention. I lean against the wall, standing out of the way, waiting for whoever is on the other side to enter.

None other than Celeste steps through, looking much paler than usual. The difference when she doesn't have makeup on is amazing. She also looks like she hasn't gotten much sleep; her hands tick nervously as she twists them together, while the nurse speaks to her in passing. Her eyes catch mine briefly, and without thought I mouth the words "Thank you," to her.

She discerns the translation and nods her head, but not without mouthing back, "I'm not doin' it for you."

Well... can't say I blame her for that remark. But if she wasn't about to save Jax's life, I'd still very much like to slap her upside the head one of these days.

CHAPTER ELEVEN

The next couple days are somewhat uneventful aside from our pagers going off to indicate a new pulse on the radar. Otherwise, each day is routine: At night I sleep in the hospital bed with Julian, propped on my side and head on his chest, unmoving for fear I'll mess up all the attached monitors and IVs. During the day, I help him with his hygiene, even assisting in his attempts to shave. Though, after seeing him so smooth, I decide I just might sneakily hide all the razors from this moment forward; Julian always had stubble kept trimmed close, and I decide I prefer him that way. Tobias and Jax are the clean-shaven ones. Julian and Bram are not. I quite like the disparity.

In addition to our morning and night routine, Julian and I even eat all three meals together. I joked that once he got out, he'd probably try to get as far away from me as possible. But he assured me that would not be the case.

News of Jax's transplant comes sooner than expected. Celeste bounced back almost instantly, thanks to her excellent… health.

The best news is that Jax is on the mend and should be able to have visitors within the week.

Today, however, after receiving the dismal news of yet another pulse, we learn that Julian gets to leave the hospital wing. It's a bright and shiny silver lining in an otherwise dreary situation.

More than eager for escape, Julian threatens to rip the tubes and cords off and dash outta there if the discharge process is "anything like in a real hospital."

Thankfully, that is not the case; within the hour, we're leaving the Medical wing, walking hand-in-hand through the waiting room and into the lower level's intersection.

An impatient buzz still hums through our bond though. He expresses that he'd nearly been driven mad by the cords and tubes contributing to his inability to touch me unhindered. To hold my hand without restrictions. To scoop me in both arms and squeeze me tight.

And to kiss me.

Needless to say, it takes a while to get to the room. In fact...

We don't make it there. First, he has to secure that bet he made with Jax. Knowing Jax is going to pull through and we'll be able to see him soon, Julian doesn't hesitate to prove to me through action just how much he missed me. He tugs me hurriedly into a room I remember visiting during my first tour with Tobias — the storage area.

In a heartbeat, my shorts and underwear are in a pile at my feet, and the t-shirt I'm wearing is being lifted over my head as Julian backs me against one of the shelving units.

As soon as I'm completely naked, he pushes cans and other nonperishables to the side, hoists me up, and sits me on the shelf's edge. My legs immediately wrap around him as our mouths clash together, our tongues battling for dominance as they tend to do with each other.

My fingers go to the waistband of his sweatpants, and I push them down as far as I can before he takes over, bending over to take them off the rest of the way while still attempting to keep our lips locked. Now bare from the waist down, he races to remove his shirt. The momentary separation happens so fast, and our mouths

119

unite again so instantaneously, my head swims with the thought that perhaps they never separated at all.

Julian slams into me with a grunt, and his head falls back, those green eyes closing in bliss. My breath catches on impact. I'd missed this rough and tumble intimacy with Julian — the no questions asked, "fuck-me-hard-and-now" lovemaking. I'd never have imagined being able to make love and fuck at the same time, but Julian ensures it happens. The intensity is so overwhelming we go from starting to finishing in a matter of moments, and I scarcely have time to breathe. My legs squeeze around him tighter as my entire body trembles. My hands come to the shelf's edge, and I grip tight as Julian drives himself inside me. My inner walls ache and explode. As I come down from that energy-stealing orgasm, his arm wraps around to steady me, and he plunges deep once more, filling me with a groan of release.

Only then does he lay me back and kiss me so passionately that our coupling is ardent and dizzying, turning from rough to gentle in an instant.

Still inside me, Julian looks around until his eyes catch on what he's seeking. Placing his hands under my butt, he picks me up and waddles us over to a different shelf. He puts me back down on a small clear space and grabs a handful of napkins, gently shoving them between us. "Food safety," he says.

A bubble of laughter escapes me, and I take over from there, extra diligent not to make a mess this time. Because, like Julian said, "Food safety."

To my further amusement, Julian even goes to the length of grabbing a large bottle of sanitizer and wiping down everywhere we'd touched. When he finishes, he finally puts his clothes back on.

"I don't know," I say. "I think I prefer watching you do things in the nude."

"We can make that happen more often if you'd like." He winks at me, taking the bunch of napkins from my hand, tossing them in a nearby garbage canister along with his own, and stealing another couple squirts of sanitizer.

"You know, I think this quite possibly is the cleanest I have ever been right after sex," I joke. When he's done rubbing our hands together, I quickly put all my clothes and pagers back on.

Julian chuckles, and we nonchalantly exit the storage room as though we weren't just in there utilizing the shelves for non-food-related needs.

Distracted by a naked, cleaning man, and the humor therein, the previous buzzing of our pagers only now comes floating to the surface of my thoughts. My hand moves to the UR pager, and Julian peeks at the screen with me.

"What does that code mean?" he asks.

"Another pulse. This one in Florida again." My shoulders droop, and I let out a frustrated growl.

"Maybe the other facilities aren't up yet." He stops looking at the pager and stares ahead, suddenly hyper-focused on where we're going. That's when it dawns on me... none of the guys have talked about their families and what this might mean for them. We'd all been so concentrated on the big picture and on getting our group back to good health, that we hadn't considered their families.

Rather, *I* had not. Guilt and mortification begins to smother me. Julian's hand squeezes tight. "There's nothing to be done about it," he says, picking up on the dramatic change in my emotions.

121

"I didn't even think to ask. To check in with you all."

Julian shakes his head. "What, and remind us by doing so?"

"Well… still…"

"There's a lot on your plate, *cuore mio*. We haven't asked about your family either."

"That's true, but we all know my parents are in the Eastern UR."

Julian shrugs. The UR pager goes off a second time. Again we both look at it, but this time he tries to interpret. "So, a pulse in the… what's that… three dash two?"

My heart stops along with my feet. "Three is Central. West to East. They kept it simple. The two means they found the supplementary facility. I pull out our group pager to message Tobias. First, I type my code followed by the transposed numbers for the word "Where?" Then, I finish with Tobias's code.

"How many more do we need before we can move forward?"

"At this point, they're under the assumption there are two locations per region. We've got both Pacific pegged, now both Central, one in the Mountain region, and Eastern is a no-go currently."

Julian nods. The pager buzzes. "Nebraska," I say, updating him. "The Central Region is pretty damn big; I wouldn't be surprised if they had a third location. But, then again, I also wouldn't be surprised if they're transporting people outside their home regions at this point. In fact, Zinna sent me to the Central Region since it was closer to where I was at the time. My home region is just minutes away from the Central facility in Florida. The facility there is almost right on the Eastern-Central border. Depending on where the Nebraska one is, that facility might be placed on a zone border too. Plus, I know for a fact NAB Sweep Teams were crossing Region borders as well since Roux was assigned to the Eastern Region Sweep, but his group still made its way over here."

There's really no point to my blabbering; it's more just thinking aloud than anything else.

Our group pager buzzes again, followed in quick succession by the UR pager. "Jeez," I say, tossing one to Julian to check while I check the other.

"Tobias wants all of us to meet in the room," Julian shares.

"They found a new location... again..." I whisper equally excited and disappointed. "The Eastern Region is finally on the board. Not too terribly far from the Eastern UR, in fact."

"From the sounds of it, Becky is going to have her work cut out for her."

"Yeah, no kidding." At that, I'm reminded Julian hasn't yet met the baby — Leta. I make a mental note to ensure that happens after our impromptu meeting with Tobias and Bram.

We hurry through the crowds of members, making our way to the room in no time. Tobias, Bram, and Auden are already there, the three of them looking downright exhausted. Most everyone with a job down here has been pulling shifts around the clock.

Bram looks the most worn. No doubt because he has been doing a mixture of greenhouse weaponizing, medicinal plants, and foods grown in the greenhouses that can feed large amounts of people. "Like potatoes and such," he explained. Who would have known botany would be so beneficial? Bram knew, of course. The plant people have their fingers in just about every aspect of the UR.

I sit beside him and run my hand through his hair. He gives me a tired smile, wrapping his arms around me and tugging me over to his lap.

Tobias stands and embraces Julian, the two men clapping each other on the back.

"Man," Tobias says, "never thought I'd be saying this, but it's damn good to see you."

Julian laughs, stepping back and taking Bram's extended hand. "Glad you're back with us," Bram says.

Auden takes a turn next, giving Julian one of those brief, side-hug-shoulder-slaps.

"So, what's going on?" Julian asks mid-air as he jumps onto his bed and proceeds to do a sheet angel on his belly, groaning. "No offense, *i miei amici*, but I missed this bed way more than I missed you guys," he says, drawing laughs from the bunch of us.

Once he's flipped over and ready to listen, Tobias starts: "Robbie and I have been working on something behind the scenes. We didn't want to reveal anything at first, because the idea was just so far-fetched we figured it was all just a bunch of blowing smoke on our part anyway. Until it wasn't. Until the idea became more and more feasible."

All attention in the room on Tobias, he swipes a hand through his hair, takes a deep breath, and begins: "After the reminder of Robbie's trojan, he popped in there to look around a bit. Of course, because she hadn't been active in the database since, there wasn't much. However, he did find an activity log, which apparently syncs to her account no matter what. So, for example, if she has to use her keycard or code to log something, it'll show in her activity log."

124

"So, I'm assuming you saw something in her log, and that's what drove this new idea?"

"Exactly." Tobias smiles. "And what we found is that she logged a work trip back to New York — date and time to-be-determined."

"For what purpose, do you think?"

"We're unsure, of course, but are assuming it's to get access to her account back."

"Okay, so what role do we play in this?" Julian asks, now propped up on an elbow with a fierce determination in his gaze.

Again Tobias rubs the back of his neck. "A few, if it pans out the way we'd like. For one, we'd like to stop her while, at the same time, finding the admin building. In turn, we're hoping to locate the host system. Having shadowed at the National DNA Database, I already know their storage virtualization doesn't send all the information in the database to the networks there. So, unfortunately, we need to figure out where it pools."

"So, like the device that holds all the information the exacentrifuges send? Everyone's scores and personal information?" I ask.

"That's right."

"Remember when Robbie said something about we 'won't know how much we can blow up until we get in there,' but he also mentioned not doing anything too obvious?" Julian asks.

"Yeah…" I respond.

"I think that's what Tobias is trying to say. Well, kinda."

"It's time to blow things up?" Auden asks with a grin.

"Not exactly…" Tobias gives a small grimace. "Or, rather, not entirely. The information is too valuable to just blow up. What a shame it would be to lose all of those decades of scientific work. The sad truth is that all that consequential information is what drives The Program. That storage pool is what provides the NAB and facilities the information they need to take further action."

I find myself nodding, starting to see a visual of what Tobias is talking about. "What they're doing is ruthless, but even so, they don't want everyone dead. Killing the Lows would be counterproductive to their plans. If they don't know who is who… they'd likely not be willing to take that risk. Lows are a much smaller commodity than Highs." Collective nods take place throughout the room.

"So, how do we keep the information while still 'blowing up' the device or program that consolidates and manages it?" Using key terms, I try my hardest to deliver the details back to Tobias in a way that might help confirm I'm understanding all the particulars.

Tobias gives me one of those rare, full smiles before letting out a breath of air. "Have you heard of DNA data storage?"

"Of course. The advancement of storage is nearly as prolific these days as the advancement of the DNA-reading technology." That's about all I know, though, so I stop there.

"Yes. So… what we're thinking… is that we can store the database directly in your DNA." The last part comes out in a rush, Tobias's nervousness evident.

Bram tenses around me, and Julian shoots up to a sitting position. "Thes-sal-ee? You want to store the database inside…"

"Inside my body?!" I finish with a squeak.

"Yes... *then* we 'blow up' the storage, so to speak. Well, not 'so to speak'; we'll actually blow up the hardware. And I don't just mean the storage hardware." He pauses, his shoulders drooping. "We're proposing to demolish every exacentrifuge too." Technology Tobias was once in awe over. "To anyone who doesn't know better — the Commission, for instance — will just assume it's gone. All that money, time, data... gone. It would take them years upon years upon years to rebuild and gather that sort of information again. While the equipment will, indeed, be gone, it doesn't mean the data needs to be. Maybe one day, a long time from now, the information therein can be used to *help* our nation... not kill them."

"But... why... me?"

Bram, who'd been so quiet, finally speaks up. "Because you're the perfect vessel for keeping it preserved... and the last person they'd kill. Zinna may have put you in some compromising situations, but she'd never physically hurt you enough to take your life. You're the safest bet. Plus, a DNA storage transfer? They'd never know. Not if we get it done without being seen or caught."

"Speaking of Zinna. What about her? Does she survive this? The Board? The COMMIES? What of them?"

"No one has to die. Plus, I think the loss of control of The Program is basically like giving Zinna a slow, painful death anyway. She'll live the rest of her life miserable and ornery. She's powerless without The Program to back her."

"Okay, so assuming we're all on board. How do we make this happen?"

"Honestly? That's where things get tricky. We'll need to gather certain supplies, demolish the exacentrifuges, then find, access, and extract the data. Getting there won't be a walk in the park either, I'm sure."

"Getting *where*, exactly?"

"To New York. Timing will be everything. The NAB is a strong unit, but they along with the facility guards are low in numbers. For this to work best, not only will the UR need to attack the facilities at the same time, but we'll need to take care of the exacentrifuges, extract the data, and wipe the storage at roughly the same time too. And hopefully accomplish it all before Zinna gets her permissions back and does something to interfere. There might be a little wiggle room with the exacentrifuges, but not much. As you all know, those aren't heavily guarded." *They really aren't. When we went to the Central Region's, one guard was on night duty. That's it.* "But, still, taking those out around the same time sure wouldn't hurt."

"And how are you proposing we get to New York?" Bram asks.

Tobias smiles at this question. "Well... Betty hasn't let us down yet."

"She very well might if you make her drive to New York!" I squeal.

Tobias laughs. "Well, if you're not opposed, Robbie would like to... doctor her up a bit."

My eyebrows rise. "No, not opposed. Betty can always use a little love. Who will be going?" I ask, feeling a bit anxious about the answer. Jax still isn't in the clear, and I don't intend on us being separated.

"Just the five of us." With Auden in the room, he makes five.

I dart a glance at Auden, and his eyes widen, his hands going up, palms out. "No, not me," he interjects.

"Oh," Tobias says, "no… Jax too, assuming he's discharged in time."

"But in less than a week? I hardly think they'll let him leave the Medical wing, much less travel cross-country that soon," I explain. The option seems so far from likely, it hurts.

Tobias places his hand on my knee. "It's basically the end of the world as we know it. We need all the bodies we can get. Jax has been healing since before they discovered he needed the transplant, and the doctors believe he'll bounce back pretty fast. Even if he doesn't, and he's still in well enough spirits to travel, he won't be letting them keep him in there anyway."

I nod, resting my head against Bram's shoulder. But then I think about Auden staying back and hate that he had to see the disappointment in my earlier response. "What about Auden though?" I inquire.

"We have plans for him here."

Still leaning against the stone near the opening to my portion of the room, Auden looks at me with a small smile. "Oh, that's great," I say. "And will we be able to keep in contact?"

"Yes," Tobias answers. "Robbie is going to give us a direct connection to the Tech room via Betty's navigational screen, provided he can get it to work properly and there isn't any issue with the satellites. But… ah…" There goes the hand through his hair again. "We had another idea too." Tobias's eyes dart toward Auden then back at me.

When I follow the check, I find Auden's head is low, his hands shoved in his pockets, and his cheeks and nose as red as a tomato. My eyes, widening in anxiousness, dart back to Tobias. Tobias takes a breath then clears his throat. "We're hoping you'll open a stronger connection with him," he whispers, dropping his gaze.

Everyone in the room stills. Every sound becomes muffled. "But he's seventeen…" I shake my head. "Even if I did like him, I'm only five years older than he is… but… still…" The blabbering doesn't end.

"Eighteen." His voice cuts me short.

"You're… Since when?! No… wait… When we met, you said you had just turned seventeen!"

"Yeah… I lied." He puffs out his cheeks and blows out a rush of air. "When Robbie started doling out duties to the group of new members I was part of, he handled it in age groups. Eighteen and older were given higher risk jobs, and I… wasn't sure I was cut out for those types of responsibilities. Since I had only just turned eighteen, I figured lying about my age would be a good idea. At least at the time I did. So… when I met all of you, I was still trying to keep up the ruse. The other day, I accidentally let it slip to Ruby."

Words fail me for a time. But before long my shocked surprise turns into laughter. "Oh, I bet that was fun."

"Well, she gave me a good swat upside the head first. But after calming down, she insisted on throwing me a birthday party since it was only a few months ago, and in her words 'you only turn into a man once.'"

Tobias laughs. "Sorry to rain on your parade, but being eighteen hardly qualifies you as a man."

I don't necessarily agree with that — nor does Auden based on the narrowed glare he gives Tobias. To snuff out the growing fire, I chime in: "That definitely sounds very Rubyish."

130

Auden's attention leaves Tobias and returns to me. "Yeah. With everything going on, though, having a party just doesn't feel right. So, she agreed to wait until…" his voice trails.

My eyes dart from Auden to the guys and back again.

Tobias finishes what Auden couldn't say, "They're waiting until Jax recovers."

"You're waiting on Jax… to have *your* birthday party?"

Auden nods.

Wait… why? "Why are you… oh my gosh… is it Jax's birthday too?"

Auden chuckles. "No. Well, at least not that I'm aware of."

Once upon a time, I had the opportunity to look at the database. Each guy's profile. Never once did I pay attention to anything other than the pertinent information. I didn't even notice their last names much less think about checking their birthdates. And in the big scheme of things, we hadn't been together very long at all. What feels like a lifetime, both in memories and experiences, has been nothing more than just a couple of months. Meet the right person and time moves differently — a moment can seem like an eternity and an eternity like a moment.

Brushing aside the notion for a time, I ask, "Okay… can we, like, handfast or something?"

Auden's head lifts, a look of relief washing over his features. The hint of a cocky smile crosses his face as he darts a look at Tobias. Tobias's returning eye roll doesn't go unnoticed either.

"Handfast? So you'll marry me, but you won't kiss me?" he asks with a smile.

131

I press my lips together and narrow my eyes at him. "No… plus, despite what people might be beginning to think, I'm not a kissing whore." Julian laughs. "Well, what do *you* propose we do?"

Auden pushes off the wall and steps to me, holding his hand out. I take it without question, and he pulls me to stand. Behind me, Tobias begins speaking, "We want the empath connection you have with us to be with someone here in the UR. That way we have a back-up plan for being able to sense your wellbeing, in case communications go down."

Auden squeezes my hand. "Like a temporary… boyf—"

"Nice try," Tobias scoffs.

Auden chuckles, throwing me a wink. "So…" — he looks down at our hands — "I don't think your idea is working."

My eyes dart to our clasped hands. "I wasn't trying." But my attention turns to Tobias, Bram, and Julian.

Bram shrugs. "I like him."

Julian nods his head.

Tobias sighs. "Yeah… he's a good… kid."

My eyebrows curve in, and I look at Auden again. Auden does not look impressed. "Not a kid, Toby," he says, using the nickname Ruby had coined early on for Tobias.

Bram turns to Tobias. "Wanna talk age gap?" He raises a brow.

Both Tobias's brows rise in return. Tobias is six years my senior. There's no room for comparison there. If Auden is eighteen, that makes him only four years younger than me. He might be shy and awkward at times, but he doesn't act like a child by any means.

Our palms become slightly damp where they touch. Either from nerves or the temperature in here, I can't decide. But I once again drop my gaze, studying my hand in his. There's been a small connection between us since we met. A connection I've casually avoided not just because of our situation but also because I already have four "boyfriends."

In light of what we've learned over the course of all this, I'll have my fair share of "connections" if I'm not careful. Opening a line between Bauer and me at the facility, for example, was easier than anticipated. For a number of reasons, the plan had been for me to get in his head without intimate contact. However, as eager as he was to act older than his age — still just a child at fifteen — he'd kissed me. Thankfully, it only served to trigger his empath abilities.

Securing a bond would have taken a mutual attraction, and there was most certainly not even a modicum of that on my end. Thing is... I can't say an attraction between Auden and me doesn't exist. A kiss with him might come with more than just an empath connection. It might come with a bond too.

If I'm following what Tobias has planned, a bond forming is exactly what they're banking on.

All the guys stay quiet while I think things through in my mind. Right now? I just can't bring myself to go that far. Auden somehow senses the conclusion I've formed, whether it be from my readable facial expressions or the speck of a bond already formed, I'm not sure. He squeezes my hand lightly and scoops his arm around my shoulders, instead, giving me a small hug.

Not a word is said from there. He simply steps away and returns to the wall. Bram takes over, wrapping his hand around mine and pulling me down into his lap again. "There's still time," he mumbles into my hair before giving me a reassuring kiss on the head.

"Even then, it's not a requirement," Tobias reassures.

"It's a smart idea," I respond with a sigh. "But if the bond *is* created, what then? Why would I want him to stay behind any more than I want you guys to?" A million more questions about the overall plan surface in my mind — too many to pick just one. For that reason, I open and close my mouth a number of times, eventually choosing to simply not ask any more questions at all, nor listen for the answers to the ones I already verbalized. Not right now at least.

Right now we wait. Wait for news about Bauer and Roux. Wait for more pulses. Wait for Jax.

CHAPTER TWELVE

Julian

"We've got new blood, fellas." Harvey, the Search and Rescue leader, pats me on the back in front of the room of crew members. "Combat likes to puff up and say they're the brawn of the Resistance, but we all know it's the S&R, right?" After being discharged, I spent a lot of time in the Combat room, doing as much as I could to get my strength back up. But news had gotten around that I was looking to join S&R, so Harvey, desperate for more bodies, intercepted me and said I was fit enough for the job.

The room *hoorahs,* and Harvey leans over, lowering his voice. "Combat hasn't been above ground since training started. When the time comes, they're in for a rude awakening."

He raises his voice again, addressing everyone: "Fuck training… Training is for the weak. Am I right?" The older man grins down at me, and for a moment I'm not sure I've seen anything more intimidating in my life. The crew laughs.

"Alright… Let's get on with it then. We've got people to save and supplies to collect." He claps his hands together, turns, and walks out of the room. Everyone in attendance follows, leaving me standing there.

"*Merda,*" I mumble under my breath, turning around and sprinting to catch up. They wind through the Underground like they own the place until they reach the steep incline we had used upon our return from the facility.

One by one they climb upward, each disappearing through a hole in the ground at the surface. The bright light outside is always such a sensory shock after being in the ambient lighting of the Underground for so long. I use my hand as a visor until my eyes adjust, then continue following along as everyone piles into a few large vans. Similar in appearance to the one Robbie likes to use, minus all the fancy tech inside, they're big enough that there's no camouflaging them... especially traveling as a caravan.

Their tactic might be *gettarsi in pasto ai leoni,* but I'm no fool; I take the van with the leader. If I'm going to learn by example, I'd prefer to learn from someone who knows exactly what they're doing.

My first misconception is regarding the tech, however. While these vans don't have the myriad of tech gear like Robbie's, they still have some. Harvey and the crew inside this van are lifting the seats and pulling gear from beneath. The group of them slip on devices similar to a com-band over their heads and flip small, glass screens over their eyes. As though reactive to touch, the devices power on. Harvey tosses me one, and I catch it and put it on just in time to be able to grab the butt of the gun he hands over next. As I study and check it over, I immediately notice my gun is different from everyone else's.

"With help from someone from Group T, Robbie was able to procure a stash of the new gripprint guns." He tilts his head toward the crew member beside me as he — she, on closer inspection — wraps her fingers around the handle and it flashes blue on contact. With a tighter squeeze, the safety clicks, and she holsters it.

136

"When you get a chance, head to Tech and tell them to program you one. For now, you're gunning old-school."

"I'm not complaining; both get the job done." After grabbing a holster from the still-open bench seat, I slip the gun inside. The device around my head powers on as soon as I flip the screen over my eye. Everyone around me shows up through the glass as red, pulsating globs of light. "Heat sensors?" I inquire.

Harvey's finger lifts to his ear, and the hum of an audio connection buzzes through my head, stemming from the pad that rests behind my opposite ear. "Yes," he says into the device. "Otherwise, it'd take us too long to find people. And time isn't exactly our friend right now."

At that moment, the van lurches forward and everyone is quick to finish up as we bounce over the rugged terrain at the far back of Robbie's property. I lift my finger to the same area of my device, finding the rubbery button right away. Depressing it, I respond with "*Sì, Capo.*"

"I'm going to pretend whatever you just said wasn't insulting." Harvey smirks as he stands, hunched, and approaches the van's cab, turning to address everyone. "Everything in a fifty mile radius is clear unless people are crossing over by foot. Today, we're the lucky fucks who get to attempt crossing the state line. Last we heard, there's a good stretch of unincorporated land there. As most of you know, the border patrols prefer to stick to the areas with more traffic. We'll get as close as we can to the next residential area, find a place to park, and handle the rest on foot." He then addresses me directly. "You ever killed anyone?"

I shake my head. "Thought about it. Shot someone once — but he didn't die."

"Heh, yeah, well thinking and trying versus actually *doing* are entirely different. You'll kill someone today. Every time we leave base there's bloodshed. *Unis* get capped on sight, no questions asked. That's jargon for 'people in uniform.' The fewer guards, the less backup they can send to aid the facilities and pulse areas when the attack starts. Plus, unlike us, they're instructed *not* to shoot on sight in case we're helpful to The Program. But they *will* shoot as soon as a threat is evident which happens fairly fast. Shoot first, think later. Got it?"

"Got it," I respond with a sharp nod and hard swallow.

To pass the time, I focus on the road through the windshield ahead, feeling the coolness of the gun's metal beneath my fingers as I absentmindedly run them over the grooves and curves. Thessaly, the guys, and I had driven this route so many times at this point that it doesn't take me long to realize exactly what unincorporated stretch of land he was referencing.

I squint my eyes, contemplating. The sudden rush of dread has my head shaking side-to-side, eyes widening, and words tumbling out of my mouth before I can consciously process my reaction in time to take a breath and think first. "The area you're headed into isn't going to be clear. Unincorporated or not, it'll be hot. You have to go a different way."

Harvey's eyes shoot to me and his brows rise. "There is nowhere else unless we head south for an hour before crossing over. And everything from there into Florida is swarming with Unis. It's too close to the Region's main facility. We've gotten word from our sources that this spot is as good as it gets."

"When?"

"Ah, about a week ago, I believe."

"*Cazzo!* Thessaly and one of the Group T agents used this area as a fake hideout in order to get the coordinates to the facility. The location is in the enemy's nav system. Zinna will have people posted there. Several. She'll cover anywhere we've left a trail... and we definitely left a trail there."

"The hot spots have been updated since."

"Well then, whoever updated the hot spots, didn't know about our espionage efforts 'about a week ago.' We're fucking screwed."

He looks at me intently as he contemplates this new information. When he comes to some sort of decision, he nods once, moves to the cab, and plops down into the passenger seat to have a chat with the driver.

The conversation doesn't take long. Soon he returns, addressing the team again. "We're stopping short and walking the last couple miles. I'm not taking any risks with the crew; you see red, you shoot." Harvey points at the lens covering his eye. "I don't care if there's a chance it's a normal person. Hesitating gets the wrong people killed... every time. We're not a proper organization, and we don't act like one. We're lawless. You have a problem with it, stay in the van."

He clears his throat, swallows thickly, and sits back down. Everyone is so silent the only sound heard for a few minutes is of the tires roving over the asphalt. The cool metal of the gun returns to my senses and I look down, checking and rechecking that it's loaded.

The van curves off the road, parking alongside the back of a small, deserted charge station. No one wastes a moment commiserating; as soon as the van stops moving, everyone but the driver piles out, Harvey and I the last to exit. Just before he slides the door closed, he grabs a canvas bag and carefully tosses it over his shoulder.

Outside, teams from each van convene, each person holstering a weapon. Most of them have a handgun, but a couple have daggers. Two members, most likely snipers if I were to guess, carry rifles.

My guess is proven accurate when Harvey points his finger at each. "You two in the front. Use the scopes to look ahead. Let us know what we're dealing with."

"You'd think this far into Mississippi there would be more higher points to work with," one of the men scoffs. "Livin' my whole life in the deep south, I'd assumed everywhere but Florida, South Alabama, South Georgia had hills. Clearly not." He holds out an arm, gesturing towards the very flat land stretching ahead.

"All of Mississippi is still considered the deep south," Harvey corrects. "On that count, it sounds to me like you won't have a problem since your past training was in the flatlands, hmm?"

"Nope. Just disappointed is all," the man explains.

"We get through this, you'll be able to see the mountains one day. Today's not that day though."

The sniper side-grins and leaves without further discussion, his companion in tow.

Harvey walks from van to van, giving each driver a directive.

"You nervous?" the woman in my group speaks up, a tremble in her voice.

"Not yet. Sounds like you are though." She doesn't respond, just looks off into the distance. "Why are you here?" I asked, now somewhat irritated if she is, indeed, nervous.

She darts a glare at me, scoffing. "Don't worry about me, I can hold my own. Pre-game jitters is all. As to why I'm here? I like to kill people."

She then walks away, circling the tension out of her shoulders. Not even ten minutes later she's hurling into a bunch of overgrown weeds nearby. Once done, she simply stands and wipes her mouth on the black sleeve of her UR shirt. Our eyes meet, and she shrugs and smiles.

Behind me a man speaks up. "Don't piss her off." He laughs. "She's a beast out there. Might mistake you for one of them if you make the wrong move."

"Doesn't look tough when she's heaving all her meals from the day into the soil."

"Hey, whatever gets the job done, right?"

"Sure."

"We're up!" Harvey yells.

The woman takes in a deep breath and pats down her holster ensuring everything is in place. Taking the cue, the man and I do the same.

The woman steps up to us, and we all turn in unison, heading in the direction Harvey is leading.

"We'll keep behind the buildings en route. Afterwards, just sprint and pray," Harvey instructs.

"Name's Walsh." The man holds out a hand and I accept, giving it a firm shake.

"Julian." I turn my sights on the woman, wondering if she'll introduce herself next.

"Aubrey," she says.

I nod, holding back a chuckle. Aubrey... such a sweet name for someone who's supposedly so tough.

Not that a name necessarily defines personality.

Traveling the number of miles from where we parked to the border of the woods doesn't take long at

141

all. About midway there, the two snipers perch on the roof of a convenience store. A store that had been gutted of its products.

Through the scope they verify a group of Unis spread to cover the area. "Find a tree," Aubrey directs, eyeing me from head to toe. "Shouldn't be tough, considering your size."

Walsh, much wider, laughs beside me. "Takes two to cover this gut." He pats his stomach. "Being small has its benefits, I'm sure."

"We're faster, for one." I state the more well-known fact. "And, yeah, if it means I can take cover behind a tree, I'll take it." Looking at Aubrey, she's about my size pound for pound. A bit larger in the chest though.

And less weighty in the pants, I imagine.

"The snipers will take out the first couple at the same time. As soon as they fall, we'll need to act immediately."

"Makes sense."

The groups step lighter, breathe shallower, and search with keen eyes. As soon as we hit the tree line, everyone takes a tree as Aubrey had predicted. We move through the woods like this, one tree at a time, each team member darting at their own discretion.

This seemingly freeform tactic spaces everyone out in a surprisingly strategic way. Come to find out, as soon as Thessaly, the guys, and I left for the facility, Robbie put the S&R crews into effect right away, starting with the most knowledgeable of the Combat teams — excluding Roark, of course. The reassignment of their strongest members caused chaos and a bit of contention, but only for a short time; once Thessaly got her hands on the rosters, she built their teams in a way that strengthened the groupings rather than weakened them.

The two outfits like to poke fun at each other though. Seeing firsthand how this crew works on the field, I now understand why having experienced people out here is a necessity. As fast as the world around us is falling apart, there's no time to train. Once the call came through, they went out that same day, working in shifts around the clock.

According to Harvey when I signed up, they haven't lost a single member yet... all because of their one rule — kill on sight, no questions asked.

Essentially, kill or be killed.

Ahead, one of the members looks back toward those of us behind him. I spot him first as he holds up four fingers, points at his eyes, then jabs a thumb over his right shoulder.

My eyes dart around from tree to tree until another member catches my eye, and I take the cue, motioning in a similar way, but pointing ahead and to the left. The guy nods, and passes along the message to another crew member.

Only a couple minutes go by, no one moving from their current trees, when Harvey's voice filters through the com-device. "Snipers are ready," he whispers. "Let's do what we do best. On my count."

The woods become eerily quiet, not even the sound of Aubrey adjusting in a tree a few paces away can be heard. The whistle of two bullets fired back-to-back zooms past quickly, followed by the thump of two bodies falling to the ground in the not-so-far distance. "Now!" Harvey's voice rings through the woods, bouncing off trees and mingling with the pandemonium of shocked and panicked Unis calling orders and unholstering their guns.

Shots ring out from every direction and red spots populate on my com-lens as we leave the cover of the trees and set our sights ahead. The first Uni in clear view pops into my peripheral, and I draw my gun, switch off the safety, and shoot. Aubrey's voice comes from just beyond my left shoulder: "Cyclops! Nice one." I don't dare look back and break my concentration. Rushing ahead, I pause only briefly at the body to remove his gun and slide it into my holster before leaping over him and moving on.

A shot fires far too close to my ear, and my pulse thuds as I propel myself forward and stay balanced despite the ringing. Beside me, Aubrey reloads her gun.

I never saw the guy, but I hear his scream even over the echoing in my ear. The scream is followed by a gurgle as someone behind us finishes him off — with a dagger I assume.

Aubrey, two more crew members, and I come to a screeching halt at a dilapidated cabin. An all-too familiar one. Our heads and feet pivot, as we scan the area. Through the woods, more team members join us, Harvey included. Blood splatter covers some of their faces, and a couple men start throwing up. Two team members walk toward the cabin, guns drawn. Something about it sends major red-flags through my veins, and I holler out: "Wait!"

That sensation. It takes me a moment, but I soon recognize it as my empath sensors picking something up. At first I reach out for Thessaly in a panic, but everything feels fine there. About the same time I notice the small red speck of heat on my com-lens, that's when I realize I'm picking up a projection from whomever is in the cabin. "Someone is in there." I keep my voice quiet with a note of caution. "Don't shoot... just... Just give me a second."

Shit.

Over time, I've grown accustomed to Thessaly's signature and how to interact with it. I've never tried to pick up on someone else's. But I take a stab, attempting to figure out... something... anything.

Whoever it is, is definitely afraid. So much so, I can't read anything other than that. My mind searches through what I know about empath connections. It dawns on me that the person inside must be on the low end of the line otherwise I wouldn't feel his or her presence.

"Unis... they're all Highs or close to Neutral, right? Disposable to The Program?" I ask, hoping Harvey knows.

"Usually, yes."

"Whoever is in there, isn't an enemy then. They're a Low."

"Ah, that empath magic I was warned about. Well then... let's see if you're right." He nods, encouraging me to take over and enter the cabin in place of the other two guys that were originally headed that way.

My confidence is so strong, I don't even bother to pull out my gun as I gently push the door open. As soon as I enter, I flip my com-lens down and hold my hands up, palms out. "We're here to help," I encourage with a calm whisper. In the far corner cowers a young girl, her clothes torn to shreds. Rage fills me, blackening my vision. No longer the safety net, I now appear very much a monster to the girl, and Harvey has to step between us to do damage control on the situation as she starts to tremble and wail, pushing back against the wall in an attempt to escape further.

Fists clenched, I watch through vacant eyes, as I'm lost in my own mind, seeing not the girl, but my sisters, mother, and Thessaly — every female who has ever mattered to me.

Harvey unzips the canvas sack, whips out a small cloth and a dime-sized, clear, marble-looking thing. He wraps the little ball into the cloth, takes a careful step forward, squeezes his hand, takes one more step forward, and when the girl uses the last of her flight instincts to attempt slipping past him to the open door, he scoops her up and covers her mouth and nose with the cloth until she relaxes in his embrace.

My chest heaves and bile seeps into my throat. The anticipation, the kill, the girl, how Harvey is detaining her — everything triggers me all at once. I turn away from them and slam my fist into the wood-paneled wall. It shatters instantly, rotten from time and weather. The sting of splintered wood digging into my knuckles brings me back to the cabin, and I look around, finding myself alone aside from someone leaning against the doorframe, blocking the light.

"Come on," Aubrey's voice meets my ears. "Harv's about to start the count."

I don't know what that means, but I follow Aubrey out anyway, taking a deep breath of cool air once I step over the threshold. The three vans in our entourage are approaching, and Walsh now has the girl, holding her in his arms and taking her to the nearest van.

"One-one!" Harvey yells. "She's going to be fine. It's a laughing gas. It will calm her down long enough for us to get her back to the UR and will also help her talk to us without fear muddling the conversation."

"Two-one!" someone yells from the woods.

I shove my hands into my pockets and toss my head back, closing my eyes, taking in a deep breath, and reveling in the feel of the cool material acting as a balm against the heat radiating off my bleeding fist.

"Three-two!" another voice follows.

Next, Aubrey hollers, "Four-one! And an assist..."

Harvey chuckles. "You're slacking, Saint."

"Yeah, well the Italian here stole one."

"Five-zero!" Yet another team member yells.

Harvey claps me on the back. "Still standing, I see."

"For now," I respond.

"Six-four!"

"Goddamn, Font! Killing spree!"

"Did my best!" Six — Font — yells back.

The count continues, not a single number missing, until we hit twenty-four and no one answers. Aubrey nudges me in the arm. And I take the cue, yelling out, "Twenty-four-one!"

"Great; crew's accounted for, and we have a tally of thirty-five Unis down. Nicely done, everyone."

"They're looking for Thessaly," I mutter to myself, clenching my hands again. This time they're still in my pockets so no one can witness my continued lack of control.

"Maybe..." Harvey answers. "But it appears they've doubled back up on their search efforts for possible Lows who are hiding too." He tilts his head toward the van that holds the young girl. "Thing is, I'm sure she wasn't alone when they picked her up. They probably decided to stick around and wait for her family to show."

Changing the volume of his voice, he yells over my head at the recovering group of crew members. "There's

147

a tiny town about two miles from here. Can't be more than three miles tall and short. Walsh is talking to the girl now, seeing what information he can get about her family. A train track runs straight through there, though, so it's unlikely we'll find anyone. Supplies, definitely. But people? Unlikely." He then addresses me. "Once they got those trains back online, stations cropped up in every town, loading people as they did. Same with the monorails that run through the bigger cities."

The small-town residents along the rail lines must not've stood a chance. Everything happened so fast with the sweep, it's a miracle the girl got away at all. "What about the subway systems?" I ask, remembering the one back in Chicago.

"Since they don't interconnect on a national level, the subways didn't prove useful at all. They shut 'em down, in fact. Not too long after the sweep started, it was proving a problem with people trying to travel to connecting cities or hide in the ones with underground tunnels."

Just as we're wrapping up our short conversation about subways, Walsh steps out of the van and approaches. "Girl said her family is still hiding. Apparently their local church has a small basement, which is probably how they remained undetected. Basements being a rare thing here in the south and all. She'd gone above surface to get something — a toy out of the nursery. Wrong place at the wrong time sort of deal. The town had been quiet for a long time, she said."

"Alright then..." Harvey addresses the crew. "Time for some worship, gentlemen — and lady. Clean our souls... and the town... while we're there, hm?"

CHAPTER THIRTEEN

Thessaly

Attempting to get things done with Julian out in the field for the first time is fruitless. A million "What ifs?" and the construction of horrible possibilities have my concentration completely shot. While quite a bit of time has already passed since he was discharged from the Medical wing, it still wasn't enough. And despite my best efforts to convince him to wait longer, he wouldn't.

The request was selfish anyway. The UR... our plans... can't wait "a couple more days" for anything at this point. Everything is down to the wire. One more pulse is all we need for the attack to go into effect.

When I get word that Julian's back, it comes with news that Jax can finally receive visitors too. I'm lying in my bed counting pockmarks in the stone ceiling the moment Tobias pops his head in and delivers the updates.

Hearing both Jax and Julian's names fall from Tobias's tongue has me jolting upright in an instant. However, instead of getting out of bed, I remain otherwise immobile, unsure which of my guys to check on first. As filled with worry as I'd been about Julian, I'd been waiting for Jax to get better far too long. "Can you send Julian to the Medical wing for me?" I ask. Tobias nods and dashes away. These past couple days, Bram and Tobias had been rushing around with no rest. Constantly gone working in their respective fields. Hopping from task to task. No dawdling.

149

Pushing the thought away, I get out of bed, slip my shoes on, grab my pagers, and meander to the Medical wing. As eager as I'd been, now that the day to see Jax has arrived, I'm suddenly dragging my feet.

Why?

Fear of what condition he'll be in?

Worry about the consequences of the transplant with Celeste?

I don't know… but every bit of me is filled with apprehension.

My wayward thoughts are put on a momentary hiatus when I arrive in the waiting area and Julian is there with Harvey. The two men are ushering in a group of new UR members to be checked over by Medical — two adults, a teenage boy, and a younger girl.

Julian's eyes meet mine right away, no doubt having sensed my empath presence first. He bends down to the young girl, placing both hands on her shoulders, and says something to her. She smiles, shaking her head. He speaks again, earning another toothy grin. She gives him a hug, and he stands, patting her head before walking toward me.

"Saving lives, hm?" I say, wrapping my arms around his neck.

He kisses me and rubs our noses together. "Taking them too," he whispers. Not only do I hear the pain in the tremble of his voice, but I feel it through our bond as well.

I pull my head back and search his eyes, bringing my hands to each cheek. "Want to talk about it?" Truth is, I'm not sure I really want to know why he had to kill someone. Everyone in the UR is aware that the S&R's rule is "Kill or be killed." The thought that any of my guys would be in that position — or really anyone, for that matter — is terrifying.

Julian shrugs, leaning down to kiss me again. "*This* is what I want," he breathes against my lips. "*You* are enough. The rest doesn't matter."

"It matters to them," I insist, darting my eyes away from his serious green gaze only long enough to indicate that I'm referring to the family he'd helped bring to the Underground.

"Shh," he says with a breathy chuckle, kissing me again. *"C'ho il dente avvelenato."*

For once I recognize one of the words… *dente*… meaning tooth. I pull back and look at him with an eyebrow raised. He chuckles. "Translated literally it means *I have a poisoned tooth*. If I speak on this subject, I will have nothing good to say, and it will only serve to anger me."

"Oh." I smile and waste no time before changing the topic. "How'd it go with Aubrey?"

Julian's eyes widen, and I can't help but laugh. Yeah, I'd paired those two on purpose. He'd need someone to make sure he's okay out there. Someone who could get through to him if anything happened. "You're sneaky, *cuore mio*."

"Am I?"

"*Sì*. To answer your question, it went well. She's tough…" There's more, I know there is, but whatever details he's leaving out can wait until later.

"Oh! Jax is awake, and they're allowing visitors." I hadn't forgotten, of course, but to reroute the conversation before he gets uncomfortable with the knowledge that I paired him with a Low female on purpose, I overact the news about Jax. The excitement, however, isn't an act.

"È un'ottima notizia! That's great news!" Julian wraps his fingers around my wrists and moves my hands away from his cheeks. "What are you waiting for? Go!"

"Had to make sure you were okay first."

"I'm okay, *cuore mio.* Go see him. I'll be here when you're done; then I'll take my turn."

"Okay." I smile and place a quick kiss on his cheek before turning around, the pep in my step now much more spirited.

WHEN I REACH THE CONTAINED AREA, I slow down. My pulse thumps hard and fast in my ears. The guard, remembering me from when I'd stayed with Julian, lets me in right away and points in the direction of the clean room. He waits patiently for me to complete the process before leading me to Jax.

When I peek my head in, my pulse feels as though it drops several beats in an instant.

Celeste is there, the two of them talking. Jax has his head turned toward her, and although he can't see me, she can. Our eyes meet briefly, but she doesn't keep the connection and instantly returns her attention back to Jax, no doubt pretending she didn't see me at all.

She has just a couple minutes before I bust in there. Two minutes. I press against the wall, close my eyes, and let my head fall back against the stone.

With nothing else to do for the next one-hundred-twenty seconds — one-hundred and counting down — I toy with the special, telepathic empath bond Jax and I share. Almost instantly a burst of *frustration* hits me hard. Then *annoyance.* Soon followed by *exasperation.* Jax's emotions are a multipronged attack of their own. While I try to keep it quiet, apparently my ensuing

152

chuckle doesn't go unheard. The smoky mumblings of his conversation pause, followed by the clearing of his throat. Then comes the repetitive word talent he has: it only takes a moment to receive his "idea" signature. The word "help" echoes repeatedly through my mind, flavored with all things country.

If it hasn't been two minutes yet, I determine it's close enough, and I step around the wall into the room.

Jax's head turns toward me instantly, a larger-than-life grin lighting up his face. "Hey, Darlin'," he says, holding out a hand. "If I didn't know better, I'd say ya could read my mind or somethin'. I was just thinkin' about ya."

"Funny thing, that," I say smiling down at him as he pulls me closer. I fall onto the bed at his side, and he wraps his other arm around me, bringing my head to his chest.

The room falls silent, aside from the steady drum of his heart beneath my ear. I'm only able to close my eyes for a second before Celeste's petulant huff ruins the moment.

"I can only say thank you so many times, Celeste," Jax mutters. "Truly, I am thankful for what ya did. But that doesn't change things for us, so I'd appreciate it if ya'd stop tryin'."

My eyes widen and dart up to the woman in question. Her bright-blue eyes redden, but she doesn't say another word. Instead, she heeds his wishes, stands, and leaves. I prop my chin on his chest and peek up at him with a stern look. I'm not taking her side... not really... but even a fool could tell his words hurt.

Jax rolls his eyes. "You too?"

"No." I chuckle and run my finger along his jawline.

"She'd been in here givin' me a guilt trip since I woke up. Don't feel sorry for her. I'm thankful; I really am. But she did it ta get me back. Or at least with tha hope ta. She even said as much."

"Did she now?"

"Yeah, she did. I mean, can't say I blame her." Jax waggles his brows. "Hard ta let go of somethin' so damn amazin'."

A smile comes and goes in a blink. "You're right, I can't blame her."

"No, none of that, Darlin'. Bring it back."

The smile, that is.

I try one on for size, but it falls flat. "There were a couple moments I thought I'd be the one having to let go."

His eyebrows curve in and eyes dart between mine. "Ya don't... not ever. Not in tha way she needs ta let go at least."

"Remember when we were first getting to know each other?" I ask.

"All of it," he responds.

"The game we played, where you had to name an animal that best described you?" He nods. "At the time, I couldn't think of one, but I think I know now."

Jax watches me, waiting intently for my answer. The serious expression makes my heartbeat go crazy. "Um... I mean... it's not as cool as yours." I shrug, and he lifts a brow. "I was thinking a mockingbird. They're smart and can sense when someone is a threat to its nest. And they're aggressive when it comes to defending." Jax smiles, his eyes getting glossy. "I may not have been that way before... but now? I'll do anything to defend those whom I love. To defend my nest."

154

He crunches up and kisses my forehead. "Like includin' lettin' Celeste do the transplant because she was the best option?"

"Yeah," I whisper. "Trust me, I toyed with the idea of dismissing her as an option."

He chuckles. "Thank ya, Darlin'. Though now I have to carry a part of her inside me everywhere I go." He shudders.

I swat his chest. "You were carrying a part of her with you anyway."

He doesn't respond right away. With a sigh, he admits the truth: "Yer right. Guess that's part of life though, hm?"

"It is. Just like how Tobias will always remember Amber. No doubt he's already gone through the steps to check on her safety."

"Well now… Celeste played a big role in my past, but we never had anythin' like what Amber and Tobias had. And definitely not anything like what you and me… and Tobias… and Bram… and Julian…" — he takes in a deep, exaggerated breath as though listing my men winded him — "… have."

I laugh. "Speaking of Julian… I have a message for you…" Again Jax's eyes focus on me with utmost seriousness, news of his friend now consuming him. "*Maledizione, quanto mi sei mancato, fratello, ma la ragazza è diventa mio,*" I say in my best Italian accent.

Jax groans and throws his head back against the pillow. "That fucker," he says. "Glad he's okay though." He rights his head and looks down at me again. "What does it mean?"

I shrug and laugh. "No clue. All I know is that he won the bet you two made."

155

Jax's voice drops low. "Neither of us could stop thinkin' about you after our night together. Both of us wantin' you to ourselves again after that." His hand slips down my back to cup my butt.

"Guess you better hurry and get out of here then, hm? Julian's already had his turn." I speak in the same hushed tone in return.

"Is that so?" he says, something growing hard under the thigh I had draped over his midsection.

"Yeah, fucked me hard and fast in the storage room," I respond with a grin.

"Mmm… damn I love hearin' those filthy words come from those sweet lips of yours." His thumb drags along said lips.

"Don't torture yourself," I say, laughing and wiggling against his hard-on. "Not sure the nurses would enjoy trying to clean cum out of the bedsheets and tubing stuff."

Jax groans again. "All I heard was 'cum'."

"You're impossible." I laugh.

"Impossibly amazin'," he quips back.

The two of us quiet then, being content just to hold each other. We lie there long enough that Jax eventually falls asleep. Careful not to jar him awake, I inch out of the bed on a mission to get a few items for him like I did for Julian during his recovery.

As promised, Julian is in the waiting area still. So are Tobias and Bram. Plopping into Tobias's lap, I join them.

"How is he?" Julian is the first to ask.

"He looks great and is in good spirits. Like you were, he's tired, though, so he's resting now. I passed on your message. Pretty sure it got the reaction you'd hoped for. However, he did ask what it meant. Care to tell me so I can pass it on?"

Julian's lips quirk up in a side grin. "*Maledizione, quanto mi sei mancato, fratello, ma la ragazza è diventa mio. Damn I missed you, brother, but the girl is mine.*"

I press my lips together and roll my eyes at him.

"What?!" he exclaims, tugging me over into his lap instead of Tobias's. "It's true, is it not? You're mine, *sì, cuore mio?*"

"Mm, I am… with a bit of a pronoun tweak."

One of his eyebrows disappears under his curly hair, now so much longer than it was when we'd first met.

"I'm *yours,* plural," I whisper, kissing him. When I pull away I look at both Bram and Tobias. "All of yours."

Julian throws me a wink. Tobias steals me back, throwing him a playful scowl.

Bram then steals me from Tobias. "Just remember who had her first."

"Oh I do…" Julian eggs. Bram talking about the friendship — Julian talking about the intimacy.

"Hey, she saved the best for last, so I'm good with that," Tobias adds to the competition.

With a deep sigh, I stand to separate myself from the tremendous amount of testosterone I can practically see rolling off them. "Well, I'm going to collect some things. You all can spend some time bonding with each other for the next few days while I stay with Jax. Seems you need it more than I do."

CHAPTER FOURTEEN

"Family meeting?" Tobias jokes. Joking aside, he's right; we desperately need one... without Thess for now. She deserves a much-needed break anyway.

Julian nods, and we all stand and head straight to the meeting room, deciding to come visit Jax later once he's done resting.

A surprise to us all, Julian is the first to speak up, eager to get something off his chest before we start going into the heavy details about our upcoming trip to New York. He turns to Tobias and takes a deep breath. "Have you tried figuring out a way to check on Amber and your parents?"

Tobias leans against the office chair's backrest making it squeak, temples his fingers at his mouth, and glares at Julian. His irritation for having mentioned her name without Thessaly in the room is quite evident.

"For the record," Tobias starts, "this isn't something I'm keeping from her. While I haven't straight out said it, she knows."

Julian nods. "She definitely knows. It dawned on her the other day that we might try."

Tobias agrees. "Yeah, I've been keeping in contact with the main Eastern Region UR and asked them to keep on the lookout. But I haven't heard anything yet."

Julian looks at me then, and I shrug. "I'm not close to my parents, but they'll either end up here or in Rhode

Island with Thess's mom and dad. Lena and Harris told me they'd let me know if they showed up there."

Thess is the closest — and most important — family I have. For a long while after the guys and I took her, guilt consumed me. But seeing the alternative? Hearing about the S&R crew's experiences? What Thess witnessed at the facility? Before this all started, we were going off a hunch — a single trigger: her flagged account and our names being attached. Nothing more.

In other words, sometimes those gut feelings change history. No way can I any longer regret being part of her abduction back then. She's here. We're all together. And because of her, we can help the nation.

Julian's lips press together, and he leans forward, resting his elbows on the table. "Do you know if S&R crews have been formed in the other regions yet? If so, we can give them our addresses and request they check there as quickly as possible. From what I learned today, they start at the UR and work in a radial pattern. It might take a while, but at least they'll know where to look once they get that far out."

Tobias nods. "We'll bring it up during the next leadership meeting. Maybe get together a list for all the leaders' loved ones and make sure the S&R crews keep it handy. That said, Michigan is a long way from Rhode Island. And Chicago is a ways away from here."

"Right, and for today's search, we went east not north. If the number of Search and Rescue crews per region is as slim as ours, it'll take ages to search everywhere. A year or more even."

"Well, if we make it through this coordinated attack, our numbers will increase by the hundreds of thousands — if not the millions. Those who survive the facilities and recover from any lingering radiation or

159

drugs they've been given, can then join forces with us to help locate anyone still hiding."

"Hopefully we won't have to lose many more people between now and then." Julian voices what everyone in the URs nationwide is collectively thinking.

Our combined silence following his statement speaks louder than any words could.

"Alright, we have shit to do." Tobias leans forward. "Bram, how's the research going?"

"When I'm not being tugged in a million different directions you mean?" I sigh. Damn, these past couple weeks have been taxing to say the least. "It's... going; the bacteria is ready. How about you? Any progress on your end?"

Tobias nods. "Yeah, not sure you're going to like what I have to say though." He pauses for a moment before continuing. "As I'm sure you both know, the Center for Disease Control is located in Atlanta. Now, I'm not saying the CDC is the only place we can find the necessary tools, but I *am* saying we know for certain the CDC has them. Not to mention, it's relatively close considering our other lab options. Better yet... I held a high enough position as a Database Tech where I should be able to gain access to the lab. That is, if The Program doesn't hold any sway with them and they're still... functioning."

Nowhere is 'functioning' right now. Not that we've seen, at least. Stores, charging stations, restaurants, schools. Nothing. The outside is desolate.

"Whoa... hold on now." Julian raises a hand. "Clearly I missed something. Bacteria? CDC?"

"To record the data directly into Thess's DNA, we need the proper resources. First, a live bacteria that will hold the data — that's what I'm working on. Data has been saved in plant DNA this way in the past, which is why Tobias reached out to me."

"Next," Tobias continues, "are the various tools to transfer the data. Those can be found at the CDC laboratory. Unfortunately, even with everything in hand, nobody here is equipped with the knowledge in how to perform this task. So we'll be collecting the bacteria, the tools, and the data… then heading to the Eastern UR.

"Robbie has been in contact with someone there who has worked in one of the largest computer software research centers in the nation in Richmond, Virginia, not too far away from the Eastern UR. Before the sweep, the guy worked in the center's molecular biotech division."

"So this entire plan is in the hands of someone we don't know?" Julian asks.

"The entire plan has a lot of unknowns. Like a cookie recipe, Chef Curly," Tobias jokes. "If you're missing one of the key ingredients, they won't turn out. And without a chef, the ingredients are useless. The plan isn't foolproof, but it's all we've got. "

"Cute," Julian says. "You think one of these days we'll eventually know what the hell we're doing?"

"Nope." Tobias laughs. "Can't believe I'm saying this, but I guess we've just got to trust our intuition — and those close to us."

"I was just thinking the same thing," I say. "That intuition got us this far," I add, giving him a knowing glance.

Tobias nods at me before turning his attention back toward Julian. Julian's sporting a shit-eating grin. "Ah ha, she's hooked her claws in deep, *amico*."

"You're one to speak," Tobias quips back. "She's had you hooked from first sight. I can still picture the moment we walked in on her getting dressed in the abandoned facility. Pretty sure there was drool mixed in with the drops of water on your jacket from the rain."

"You're probably right." Julian chuckles, but then his smile fades. "So, what can I do to help? Maybe try to sway S&R to head to Atlanta and you can tag along? Get that part taken care of first?"

Tobias is quiet for a moment. "It's not a bad idea, but I don't think it's smart to take two of us out of the UR."

Julian nods, understanding. "What if you go and I stay behind? I can help in Tech or serve as a temp guard while you're gone. Take care of Thes-sal-ee for you." He throws Tobias a cocky wink after the last suggestion.

"Well, you almost had me convinced. But then you fucked it up." Tobias's voice is flat, but the smile on his face proves otherwise. "Eh, I'll think about it. When do they leave next?"

"Every day," Julian answers. "The trick will be convincing them to take it that far north without clearing the areas between here and there first."

"What if we just hit it up en route to New York? Make a pitstop?" I suggest.

"That was my initial thought. We're already on a time constraint though, so getting the equipment in advance might help us get ahead. Plus, in the event we can't get our hands on what we need, we'd have a little more wiggle room to come up with an alternate plan."

His comment makes me wonder how we intend on communicating from so far away. Tobias had mentioned Robbie fixing Betty. Even then, as far as I understand the pager system, the pagers range only goes so far before we hit the other Region's system.

"That got me thinking... I'm not quite understanding what your plan for communication is while we're away; things aren't adding up for me. Also, I played along with whatever the hell that was with Auden earlier, but I'm not seeing how that will help us either," I explain.

"Robbie's setting up a more advanced computer system for Betty's dashboard," Tobias begins to explain. "As long as the satellites and towers are still up and running he'll simply tap into those. We shouldn't lose communication with the UR. And, considering The Program is dependent on them as well, I'm sure there are plenty still in working order even despite the nationwide power outages and such. Unfortunately, depending on where we are, we'll likely experience intermittent service or our pagers might stop working altogether.

"As for Auden... We don't know what type of empath bond she'll have with him, what with you and Julian being connected to her emotionally, me via pain, and Jax telepathically — which is still weird, by the way."

"Not any stranger than you being able to feel her pain," Julian points out.

"True. Anyway, she gets along with Auden... and none of us are bothered by him..." We all share a look. Tobias is comparing Auden to Roux — who we are trying to like despite the nefarious things he has done. Auden, on the other hand, has proven himself worthy on more than one occasion. "We — well I — want someone here that can get a good read on her in case all communication is lost and we need to have help dispatched."

"But that far away... with a new bond?" Julian shakes his head.

Tobias leans forward. "I was in Michigan when you two were taken. I felt it. I felt when she was

163

restrained — the pain radiated through my shoulders. My head hurt too." Julian gives him a vacant look. Neither Thess nor Julian remember the details about getting taken. Roux later explained exactly what happened in the cottage when Julian shot Roux's partner at the time. "We'd kissed, but nothing more at that point. And even though I fought the idea for so long, when it happened, I knew without question it was her. No training needed."

Julian speaks up then. "I didn't even need to kiss her." Both our attentions dart to him. "Mine kicked in when she passed out at the lab."

"Wait... what?!" I say, shaking my head. "I thought all our bonds were the result of something intimate..."

Julian shrugs. "Mine wasn't. I mean... don't get me wrong... we were drawn to each other immediately. But I started feeling her emotions before any form of sexual contact. It was heightened after we were intimate though."

I turn my attention to Tobias. "You kissed her before you left, correct?"

"Right..." he says slowly, contemplative. "But... I didn't feel it until the night she was taken by Roux..."

My eyebrows go sky high. "This entire time, we've been wrong?"

Tobias starts calculating; his eyes go unfocused and he finds a spot beyond anyone in the room to stare at. "Damn we're stupid... the bond isn't formed because of intimacy. It's formed for protection. Like how a mother is hard-wired to protect her children. Julian's happened when she passed out, mine happened when she got hurt." His attention moves from the spot on the wall to me then.

"I-I don't know anymore." A breathy chuckle leaves me. So many things have happened over the course of our friendship; I don't even know anymore. First, I thought it was a hug. Then, I figured it was when we practiced kissing as preteens.

"Okay... does anyone remember Jax's trigger?" Tobias asks.

We're all silent for a moment until Julian speaks up with a sigh. "His started when we were at the campground. She wasn't hurt though..."

Tobias's eyes widen. "Yes she was. She hadn't had anything to eat or drink for a while and was getting malnourished. Not to mention she was lacking sleep, most certainly not talking, and emotionally unstable too. The two of you know that part at least."

"So... having her kiss Auden then?" Julian asks.

Tobias grimaces. "Yeah, I don't know anymore."

My mind starts piling on blocks of ideas, one seeming a bit sturdier than the others. Of the four of us, Tobias has the biggest clash with Auden. It's not terrible — probably due to Auden's age and mild mannerisms — but there's always been a bit of competition between the two of them. It reminds me of the rift between Tobias and Julian but less severe for the aforementioned reasons. Poor Tobias seems to get the brunt of the High clash. "What if you provoke him. Make him think you're putting Thess in danger?"

"Thats..." Tobias says, hesitating.

"Mean," Julian finishes.

But then we all fall silent, digging a bit deeper into the idea.

"Possible," Tobias decides. "Thessaly and I have the beginnings of a Dom/sub thing; if he were to accidentally happen to see me acting like a Dom to her, it might have the potential to light him up."

"That has the potential to light me up," I say. "Please don't ever let me walk in on that. For the love of god."

Julian laughs. "Same."

Tobias shoots him a look. "You're talking? Nine times out of ten, I feel it in my nuts when you have sex with her. You're rough as hell."

Julian shrugs, the smile stuck like glue to his face. "Still doesn't mean I want to see you hurting her."

"Well if it's any consolation, kids, she fucking loves it."

I groan, running my hands over my face. "Okay, back to the idea. First of all, you'll need to tell her. I'm not being an accomplice to any more lies or secrets again. That ship has sailed. It should have never docked if I'm being honest."

Tobias nods. "Always. Don't have to worry about that with me. But... yeah... I'll get it handled."

Julian's head jerks up. "Speaking of these empath bonds and stuff... Did you all know Thes-sal-ee paired me with a Low female on the S&R crew?" Tobias and I shake our heads. He addresses Tobias directly, the two of them having formed a special type of friendship through somewhat recent trials. Shaking his head, Julian sighs. "I almost lost my shit on the field. Aubrey pulled me out."

At that my eyebrow rises. "In what way?"

"*Non, non*... nothing like that. She just was there; her voice was enough to bring my focus back. When I saw Thessaly, she said she'd paired us on purpose."

"Probably for that reason then," Tobias says.

166

"Thess isn't the over-jealous type. I mean, it happens, but I imagine she's only jealous if she senses a threat. Something about Aubrey must make Thessaly not worried about you two being on the field together," I rationalize. In that moment, we all realize exactly what that factor might be, and the three of us burst into laughter.

CHAPTER FIFTEEN

Thessaly

Waiting for Jax to be discharged is excruciating. Under any other circumstance, they'd have kept him in there. Here in the UR, rules change. For me, those couple days after he'd woken up was torture. Ironically enough, waiting while he was in the coma was easier. Knowing something you're super excited about is quickly approaching makes the anxiousness even worse. Want it bad enough, and time crawls.

As soon as I was told more specifics regarding the date and time of Jax's release from the Medical wing, I delivered the news to Auden so he could follow through with the combined birthday and recovery celebration he had previously mentioned. His plans included something extra special for Jax... something he wouldn't tell me because part of it was apparently a surprise for me too.

"Fuck, it feels fantastic to get outta that room," Jax groans, stretching in an exaggerated way that lifts his shirt up just high enough to where I can see his lower belly and that defined v-shaped line of muscles. Even without working out as much he used to, that man's body is something else.

"So... we have a 'thing' to do," I reveal, having saved the announcement for after he was discharged. Mostly because I don't know what all is planned... but also because Auden threatened to sic Ruby on me if I didn't wait.

"Why yes we do, Darlin'," he says, slapping my ass. "Gotta make sure this thing still works." He grabs his junk and waggles his eyebrows at me. "Also, I wanna make you scream my name somewhere in the vicinity of where Julian is so he knows where your loyalties lie."

His competitiveness makes me laugh. "Oh, speaking of… I asked Julian what that phrase meant that he wanted me to pass along to you. *Maledizione, quanto mi sei mancato, fratello, ma la ragazza è diventa mio. Damn I missed you, brother, but the girl is mine.*"

Jax frowns, wrapping his arm around my waist and pressing our bodies together as we walk side-by-side. "We'll see about that." His smile returns, and he turns his head toward me, pulling that eyes-from-under-the-lashes look that makes me want to immediately have sex with him every time.

"Um… seriously though… there's a get-together in which our presence is requested. Are you feeling up to it?"

"Well, if I'm feelin' up ta gettin' with you, I'm pretty sure I can handle a gatherin'. Last gatherin' I went to, though, I was tha main event."

I chuckle. "I don't think that's what Auden has in mind. In part, it's for his birthday… and um… as far as I know, male strippers aren't really his thing."

"Birthday, huh? Eighteen? Have ya already forgotten that we have female strippers down here too?"

Jax's blue-gold eyes meet mine, amused. My heart rate doubles. I hadn't thought of that. I mean, of course I hadn't forgotten; I just hadn't put the two coincidences together. Strippers and Auden's birthday gathering, that is. Plus they'd said something about a celebration of recovery. My gut twists at the thought.

I try to form words but instead just end up looking like a fish out of water until the sounds join the movement. "No... they wouldn't have planned that and invited me to it. Surely." Not that I don't want the guys having a good time. But considering *who* the entertainment would likely be, and how shaky things are down here, well, the idea just doesn't sit well with me right now. Or ever, possibly. Not where Celeste is concerned.

"Ya know, Darlin', I think you're right. Don't mind me; I say stupid shit all the time." I give him a halfhearted chuckle. "Let's go see what's up their sleeves, shall we?"

"We shall." I smile up at him and place a quick kiss on his cheek.

THE GATHERING, I was told, would be held in Auden's room. We walk that direction, following the smell of food and the crowds of bodies moving that way for lunch.

When we get to the line, unsure where to go from there, I notice Ruby isn't manning the table this time. Someone has taken her place and another person — one that's not Auden — is helping. This worker is much younger than Auden.

Jax and I step around everyone and head straight to the front, and the two standing there immediately notice our rebellious presence. Something about us must form a recognition in the boy's mind, because he is the one to speak up, "Thessaly and Jax?" I smile and nod. "Great! I was told to watch for you then take you back." He finishes what he was doing and lets the server know he won't be long. "Follow me," he says with a grin.

"This is creepy as fuck," Jax whispers in my ear, a smile coating those words. "Think he'll notice if you and I disappear into the kitchen for a bit?"

"Now, why would we do that?" I whisper back, weaving our fingers together.

"You make jokes," he says, nudging me with his shoulder. Happiness fills me in this moment. I'd sure missed our playful nature.

There isn't time to slip away though. Our banter comes to an end as our guide steps into Auden's room.

The room is full, and everyone is speaking in hushed tones. Jax and I both freeze... probably for entirely different reasons. As expected, Auden, Julian, Bram, and Tobias are there, but when my focus drags from face to face, I recognize more than one person that I most certainly have never seen in the UR before. In fact, I haven't seen them since my real life before the UR.

The faces of the boys from the behavioral center where I'd been an intern look back at me. There was a time in the early stages of this insanity that I'd wanted nothing more than to reach out to them and make sure they were okay. I'd thought of them a time or two since, but... the fate of everyone at this point was about the same.

Back then, Jax had suggested—

Wait a minute.

In one exaggerated motion, I turn sharply toward Jax. However, he is standing there seemingly just as confused and shocked as I am. "Did you have something to do with this?" I ask.

Jax shakes his head. "Was gonna ask ya the same thing."

A man about our age steps forward. Jax apparently hadn't noticed him yet because his expression goes from dazed to surprised... and then to... angry? Of course, all his internal emotions match, stabbing me like darts on a board, one by one. "Celeste," he whispers right before putting on a huge grin and embracing the man.

As profuse as his emotions are, paired with the revelations that Celeste had something to do with this, the reddening of his eyes when the two hug each other doesn't help me understand anything.

Confused, I leave them alone and turn to the boys I recognize, rushing over to them and squatting down to place my hands on their knees as they sit in their seats. But then I toss all protocol aside and wrap them both in my arms, squeezing tight, which makes them squeeze together too. They both grimace and begin releasing a string of swears and complaints, causing laughter to bubble out of me.

"Those mouths, boys. Watch it."

Despite their objections, I hug them once more, rocking back and forth. When I let go, I drop to their level again. "Staying in trouble, clearly." I look around the room, joking about the fact they're in an underground cave system.

"You know it," Mark states, jutting his chin out.

"What's going on here?" I ask, dropping my voice a bit.

"You tell us," Stanley whispers back conspiratorially. "We were here for a meeting and to celebrate Auden's birthday. Ms. Ruby has been helping us. All of us." He looks around the room.

"Are all of you from behavioral health centers?"

The two of them nod, but Stanley is the one who elaborates: "The center was ambushed, but instead of being taken, they were locking more people in there. Me and Mark managed to get out. We found a hideout, but some of the UR people found us."

"Wow." I blow a raspberry from my lips. "You boys did really well." All silliness is gone for a blink as the reminder of their experience before being found swims in their gazes.

To help them avoid any lingering negative thoughts and enjoy the get-together instead, I smile and look at Jax over my shoulder. "So, the guy talking to my friend over there? Is he a center boy too?" I ask, wondering if the coincidence applies to Jax's acquaintance as well.

"Yeah... well... used to be, obviously." Mark pokes fun at the man's age which is still quite young, but apparently not young enough.

"Obviously." I laugh and roll my eyes. "It's great to see you two." I hug each of them, separately this time. But my mind is still trying to piece together what Jax has to do wi—

Oh.

I stand and blink stupidly. Over his friend's shoulder, Jax's eyes meet mine. *Worry, guilt,* and *frustration* are tossed through our bond on a Jax-infused wave of emotion.

With a sigh, I pat each boy on the shoulder and walk over to Jax, sidling up to him. He immediately wraps his arm around me, letting it settle on my hip.

"Thessaly?" the man asks.

"Yes." I put on my best smile and hold out my hand. He takes it, and shakes lightly. "Tanner. Nice to meet you."

Jax squeezes me harder, clears his throat, and says, "Tanner and I met years ago at the boys center."

Tanner leans forward and whispers, "Between you and me, he was the bigger trouble maker."

173

Even though the information unraveling is surprising, that comment is not. A laugh bubbles out of me, and I look the man dead in the eye. "I believe it."

Jax groans. "He's lyin' to ya, Darlin'."

"I somehow doubt that."

Jax gasps and places his hand over his heart. "You'd believe a stranger over me?"

"No, I believe what I know about you already... over you... or something." The two men laugh.

Jax's unease about me discovering this little bit of information from his past leaks into me through our bond. Not at all feeling disappointed or upset, I meet his eyes and give him a warm smile.

His chest rises and falls on a small sigh, and he squeezes my hip. "Mind if we break away for a moment?" Jax asks his childhood friend.

"Of course, man. Hey" — Tanner turns his attention toward me — "it was nice meeting you again."

I give the man a smile and nod before Jax adjusts his grip from my hip to my hand and pulls me toward the exit. My gaze catches Bram's, and for that brief moment, I see a cautious protectiveness in his brown eyes.

Jax is clearly worked up, and it wasn't too terribly long ago that Jax and Bram were at odds with each other. Bram's on the watch now for anything amiss.

Me? I'm not worried about it, so I quickly smile, hoping it's enough to cool Bram's worry before Jax and I are around the corner and the connection is lost.

Once we're out of the main party area, Jax instantly spins me around to face him. "Are ya upset with me?" are the first words out of his mouth. Not "What's going on?" Not an explanation. First and foremost he's worried about... us.

"No. Should I be?"

174

"Probably," he replies. "There's a lot I haven't told ya."

"Oh, I'm sure. There's a lot I haven't told you too." I cross my arms, irritated more by the fact he's so worried than by the revelation that he's kept information about his past from me.

"So… you *are* upset then?" he asks again, noticing my actions over my words.

"A little… but not for the reason you likely think I am. I'm more upset that you're so nervous and unsure about telling me whatever is going on." I gesture toward the room. "Unless you have a child I don't know about or are some sort of horrible convict, I'm not upset or concerned."

Jax remains quiet for far too long… which, I admit, does begin to worry me. Enough so that both Bram and Julian end up popping their heads out of the room's opening.

"Everything good, Thess?" Bram asks, meeting my gaze, while Julian turns his attention toward Jax and asks the same question with his eyes.

"Yeah, we're fine," I respond with a small huff of impatience and irritation as I turn back to Jax and ignore the other two. Jax's eyes remain riveted on the doorway for a couple more seconds until Bram and Julian are gone.

"No, Darlin', it's nothing like that," he immediately picks back up where we'd left off. "I was wild but not stupid."

The unexpected tension in my shoulders eases, and my arms uncross, my hands dropping to my sides. "Now *that* I already know."

He tries on a small smile before blowing an exaggerated breath from his lips.

"Look," I say, holding up two fingers. "We've known each other for two months, had one official date, and have only been intimate a few times. In between all of that, we've been... busy. It comes as no surprise that we don't know things about each other. There are married couples who still learn about each other on a regular basis. Not every moment in a relationship is the right time to deliver news about the past."

Jax's attention had been fixed on the ground between us, but at this comment he lifts his head slightly, looking at me the way he does from under his eyelashes. This time the look isn't an intentionally sexy one, it's a serious one. Albeit still sexy nonetheless. "Well ya know now, or probably figured out that I was once just like the boys ya worked with?"

"Why didn't you tell me in the car?" The only reason I ask is because I clearly remember him being the one who suggested I write a letter to my boys one day, when things calmed down. Memory flashing so brightly, I marvel at the fact I didn't catch the meaning behind his sympathetic response.

"There was so much goin' on. We'd just taken ya. None of us knew each other well. The time didn't feel right. Plus I wasn't sure I wanted to recall those memories for myself anyway."

"See? No harm then. Do you want to tell me now?"

"Yeah, I believe now is about as good a time as it's gonna get. First of all, Celeste did this... or at least had a hand in it. She bein' the only one here that knows. She probably thought it was a nice gesture. But, really, I'd been workin' up the nerve to tell ya, and this sorta ruined that."

Jax is usually short on words but this time he doesn't stop, wanting to get it over as quickly as possible.

176

"So, my ma left when I was eight years old; she didn't say goodbye or nothin'. In fact, she said she was headed to tha store to get ice cream. Found out years later she'd left because she couldn't handle me or my da anymore. Not that I blame her; my da was a piece of work and so was I, if I'm bein' honest. Time went by, as did the women he brought home. Sometimes I'd grown ta like 'em quite a bit, but clearly they didn't like me enough ta stick around. Eventually my da couldn't handle me either, so I was sent to the center. Tanner and I became good friends; the two of us were... stupid. Most interns dropped like flies. They'd come in happy and determined that they were the ones who'd be able to turn us around. Didn't happen. Each time one left was a small victory for us.

"Or so I thought. But honestly, each one that left only served as another blow to my heart."

My eyes drift to his tattoo, and the redirecting of my focus doesn't go unnoticed. He pauses briefly, only to pick up the conversation on the exact topic my mind had wandered to. "Got my tat the day I left there."

He'd already explained the meaning of the angel with a scythe and the rebellious rider a while back, but the true meaning comes crashing in at that moment.

"Celeste's family owned the tat shop. That's how we met. Just like the others, she thought she'd be able to tame me. Took me in and convinced me to join the dance crew. I hadn't danced a day in my life." He chuckles. "The whole time she'd thought it was her that changed my life. But it was the music. I got a little of both worlds. The music never left, but the women did. I didn't want them anyway. Not for more than a night. Celeste was never terrible to me, but she wasn't the woman with the scythe. The hard truth is that she was too promiscuous —

177

still is. I was, too, but eventually that wasn't the life for me anymore. She, on the other hand, can't turn away from that lifestyle. She'd promised me time and time again she was ready for it ta just be the two of us."

Dread fills me from head to toe. In a way, I now feel like Celeste and I aren't much different. It's not just Jax and me... I divide my time with more than one man.

In an instant, all the insecurities I thought I had dropped come down on me like an avalanche.

I'd been better lately at keeping my facial expressions in check, but in this moment I quickly learn that I haven't mastered the technique. Jax's face blanches and he shakes his head. "No... no. Wait, that's... it's different... just let me finish."

With a hard swallow I nod, chewing on the inside of my bottom lip. Jax's hand reaches up to run his fingers over the indentation just above my chin. "It wasn't the sharin' of her body that bothered me, it was the..." he sighs deeply. "Ah... fuck... how ta explain... ya see, you share all of you. And you care about each of our opinions. The five of us are a team. To Celeste it was a game of numbers, and her heart wasn't there. Not the way it should be. She has an addiction, and it's dangerous. She's not smart about it. It's... I talked ta Tobias about Amber, and while it's similar, it's still vastly different. In other words, she's puttin' the people she becomes involved with in danger. So much so that she was kicked from the dance crew just before I left. She became a liability.

"Before I continue, I want ta reassure ya I am completely clean. I would have never touched ya otherwise. If I need to take the tests again ta prove it, I will. But, I do have the paperwork from my last lab."

It's not something I usually worry about what with the implants taking care of both preventing pregnancy and an extensive list of sexually transmitted diseases, but if Jax had himself tested, there must've been something that concerned him. Part of me wants to ask him to do just that, but the other part feels like it'd be a major step back from the trust we'd built during our time together.

For now, I don't give him an answer, I just remain quiet, ready to hear the rest. "Also, I'd stopped fuckin' her pretty damn fast, once I realized she was gettin' carried away and wouldn't stop. Now, I realize I'm sharin' an awful lot of information about someone else, without her permission, but with Celeste so closed off to ya, I don't know another way. She hasn't much changed. She's still up to her old ways, if not worse, but at least now she has the smarts to get tested on a much regular basis. Somethin' I'd encouraged for a long-ass time. Plus, rumor has it, she's actually warnin' guys before they stick it in." He shudders and rolls his eyes. "I cared for her for a time. I still do. I wouldn't want anythin' terrible ta happen to her. But Celeste and I are never going to be a thing. No matter how hard she tries."

For a time, I just stand there staring at him, the bombardment of information bogging down my ability to speak.

With a shake in his voice at my delayed response, he continues tentatively. "I wanted ta tell you all these things in small bits, over time... but..." The explanation trails while his eyes bore into mine and his back straightens. "If ya wanna leave me—"

Words return to me in an instant. "Shut up."

Jax's mouth slams shut and his Adam's apple bobs.

"I'm not leaving you, Jax." I press my lips together. "You're a good man. Better than most. That last thing

179

you said was pretty damn stupid though." At that, his eyebrows lift high. "I'm not leaving you," I say again, softening my gaze and truly meaning it.

Other than that, there's not much more for me to say. His past is his past. Celeste is here, and that's not going to change. Most importantly, he trusted me with this personal information, and I trust him. What he went through made him the man he is today, but it doesn't define his future.

With the hard part now behind him, he slips his fingers along my chin until his palm rests against my cheek, cupping the side of my head. "I don't deserve ya, Darlin'."

"No, Jax... you very much do," I respond, leaning in to kiss him. Just like the day we'd first hugged, he melts into me, bringing up his other hand to cup the other side of my face.

"No, Darlin', I don't," he whispers against my lips. "But I'll spend the rest of my life tryin' ta prove myself wrong."

Damn this man and his words. There's nothing remotely coherent I can say to that, so I hum and kiss him deeply this time. To which he responds by swiping his tongue skillfully against mine, and pressing his pelvis toward mine so I can feel the other way I imagine he'll try proving things to me.

Before I squeak, or moan, or do an unbecoming combination of both, I pull away, clearing my throat. "Ready to go back in?" I ask.

Jax raises an eyebrow, shoots a glance down at the tent in his shorts, then back up at me shaking his head. I chuckle and turn around, escaping into the room.

CHAPTER SIXTEEN

After the initial shock and introductions, the gathering proves to be a blast. Everyone celebrates Jax and Julian's recovery and enjoys an array of foods Ruby prepared. Auden has a good time, and I'm able to reunite with my center boys and get the lowdown on their arrival and how things are going otherwise.

Jax, being the entertainer he is, eventually encourages everyone to head to the Oracle Room... which doesn't take much tugging on his part.

Once there, he first directs Kait to her rightful side of the bar, insisting that no one can make a drink like her and Auden deserves the best for his eighteenth birthday celebration. He then orders a drink for Auden, much to Kait's chagrin.

"Now ya know he's underage, pretty boy," she laughs, all the while grabbing a glass and filling it anyway.

"My da gave me a drink on my eighteenth birthday after I got out of the center" — Jax puts the back of his hand to the side of his mouth, leans over and whispers — "though I'd already been sneakin' drinks for a number of years by then." Auden laughs, taking the drink in his hand once Kait passes it across the bar.

"He'd said" — Jax's voice deepens to mimic the sound of an older man's — "'back in your grandpop's day, legal drankin' age was eighteen. So he'd thought it only fair I get a drink on my eighteenth birthday too. And now, I'm givin' ya tha same thing.'

"Was tha only nice thing my da did for me," Jax finishes, picking up his own drink and holding it up high, raising his voice for the next part. "Here's ta becomin' a man… and savin' tha nation." Everyone hoorahs, but Jax doesn't drink. Not without first leaning over to me and adding, "… and to tha most beautiful woman I've ever met."

I had already lifted the glass to my mouth, pausing when he'd leaned in close. I smile over the rim, and he gives me a quick kiss on the cheek before taking a big swig of his drink.

Julian, Bram, and Tobias wait until after the toast to join us, choosing to leave Jax and me by ourselves for a short time since he'd just gotten discharged.

Tobias approaches behind me, wrapping his arms around my waist and nuzzling his nose into my neck. Bram takes the stool on my free side, and Julian steps beside Jax, plastering a big, Italian kiss on his cheek.

Jax grimaces and sticks his tongue out with a *blarg*, then wipes his cheek on the top of his shoulder, nudging Julian aside. "I like ya, friend, but not that much."

Julian laughs, reaching around him to push his glass to the other side of the bar for a refill. Having everyone here, enjoying themselves, is such a balm. Kait's hustling behind the counter, thoroughly enjoying being back to what she loves doing. All my guys are around me, safe and happy for the time being.

A throat clears nearby. It's recognizable but definitely not one of my guys. One thing is for certain, though, there's a rush of panic interwoven in his interruption. The guys and I turn around.

Standing there, wide-eyed, is a member of the Tech team. Anxious and out of breath, his attention lands on Tobias. "Roux?" the guy asks before taking a deep breath and clearing his throat. "They said that name would ring a bell."

I nearly tumble off the stool in an attempt to get to the man and extract more information. Tobias and I both approach at the same time. "Yes, it does." Tobias beats me to an answer, his ability to remain calm and collected far superior than mine.

"Per Robbie's instruction, we've been checking his feed occasionally. The lens was damaged during his interrogation, so anything that came through was short-lived and intermittent. Until a few minutes ago. When the feed cleared, it was of him looking down into the camera — working on fixing it, I guess? Anyway, he put it back in his eye and turned to a monitor. After that, he opened up a word processor and typed *Thessaly*. Hasn't stopped since," the Tech guy explains.

Tobias nods and shoots a glance over his shoulder at the rest of the guys. Bram, Jax, and Julian are quick to get off their barstools and join us, ready to move the party to the Tech room. "Thanks, we'll be right down," he responds.

Once the man leaves, Auden walks with us to the Oracle Room's exit before we insist he stay back this time since the gathering is mostly honoring him.

The rest of us, on the other hand, head to the lower level, straight to the Tech room.

NORMALLY, WE JOURNEY THROUGH the Underground on autopilot, getting from point A to point B seemingly in a matter of seconds. That isn't the case this time though. Every rushed stride is more like a slow-motion movie scene. Each twist, turn, and step is suddenly too far away.

With every passing second, I worry the feed will be gone by the time we get down there, and we'll have missed him. But going any faster is impossible with all the UR members to push through en route. The place has been steadily getting oversaturated, but it isn't until a need for speediness and accessibility of the passages is imperative that the numbers become overwhelming.

When we arrive at the Tech room, the density there isn't much better; every member of the team rushes about, each doing something important to support the UR's efforts. Even Tobias takes in a deep breath and lets it out before blinking the overwhelmingness away and scanning the room for the team members — and portion of the wall-screen — hopefully still working on Roux's feed.

Tobias's attention locks somewhere above the crowd and his head nods. He then takes my hand and weaves us ahead. Team members part to let Bram, Jax, and Julian through before the crowd closes in again, returning to their assigned tasks.

There on the screen, just as the guy had described, is my name in caps and bold. Occasionally, the feed moves down and shows a holographic keyboard, fingers pecking away at the letters *T-H-E-S-S-A-L-Y* before looking back up at the screen and down again to depress the backspace button and start over.

"How long has he been doing this?" Tobias asks.

"As soon as he typed it the first time, we sent someone for you right away," the assigned Tech member explains. "So… ten minutes, maybe? This is all he's been doing, over and over again."

"He's giving us time," I ascertain. "He can't keep on like this for long though. Looks like he's in one of the lab rooms at the facility." Unfortunately I know from experience, having initially been processed in one prior to being assigned a pod during my "visit" to extract Kait.

"Does his contact have the holographic features like the ones Bram and I used when we got Thess and Julian out of the Exam Center? We could send him a quick message lettin' him know we're here," Jax suggests.

"It did. However, we think he must've given the younger guard the lens that wasn't zapped by the radiation pulse and attempted to 'fix' the one that was. That correction apparently didn't include the holographic feature, because we tried to send him something but it didn't garner a reaction," one of the techs responds, deflating Jax's idea.

I watch as Roux types my name out for the third time already since we've been down here. He presses the first S before an idea hits me. The thought starts a little like, *"If we can't send him a holographic message, how will he know when we're paying attention?"* and ends with a mental slap to my forehead.

To test the sudden theory, I focus all my mental energy on the empath connection between Roux and me — the one both of us have strategically avoided since the moment it sparked. Similar to someone emerging from a crowded subway car and brushing shoulders with a nearby passenger, I lightly skim the bond between us while narrowing my focus on the screen.

T-H-E-S-S-A- Roux's typing stops.

In response, my pulse quickens, and I instantly open up our line of communication more, reaching for his emotions. A rush of *fear* and *panic* hit me hard one moment, and in the next, they're gone. Roux cuts the empath connection, leaving only the contact lens to relay his message.

Sometime during my short emotional separation from the guys, they had discontinued their conversations and turned all attention to the feed in order to watch in real time as the result of my empath attempts materialized on-screen.

Roux begins moving at a pace even quicker than the wild beating of my heart. First he deletes my name and shuts down the word processor. What he does next is a blur of activity. Roux's focus moves from the monitor to the keyboard over and over again as he types an intricate code into the screen.

"He's figured out a way to hack into some of their files," Tobias explains, eyebrows raised.

"You sound surprised," a recognizable feminine voice responds from directly behind us.

Tobias huffs out a short laugh. "I am," he replies to Becky without looking back, lest he miss anything Roux is doing.

"Of all the Group T members across the nation, Roux has always been one of the best," Becky reveals. Considering everything we've witnessed him do first-hand, none of us can argue that point. When set on a task, Roux has proven more than once that his efforts are all or nothing. No matter the cost. Unless the cost is his daughter, which, of course, is the very cost that drives everything he does.

"Hey!" Tobias yells, knocking my attention back to the present moment. "Is this being recorded? Get me a copy!" My eyes move back to the screen as Roux clicks past a map of some sort. "Fuck," Tobias grinds out. "He's going too fast."

After several heartbeats too long, a member of Tech finally responds. "Got it!"

Roux's eyes dart over his shoulder to the door and back to the screen again. What might have been considered fast a moment ago, moves at super-speed as he swipes through one map after another — all in the shape of the United States, each one showcasing something different. A new piece of vital information, no doubt.

Tobias sighs and swipes a hand through his messy hair.

"We'll need to wait for the playback to make any sense of this," Bram includes. Even still, he and Tobias scrutinize the screen, attempting to capture as much of the information as possible, even if it all feels for naught at the present time.

Unable to follow Roux's efforts myself and knowing we'll be reviewing the playback at a much slower speed, I break from the screen in search of Jax and Julian; both men have been oddly quiet.

Come to find out, Becky had passed Leta to Jax. Jax holds the baby out away from his body like she's a toad that's about to pee on him. Julian begins wooing her in Italian while Jax continues keeping her at an arm's length.

It only takes a few more seconds before Jax realizes he can touch her without any dire consequence. He draws her to his chest, holding her with one arm under her butt and his other hand supporting her head.

My attention moves to Becky, and her eyes meet mine. She gives me a smile and a shrug before returning her attention to the screen. "She started crying," Becky explains, watching as Roux moves on to shutting all the open folders and files and returning the computer screen to its original state.

Attention back on the contact lens' feed, I watch as Roux glances over his shoulder again and again in much quicker succession this time. Still, our bond remains quiet even though his increasing panic is evident on the monitor.

After a few more clicks and swipes, the screen he's looking at powers off and he rolls backward in what I presume is a chair. He then turns to face the door, still remaining seated.

The anticipation of what's next has the entire room silenced now. Everyone. Each and every Tech member has halted their activity, all eyes fixed on Roux's feed. He lifts his hand in front of his face, brings his thumb and pointer together, and inches his fingers closer and closer toward the contact lens.

Roux removes the contact — which translates as a quick blur of white — and flips and steadies it on the tip of his finger. Holding the lens out at an arm's length, Roux now aims the camera toward his face.

My mouth and throat go dry, and I swallow hard as my body seems to move forward of its own accord, approaching the screen. I place my fingertips on the deep gash and trace the cut on the side of his face from eyebrow to cheek.

The movement of his lips draws my gaze away from the brutal wound to his mouth. With slow and deliberate effort, he says something. When he's done, he does it again, his mouth moving in the same pattern.

Since I wasn't expecting it, the first time I couldn't make out what he was enunciating. The second time, I catch the words *"Tell my..."* but nothing more.

He tries a third time, but the sentence is cut off and his attention darts over the camera, toward the door. Eyes wide, he looks back at the lens, and his Adam's apple bobs over a hard swallow. "Tell my..." he says, blinking fast, but his efforts don't stop the single tear that tracks down his cheek.

Again his eyes dart over the contact and back again. He presses his lips together and takes a deep breath. When his lips form my name, there's no mistaking it. "Thessaly," he mouths. But the next part is difficult to translate. *My... pack? My... bad?* I don't have any more time to try. His eyes go wide again, and the visual turns into a blur.

When the video clears the ceiling is in view.

Another second later the cuts and grooves of the sole of a boot appear clear as day above the camera.

Then the monitor goes to white noise.

"Play it back!" I screech. When I realize the whole room is still quiet, I clear the shake out of my voice and try again. "Play back the parts where he's talking, please."

Beside me, Tobias gives a directive to someone nearby: "Go get Ruby."

"I'm already here." Ruby's aged voice is quick to respond from the back of the room.

Meanwhile, a Tech guy begins buffering the playback right away. The screen rewinds in fast motion until the part just after the tear had dripped from Roux's jaw. I watch his lips intently as he mouths *Thessaly* followed by the word *my*. In slower motion, I can now tell that his lips press slightly inward and completely together for the first sound of the next word... The sound "B." Then his mouth opens to create the sound of a vowel... "Ah."

From there, his mouth doesn't do anything at all; he just kind of holds it open. I turn to Ruby. "Maybe a sound that comes from the throat, instead of the lips and tongue?"

Only a few consonants of which I can think of…

The letter C, the letter G, and the letter H come to mind.

Ruby nods. "Bag," she says with confidence.

"Bag," I repeat. "'My bag.' He wants me to check the bag he must've left behind in his room." Feeling pretty good with that assessment and feeling great that the knowledge gives me something to do after this, the tension building in my shoulders lessens. "Go back farther," I request.

The playback rewinds, yet again, to the point where he'd just turned the lens over. We all watch closely as he takes his time to mouth his first message.

This time, with Ruby helping, it doesn't take long at all to decipher.

Ruby's dark blue eyes blink up at the screen and redden.

"Tell my daughter I love her," she translates. "Every day."

GROUP T'S PURPOSE has always been to find out anything and everything possible about The Program. Roux had done exactly that. After we translate Roux's personal message, the Tech team rewinds the playback to where the first map flicked onto the screen. One by one they capture, save, and study each.

One map in particular is riddled with location markers. If I had to guess, there's somewhere in the vicinity of over a hundred thousand dots. In comparison to the other maps, this one is far more glutted with specific spots. Even so, each is nothing more than a mark. Since we don't have direct access to the file, we can't zoom in to determine their significance. The concern is great enough, however, that while a portion of the Tech team moves on to study the remaining maps, several more begin attempting to discern what the dots on this one might mean.

With the combination of talent in the room and available technology, it doesn't take them long to figure out a way to make it happen. By layering The Program's map on top of a live, satellite map, they are able to lock the dots as a separate, transparent layer onto the live screen before removing the copied image. Doing so provides them with the ability to zoom in on the real map with the dots intact. The placement isn't perfect, but they get close enough to find a pattern: schools, hospitals, prisons and jails, commitment facilities, work camps... all large-scale, pre-existing establishments that can hold and contain millions of people when collectively used for that purpose.

The visual is overwhelming but brings with it clarity to some of the big questions we'd not been able to answer before. For instance, the fact that there appears to be far fewer pulse facilities than what could contain a nation... yet entire counties are so desolate.

With this new information, we come to the harsh realization that these buildings are being utilized as holding centers. They are likely shipping out Highs as quickly as possible while keeping Lows separated and secured.

It also segues into the conclusion that not all military, law enforcement, and federal agencies are likely friendly. At least those who haven't already been separated, drugged, and pulsed or sent to Low holding areas. Because, after all, jobs or careers before the sweep don't matter where the DMISs are concerned. Considering the number of Lows is far fewer, once all this is said and done, there may not be very many trained personnel remaining.

Even if our efforts result in a balance and power shift, the nation will be left in ruins.

A real life post-apocalypse.

CHAPTER SEVENTEEN

Tobias is the one to call it quits after a time because, according to him, "The Tech team can get the rest of this handled and give the leaders a thorough update as soon as they have all the details."

We'd already had an incredibly long day and there's an active party requesting our presence still going on. In between all the action, the UR's world turns. And, if I'm being honest, I am grateful. I'll gladly welcome every bit of faux-normalcy and distraction.

The five of us rejoin the party in the Oracle Room, only having missed about an hour even though it feels like triple that amount of time. To help us take our focus off Roux's message and the information he unearthed, we all cave and enjoy "one more" mind-numbing drink.

Another couple of hours go by along with several more drinks. Not too much later, Jax becomes quite vocal about him and I "Gettin' some one-on-one time."

However, before Jax can whisk me away, Tobias pipes up and pulls me to the side. Jax curses and mumbles complaints under his breath to which I throw him a wink and hold up a finger, promising this should only take a moment.

Tobias leads me to the hidden spot in the stairway area — the same one where he told me about his pain kink. "First," he says, wedging us between the stone walls, "do you and Auden have a bond?"

The question catches me off guard, and for a moment I stutter and blow out a breath. Tobias's eyebrow rises. "Why?" I ask a bit too defensively.

Tobias blinks at me, but then he smiles. "Because we need someone who shares a bond with you to stay here while we're in New York."

Oh... right. I take a steady breath, unsure how comfortable I feel admitting anything of the sort to the guys... nor to myself for that matter. Instead of a helpful response, I nod, shake my head, then shrug.

Hey, at least it's better than squeaking or any other form of embarrassing noises that I usually tend to do when in a compromising situation. After a long, drawn-out sigh, I finally respond in a helpful way: "Yes and no." Okay, probably still not helpful.

"How so?" Tobias encourages.

"Yeah, there's something there. He's not holding back though. Hasn't since the moment we left for the facility. Dare I say if I were to compare him with my 'official' Highs, he's more confident and less flighty than the rest of you were. But a bond? Eh." Again, I shrug.

"Well, damn. I thought I was doing a good job scaring him off." Tobias winks and tilts his head to the side. The small adjustment makes me all too aware of our extra-close proximity.

When I hesitate to finish my thought, he reassures me the question is platonic in nature. Well, as platonic as this bond mess can get between an extreme Low and extreme High counterparts.

"A fate-driven bond can't be scared off," I explain. "Do you think someone could scare you away from Leta?" It's my understanding that Auden is one of the highest out of the UR members, the guys notwithstanding. Roux is up there too.

There might be an age difference between Auden and me, but apparently we're close enough that the bond will morph itself accordingly. Add in his good looks and kind personality, and the start of a bond has nudged between us with ease.

"Nope… no one could scare me away from you either. Except for myself, of course," Tobias answers.

"Right. The four of you have each struggled with that throughout this process."

"Indeed." Tobias grows quiet, working through his next words. His attention moves from my eyes to the opening at the stairwell, then back again. "So…" His hand leaves my hip long enough to push through his messy hair before returning. "Um… like I said, we want someone here that has a bond strong enough with you to be able to sense you empathically from a distance like the rest of us can."

Groan. "Right, I remember."

"Julian, Bram, and I were talking about it, and we think we've been wrong all this time about the bond strengthening or starting because of intimacy." I raise an eyebrow at that revelation. If anyone were to get down to the science of it, it would be Tobias of course. He doesn't wait for me to respond before finishing: "We're pretty sure it has to do with protectiveness — the partner's need to keep his or her match safe."

The many scenarios over the course of our relationships cycle through my mind. I do remember Julian saying his empath connection started when I passed out at the lab. Thinking back on all my time with Bram, though, I can't pinpoint one particular memory that had a similar response. Unless, of course, *I* triggered it instead of the other way around; Maybe it happened when his parents were going through their divorce. Then it dawns on me that Tobias might be right once I realize his hit the strongest when I'd been abducted, and Jax's happened when I'd secluded myself from them at the campground.

My mind goes back to Roux and our dealings. When my memory returned about my time in the lab, he'd kissed me, and I'd assumed that's what triggered our bond.

As all the puzzle pieces fall into place, my eyes widen. My reaction to the Dub. Roux had to watch me go through that and at his own hand nonetheless.

It wasn't the kiss that triggered our empath connection... It was me nearly flatlining on the table in front of him. Or appearing to, at least.

Huh.

Tobias's eyes had been studying my features — and facial expressions, no doubt — while I worked though the concept in my mind.

"Okaaay..." I draw out the word, trying to piece together how he'd converted this knowledge into a plan involving Auden. Nothing comes to mind, so I stare blankly up at him.

"We want to see if we can trigger Auden," he explains. At that, my eyes widen; I can't imagine what they could possibly have in mind... and why he is telling me in a hiding spot...

"You... want to scare Auden into thinking I'm in danger?" I ask. Tobias nods, running a hand through his hair again. "How exactly?"

He then grimaces, and his previously dropped gaze lifts to meet mine. "Thought maybe I could... uh... do a little light-choking, breath play with you... in here... right now... so when Bram comes by with Auden and they 'accidentally' happen upon us, it riles him up a little."

196

Worldless, I blink up at him. His nervousness is endearing — I'll give him that much. "Right now?"

Tobias nods again, bringing one of his hands to my shoulder. The other remains on my hip. He then looks back to the opening again before meeting my gaze once more. "They should be coming toward us any second." Tobias clenches his teeth together, displaying a part grimace, part smile.

Once again, my eyes pop wide, and I'm rendered speechless. When I don't provide an answer as fast as he'd hoped, Tobias turns his sexy prowess on me, curving in his shoulders and leaning his head down so that his lips graze my ear. "Say yes," he whispers.

My throat makes an odd squeaky sound. Tobias laughs and responds, "With words not indiscernible squeaks."

Not sure what's going on anymore at this point due to my brain turning to mush, I try again, still not quite getting it right when I nod instead of speaking.

The hand that is — was — on my shoulder now moves up and around my neck, until Tobias's thumb is on that sensitive spot just below my ear, while the rest of his palm covers the width of my throat. "I'm only going to ask one more time," he warns and promises all-in-one.

This time, I have enough sense to use my words in defense, albeit a very breathy one, "You never asked a question in the first place."

Tobias's hand loosens a little, not that it was getting tight just yet, but apparently it was tight enough that my quite-accurate comment set off his Dommy warning bells.

He tilts his head to the side, now running his thumb down the middle of my neck to that little dip in the center just above and between my breasts. "Fair enough. Will you let me play with you in here… right now… while we have someone watching us?" Tobias makes sure he covers each aspect of what he's expecting this time.

"You're hard to say no to," is my response. "I hardly think that's fair."

"That's not an answer," he says with a side-grin. As much as he admits his affinity for being in charge, the steel rod pressing into my pelvis right now tells me he likes my rebellion just as much.

Or maybe I have it all wrong. Curious, I ask, "An answer for an answer?"

Tobias glances anxiously at the opening again before returning his attention back to me and nodding, all the while using his thumb to caress my skin in all the most sensitive of places. Before asking my question, I place my hand over his and aid in curving it back around my neck, keeping my hand there, with my fingers gripping him as though I'm trying to pull his hand away.

Honestly, it's pretty much saying yes to his question, but if I have to pretend, I'm at least going to have a little fun myself. "Do you like it when I resist?"

Tobias adds a little pressure to my neck, "Yes, but not for the reason your innocent mind probably thinks."

Guess I do have it all wrong. I raise an eyebrow, "Oh? Care to elaborate?"

He shakes his head. "Nope. I gave you an answer, now it's your turn. That was your deal, remember?"

I lean my head back against the stone wall, lengthening my neck against his hand. Tobias groans, sliding his palm upward closer to my chin, which in turn causes my head to tilt back even farther.

"I think you know my answer," I breathe out.

He chuckles, drawing his nose against my cheek. "Of course I do, but I like hearing you submit. In more ways than one."

"I have… forgotten the question."

"Maybe if I elaborate on my previous answer after all, you'll suddenly remember."

My shoulders shrug, and he chuckles and shakes his head, pressing our foreheads together. "There's a time for resistance, which you happen to play off so well. But what's nice about it, is that once you do bend, I get to punish you that much more. So, yes, a little resistance is… fun. But it's not the resistance that turns me on, it's knowing what I'm going to do to you later — because of it — that does."

Oh… well crap. "Fair enough." I give a nervous chuckle, using the same words he had a moment ago. Then I flutter my eyelashes, smile, and give him the answer he'd been looking for, not entirely sure it'll work to trigger Auden but also not caring much right now because… Tobias… and reasons. "Yes."

Tobias's fingers constrict around my throat. "Damn I want to kiss you so bad right now."

I snake my tongue out and capture my bottom lip before releasing it and saying, "So why don't you?"

Tobias hums and tightens his grip a little more. This time it's tight enough that my next breath is restricted. "I suggest you stop your teasing," he says. "You bend to my will, remember? I officially have your permission to… do what I please."

What I want to do is say *you're the one doing the teasing, hot stuff.* But instead, without words, I close my eyes and relax under him, letting my hands drop and my head, neck, and shoulders go completely lax.

Our lips meet, but he still doesn't kiss me. Instead, he brushes them lightly against mine, and says, "Good." But then, for a moment, his voice changes to a more serious tone. "Pretty sure we have a visitor."

My eyes spring open at this revelation just as his hand tightens. The pressure is stifling in a way that I'm not used to; even though I trust him, both my hands still come up reflexively to wrap around his hand in order to pry it away. With rapid, choppy breaths, I close my eyes, trying desperately to calm down and remind myself he would never purposely hurt me. Then, I have the sense to open my empath sensors, remembering why he's doing this to begin with. Pure, unadulterated rage slams into me with a very definitive Auden signature. A rage full of terror and protectiveness.

With the hand still gripping Tobias's, I make bunny ears and scratch them against the back of his hand. Tobias immediately loosens his grasp on my neck, and his mouth slams down over mine. The same hand that had been testing my resolve just moments before, wraps around the back of my neck and he pushes his fingers through the hair at the base, swooping his tongue in for a remedying kiss.

Auden's anger only strengthens, damn near causing me to tremble beneath Tobias for reasons associated only in part with his knee-weakening kiss. Also, this isn't the kind of rage I've felt from Julian. Julian's has always been a bit manic. Auden's is... controlled...

I'd put money down that, should I break the kiss with Tobias and steal a glance in Auden's direction, he'd be lurking in the shadows, eyes flat and piercing. Honestly, at this point I think I prefer the lashing out type of anger over the brooding, planning kind.

We might have been wrong about what triggers the bond, but one thing that has been equal and certain across the board is that when my matches get worked up, touch — mine in particular of course — helps calm them down.

Which, for the record, I do still find quite odd, but I'm not going to argue against what works.

Desperate to get the festering emotion out of me, I extend a hand toward the hiding spot's opening and wiggle my fingers. Yes, all the while still kissing Tobias.

Just like that, the calculative anger inside Auden flips to confusion. Nevertheless, after a few echoes of footsteps in the tight passage, a warm hand is in mine. But Auden doesn't pull me away from Tobias nor does he tighten his grip.

Since I'm a bit pinned and can't exactly pull the kiss away myself, with the hand Auden isn't holding, I bring it up to Tobias's forearm and use our bunny-ear code again.

Tobias pulls away. "Is there a problem?" Tobias asks, turning his attention toward Auden. There is neither venom nor condescension in his tone; it's simply a question. Nonchalant.

In the outline formed from the light filtering through the stairwell, I see Auden's Adam's apple bob hard as he shakes his head. "No, I suppose not."

Tobias chuckles. "Did you think there was?"

The bit of tension that had knotted in my shoulders when Auden's empath signature made his presence known, seeps away. Truth be told, while I do trust Tobias, I wasn't quite sure how ruthlessly he was going to handle getting Auden worked up. But Tobias's calm demeanor proves he doesn't mean to cause problems; he wanted to set the trigger and do what he could do to keep it at that.

If it worked, I'm not entirely sure. Auden is definitely impressing strongly enough to set him apart from the other people around me, but as to whether or not the connection goes both ways, I suppose he'll need to be the one to divulge the details.

With all the calmness in the world, betraying the rage I felt inside him just moments ago, Auden says, "Of-fucking-course I thought something was wrong."

Both the calm expletive and the fact his calculative rage is downright impressive and shocking, an unintended laugh bursts out of me which I quickly attempt to cover with a cough.

Oblivious to just how much of a threat Auden might be to Tobias after all, Tobias tests him further, "In ten years maybe you'll have enough experience under your belt to be able to tell the difference between a woman who is wanting versus a woman who is refusing. Sometimes, the two can look similar to the untrained eye."

Tobias's simple statement serves to lash at Auden by poking fun at both his age and his lack of sexual experience.

"Tobias…" I warn quietly, while lightly squeezing Auden's hand.

To the 'untrained eye' Tobias is unintentionally digging himself into a deeper pit than he realizes.

However, Tobias is smart — that much is consistent — and he doesn't brush aside my warning, thank goodness.

The cockiness in his voice fades, and he drops his voice, lifting his hand to my neck again. "She likes it. Don't you?" This time Auden's hand does squeeze mine and that rage reappears. Tobias's words, nor mine at this point, are enough to convince Auden nothing is wrong here.

In response to Tobias's question, I nod, feeling the heat of his palm against the length of my neck. But when I open my mouth it isn't to say yes. Instead, I say, "Auden, you're allowed to check through our empath bond. There's more proof there than my words can relay."

At that, Auden's hand loosens. But the problem is that he doesn't know how to check through our bond. As a result, disappointment overrides the anger. However, simply hearing me say that if he could check empathically, he'd realized there isn't a threat like he'd worried there was, Auden lets go of my hand, straightens his shoulders, and… apologizes. "Sorry I interfered in something… private."

Tobias lets go of my neck and slaps Auden on the shoulder, dropping his voice to a whisper. "Another tip… she likes to be watched. And to watch."

"Tobias!" I squeak. My face heats to a level it hadn't heated in quite some time.

Tobias chuckles and shrugs.

Auden stammers, "Oh-oh-okay," then takes a deep breath, and spins on his heel, exiting with haste.

Once back in the stairwell his flustered voice meets my ears, but it's not me or Tobias whom he's addressing. "You did this shit on purpose!" he grinds out.

Bram's husky chuckle meets my ears next.

CHAPTER EIGHTEEN

"Come here, Darlin'," Jax sing-songs in his smoky voice, stealing me from Tobias as soon as we enter the rooms. Turning to Tobias he says, "Thanks for warmin' her up for me."

"W-warm… wh-what the hell is that…" I stammer and squeak as Jax yanks me away from the guys' shared bedroom toward mine. Once we're close enough to my bed, Jax puts a finger up to my mouth to shush me, then slips his fingers under my shirt and lifts it up over my head.

It's not the finger that shuts me up; it's when he steps back and takes off his own shirt followed by his pants, that does. I had opened my mouth to lecture him, but all those lines… and stuff… and things…

…and then the eyes.

"Yer starin', Darlin'," he chuckles, causing my nipples to harden. A telltale dampness also suddenly forms between my thighs.

He steps toward me… all skin and tattoos… and equipment.

Here I stand, still as a statue — aside from my vagina which is pulsating like it's attending a damn rave.

Jax's fingers and thumbs find both of my nipples, and he rubs them lightly before sliding his hands between us and unbuttoning my pants. While he skillfully and thoroughly removes all the clothing on my lower half, he leans his head forward and whispers, "For as smart as you are, I sure love makin' ya stupid," he says.

I respond with a very educated, classy, and odd gulping sound. Jax grins, slipping his hands to my thighs and lifting me up just long enough to toss me onto the bed. As soon as I'm on my back, he has my legs wrapped over his shoulders and is on his knees, his tongue flicking places I'd momentarily forgotten having.

The overwhelmingness of it all has me turning into jelly — melting into the mattress — and moaning. My hands seem to know what to do, thank goodness; my fingers slip through his black hair to cup his head and press him against me more.

Jax slips his tongue inside, reaching up to tease my nipples concurrently, and I let out a soft groan, lifting my hips before dropping them and arching my chest into his palms instead — unable to choose which I want the most.

My body clenches around his tongue the next time he inserts it, and he quickly pulls away, much to my dismay. Assisting my thighs back toward my torso, he readjusts and slides his length inside me, gliding his hands up my thighs to the underside of my knees as he tests my flexibility and depth.

With my legs straight up, more of him fits inside me, hitting places I've not felt before. His hands drop to where my thighs meet my hips and he wraps them around, using them as grips with the next thrust, and the next, and the next.

Chest heaving, head tossed back, and hands clenching the sheets at my sides, every pump procures a breathy moan. When Jax's grunt and deep-chested growls add to the music of our intimacy, my body explodes from the inside out. Like pulling the trigger of a gun, he releases inside me, never once stopping the desperate plunges until both of us have ridden the wave of our orgasms through to completion.

He then wraps my legs around his waist, lifts me off the bed, still keeping us joined, and waddles us over to the bathroom. I slide off his body, and the two of us promptly clean up before he pulls me back to the bed and plops me on top of him as he collapses backward.

When my hair falls over his face, he reaches up and tucks it behind my ears, dragging the knuckles of both hands down the sides of my face once the hair is secure.

"It still works." He grins ear to ear.

The grin is contagious, so I smile down at him with a chuckle. "Mm hmm. Sure didn't last long though." I shrug, and he gasps, eyes wide. But he quips back, "Ya sure didn't last long either," with the waggle of his brows.

"Guess you did your job."

"Damn straight I did." He winks at me with those addictive blue-gold eyes.

Since we're both still naked, the fact his shaft is growing hard again does not go unnoticed.

He then flips me over, hovering above me. "And I'm about to get the job done again," he says with all the confidence in the world.

"We'll see." I wink back at him. Though, based on the way every nerve in my body tingles at the suggestion, I'm guessing he's right. In no time he'll have me tumbling over the edge again.

This time, he takes me slow, hands exploring every inch of my skin all the while his shaft explores every muscle and crevice inside me. Slow, deliberate pumps. Watchful, hungry eyes. Soft, explorative touches.

The careful passion is so much more harrowing than the intensity of before, and the two of us finish even faster this time. When we fall onto our backs, Jax turns his head toward me and says, "Ugh, I can't get enough of ya. Fuckin' thirsty... that's how you make me feel."

Pink flushes across my cheeks, blending with the remaining red that had already been there due to our lovemaking. "Undeserving... that's how you make me feel," I whisper, scanning every inch of his handsome face.

"No—" he tries, but I stop him, leaning forward with a kiss. In my mind — and my heart — I repeat the word 'yes' over and over again until it makes a firm enough impression though our bond.

He sighs against my lips and takes my cheeks in the palms of his hands. When we part, his blue-gold eyes pierce mine. "I love you," he whispers.

I close my eyes, nod, take a deep breath, and let it out. "I love you too."

The aftereffects of our union are quiet and calm. The two of us simply lie in each other's arms, no more words needing to be spoken. The three most important words already said.

Lost in our individual reflections, I become so relaxed, so at peace, that I make the grave mistake of letting my empath barrier crumble — something I haven't done in a very long time. Something that would undoubtedly be habitual were we to live together in a normal world, under normal circumstances.

But we don't.

A barrage of *fear*, *worry*, and *panic* hits me so hard, I fear it has pinned me to the bed with a tangible force. Needing proof that I can, indeed, still control my own body, I shoot up into a sitting position, closing my hand over my chest.

"What?" Jax asks, shooting up beside me.

"Everyone... the UR is up in arms."

207

"Oh yeah… 'bout that."

"About that?" I screech, jumping out of the bed and rushing to get clothed.

"Yeah, so…" I look over my shoulder, buttoning up my pants, to find Jax rubbing the back of his neck. "We got tha final pulse location."

"The fi—when?!"

"When you and Tobias were screwin' with Auden. It was on one of the maps Roux showed us."

Jaw dropped, I stare wide-eyed at him. "My pager didn't go off. The UR alarm didn't sound."

Jax shakes his head. "No, it didn't because Robbie wants ta make the rounds in person. He's been goin' to tha different levels and notifyin' leaders one-on-one. There was nothin' for ya to do… not yet." Jax slings his legs over the side of the bed and reaches down to collect his clothes. "And there was no fuckin' way we were goin' out there guns a-blazin' without me bein' with ya first."

His gaze dares me to challenge him. But I don't dare. There's no way I'd take back that time with him.

Letting the momentary panic seep from my tightly-wound muscles, I throw my head back and exhale before rubbing my hands down my face. "You're right. Sorry. It's just… we've been waiting for this moment."

"Yeah, I know, Darlin'. But ya can run or ya can walk, and either way, down here, things are gonna progress at the same pace. There are too many workin' parts — too many people involved. One person can rush things along, but it's pointless if no one else does."

Dropping my hands to my sides, I turn around and sigh. A now fully-clothed Jax steps around the bed and takes my shoulders into his hands to reassure me more, but Tobias comes rushing into the room. Jax drops his hands in an instant and steps aside.

"Hey," Tobias says, his voice higher in pitch from what sounds like both adrenaline and excitement.

"I heard about them finding the pulse location," I respond.

"Good! Umm..." Oh boy, there goes his hand swooping through that untamed sandy-blond hair. I look up at him, waiting patiently. "I'm leaving with the S&R crew. Gotta make a quick trip to Atlanta and get some of the equipment we'll need to do the data transfer."

"R-right now?"

"Yeah," he sighs.

"How long is it going to take? And when is everyone scheduled to leave for the attack?"

"Shouldn't take more than forty-eight hours... and they're waiting on Group T to return from the last pulse location so they can dispatch them to this new place. Once they've scoped it out, everything else will go into motion."

"And, when do *we* leave?"

"As soon as I get back. We need a couple days' head start. Ideally, we'd like to be in New York gaining access to the host system at the same time the attacks are scheduled to hit. Ideally. Give or take."

"Okay... so it'll still be a handful of days before the other URs are ready too?"

"Yes. Oh, and the Auden thing is official."

"The Auden... thing..."

Tobias gives me one of those rare, huge grins before darting a glance from me to Jax and back again.

Blood rushes down to my toes, and I stumble to the bed, falling dramatically onto my back. "Say it isn't so."

Tobias walks over and looks down at me, still smiling. "Oh… it's so."

Meaning, everything Jax and I just did, projected. *Super.*

"Maybe one of these days you'll learn how to keep that barricade up when you're doing… stuff." Tobias winks at me.

Yeah… I'm too… involved… too relaxed in those moments to keep all the feels from projecting; it's usually the recipient's job to compartmentalize it.

"We aren't like… in a relationship though. How is he connected to me that strongly?"

Tobias's eyes twinkle. "Uh, I believe intent has a thing or two to do with it as well."

"Ya keep actin' like the connection between you and Auden is strictly friendly… but tha bond begs ta differ."

Instead of humoring them with a response, I roll over to my stomach and shove my face in the mattress. Tobias slaps me on the butt with a chuckle. "Get up and give me a proper goodbye."

I bounce to my back and shoot up right away. "You're leaving right this minute?!"

"Yes. The sooner I can go, the sooner I can get back."

I stand up, wrap my arms around his waist, look up at him, and say, "I don't like it. Why you? Why can't someone else go?" Sure, that's selfish and not entirely fair to the 'someone else' — which I obviously mean no one in my direct circle.

"Because I'm the only one who knows what we're looking for and who is most likely to be able to gain access. But this is it. We'll separate this one last time, and then we'll be sticking together."

When I drop my gaze, he places a finger under my chin and lifts my face upward so that I'll reconnect. Unfortunately, when he gets what he wants, it also comes with what he doesn't want; my eyes are reddened, no doubt. There are no tears, but given a few more minutes, I'm sure they would have appeared.

"Ah, now... none of that. Another benefit of this particular run is that we get to test out another one of the maps Roux gave us. We're pretty sure one shows all the border-patrol hot spot locations." Tobias offers me a small smile before kissing over each eye.

I take a deep breath and let it out, nodding. "Hurry back."

Jax clears his throat. "So, um, hate to be the bearer of bad news, but I've seen this shit in movies. Never turns out good."

Tobias shoots Jax a stern look over his shoulder. A weight settles in my gut. Jax is right. Books too. As soon as the love interest says they'll see the other soon, or something along those lines, yeah, that doesn't happen.

My arms tighten around him and he wraps me in his, hugging tight. After giving me a kiss on the top of my head, he says, "Well, in the movies and books they never have a back up plan, right? So how about we change the pattern?"

I pull back from him, but still don't let go, resting my hands in his back pockets. "Yeah... at least that's something."

Tobias nods. "If I'm not back in time, I want you to go ahead and assume it just took longer than we'd expected. Leave here without me... and swing through..."

"There's a national park up there in tha northwest corner of Georgia," Jax pipes in, more familiar with

Georgia than any of us, what with it being his home state. "Should be an easy stop on tha way."

Tobias nods and looks down at me, eyebrow raised. "Sounds good to me. Swing through there, and I'll be waiting. Good?"

"Sure. Not much else we can do, hm?"

"Not really, no."

I inch up on my tiptoes and he bends his head down, meeting me for a kiss. "Same 'safe actions' as before? Pad of thumb if you're in danger... bottom lip if you need me?" He waggles his eyebrows. "I might not be able to respond this time, but you can still do something yourself, and I'll sure as hell make sure I'm thinking about you while you do."

"Thirsty," Jax whispers behind Tobias.

I roll my eyes but chuckle all the same. At some point, apparently we all became comfortable enough in our group dynamic that it's no-holds-barred with our sexual innuendos and what would under any other circumstance be private conversations.

Tobias doesn't disagree; he throws me a wink and leans down for a goodbye kiss, which I gladly provide.

The three of us head out of my bedroom. "What time is it?"

"Late-thirty," is Tobias's response. "Seriously though, I'm not sure on the exact time, but I do know it's super late. We didn't want to drive that distance in the daylight, so we're trying to leave before the sun rises."

"That makes sense, I suppose. Unless, of course, your awaiting enemies see your headlights before you see them."

Tobias lifts a finger as we join Julian and Bram, who apparently had been sitting quietly on their

212

respective beds waiting for us. "And that's why we won't be using lights. Night vision goggles."

"Even still, the roving of tires over asphalt is loud enough — especially at night. Got any fancy tech to take that away?" I'm kidding. There's no tech to eliminate sound.

He just looks down at me with a side-smirk and shakes his head. "Guess that's a risk we're willing to take. The alternative would be walking, and like hell am I doing that. We wouldn't be back for a month or more."

I want to suggest he take Betty. The smaller the car, the quieter it is, especially with electric tech these days, but I know what his response would be. Robbie had been working on getting Betty ready for the trip to New York… not for the trip to Atlanta. Gotta save her for our group travels.

The one that will include Tobias.

"See you in Georgia," I say, feeling much more convinced something will go awry and he won't be back in time. I feel it in my bones.

Tobias swoops his hand through his hair but nods in silent agreement. Truth is, I think he feels it too. But as much as the five of us — heck the thousands of us if we include the UR — each individually want to make self-serving decisions, there's a much bigger goal we need to achieve. One that is still self-serving in the end, but that requires risk and service to save others as well in the process. A lot of others.

An entire nation.

Neither of us say anything else. Tobias gives me one more quick kiss, whispers "I love you" in my ear, and rushes out of the room, unable to stand there and put it off any longer for fear that should he stay too long with me, he might change his mind. Even the smartest, most determined of personalities have their weaknesses. Apparently I am his. I'm glad for this quick departure, though, because, truth be told, I was super close to begging him not to leave and testing his control where I'm concerned.

Without Tobias to focus on, I now meet the watchful gazes of Julian, Bram, and Jax. However, I know I'll be spending an extended amount of time with them soon. In a cramped vehicle. So, it's not them who is on my mind... but rather Auden. I narrow a glare at Bram, who was apparently in cahoots with Tobias to set Auden up. "Where is he?"

Bram wastes no time, having known me long enough to anticipate my thoughts and actions before I even do in many scenarios. "In his room."

I give them all a sharp nod, spin on my heels, and leave toward the lower level to do a little damage control.

CHAPTER NINETEEN

Auden

When I shove my head into the pillow, the case is much cooler than my face in comparison. Once the pillow is done muffling the swears of frustration, I roll over to my back and stare up at the stone ceiling.

I'm always interested in the ones I can't have. Fucking figures.

What's worse, though, is that I'll always feel the need to protect her; something deep inside tells me so. Even if I'm not qualified and there really isn't a need. Like during the situation earlier with Tobias; there wasn't a need. I overstepped. Even if they had set me up.

Bram tried to explain everything to me afterward, but I was too angry to hear anything he had to say. But then... the *thing* happened: all these crazy hot sensations and thoughts popped into my head — and in my pants. I freaked out and went running to Bram again, knowing right away they weren't *my* thoughts. Not that I don't have those types of thoughts about her. I do. But... nope... those were not mine. Definitely not mine.

Julian was the one who had to help me though. Something about him being the main one who can feel her in that same way and being good at "compartmentalizing."

He'd tried to teach me how to compartmentalize, but... I can't get the hang of it. So, while her and Jax were having sex I had to rub one — or two — out.

How do the guys not let their anger, jealousy, and insecurities get the better of them?

With a groan of frustration, I squeeze my eyes shut.

It's not fair that I have to feel her in that way, while not having a chance at being with her myself. That's all sorts of fucked up destiny fate shit right there. No wonder there are people out in the world with mental problems; it wouldn't surprise me one bit if it was because of this opposite bond crap.

"You're sulking," a very recognizable female voice shocks me out of my thoughts, and I sit straight up in an instant, flinging my legs over the side of the bed.

There she stands, in all her stupid-sexiness. Hair messy — no doubt from what just happened. The swelling in my pants starts back up as if I hadn't just taken care of it more than once. With a nervous chuckle I casually palm myself, shoving it down between my legs.

If Thessaly notices, she doesn't say anything. Based on her decision to walk to the bed and plop down beside me, my guess is that she didn't notice.

She then scoots closer — too close — and rests her head on my shoulder with a big sigh.

The awkward smile I had plastered on while trying to distract her from my boner is still spread across my face. I side-eye the top of her head and pat the top of her bun.

She blows one of those loud raspberries from her lips and says, "Yep."

Clearing my throat and wiping the stupid awkward grin off my face, I ask, "Is something wrong?"

Why else would she be in here?

However, I immediately regret asking because then her head leaves my shoulder. Funny how you don't realize how much you like something until it's no longer happening.

Still far too close, she turns her face toward me and smiles. "Yes…" she says, but her eyes shine in amusement. "You can feel it when I'm turned-on… and stuff."

As she spoke, she lowered her voice, probably due to embarrassment, but my brain hears it as this sexy, whispery tone. When I look away to escape my unwanted thoughts, I catch her doing the same. This time, though, I'm thankful for the loss because her looking at me doesn't help matters at all either.

The two of us sit there, quiet — me trying to talk my dick down, her staring ahead at the door, fingers twisting. When the silence becomes uncomfortable, I try saying something at the same time she does.

"How oft—"

"I think I kn—"

I look at her and smile then, and she does the same before laughing and shaking her head. When I don't continue right away — a wordless offer that she should go first, she tries again: "I think I know what famous figure from history Ben used as his inspiration for the communication system," she says.

My interest piqued and exceedingly grateful she brought up a topic having absolutely nothing to do with the real reason why she's down here, I crook an eyebrow. Truth is, I already know the answer, but since I work in the kitchens, I figured someone else could benefit from our Communication instructor's reward of hand-delivered meals for the lucky person who solved the riddle.

As far as I've heard, no one has mentioned anything to him despite Ben bringing up the offer in every single class.

Thessaly squints and presses her lips together.

"What?!" I exclaim at the sudden change in expression.

"You already know!"

"Wha—yea—well, no. Well, yes and no... I mean yes, I think I do... but no... I... not officially." *Just stop talking, Auden. Stop.*

This time her lips press together for an entirely different reason — to stifle another laugh. When she's done being amused at my expense, she coughs and clears her throat. "Same time?" she suggests.

With a shrug and nod, I agree.

"On three... you count," she says.

"One... Two... Three."

"Genghis," we share in unison, both of us beaming proudly.

"When did you figure it out?" Her laughter calms any worry I'd had that she'd be upset I already knew.

"The first day of class." I shrug it off. "You?"

"Not until we started planning the multipronged attack. Why haven't you claimed your prize?"

"Hand-delivered meals?"

I don't have to finish the explanation because she pieces it together right away. "Oh, right." She waves a hand, and just like that we fall quiet again. After a minute or two, she speaks up. "What were you going to say earlier?"

Truth is, I'd worked myself up to ask a certain question, but now I'm not feeling as brave. My face gets hot, and I'm over-aware that it's likely turning red right in front of her. "Eh, nothing really," I stammer.

She scoots backward on the bed until her back rests against the wall and draws her legs into a criss-cross position. "Ready to talk about the elephant in the room?" she asks with a sigh.

No. "Yeah, sure."

"Starting with your question," she pushes.

"It wasn't exactly appropriate. Well... I mean... it's on topic... but I could have done better—"

"Try me," she says with a smile.

I blow all the air out of my cheeks and give myself an encouraging nod. "How often do you have sex... and other things?" I spew it out, having built up the nerve to ask the question but not look at her while doing so.

The room becomes so quiet that even my breathing sounds exaggerated. I hold my breath while waiting for her to respond. When she doesn't, I finally let out the breath and apologize, "Sorr—"

"Well now, hang on... It happens so frequently I'm trying to calculate it; I've had so much sex that I can't math right now," she says, and my eyes dart up, finally meeting her face. Her expression isn't nearly as serious as her tone had sounded. She holds up four fingers. "Four of them, so one for each meal — plus a snack — each day."

As red as my cheeks had been, all the redness drains away, being replaced by a ghostly whiteness — if the numbness in my face is any indicator.

"Auden," she whispers, leaning forward and placing her hand on my shoulder. "It was a joke. Pretty sure I can count on both hands how many times I have participated in forms of sexual activity since our group dynamic became a thing. Well... not including the times with Jax because he tends to keep goi—"

"Yep, got it."

"Sorry." She makes this cute grimace, biting her teeth together, drawing her lips back, and darting her eyes away. But then she sighs and says, "It has been more frequent lately though — now that we're all comfortable with the idea."

"Did Julian tell you that I wasn't able to compartmentalize it?"

She shakes her head. "In your defense, it took me a while too."

"Really?"

"Oh yes. Years. I was shocked when I learned Julian was able to do that so easily. Bram too. Apparently he was compartmentalizing soon after our bond formed." Hearing that she struggled with it does make me feel better. "I'm curious though... is that the only thing you feel from me?" she asks.

I pause to consider my answer for a moment, really digging deep. But, unfortunately, the answer is yes.

Apparently I don't even need to answer; she sees the distress on my features as I come to the conclusion. Her shoulders droop and she takes in a deep breath before blowing it out. Then her face morphs into a series of expressions, and I can't help but laugh — though I end up muffling it with a cough. The guys are always making fun of her because she can't control her expressions. "What is it?" I ask. "Did you figure something out?"

Her blue eyes dart up to mine, a little panicked if I'm reading her right. She then shakes her head and gnaws on the inside of her bottom lip. "Do you know if DMIS opposite matches can... just be friends? Like, is the matching exclusive to intimate compatibility? Because, with Leta and the guys for example, they have a strong connection, but it's not a romantic connection. Because I... I can't—"

"Hey," I interrupt her. Partly because I'm not sure I can handle hearing about how intensely she doesn't want to be anything more than friends with me, but also because she's starting to freak out and I don't like how it makes me feel. Especially because it's me making her feel that way. "You and Kait are just friends, right?"

Her eyes open wide and she nods.

"Well, there you have it." I give her that much. Even though she's smart enough to know that I'm blowing steam just to make her feel better. From what I know about the bonds, they link the way we've linked only when the feelings are mutual. But there is absolutely no sign that she feels the same about me as I do about her, so now I'm not so sure.

"Good…" The word trails quietly before picking back up with her next comment, "… because I could really use a friend."

There's so much sincerity in that statement that my heart drops. Looking into her eyes, there's no way I could deny her that, even if I wanted to. But the truth is, I don't. For some reason, "You've got Bram," comes out of my mouth instead, though, and I immediately regret the comment.

Thessaly shakes her head and says, "Not like that… not anymore. He's my best friend, yes, but in a different way now."

"Okay." I can't pretend to understand, but I can at least encourage the conversation. "But if we're going to be just friends, I can't deal with feeling your orgasms inside *my* body." I laugh to lighten the seriousness of the topic.

"Practice makes perfect." She winks, and I groan, falling backward on the bed and covering my hands over my face. "Did Bram tell you the reason why they did what they did?" she asks.

"Yeah," I mumble through my palms. "What good is it if what I pick up from you is only the one thing though?"

When she doesn't respond right away, I peek at her through my fingers. Her eyes search the room for answers, as she tends to do when she's thinking. Then they widen and she breathes out, "Law of similars..." I roll to my side, propping up on my elbow and hand. "Like treats like," she continues, not making a whole lot of sense. But, like a good friend, I wait patiently while she works through whatever she's thinking.

She then turns her attention to me with one of the biggest smiles I have ever seen on her face. And I swear if I could stop time, I would. But then she starts speaking again and the moment is gone.

"Similar things happen to the brain when we are experiencing something intimate versus when we are experiencing fear. Some people seek out fear for the thrill of it all. Imagine a haunted house, for example: we go in there expecting to be afraid but our brains, instead, relabel that fear. The fear then becomes something exciting. Our breathing intensifies, blood pressure rises, heart rate quickens — all of which happen during sex too."

Wow, I sure didn't expect to get a sex education lesson. But hey I'll take it. "Yes, I see. But, what does this have to do with me being unable to help you?"

"You say you can't feel anything other than my intimate responses. However, since the emotional response is similar, I have faith that you can pick up more than you think."

I sit up and face her, now intrigued by the concept. "Okay… I'm listening."

"That's it, though," she says with a laugh. "There shouldn't be much more to it. You simply pay close attention to the sensations you feel while I'm intimate, and pay even closer attention to when I might be feeling similar sensations outside of intimacy."

"You say 'simply' as though there's nothing to it."

Thessaly grimaces again. "Sorry about that. Sometimes I forget what it's like when the empath abilities are new. It's been quite a long time since that happened to me. Are you having any headaches?"

"Yes, I have been." The fact that she picked up on that surprises me. I hadn't even thought to mention it to her.

"That's normal," she reassures. "Do you feel a little unusual or manic with your own emotions lately?"

"Also yes."

She raises a single eyebrow, and her lips pull up in a half smile. "All that hypothesizing only to discover that you're feeling more of my emotions than you realize."

"Oh really, how?"

"Julian must be a horrible teacher. In his defense, though, he's pretty new to it too."

"I thought he did pretty well; I just figured I was tough to teach."

"Now, that I believe."

"What are you saying?" I ask, pretending to sound offended.

"Oh, um, nothing like that." Now it is her turn to turn red. She recovers quickly and has no trouble continuing the conversation. "Did they explain to you what they are expecting in greater detail? Tobias, Bram, and Julian I mean? Why they want you to be able to tap into our empath connection?"

"Yes, I believe so. Something to do with a back-up plan just in case communications go down or, worst case scenario, you are in danger and none of them are with you."

"That's... reaching. I can't imagine all those situations lining up to the point where you would be needed in that way. I mean, say it were to happen: What then? It's not like you'll be able to teleport to New York in an instant."

"No, but I can get somebody out there who can. Not teleport." I laugh. "But, at least be able to get someone to you quicker than I would."

"That makes sense, I suppose."

"Something is bothering you about this," I point out. "They didn't really ask my permission. I'm sure we can decline if we would like to." She laughs at this, and I feel accomplished despite not being able to do much about the situation. "Care to tell me why it's bothering you?"

At first, she hesitates, looking down at the still twisting fingers in her lap. It's only for a moment before she sucks it up and lays everything out there: "Adjusting to and being comfortable with this group dynamic took me some time. Our situation is not conventional, as you know. But what I don't like about this thing — the one with you and me — is that you are not being brought into the fold organically. Rather, we're being forced together: You being pushed to connect with me on a deeper level than you probably should be; me being encouraged to accept it." The tension in the room becomes palpable. Both of us are feeling the true meaning behind her words on a deep level. "Now, that's not to say it wouldn't happen organically, eventually. But, Auden... four guys are a lot." She whispered the last part. "I love them all; and I'm not saying I can't love more... but right now? Right now is not the time."

Selfishly, I want to be hurt by her confession. But that's just the thing — feeling that way would be awfully selfish. I can't imagine what she's going through. Even despite thinking it might be fun to have more than one woman, I'm not so sure I'd be a good candidate for the responsibility. Fate dealt her a hand that is not easy to play. For that reason, I toughen up, and let the momentary hurt roll off. "So, what if I say you don't have to worry about that? That I promise to use our connection only as a protector? A friend?"

She takes a deep, steadying breath. "I'd like that."

CHAPTER TWENTY

Thessaly

If the guys are right — if these bonds are triggered as protective instincts — having Auden as a backup is certainly a good measure to take. However, with the final pulse location having just been determined, there's not much time to work with Auden in preparation.

Nevertheless, we do our best, pushing our empath abilities to the brink more times than I can count. Pushing them so hard, the two of us end up passing out on his bed despite the hustle and bustle going on outside the stone walls.

When I wake up, cuddled closer than I remember being prior to falling asleep, the regular-paced, rhythmic breathing under my ear tells me Auden is already awake. I tilt my face back to look up at him, and find him staring up at the stalactites in deep concentration.

"Been awake long?" I ask

He shrugs beneath my head.

I raise an eyebrow.

He sighs. "Never really fell asleep."

"What?!"

He chuckles. "You... rolled over onto me and I couldn't bring myself to get you off—move you—I mean move you."

I hurry off him, returning to the other pillow. As expected, he sits up and twists his back side-to-side, stretching.

"You could have woken me."

"Nope," he says with confidence. "I kept practicing while you slept. I think I've got it."

"Yeah? Want to show me?"

Since I'm so used to all this empath stuff, so accustomed to emotions, I can easily pull them. Pretend to feel them. Mom used to say that I'd make a great actress, especially when I threw the most dramatic, tearful fits over the smallest of things.

For Auden, I pull on my fear instinct and project it toward him.

"Fifty-fifty chance I'll get it right," he says with a grin.

"There are worse odds," I laugh, finding it hard to hold on to the feign of fear when he's being all cute and witty.

His brown eyes search my face, and I immediately shut it down. "No... you can't use my features. You won't have that element at your disposal when I'm gone."

"Well... stop looking at me then." He raises an eyebrow. "Because it's hard not to look at you when you're sitting... right here."

Oh, right.

I stand up and start pacing the room. Auden falls onto his back and closes his eyes. Again I project the fear. It's easy to do right now, even if I'm good at it, because the UR is filled with fear. A fear that has, in fact, increased since waking up. One that will soon need to be addressed no doubt.

"Fear?" Auden asks.

"Yeah."

"Felt that one pretty strong."

"That's because it's dense down here. I absorbed some — not all — of the fear in the UR and projected it to you."

Auden nods.

"Something's going on," I sigh. "Guess I'll go check it out. I haven't gone out there since I heard about the final pulse, aside from making my way to your room."

"I'll join you."

"Don't you need some sleep?"

"Probably." He laughs.

THE UR IS CHAOS. Instead of the dining area being filled with congregating groups enjoying meals and conversation, there are groups of Combat teams gathered — the teams I assigned. Most of these people I haven't met in person though; I utilized Robbie's UR membership database — the one we'd signed into prior to the classes beginning — and used the scores gathered therein to create the teams in order to save time.

There were a handful of instances where I requested one-on-one interviews in order to determine each group's leader and who would be the strongest empathic influencers, but other than that, I'm seeing these people in their assigned groupings for the first time.

Robbie and Roark are at the front. Auden and I make our way forward to join them.

As soon as we're close enough to the meal counter, though, Ruby spots Auden and hollers him over. I place my hand on his shoulder and give him a quick smile, and he returns with one of his own before walking away.

"How's it feel seeing your handiwork in person?" Roark asks once my attention is back on the assembled teams.

"Pretty cool," I respond, opening up my empath sensors so I can get a feel for the group directly in front of us as a whole. The camaraderie is instantly evident. Not a unanimous emotion but rather a combination of several — *confidence, comfortability,* things of that sort — blended together to form a group-type bond.

Sorta like what the guys and I have, I realize for the first time.

Also similar to the guys and me, these groups' leaders are either one extreme score or the other. Their team, the opposite or neutral.

My eyes search the different groups until I find Celeste.

Amid all the planning and organizing and everything going on with Jax, Celeste and I had to interact more than I ever cared to before. But, if I was being smart and fair about things, she's one of the best empath candidates the Central UR has. Not because she's a good candidate for the field, but because I've since learned that the buzz she causes isn't only an indication of a bond magnetism — it is also a sign that she is using her empath abilities — even if she doesn't realize it.

Knowing this, I realize she'd been trying to use her empath skills with both Jax and Tobias the times I'd been there beside them to witness those buzzes. Even the reminder now serves to make my hands clench at my sides.

I'd approached her and the two of us had a sit-down. A sit-down which did not include the mention of my guys — no matter if one of them used to be hers or not. This sit-down had nothing to do with them and everything to do with saving lives.

Thankfully, even despite our dislike for one another, she was receptive to what I had to say. She even went to the length of approving the process, agreeing that it made sense, because she'd now understood she'd been tapping into that empath ability in her career — to get a fatter pay at the end of the night.

She wasn't happy, however, to discover that she would be expected to converge on the enemy first hand. I assured her that the Combat team she'd lead would be instructed to make sure their leader — her — is covered at all costs. But I also told her she'd best keep her clothes on and head down.

In fact, after that little comment and thought, it dawned on me that she'd be better off heading up a woman's regiment since her sexual preference seems to be men. Last thing we'd need is a bunch of guys fawning over her or becoming too physically or emotionally attached to focus on the field.

And so, that's how she came about leading a mostly-all-female regiment. However, I placed the overall leader, Roark, and a few of his best men in there too. Neutrals mostly. My only fear was that she wouldn't be able to fight should it come down to it. But, thankfully, Roark promised he'd be working with the leaders separately to prepare them.

Roark, having a heightened knowledge on all things empath-related, also explained to all the leaders and their teams that hostages are to be taken and given the chance to change their loyalties by a UR Combat team member that is roughly their opposite score-wise. And, in many cases, they very well might convert, which will serve to improve our numbers significantly.

The one biggest obstacle is that our time in converting them will be short. With the coordinated attack planned, the goal is one hit... and done. Conversion will need to take place on the spot, amid battle.

While we'd technically like to take the "subjects" as our allies and fighters, the sad truth is that they'll be too drugged to help. As a result, we're looking at defeating the opposition before even being able to make a move on our preservation efforts.

Getting them out of there will come last, after the facilities are secured, and the power is granted to the UR.

The conversion efforts are where select groups of Low team leaders — like Celeste — will come in. They will not only lead Combat teams but also pull the opposition like weeds in a garden.

In other words, they are charged to order the kills — and to collect the proverbial flowers.

The blood of so many on the hands of so few.

I'm not sure how I feel about that. Aloof, I guess? Surreal?

Anyway, this recruitment process had continued daily until there were no more qualifying Lows to assign as team leaders. Things were looking good, and as the teams started training together, I began to witness first-hand the effectiveness of this plan.

Taking another pass over the crowd, a significant item of note that I hadn't expected to see is all the white uniforms. When we'd received our UR bags — with the pagers and uniforms — the clothing was black. These look exactly the same, but white, instead.

"White?" I ask. "That's not very sneaky. Also... where did you come by so many so fast?"

"That's thanks to Bram and the other botanists," Roark explains.

"Of course it is." Seems most everything is thanks to them down here.

"After the radiation scares" — Robbie's eyes fixate on a point in the crowd, but when I try to follow his sightline, someone steps in front of me, blocking my view — "we decided we shouldn't send anyone there in all black. The color is too absorbent. It's not a full-blown safeguard against any lingering radiation, but it's something. Bram and the crew whitened them all with a plant-based bleach alternative of some sort."

Well, that explains why they're more an off-white than the blinding white of some materials. Still somewhat distracted by what Robbie keeps looking at, I stand on my tiptoes and lean side to side until I find exactly what he'd been so intent on watching. Kait.

I spin on my heels and face both Robbie and Roark. "You're letting her participate in the attack?" The question isn't mere curiosity but filled with accusation and worry as well.

"No, I'm not," Robbie says. "She's letting herself," he grinds out. "Put up a good fight too."

"I'll talk to her."

"Go for it." He doesn't sound confident it'll do any good.

I don't waste a lick of time. I stomp through the groups, straight toward the woman who'd won her way into my heart, and who I'd worked awfully hard to save.

"Just what the hell do you think you're doing?" I grind-whisper.

"Oh, not you too." She rolls her eyes. "I thought surely you'd be smarter than Robbie."

"Well if we're comparing on account of you going out in the field, I guess I'm not then."

Her dimple indents, but not because of a smile, rather due to her pressing her lips together instead. "Imma get them back. I don't remember what happened in there, but I'm gonna help. Help get the other women — and men — out of there. I can't just sit in here serving people drinks anymore. You out of anyone ought ta relate."

Of course I do. Feeling helpless is the worst. That's what led me to go get her out of there to begin with.

I look around at her group and open my empath sensors. Whoever placed her, did a pretty damn good job. A couple Lows, a couple Neutrals.

"Who assigned you?" I ask.

At this she darts her eyes sideways, refusing to look at me. Whoever it is worries her more than being discovered as a team member.

Oh, of course. "Celeste?"

Kait's blue eyes meet mine and she nods. "I cheated on ya, Sweets. Girl, I'm so sorry. Ya just had too much going on, and I didn't want ta both—"

"It's okay." I place my hand on her shoulder. "She did a good job with your team; I think you all will work well together. This is bigger than our dislike for each other. Pretty sure the two of us have set our issues aside for now."

With the entire scene now absorbed — the gathering, white clothes, Kait's participation — I finally think to ask what the heck everyone is doing out here.

"Drills in preparation for leaving in a few days?" I inquire.

"Oh... no, Sweets," Kait says, her eyebrows curving in. "We're leaving today."

233

"Today?! But—" A loud, recognizable whistle mixes with the quiet and nervous conversation of the gathered groups, and I instantly scan the top of the crowd for Bram's head. As soon as we make eye contact, he waves me over.

"What's going on?" I ask over the noise before I can even make it all the way to him.

More patient than me, he waits until I've approached before responding. Even still, he makes me wait longer, pulling me out of the dining area, past groups of members, until there's enough quiet space for him to speak without the distraction of a crowd.

With his free hand, Bram handles one of his pagers, quickly typing in a message. When my own buzzes, I know he's sent it to our group. As we wait near the opening passageway that leads to several dorm rooms, I am reminded of Roux since this is where he stayed during his time here. The contact lens' feed playback comes rushing back, and I remember I need to make a visit to said room. "Want to talk in Roux's room?" I suggest, pointing in that direction.

Bram nods and plugs another message into the pager to specify where the other guys can meet us.

Once inside, I sit on Roux's bed. Bram paces, looking up at the ceiling, clearly calculating or contemplating something. His finger taps over the pocket that holds his pagers.

Knowing it doesn't matter how much I dig or how many times I ask, Bram's going to answer me on his own timeline, so I sit and wait.

When Jax and Julian join us a few minutes later, Julian sits on one side of me while Jax takes the other. Then, like teenagers, the two squeeze in, wedging me between them. Jax slips his hand between my thighs, and Julian weaves our fingers together.

"Are you two still trying to stake your claims on me?" I ask, laughing. "Because" — I drop my voice low — "spoiler alert... the answer is 'both.'"

Jax leans his mouth toward my ear, "Spoiler alert... We know you like us both... at the same time." His hand inches up higher, and Julian's amused laugh meets my other ear.

Bram clears his throat, and the three of us hurriedly inch apart, suddenly reminded we're here for an important reason.

"Pulses are going crazy," Bram announces. "Seems they were pulsing separately until every location cleared protocol. The final location pulsed, and now they're coming in more frequently and from every facility. Robbie turned off the UR notifications because it's... it's just too much for the members to deal with. To make matters even more challenging, Zinna's activity log shows her flight for New York is tomorrow."

A heavy weight sinks into the bottom of my gut, and all the blood drains from my face. Julian squeezes my hand tight before rubbing my knuckles with his thumb. Once the news sinks in the rest of the way and my initial shock wears off, I am able to take in a breath and exchange glances with everyone in the room.

There's no time for worry to debilitate us. We have just a moment to take a breath, and then it's time to put on our serious hats and get to work. "Okay... so the UR teams are dispatching across the nation... today? What about that final pulse location? Was Group T able to scope it?"

Bram shakes his head. "They're going in blind. Group T will be going to the last facility alongside the Combat teams assigned to that spot though."

"When does everyone attack?"

"Based on all the distances, travel, and prep time, we are estimating the attacks will begin approximately twenty-four hours after arrival, give or take for each group. Our hope is that everything lines up."

"And they all have predetermined places to set up camp? Relatively near each facility?"

"That is my understanding, yes."

I can practically hear the mental tick, tick, tick as I run through the list of questions stacking up in my mind.

"But... wait... Tobias," I announce. Bram gives me one of those looks — the apologetic kind. "No! He only just left, what" — I try to do the math in my head — "less than half a day ago?"

"The UR pagers may not work because the UR messaging system between regions is different than the one with our group pagers. Tobias's group pager worked when he was in Michigan, so I've sent him a message to decode, informing him of the changes," Bram tries to reassure me. That is until the next part: "Haven't heard back yet though. We'll need to leave without him. Maybe meet him en route."

"Maybe?!" I squeak.

Bram steps toward me and squats to look at me eye level. "He knows everywhere we're going, Thess. And now that I've paged him and the leaders have no doubt gotten news to the S&R crew, he'll know not to come back here. Worst case scenario, when it comes down to our timelines crossing, he'll just meet us at the Eastern Region UR's headquarters."

"What, exactly, is our route?" I ask. Because if it doesn't go through Georgia — the northwest corner to be precise — that route is changing whether or not they agree.

"We'll go to Alabama for the exacentrifuge, then up to New York, followed by Rhode Island," he answers.

"Like hell. Better find me a route that hits both the CDC and the National Park in northwest Georgia too. Otherwise, I'll just throw caution to the wind and drive."

Stupid?

Maybe.

Happening regardless?

Definitely.

Bram pats me on the knee and stands. "We'll make it work."

"Thank you." With all this talk about Tobias, I unclip the pager from my pocket and catch up on the group messages. Sure enough, Bram's appears on the small screen; apparently he'd sent that one while I was asleep in Auden's room. So much for being of use when any of the guys — or sleep — are distracting me. I'm beginning to think that they often do it on purpose. Like that whole Julian and Jax sandwich a bit ago.

I continue flipping through the messages, and sure enough, there's no response from Tobias. "When are we leaving?"

"Tonight."

The word hovers in the room like a dense fog.

We knew this moment was coming, but that doesn't make the reality and decisiveness of it any easier to swallow.

"Well, *amico,*" Julian sighs, "guess we shouldn't defile Roux's bed right now after all."

"Such a shame," Jax quips back.

237

Bram mumbles a string of complaints, throws his hands up in the air, and leaves the room. But he quickly pops his head back in, and his gaze meets mine. "Try to get a little bit of sleep at least?"

A laugh escapes me, effectively clearing the dense fog in an instant. One thing is for certain, I love that my guys know how to lighten the mood during intense moments. "I'll try, but I can't make any promises."

Bram gives me a sharp nod before disappearing.

Jax and Julian don't remain seated at my side for long.

Jax gets up and bends down to give me a kiss on the forehead.

"What can we do to help you get ready?" Julian asks, standing beside Jax and stuffing his hands into his pockets.

"Honestly? Right now, I just need to process everything. Make a list of things to do. Stuff like that," I explain.

The two of them nod. Julian takes a hand out of his pocket and extends it toward me. Instead of taking it, though, I give him a wave of dismissal. "I... I think I'm going to stay in here for a bit. It's quiet... and I need to see what Roux wanted me to find in his bag."

"Okay, Darlin'." Jax gives me a reassuring smile before both of them leave. Jax's Southern accent travels down the passage when he hollers out, "Page if ya need anythin'!"

THE EARTHY SCENT OF STONE fills my lungs, along with a very faint hint of the remnants of cologne — a distinctive smell that instantly makes me think of Roux. I never consciously paid attention to how he smells; only now in his absence does my subconscious prove otherwise.

A few of the happier moments between us flicker through my thoughts in order of when they'd happened; each replay until his most recent messages imprint themselves clear as day in my mind's eye.

Roux's requests seemed so… final.

Desperate.

The weight of dread presses in on me, wrapping over my shoulders and around my throat like a thick scarf. I criss-cross my hands over my chest and take in more air, willing the invisible scarf to unwrap and fall. After a few more isolated breaths, I get off the bed and search around every corner and edge of its base until I find Roux's bag. The black backpack is curiously light when I lift and place it upright on the mattress.

What's even more curious is that, upon searching every pocket, I discover the bag is empty. Again, I search every pocket, make sure every clip and velcro strap is open, flip the bag upside down, and shake it. Again, I find nothing. When I toss the bag back onto the ground, however, a faint *ting* bounces off the room's stone walls. Eyebrows drawn inward, I pick up the bag and try once more. At the very bottom of the main compartment, my fingers brush against the metal grooves of a zipper. Since the main section is empty, I turn the entire thing inside out and a somewhat-hidden, zippered pocket reveals itself.

The metallic click of each prong opening echoes through the quiet room. Once open, I peek into the little compartment. A small glass vial, filled with a familiar white powder and a slew of memories, lies inside.

CHAPTER TWENTY-ONE

Not too long after the groups gathered in the wee hours of the morning, the first half departed — the trip to Nebraska more than triple the distance than the estimated travel duration for the second set of Combat teams. This, in turn, means a much, much shorter time between setting up camp and initiating the attack for them. About midday, the Combat teams assigned to the Florida facility left.

As for us, Bram said "Tonight," and we wasted no time rushing around and ticking off items on our mental to-do lists: See the Combat teams off, tie any loose ends with our assigned responsibilities, try to get as much sleep in as possible, shower, eat, pack…

One item on the list is to make sure Tobias's stuff is handled too. While Bram and Julian double check with Tech to make sure he doesn't have any outstanding tasks, I am in charge of collecting his things. However, I soon learn that he'd already thought this far ahead, because his belongings are nowhere to be seen. I guess he'd brought everything with him just in case, which isn't too surprising. At the rate everything is going, and how last-minute his departure was in addition to our equally last-minute backup plan, Tobias's odds of returning were looking slimmer and slimmer anyway.

After the bigger tasks are accomplished, getting ready takes the guys hardly any time since they all are still living out of their travel bags. Plus, when Robbie had been fixing up Betty, he made sure her trunk was packed with meals, a couple first aid kits, and other necessary items like the small generator that now aids our upgraded solar-charging system. Quite honestly, it's a miracle we were able to fit our bags in there at all.

Just as we're wrapping up forcefully stuffing the trunk, Auden emerges from the Underground to see us off. I'm quick to approach him with a big hug. "Let's hope you don't feel anything alarming," I say as we break our embrace.

"Well, if I feel the *other* alarming thing, at least I will know you're okay."

"This is true; though I can't imagine how we'd fit *that* in."

"I can," Auden is quick to respond. So quick, in fact, it's almost as though he'd already been thinking it. One of my eyebrows rises. He laughs. "You're going to be in the car with *those two* for over twenty-four hours." Auden's attention flickers over to Jax and Julian.

Being stuck inside a tight vehicle with the Country-Italian duo is indeed... concerning. However, "There's no way Bram would be okay with anything happening. He's still... I don't know... out of sight, out of mind kind of thing?" But goodness, twenty-four hours? Guess I had mentally underestimated how long it was going to take. It's no wonder we need to get out of here as soon as possible.

Auden nods, but the creases at the corners of his eyes negate his agreement; he's not convinced. Unfortunately, we didn't really get a chance to practice the compartmentalizing part, just the association stuff, so if something does happen, eh... it is what it is, I suppose.

Bram slaps the top of Betty's cab a couple times with an "Alright, let's get this show on the road!" and Auden gives me one more hug before making the rounds with the guys: handshakes, man-hugs, dirty and random

241

remarks that sound awful but are apparently their way of saying goodbye… things of that sort.

Bram hops behind the wheel, and Jax and Julian take the back. Before ducking my head inside the front passenger seat, I smile at Auden once more, and he mouths "Good luck!" with a grin.

Due to Tobias and Bram's need for extra leg space, it has been quite some time since the rest of us have claimed shotgun. As a result, the passenger seat is adjusted as far back as possible, serving as a dismal reminder that we're missing an important part of our group.

When I reach down to adjust it accordingly, the gravity of his absence heightens tenfold. I change my mind, choosing to keep the settings untouched instead.

* * *

THE FOUR OF US have been in and around the lab in Alabama enough times now to be able to drive there on autopilot. With it being just barely over the border, the drive doesn't take long. For that reason, every second is spent hashing out a plan.

In addition to the upgrades Robbie gave Betty and the meals and other helpful supplies he put in her trunk, I also learn he stocked us with a number of tools and weapons, chosen specifically with our assigned tasks in mind. Demolishing each exacentrifuge, for instance.

This particular task, I am told, will be a two-part process: For part one, we use a special device to overload the equipment with electricity. From what I am able to translate about capacitors and circuits, this will mimic what a bolt of lightning could do to household appliances that don't have a surge protector. In short… it'll fry the hardware. For part two, we then take a sledgehammer — or four — to the equipment and leave it in as many pieces as possible.

Of all the tools and weapons Robbie gave us, the fact he included sledgehammers has me in a fit of temporary laughter. No wonder poor Betty is a little droopy in the rear. Also, I'm not entirely sure I can so much as lift one of those things. Even if it is possible, Roark failed to include "Sledgehammer Wielding" as part of the Combat course.

Our conversations naturally lead to the most important part of the discussion: planning how to get inside the lab. Our first — and last — attempt ended with a drugged guard, a wounded Tobias, and some video footage tweaking. Since our first rodeo, we've all had training in various areas, namely technology and combat, that should make our attempt this go round much easier.

This time, however, we have no need to take the same extra steps we did during our first visit. For instance, we have no desire, or need, to shield our identities. To say we have nothing to lose, though, isn't entirely correct. If we fail we lose everything. Losing is not an option.

In preparing for this plan, apparently Tobias had a lengthy discussion with Becky about the different exacentrifuge labs. Becky explained the labs were mostly unused now that the sweep was done, and just about everyone's samples had been submitted. She also mentioned most laboratories didn't typically have security anyway, despite the high-dollar equipment therein. The labs with exacentrifuges were an exception to this rule. But even then, they only had one guard on duty when they were open and functioning.

In short, she predicted we should just be able to break in, and if not, there would only be one guard to overthrow.

Just as we had done before, Bram pulls into the wooded area between the Exam Center and the lab. Because even though we don't care if we're seen, doing so at least gives us a few minutes to finish getting ready — mostly mentally and emotionally — without the risk of getting seen in the interim. Like last time, the plan is to approach the building in pairs, staggering our arrival. The woods prove a good base, and the extra cover is a useful addition to that tactic.

When we arrive, we notice a big difference with the parking lot lights in comparison to our first visit; the area is nearly as black as the surrounding woods. A speculative excitement buzzes through our group: if there is no power running to the lab, what are the odds they'll have employees — guards — on the clock?

"Can you still fry the hardware if it doesn't have any power running to it?" I inquire.

Julian responds, "Thanks to Tobias suggesting we bring an external power source, yes. Otherwise, no, we wouldn't have been able to."

Julian returns to the conversation he'd been having with Jax, and I turn to Bram instead, unable to sit there silent when my mind is anything but. "How long will it take to get to the second centrifuge? We're doing two, right?"

"Roughly sixteen hours not including the stop for Tobias," Bram explains while Jax and Julian wrap up rehashing their part of the plan. "It's in southern New York."

"My butt hurts just thinking about how long we're going to be in this vehicle. Sixteen hours is a long time between hits. Surely word will have gotten out that someone destroyed one of the exacentrifuges by then?"

"That's one of the many risks we're taking. Hopefully we'll have Tobias back by then. If not, hopefully news won't have traveled that far. Or, better yet, not at all if this place is as abandoned as it appears."

"And if news does reach the second location?"

"We just might hafta get a little meaner," Jax pipes in from the backseat.

One thing Roark warned all his students about is that this could — and would likely — get bloody. Doesn't matter if you're staying in the UR or if you're on the field, everyone needs to be prepared to do whatever it takes to survive. Even if it results in bloodshed and lives lost.

There's already enough of that with the pulses. Not so much the blood part, exactly — not with how this advanced radiation melts them from the inside out, turning them into... into... I'm not sure what. Nothing, I guess?

The mental image is horrible. If I allow my mind to dwell on the reality of the situation, it'll debilitate me. In an effort to redirect those thoughts, I begin mulling over the roles the guys and I are playing in comparison to the multipronged attack. Although we're not hitting these two exacentrifuges at the exact same time as the others and the facilities, it might prove as a good distraction to what's going on much closer to the pulse points.

With the limelight on the Central and Eastern exacentrifuge locations, we hope the people in charge won't be overly concerned with what's brewing right under their noses elsewhere.

As for our part, were we to drive straight through, the estimated travel time to New York is twenty-three hours. We're not, however, driving straight through. With the multipronged attack due to go live in less than forty-eight hours, and all the stops we still have to make...

...we'll be cutting it close.

Jax and Julian exit the vehicle, open the trunk, and take out everything they need to put our plan into action. Julian taps on the window and I roll it down so he can bend inside and give me a quick kiss. Jax stands behind him, and when our eyes meet, he tips his invisible cowboy hat.

They disappear between the trees, sledgehammers propped over their shoulders.

Bram and I stay behind temporarily, watching the minutes pass on the clock on Betty's newly revamped navigational screen. There's a good chance all four of us aren't needed to get the job done, but when the guys suggested I stay behind and be the getaway driver, I countered the motion.

If nothing more, I'd at least like to get one good whack in.

That is assuming I can carry the sledgehammer across the parking lot without my arms turning into jelly.

With a deep breath, I rest my head back and close my eyes, mentally preparing myself for the longest couple days of my life...

...beginning with the longest fifteen minutes.

CHAPTER TWENTY-TWO

Tobias

"There are so many of them," Aubrey whispers, doing another check of her gear. "I thought you said the map Roux shared was a near-guarantee this place wasn't hot."

"From border patrol," I speak low, hoping we're not discovered. "There were no promises the selected route would protect us from anyone else in a uniform."

"They look like the same type of group we took down in Alabama the other day," she points out. But I wasn't there the other day... Julian was.

What I do know is that our entire crew walked right into them — whoever they are. Thankfully, the S&R crew all know how to hide well. None of us have been spotted... yet. The first directive Harvey gave us, though, was to turn off all our com-devices, pagers included. If we're going to get through this, we can't risk interference or the vibrating buzz of a pager going off.

While I certainly don't like it, because I need to be able to hear from Thessaly and the guys should anything come up, I understand the need for safety.

Getting to Atlanta wasn't a problem. On arrival at our destination, however, we quickly discovered the CDC must be a major player in this entire debacle. The place is crawling with people in uniforms.

Since I swapped places with Julian, Aubrey and I paired up. A couple other team members are nearby, taking shelter behind the catty-corner building. The CDC is housed in an area similar to an oversized university or, rather, several universities rolled into one. Not all buildings are CDC-specific though. Right now, the entire S&R crew is hiding behind several buildings in what appears to be a commons area of some sort. When I'd been here in the past, it was only for a brief visit and tour. Unfortunately, I never paid any attention to everything else around the area.

For the better part of an hour, we've been sitting ducks, hoping for a shift change or some miracle to come along that gives us a window of opportunity to move. The entire crew — including our leader — is unsure what to do, and no doubt pissed off. Due to reasons like this, they perform cleanups one small area at a time — less intrusive, more effective, and a much lower risk.

"I need to just walk right up, and pretend I'm supposed to be here," I blurt out.

Aubrey stays quiet, thinking it over for some time. Eventually, she nods. "If you go in alone, at least you're confident someone knows where you are. We — or at least I — can lie low and plan an extraction should one be needed." Her specifically, because right now there's no easy way for us to communicate and explain the plan to the others.

I remove all my gear, take off my UR shirt, leaving the white undershirt on, and place everything on the ground beside her.

"You're going in unarmed?" she asks, eyebrows raised.

"A Database Tech wouldn't show up with weapons."

Aubrey picks up my gear and adds it to her own. "Well, at least you've got size on just about everyone over there — from what I can see at least. Please tell me you know how to use it."

Freezing, I look at her, eyes wide. Maybe we were wrong about which way she swings after all. "I… know how to use it…" I answer cautiously.

She nods, unfazed by how her comment caught me off guard. But then her eyes widen to mimic mine. "Oh, shit," she laughs, covering her mouth to muffle it. "Yeah… not what I meant," she mumbles through her fingers. "Nothing to worry about with me. I've got your back. No distractions."

Deciding to leave it at that, I peek around the corner once more. "I don't want to appear from this spot, so I'll try moving to another section of the grounds and step out from there." I look around, weighing my options. "There… that fire station. A road butts up to it. I'll hustle over there, then step out onto the road and enter from that direction."

"Okay, I'll double back and let Harvey and the others know," Aubrey responds.

With a grateful nod, I run from one covering to the next until I'm hiding behind the side of the firehouse. For as abundant as the Unis are, I would've thought they'd be spread out a lot more. Instead, they're so localized around the main CDC entrance that it's quite easy for me to step out and start strolling down the road as if I haven't a care in the world.

My suspicions regarding their aptitude rise when someone finally spots me, yells, and about ten more bodies aim their weapons at the same time. After all, I'm only one man — hardly a startling threat.

Heart pounding, I put my hands up. "Whoa. Hey. Name's Tobias Revard; I'm with the DNA Database Office."

Apparently that was the wrong answer. No less than three men rush toward me and bring me to the ground, wrenching my arms behind my back to secure my wrists with cuffs.

Fuck.

CHAPTER TWENTY-THREE

Thessaly

Longest fifteen minutes of my life indeed — if the first few minutes are any indicator. Quite anticlimactic, too, considering my current lack of participation paired with Bram's and my decision to memorize our travel map in the meantime. That is until the nav screen starts flickering.

Heart rate accelerating, eyes wide, I inch my body away from the screen as if something is going to pop out of it. I know that's impossible, but with everything going on, my nerves and anxiety aren't in the best place for unexpected technology complications.

Robbie's face appears on the screen, his affable smile lifting. "I think we're connected," he says to someone off-screen. The person beside him tilts his head in front of the camera. Auden.

"Anyone there?" Robbie asks, moving a curious Auden aside.

The unexpectedness of it all leaves me mute for a time. Bram clears his throat, waves at the screen, and says, "Yep, Thess and I are."

"Oh good!" Robbie exclaims. But then his smile drops, no doubt the accomplishment in tweaking Betty's features now replaced by the reason he's reached out.

"Can you see us?" I ask, needing the heads-up… should things go… down… in here at any given point of this adventure. Not that I'm planning anything crazy — nor planning anything at all really — but privacy and all that.

"No. Can you see me?" he asks.

"Yes, we can. It's a bit staticky though," I respond.

"Ah… okay. Sounds like we won't reach as far as I had hoped then."

"Why didn't we just use the burner phones?" I ask, prompted by a random memory from our past travels.

"Because we had to toss the ones you already used — since they're a 'one and done' sorta deal — and we want to make sure we have plenty left to be able to communicate with people at the facilities in the aftermath. Anyway, look… I've got a couple items of news."

I nod before remembering he can't see me. "Okay… shoot."

Robbie swallows hard and takes in a deep breath. "Good news or bad news first?"

"There's good news?" I ask in jest. "Shocking."

Bram laughs beside me, and Robbie gives a halfhearted smile. "Okay, we'll start there… we've got a few members of the Eastern Region's Relay Division set to meet you at the second lab location to switch out your UR pagers. Your group-specific one should continue to work intermittently though."

"Oh! Since they're already going to be over there, have them scope out the lab or stick around and help us should we need backup." The thought alone makes my concern about the next exacentrifuge location ease tremendously.

"Sounds like a plan," Robbie agrees before continuing with his update. "Almost all the Combat teams are in place, aside from a couple that had longer drives. So, as planned, the attack starts across the nation in about twenty-four hours give or take. So far, the execution is perfect." Robbie grins.

"Now that *is* good news," Bram replies.

But instead of Robbie's pride holding up, his smile drops and he rubs the back of his neck. Auden's voice comes from off-screen, "Want me to tell her?"

Robbie steps aside and Auden's face appears. "The Search and Rescue crew was compromised. We got news from Aubrey that Tobias has been apprehended." Auden doesn't pause, doesn't hesitate, doesn't candy-coat it.

Robbie urges him aside and his face fills the screen again. "Sorry, Thessaly. But what's most important about this new situation, is that I have to urge you not to go there. Let the S&R crew take care of it; that's what they're trained to do. The place is hot. Crawling with Unis. According to S&R, they think this is a new group of people. They still seem like authority figures of some sort, at least if their uniforms are any indicator."

Bram's hand slips under my hair and he cups the back of my neck in an offer of quiet reassurance.

Since Robbie can't see the dour expression on my face, it's the lack of a response — the silence — that clues him into my reticence. In his own way, he tries to ease the delivery of this news with a small smile. But, even so, there's still the business side of this conversation to wrap up. "Listen... don't dawdle," he instructs with a wink. "With the pager swap and the attack, there's not a lot of time to wait around. In fact, I need to stop parting frog hairs myself."

The amusing and bizarre comment works to lighten my mood for a heartbeat — just long enough to bring my mind back to the situation as a whole. Before disconnecting, though, I remember to inquire about his wellbeing since Kait left with the Combat entourages. "One more thing... I'll be quick, promise." Robbie gives me a sharp nod. "How are you holding up?"

There isn't a need for me to say Kait's name for him to know what — who — the question pertains to. Watching her go out there with a team... especially after what he went through during her capture... must be difficult.

"Best I can do is distract myself. Keep busy making sure everything is taken care of on our end so that things go smoothly for them."

"You're a great leader, Robbie. Thank you for everything. Seriously."

"Hey, you all are due quite a lot of thanks too. We're rooting for y'all. The whole nation is."

"Heh. No pressure."

"None at all," he says with a wink. "Hopefully next time we see each other, it'll be to celebrate, right?"

"Right. Let's make it so," I offer.

Auden peeks his head in front of the camera and smiles just before Robbie shoves him to the side, salutes, and cuts the connection.

As soon as the screen is black, news of the danger Tobias is in returns instantaneously. My heart becomes heavy and my mind reels with all the grim possibilities. Eyes threatening to fill with tears, I slip my bottom lip between my teeth and bite down — hoping that, if nothing more, Tobias can feel the twinge of pain and know I'm thinking about him.

"Thess..." Bram's quiet voice nudges my mind back to Betty's cab. "If we don't join Jax and Julian soon, they'll begin to worry. Do you want to stay here? I can go by myself — check on them and let them know we're okay then come back and sit with you?"

"No," I respond easily. "My sadness is the least of our problems right now. Let's head over there." The words Tobias has used on more than one occasion fall from my tongue: "The sooner we go, the sooner we can get back." But my final thought remains just that — a thought: *And the sooner we can get back, the sooner we can move on to the next task and the next until there are no more left and we can find Tobias.*

Without further ado Bram and I leave the car and grab our sledgehammers. Like Jax and Julian, Bram carries his over his shoulder. After my own attempt to do so, and scarcely making it through the trees without feeling the pang of its weight digging into my bone and muscle, I swap to a cross-body hold. Gripping the handle at both the bottom and up near the head, the weight is more evenly distributed, making it easier for me to hold it and walk at the same time.

About three-fourths of the way across the parking lot, the outline of someone approaching appears in the faint moonlight. Glancing around, I realize there's nowhere for us to go. We can run back to the woods, or we can take our chances and continue ahead.

Bram and I share a look, but even when the stranger comes to a sudden halt, neither of us stop moving forward.

"*Oh, grazie a Dio ce l'hai fatta.*" The stranger's words reach our ears in the still, quiet night.

Although the unexpected presence of another person caused Bram and me to slow, the now-familiar Italian reassures us of Julian's identity, and we pick up our pace again. Julian meets us in stride, turning around to continue with us the remainder of the way.

"Anyone know why the heck this parking lot is so big?" I inquire to make the last several feet go by faster.

"It's most likely that the property was something else before they demolished the original building and put this smaller lab in its place," Bram unsurprisingly offers.

"*Si.* That… or due to a different reason entirely," Julian states, his tone wary. "Come… you'll see."

The three of us enter the building's rear access easily, because the door is missing a handle. In its place, a hole. Guess Jax or Julian got to have a little fun right off the bat.

"No one is here," Julian verifies. "There is power running to the building, though, and we were able to access their security footage," he explains, popping his head into the room with the exacentrifuge. Jax had apparently been waiting in there for our arrival; on Julian's return, he steps out and joins us.

Neither of them say anything as they lead us through the center of the building, to the front, and through another busted door. Crossing the threshold, we are brought into the entrance vestibule. Images of our last visit here flash through my mind. On one side of the room is the guard station where Tobias had tweaked the video feed before we broke in to do my blood draw.

Just like that night, the glow of electronics emanates from the open door. Jax and Julian lead us straight there and stand in front of the screen, drawing both Bram's and my attention to its content. Different scenes flick on the monitor as it cycles through what appears to be several unique live video feeds.

After leaning my sledgehammer against the wall, I step closer to the screen to scrutinize each image, but they cycle too quickly. "Can we pull them all up on a grid?" I inquire.

Julian swipes his finger across the screen and taps a few different selections to get the job done. Most of the feeds are of the inside of the lab. The ones that are not, however, stand out among the rest. Naturally, my attention is drawn to the ones with movement.

Each screen showcases a room packed with people. Standing, lying, sitting... there's hardly room to shift. My eyes travel from feed to feed, trying to make sense of what I'm seeing. My focus lands on another peculiar image: a parking lot similar to the one outside this building. In the far back, however, the feed shows what our vision couldn't pick up in the dark — a large number of vehicles, similar to the ones I remember spotting from a distance while I was in the facility. These ones, however, are much bigger and more military-like in comparison to the prisoner-style ones that were transporting subjects from the train station we'd passed en route.

"So they're using this lot to park transport vehicles, I guess. How about these people? Is this footage from inside the facility?"

Julian's head moves in my peripheral vision, and I turn to face him. His green eyes, brightened from the screen's glow, meet mine, and he shakes his head. "*Io no, cuore mio.*" Julian lifts his hand and points a finger at something at the bottom right corner of one of the feeds.

PHASE TWO CENTER REGION 3

"Phase Two Center?! The one through the woods on the other side of Betty?!" With a frustrated growl, I grab the bottom part of my sledgehammer's handle and drag it behind me as I leave the security room.

The exacentrifuge isn't the only thing that's about to meet its demise. Before we enter the main part of the lab again, I lift the sledgehammer up and over my shoulder, tighten my grip with both hands, and swing with every bit of effort I can muster. The anvil crashes against the vestibules camera, resulting in a satisfying clatter of breaking glass. Heart racing, I let my newly triggered determination guide me into the lab.

"Time ta break some things!" Jax whoops, his clap echoing around the room as they follow my lead.

We each take a corner and effectively break every camera within. When the easy part is done, the four of us move on to the room with the exacentrifuge — adrenaline swimming through our veins and a swagger in our steps.

For a moment, we all just stand there staring at the large piece of equipment. After several more seconds, I whisper to Jax and Julian as though the machine might hear me and run off before we can do any damage. "Did you already fry it?"

"Yes," Jax whispers back with a quiet laugh. Instead of responding with my voice, I nod and step closer. "Ya get first dibs. Seems fittin' with everythin' ya've gone through."

When I look over my shoulder at each of them, I receive nods, smiles, and shrugs in response. But when I return my attention to the large machine, the previous exhilaration fizzles. A memory of the first night we came here takes its place. Tobias was so excited — so enamored by what this machine meant by way of science and technological advancements.

I take another step forward, letting the head of my sledgehammer rest on the ground while still keeping a grip on the handle's base, and I run my fingers over the cool metal. This piece of equipment in combination with the ExaIntel database is what brought the five of us together. Without the two working in tandem, I likely would have never met Tobias, Jax, or Julian. For those

258

reasons, my tightened grip on the hammer's handle loosens.

But then all the horrific, cataclysmic events that supervened its invention serve as a sullen reminder of why wrecking this machine is so crucial. Before I let my unstable emotions get the better of me and change my mind, I close my eyes and raise my weapon.

As if my emotions are working in tandem with the motion, a tear streaks down my cheek and drips off my chin at the same time the anvil comes crashing down on the exacentrifuge. The single swing — the single tear — zaps so much energy from me the hammer drops to my side with a thunk, and I stumble backward into the arms of one of my guys.

"I've got you, Thess. They'll take care of the rest," Bram whispers in my ear, keeping hold of me as I cave in on myself. Jax and Julian step away, both men raising their sledgehammers and following through without a lick of apprehension or hesitation. With every raise of their weapons, another tear builds, and with every swing and strike, a tear falls.

The demolition takes time and a tremendous amount of effort — the process long enough that my emotional imbalance eventually becomes manageable. Once I feel more emotionally stable, I am able to relieve Bram of his promised companionship, and he joins Jax and Julian to help speed up the task.

Unable to remain still now that I'm no longer soaking Bram's shirt with my tears, I pace. My emotions may have temporarily immobilized me, but I never once stopped watching. Every strike. Every kick. The movement of their mouths with every muttered — and sometimes yelled — expletive.

With each new successful chink in the machine's metal, a dense spine-tingling buzz of defiance spreads through the room until the air becomes alive. My heartache feeds on the electric sustenance and redirects, amalgamating with adrenaline once more and morphing into a defiance of its own.

I pick up my sledgehammer, slinging it over my shoulder, no longer sensing the discomfort — or no longer caring — and I walk to the corner of the room where the last remaining camera aims down at the destructive scene. Then I lean against the nearby wall, situating myself in a way that allows me to continue watching the guys.

As soon as they each take their final hits, I turn to the camera, position myself directly in the center of its sightline, and give it the middle finger.

Then...

...I destroy it.

CHAPTER TWENTY-FOUR

K nowing we aren't equipped to handle extracting the hundreds of people packed inside the Exam Center — especially in the event it's guarded — the best we can do is reach out to someone who can.

As soon as we're back inside Betty, I whip out my UR pager and plug in a message that should result in another video call from Robbie. Pressing the buttons is rather difficult as my hands and fingers tremble, but I manage to push through the residual adrenaline, and before long, Robbie's face appears on the screen.

"Are we celebrating already?" Robbie grimaces on screen, knowing full well not enough time has passed to accomplish anything worth celebrating — not including the exacentrifuge's demolition.

Julian delivers that bit of good news to Robbie before delving into the real reason we reached out. Each guy then takes turns delivering our findings, beginning first with information regarding the military troop transport vehicles and ending with the grim details about the people packed inside the Exam Center like sardines — and how we came about that discovery.

Robbie ends the conversation with a promise to get S&R out here as soon as he can, as long as it doesn't interfere with the progression of the big-picture plan.

When the transmission cuts, my head falls back against the headrest, and I close my eyes and take a deep breath. Speaking with Robbie again mixed with the temporary reprieve from everything outside Betty's cab, the reality of Tobias's predicament rushes back. The sudden onslaught of adrenaline that had caused my heart to pound faster suddenly subsides, and my racing heart decelerates to painfully slow thuds.

One of the guys begins to speak, but his accented tone halts and the return of his conversation is directed toward me. "What's wrong?" Julian asks, having tapped into our empath bond.

Unable to keep it to myself — unable to bear this burden alone — I recount Robbie's first message, starting with news of the meetup with Eastern Region's Relay Division, and saving the hardest part for last. Up to that point, I'd like to think I handled the delivery pretty well.

However, before I realize what's happening, Jax is consoling me. Against his shoulder, my heart bleeds.

"I... I've dealt... with... a lot... but... I can't... lose... any... of... you." And I mean every single word. If even one of them is stripped away from me, I'll no longer be of use to anyone. I'll run; I'll hide. I'll be by myself so I can live out the rest of my days in my own misery — no longer a burden to anyone and no chance of negatively impacting anyone else around me.

There's nothing any of them can say to heal the agony I feel in my heart.

We've reached a time where promises can't be made, not even promises of attempt. The old Bram, for example, would have ensured we'd figure out a way to turn the end result in our favor.

The new Bram — transformed by our situation — can only support me and be a sounding board. Same with Jax and Julian.

For that reason, no one says anything at all.

Eventually, however, Bram starts Betty, and we leave the lab and Exam Center behind.

After a while on the road — once I've calmed down — Bram breaks the extended silence. "Want to talk about it or do you need a distraction?" he asks, knowing his offer is one of my most favorites anytime something is wrong.

"Distraction, please," I answer.

Bram points to the road ahead, slows down, and turns. Having nearly memorized the travel map by now, I realize he's turned north instead of north east, and I immediately question why.

"The National Park is on our route, so we're stopping there."

"A-are you sure?"

"Yes. Robbie warned us not to go to the CDC, but he didn't say anything about steering clear of the rendezvous spot. Even if Tobias isn't there, it wouldn't feel right not to check," Bram explains.

All the breath releases from my body on a lead-filled sigh. That's exactly what I'd been thinking too. But with Robbie's warning, I wasn't sure anymore. To have Bram follow through with that portion of our plan, relieves me substantially.

The next few hours creep along — both what's ahead and what's behind still hovering thick in the confines of Betty's cab. Even with this much going on, all of us except Bram manage to get some sleep in restless spurts, making the trip seem all that much longer.

In the least, I am thankful for each task — each stop — en route. Having a few things to do breaks the day-long trip into shorter, more manageable bites.

The farther north we drive, the colder the cab becomes, even though I'm sandwiched between hot and hotter. Bram and I aren't used to the cold, the two of us living in Florida for our entire lives. Jax is probably not much different, growing up in southeast Georgia if my memory serves.

Julian, being from Chicago, is probably more accustomed; Tobias is likely as well seeing as he calls Michigan home.

The morose reminder of his absence hits again just in time for Bram to pull off the road onto the National Park's property. All of us now fully alert and on the lookout for any sign of Tobias under the unhelpful, deep-blue, extra-early morning darkness, Bram drives through the property a bit. When we don't see him, Bram parks at the edge of a huge — and tremendously beautiful — ravine with a river running through at the very bottom. As the dawn slowly begins to illuminate the sky, we see a considerable span of apartment complexes and other stacked housing units on the other side of the river where I imagine trees once used to be.

All the buildings look desolate and abandoned. Sound is nonexistent. I imagine a place like this would be quite the beautiful sight in the evening with the yellow glow of lights coming from each home, but with no one living in them, it would be nothing but solid black once the sun goes down.

"We should've been more specific as to where to meet here. The park is huge," I say absently, wrapping my arms around my shoulders to hold in warmth.

Unable to deal with the chill in the air, I walk back to the car, open the trunk, and take out my UR outfit, slipping the cargo-style pants over the comfy spandex I'd worn for the trip. Then I dig out my white pleather jacket and slip it over my white tank-top.

"Still think it'd be cooler if we kicked all this ass in black, but at least you look good in the white, Darlin',"

Jax comes up from behind, slipping his arms around me, now wearing something similar, but not leathery.

At the sight of me changing, the guys decided to do the same, gearing up for… whatever. Being anywhere near radiation isn't on our agenda, but considering the circumstances, one can't be too careful I suppose.

"I like the white," I divulge, turning around in his arms. "So much cleaner, despite the mess we're in."

"If ya say so." He winks at me and leans in for a kiss, which I'm more than happy to oblige.

Once the moment is over, he takes my hand and we return to the overlook just in time to watch as the blues turn to purples, then pinks, and finally oranges. "Been a long time since I've seen somethin' so beautiful."

"Yeah. It's a bit sad, though, don't you agree?"

When I turn to look at him, his blue-gold eyes are already on me. "Even when you're sad, you're still beautiful."

I chuckle and swat him on the arm. "You weren't talking about me."

He laughs and looks back at the view. "Not at first, but then I realized how the comment could go both ways."

"Such a romantic." I sidle closer to him and rest my head on his shoulder.

"Yer right, though… it is sad. The turn tha nation has taken."

"Yeah," I whisper, closing my eyes, appreciating having him by my side more than the silent scream of desperation from the desolate community.

I look over my shoulder to check on Bram and Julian and internally freak out a little when I don't see them anywhere.

"They went to look around now that we have more light. Want to stay here or take the opposite side of the park?" Jax suggests.

"Yeah, we can take the opposite side." Being helpful is always a good distraction.

Unfortunately, even in the daylight our search is fruitless. The company, conversation, and walk is invigorating though. After about an hour we all meet back at the car, still less one Tobias.

"Sorry, *cuore mio,*" Julian says, "but we need to get out of here to keep the timeline."

I nod, glancing around one last time. "Thanks for giving it a shot, guys."

"Next stop, New York. Thirteen more hours," Bram says, getting into the back seat.

Julian groans.

Jax offers to kick-off the drive.

I join Bram in the back. But when it comes time to close the door and leave, I find it difficult to commit. The guys wait patiently though. When I finally do, Jax is quick to start Betty and put her in gear.

CHAPTER TWENTY-FIVE

"The smoothness of our plan — minus not having Tobias — puts us all at ease for this final stretch of the trip. With the late night and early morning start, those of us not driving fall asleep easily, gearing up for the biggest parts yet to come.

In between stretch and "bathroom" breaks, driver swaps, and restless naps, the sun sets on yet another day. During one said nap, in a sleepy haze, I find myself mumbling, "Tomorrow is the first day of a different — better — forever." One of the guys responds, but I'm back asleep before I can make sense of the words.

The next time I wake up, someone is running their fingers through my hair. Bram, I presume. When I stir in response, his deep baritone meets my ear, easing me out of the remnants of my slumber.

With a gaping yawn, I arch my back, stretching. The first thing my eyes discover outside the window is crisp, thick, white snow. Even in the dark it's bright and beautiful.

I've never seen snow aside from rare flurries... most certainly not enough to stick. This snow looks fluffy and deep; I only wish I was experiencing it under better circumstances.

"The snow is pretty," I point out.

"Don't let its good looks deceive you, *cuore mio*," Julian chuckles.

Bram gives us a heads-up, and the lab housing the Eastern Region's exacentrifuge comes into view. After our cautious inspections determine it appears just as vacant as the other was, we pull up to the door instead of seeking cover.

We couldn't have hidden in the woods anyway. This particular lab is surrounded by corporations and commercial buildings — all of which have been swept and cleared. Here in this small portion of the city, broken windows, abandoned vehicles, and random personal items partially buried under the snowfall are the only proof people ever occupied the area. These few signs weave a tale of immense devastation though.

We sit in the car, scarcely breathing in an attempt to be as quiet as possible so we might hear — or see — signs of the Eastern UR's representatives.

Who, if they're already here, apparently know how to hide a lot better than we do.

After several minutes pass, Julian proposes we move forward with the plan to destroy the exacentrifuge. We have some time to spare but not enough to sit here and wait much longer.

Since our last demolition went through without a hitch, we decide to take the same steps. Jax and Julian collect everything they need and get out of the vehicle while Bram and I wait behind until it's our time to join them.

Jax and Julian aren't gone long though. In a matter of just a few minutes, they're back inside Betty, sledgehammers resting in their laps.

"The Eastern UR's guys are already in there takin' care of business," Jax explains. "Should be out soon."

"Oh... that's good! I bet they're having a blast in there."

Julian laughs, adding in his thoughts. "They were. It's not everyday people on the technology side of things get to do demolition."

Sure enough, not much more time goes by when a group of people emerge from the building. Neither party wastes any time with casual conversation. We give them a heads-up about the current use of the Central Region's Phase Two Center and suggest they have some of their remaining Combat or S&R Crew — if any — scope out the Eastern Exam Centers as an added precaution.

They give us the coordinates for the Eastern UR's exact location, swap our pagers with a new set, and explain that the messages received are now from the Eastern leaders. They go on to inform us the leaders from every region are in contact with one another and have set up a plan for making sure the "attack" code goes off simultaneously. Every pager will get the announcement, and if we can wait until after the pagers go off to take care of the database, it'll better coincide with the multipronged plan. In the same breath, one of the Eastern UR guys says that we'll have a little more wiggle room than the Combat teams, of course.

After giving our thanks, we part ways. This time, our next destination is a much shorter trip, thank goodness.

"How much farther?" I ask, hopping back inside Betty as quickly as possible, eager to get a short reprieve from the freezing temperature.

"One of the maps Roux flashed on the screen was of The Program's various operational locations in New York — including Zinna's office. Our Tech team shared the screenshot with the Eastern UR Tech team, and they, in turn, utilized a resource there that was well-versed in the area. That resource gave us instructions for where to park and how to navigate the area on foot. Not too far from Zinna's corporate office, there's an old shopping center. The raised loading-dock style storage buildings behind there should provide ample hiding space for a vehicle. So... maybe fifteen miles from here?" Bram finishes his monologue by finally answering the question. The details are all relevant, though, of course.

"Once we get to Zinna's office, what do we do from there?"

"Unfortunately, we still don't know where the host system is, so we're heading there to see what information we can find." Bram looks at his pager. "According to her activity, Zinna should arrive in New York via plane sometime this evening. Now even."

"Ah, so the airports are still in working order then?"

"Hmm... I'm not so sure. Wouldn't surprise me if it's a business jet or something along those lines," Bram responds.

"If she has to get her permissions returned manually, I imagine that means there are still people working in the admin building. Maybe the roads around the area are flatter, more traveled? Or at least from wherever they're sleeping to where they're working? Perhaps that small detail could clue us in to where the admin building is."

"That's an excellent thought, *cuore mio*. We'll keep an eye out. People have driven through here somewhat recently... and regularly... but not often enough to warrant the roads being plowed and salted."

"Wouldn't surprise me one bit if the road crew is locked up in a facility somewhere," I muse. Unless, of course, they're needed. In which case, I'm sure The Program has no problem keeping people around past their "time."

Keeping that particular thought to myself, I nod and rest my head back, choosing to watch the buildings pass rather than dwell on what I presently can't control.

I always imagined New York as overwhelmingly busy. Usually, everywhere is busy — too populated, too commercialized, too everything — but some of the more populous states like New York seemed to have been one of the first places for this to happen, urban sprawl the only thing giving its streets somewhat of a reprieve whilst smothering everywhere else in the process. My first visit vastly contradicts those expectations though. Just like everywhere else — every street we've traveled, every town we've driven through — the streets are empty and the driveways and storefronts hidden by banks of snow.

In fact, in order to pull into the parking spot, we end up having to get out and do a little shoveling with our hands — as, in our preparation, none of us considered needing to bring an actual shovel. We try barehanded for a bit, but it doesn't take long for our fingertips to redden and go numb.

Why we didn't think to get some socks or something out first is beyond me. Then again, I suppose it's not too surprising that our brains are at max capacity. After a little trial and error, we do just that, popping Betty's trunk and digging out socks to slip our hands into.

That does help… but only for a time before the snow soaks the fabric, turning them into a soppy, uncomfortable mess.

Thankfully, we're eventually able to access the handle that allows us to open the garage door. We drive Betty up the loading dock, put some dry socks on our hands, and slip back out, closing the door behind us and kicking some snow over the grip again in a lackluster attempt to hide some of our trail.

Not that it matters much. We're here. If someone's looking for us, surprise!

"They sure cleaned out well… and fast," I mention, bringing up the widespread emptiness. Zinna's office is only a couple blocks from where we parked. I don't have a big-picture view of the streets, but the alleyways provide enough of a visual to know there's really not much to see at all. "It's… quite impressive, for lack of a better word," I add. "Even with the DNA Networking Act itself taking the nation by storm, I never would have been able to wrap my mind around The Commission accomplishing what they've accomplished on such a grand scale as this. And in such a seemingly short timeframe nonetheless."

"And people are usually of the mind that one person can't make an impactful difference," Jax grunts, tromping through the snow.

While it was certainly the work of many over a long duration, Zinna single-handedly made the biggest impact. She's not overly intelligent — smart, yes, but not a genius or anything — but she's got a strong will. And where there's a will… there's a way.

She's met her match in me though. I'm not genius material either, but I'm definitely determined. In the end, I think whoever is more ingenuitive of the two of us will win this battle.

I'm not saying I'm personally more intelligent than her, but I think collectively *we* are. The guys and I… the UR. Yes, one person can make an impact, but there is still power in numbers.

What was it that Robbie said? Ah… right… *Whisper until we can scream in unison.* The URs have been whispering for a very long time. Some longer than others — Robbie's being one of the more recent to get on board.

"If my legs aren't sore after this, it'll be downright shocking," Julian says randomly, huffing and puffing as we trudge through the last section of deep snow behind the building. The road, we discover, is much easier to walk through.

A cat, surprised by our unexpected arrival, dashes across our path. It's hard not to notice the bright pink collar in contrast to the white snow; even in the dark of night, the colorful band stands out. A pet — someone's furry child — left behind in the chaos. While Bram finagles the door and access keypad to Zinna's office building, my gaze travels up the many stories of the tall structure across the street, and I can't help but wonder how many of those rooms have abandoned animals inside. Once-loved pets now left for dead, not given a chance to fend for themselves on the streets like the cat.

The gentle touch of Julian's hand pulls me out of my dour thoughts. Bram was able to work his way into Zinna's office with ease, using the same access information Robbie had pulled from the portable device he hacked a while back. The fact he could use an access code at all proves the electricity works here as well, which we are grateful for.

Perhaps I shouldn't pretend fate had anything to do with it this time, though, since we're well aware Zinna had planned on returning; she'd likely set up the power well in advance — or paid someone enough money to make sure it was never shut off in the first place.

Her office is nice; it's fitting for her, I suppose. I can envision her sitting behind the desk in the posh, comfortable leather chair, reviewing everything on her large wall-screen.

My body leads me directly to said chair, and I sit down, propping my cold and tired feet on her desk. The wetness and snow adhered to my shoes fall onto the table, melting into tiny puddles on contact.

Dirtying her desk is oddly satisfying. I place my arms behind my head and recline while Julian and Bram work on accessing her computer.

Jax walks around, pausing to scrutinize the large painting on the wall — a floral watercolor piece, full of vibrant fuchsias, yellows, and reds. The irony of it has me chuckling. Something so pretty for someone so ugly. "Zinnias," I state confidently.

Bram pauses what he's doing, looking over his shoulder from where he now stands at the multi-touch wall display. "Look at you," he says. My plant guy, impressed.

"Peak in the summer," I further display my incredible knowledge. "Easy to manage, grow fast, and bloom in high quantities. Sounds a lot like her involvement in this whole ordeal. The flowers grow so fast and so copiously, that even something so beautiful will destroy an area in large enough quantities. Dormant the other times of the year though. Hiding, just to spring up and do it all over again when the time is right.

"Guess she's living up to her namesake. This era is her summer. Thing is… they need sunlight to grow, and I'm not seeing a whole lot of that going on right now."

"Cloud that bitch," Jax hoots.

"I'm saying." I laugh.

"I'm so turned on right now. Tell me more about flowers," Bram jokes.

With a chuckle, I hound him and say, "Coming from a man who hasn't given me flowers the entire length of our acquaintance."

"The fuck?!" Jax explicates with a side grin. "What's wrong with ya, man?"

"Thess…"

I chuckle. "I know, I know; you have… ones from the side of the road."

"Exactly."

"Never been much for flowers anyway…" I give him a break.

"Yes, I'm well aware," he huffs, "which is why I usually give you food instead."

Food…. Damn… when was the last time any of us ate? "The way to my heart, for sure."

"We're in," a previously quiet Julian sighs in relief.

The first thing that pops up on the screen is a map similar to the radar map in the UR. Every facility we were so eager to find is laid out there on the screen, pinging red just like they do when a pulse is happening.

Except these fade red for only a few minutes before they ping brightly again.

"Does—does that mean they're doing back-to-back pulses?" I squeak, dropping my feet to the ground and leaning forward. We hadn't heard anything alarming from the URs. "Surely that's not what it means." *There…* "There isn't going to be anyone left by the time we attack." The tears don't come, but the conjoining watery, shaky intake of breath does.

Bram closes out of the map and opens a new screen — one that's a little easier to watch.

Zinna's activity logs.

Sure enough, she'd logged the New York trip…

And sure enough, she'd arrived around the same time we did.

But she hadn't done anything since. Robbie had said it would be very obvious once she received her permissions. So all we can do is sit and wait.

Or rather take turns sitting, pacing, leaning, lying on the floor... things of that sort.

It takes quite some time, but eventually we do get our clue. The activity log zooms with code and updates... information that doesn't make any sense to me.

"Looks like administration gave those privileges back to her after all. And..." Julian zooms his fingers over the screen. "We have a location tag... approximately two miles from here."

"Oh that's not too bad." I mean in the snow it is... but things sure could be worse. "We walking it or going back to Betty first?"

"I think I'd like to try the element of surprise if possible at this point," Julian decides. And with that, we all head out of the cozy office and back onto the dark and frigid New York streets.

CHAPTER TWENTY-SIX

At some point, I eventually become accustomed to the cold — or at least I think I do. My body stops shaking, and everything goes a little numb. The guys take turns pulling me up against them... or trying to, but walking that way makes the trek take longer.

After a while of trudging, I stop long enough to scoop a sizable amount of snow into my sock-covered hands. While continuing the walk, I compact it into a ball, much like I'd always envisioned doing if ever I had the opportunity. I set my sights on my victim — Jax, who is now in the lead just ahead of me. Julian and Bram bring up the rear of our group. Once my snowball is ready, I wind my arm back and toss it. My aim is on point. The moon is bright enough to aid in my efforts, and I hit him in the back of the head, causing him to screech to a halt.

"Oh fuck no!" he exclaims, turning around. I come to an abrupt stop, laughing. But when he tilts his head down, and he looks up at me from under those long eyelashes, my laughing ceases. Jax charges, and before I can react, the two of us are on the ground, grappling in the snow.

On my back with him over me, I scoop some more snow up with one hand and smack him upside the head. Snow sprinkles down onto my own face, and I blink to clear the wet droplets from my eyes.

Jax stills, leans down, and presses his mouth against mine, slipping his tongue inside. Every inch of me heats up. When he pulls away, and I open my eyes, both Bram and Julian are leaning over us, looking down, unimpressed.

"We have places to be, Thess."

"Okay, Bramby, fine. Just… snow…"

He sighs, holding his hand out as Jax rolls off me and begins to make a snow angel. "I know. Later, though? Our pagers should, hopefully, be going off any moment to announce the attack."

I clear my throat and allow him to help me up. "Right. Sorry."

"Nothing to be sorry about; I'm just playing devil's advocate is all."

A far-off rumble interrupts our conversation. Accustomed to the silence of empty streets, the unexpected sound of what might be an approaching vehicle has all of us on high alert. What's more concerning, however, is the distinctive, low reverberation indicating that the vehicle is most likely not small… nor electric.

Jax's snow angel, the proof of our short tussle, and our trail of footprints suddenly become more conspicuous in the otherwise untouched snow. But when the hazy glow of bright headlights appears in the distance ahead, there's no time to cover our tracks.

One of the guys' hands grabs mine and before my mind can catch up, I'm being tugged into a dark alleyway. The four of us keep quiet, unwilling to risk our hiding spot by speaking, even if the approaching trucks would drown out our voices anyway.

As the crunch of tires compressing the snow gets closer, I press my body against the wall of the wide alleyway and peek around the corner of the building. Beside me, Bram's added height allows him to do the same thing.

278

The two of us watch as a convoy of trucks approaches — ones similar to those parked at the exacentrifuge lab. "Do you think these are military troops heading toward the facility to forestall the UR Combat teams?" I ask on a quiet exhale. The warmth of my breath creates a stream of fog which then travels toward the street before dissipating into the air.

"No," Bram answers low, "the closest facility is in the opposite direction."

"So, they're leaving the facility... instead of heading there?"

"Possibly," he responds.

When the first one is just several yards away, Bram and I pop our heads back inside and slink deeper into the veil of darkness to join Jax and Julian.

As the first truck passes, a gust of air whooshes into the confines of the alley, bringing with it an unbearable smell. The four of us cough and gag, covering our mouths with either our hands, shirts, or jackets. Several pungent scents mixed into a powerful odor — a combination of mustiness, metallic-like chemical tang, and hint of fish. Blood, rot, and decay.

I bury my face inside the unzipped portion of Jax's jacket, and he wraps his arms around me and buries his nose into the hair at my neck.

The convoy doesn't seem to end. Eyes watering from the overwhelming stench, I count the transport vehicles one by one as they pass, reminiscent of the days when I was just a young girl and the old trains were still functioning. I remember getting as high as sixty-two train cars as they zoomed past us while stopped at a crossing. The more cars, the more exciting it was.

This time, every truck that passes debilitates me more and more. At twenty, my heart starts racing. At fifty-six, my eyes start leaking tears. At ninety, every muscle in my body weakens. At one-hundred...

...I stop counting.

I crumble to the ground, and Jax follows me down, never once letting go.

Yet still, the convoy keeps going.

I try to convince myself that what's inside those transport vehicles is anything other than what I know to be true deep in my soul. That maybe it's actual troops. Or supplies. Or perhaps even "subjects" they're extracting to save. Because maybe, just maybe, they're on our side.

No matter how hard I try, though, I can't get the image of the dead bodies out of my head. Bodies packed tight in each transport in order to fit as many as possible. I can't get the mental picture of genocide out of my thoughts. With my eyes closed, the visual only worsens. Instead, I'm forced to watch. Forced to witness the transportation of dead victims. Forced to sit here in a dark alleyway hiding, so close that I could walk over there, reach out, and touch them... yet still not able to do anything about it.

The familiar buzz of the UR pager vibrates in my pocket, bringing with it a sense of comfort in the midst of our present circumstances. Desperate for a reprieve, I finally let go of Julian. The four of us dig out our pagers, eager to see proof the multipronged attack has commenced.

However, when we look down at them, the expected attack code isn't what flashes on the screen.

"*Cazzo*, someone please tell me this doesn't mean what I think it means," Julian says, the words starting out almost indiscernible over the roar of vehicles, but ending loudly as the last truck in the convoy finally goes by.

Jax and I both push off the ground as he flips the pager every which way, tilting his head to try to make sense of the numbers.

My reddened eyes meet Bram's studious gaze. Wrinkles of stress and wariness frame his eyes, but instead of speaking he stomps off, eager to leave this alley far behind and make forward progress once again.

Jax, Julian, and I all jog to catch up, the desperation coming in tenfold now. Not that we can do an absolute damn thing about it… but at least moving forward with our own plan serves to temporarily distract us from the apparent attack on the Central UR.

The next several blocks are deathly silent.

But my busy mind isn't kind enough to grant such an absolution.

After a while, I can no longer keep my mouth shut. I want to scream. With Julian the only one falling back with me, he's the one that has to hear all my mumbled expletives on the matter — and the underlying anguish that pairs with each. "They don't even have any of their Combat teams there to help with defense!" I screech, not caring that the sound is absorbed by the snow around us. The attack as a whole assails me immediately, coalescing with the lingering thoughts of the convoy. But it isn't until I start verbalizing my frustration that the smaller-circle impact hits me:

Auden.
Robbie.
Leta.
Becky.
Ruby.
My center boys.
Ben.
Everyone.

281

"Well, Robbie is smart, and Becky knows insider stuff. The leaders that stayed behind are invaluable resources. They're equipped, just not with Combat. It's okay, *cuore mio*. They'll be okay." Julian is trying to convince himself just as much as he's trying to convince me, I'm sure of it. "We do what we can," he finishes as we approach what I hope is the admin building.

"This it?" I inquire.

"This is the location the activity log showed," Bram answers.

For all intents and purposes, the place looks just as abandoned as everywhere else; nevertheless, Jax offers to help Bram wrench the already slightly ajar door open.

What we see inside isn't at all reassuring. Clearly when Zinna requested the admin's assistance, they must not have been so willing after all, which explains why it took so long for the tracker to mark activity after her arrival into the city. She was too busy taking more lives. Well, not her I imagine; she doesn't seem the type that would be willing to get her own hands dirty. Acting the intermediary, though... she's definitely about that life.

My lips curl in disgust — both at the blood of her dead victims, lying on the floor behind the admin desk, and of the woman who called the kills.

For a couple minutes, we all just stand there, the tang of death filling our lungs, the sight seeping into the recesses of our subconscious to haunt us at a later date.

Numb... for now... I narrow my eyes on the scene. "Good news... While I'm sure she was desperate to have her permissions reinstated, I can put money down that's not why these people didn't survive the gentle nudge for assistance. My guess is she wanted to gain access to something much more important... that these people would have needed to approve." All three guys turn to

282

me at once. "The host system? It must be here." I raise an eyebrow. "Search the bodies for keycards... Search the desk or computer for a map of the building... Search for anything that'll clue us in."

Each of us jump into action. While they're doing the dirty work, I walk around visible portions of the floor, unwilling to go anywhere that risks our ability to still see each other in the dim light.

Unfortunately, without going into an elevator or stairwell, there isn't anywhere else I can check.

"Bottom level," Bram hollers out.

"Well, that's... not surprising... at all."

Jax waves a keycard in the air.

Julian starts down the hallway, no more questions asked. We all follow as quickly as possible. Try as I might, I can't help but glance over my shoulder at the admins who lie dead in the building foyer. Before the bile creeps up too high — before my already-shaky legs lose their last bit of strength — I turn back around and force the image out of my mind.

The stairwell does, indeed, have a keycard system. Jax swipes the card, the door buzzes, and we gain access to the stairs. The four of us rush down floor by floor into the depths of a relatively normal-looking corporate building. "I wonder if the residents of this town were at all aware of this host system. Or how the information therein would change the course of history — of their lives."

None of the guys respond since it was more a statement than an open-ended comment up for further discussion. When we get to the final door, leading to the final level, the four of us stop and just stand there for a time. No thoughts, no words, no conversation. I scarcely think any of us are breathing for a moment.

When Jax looks back at us, he raises an eyebrow in silent inquiry.

Bram, Julian, and I nod in unison.

Jax draws out the keycard process, feeling the need to take extra precautions and be extra quiet since we have no way of knowing what's behind that door.

He inches the door open, but promptly pops his head back inside the stairwell, letting the door rest but not close all the way again. He then tears off a piece of his shirt and stuffs it into the door lock's strike plate — something I remember seeing Roux do at the pod I stayed in at the facility.

Once that's set, he turns to us. "She's in there, tryin' ta gain access to another room. Lookin' quite perturbed."

"No one is with her?" I ask on the faintest of breath.

Jax shakes his head. "Not that I could see."

"There's no fucking way she took out the admins by her own hand. No fucking way."

Jax groans quietly, grabs his junk, and whispers, "Say 'fuckin' one more time."

I roll my eyes. Julian chuckles ever so quietly and Jax grins, the two of them trying to calm my ever-increasing nerves — and their own, no doubt — by bringing a little inappropriate humor into the mix.

Bram nudges Jax out of the way and peeks an eye through the crack.

Unfortunately, the real risk comes from above, when the associates I assumed were accompanying her barge through the door a few levels above us.

Since there's no way in hell I'd be caught dead waiting in a damn stairwell with guys like that, I give a quick glance and empath brush at all my guys. With that simple gesture, Bram opens the door, and the four of us nonchalantly join Zinna, letting the door close over the stuffed cloth behind us.

"About damn—" Zinna's words cut off abruptly when she realizes we're not her backup. She steps away from the door she'd been trying to access until her back is up against the wall. She's not so confident now that it's just her and us. Problem is, that's about to change, and the ball will be back in her court.

All three of my guys have their back against the door, helping me bide my time.

But to do what?

"So… um…" Since this is one of the few times I've spoken to the woman, I'm quite at a loss of words. "Cold out there. Think I much prefer Florida weather, to be honest."

Zinna tilts her head to the side, clearly stunned speechless from her unexpected visitors.

I walk up to the door she was trying to open and drag my finger down the black glass, just as I hear the stairwell door bounce against the frame. I steal a glance over my shoulder at the guys and find them bracing for the next blow. They're strong, but they won't be able to keep Zinna's helpers at bay for long. I turn my back to the door and lean against it, crossing my legs at my ankles, and start picking at my nails, suddenly intrigued with how long they've gotten. "Guess neither of us are getting in there, hm?"

I still don't know what exactly is in that room. My guess is the host system, but I could be wrong. In the least, maybe she'll give me the deets and we can figure out our next step.

Zinna's lips press into a thin line, completely hiding her fuchsia lipstick.

Another thing I don't know is why she needs to access said host system. What reason would she have? Everything she wants is presently happening across the nation. "Does it feel good being an accomplice to murder, Zinna? For what reason? So you can live in a post-apocalyptic world for the less-than-second-half of your life?"

"Of course you would think that, child." She stands up straighter, darting a sideways glance at the battle of strength at the stairwell.

"So selfish," I state.

"Think about it… all the diseases we hate? Gone," she counters.

"Surely you don't think that's forever though? Surely you're smarter than that." Unlikely.

"Forever? Won't matter, the world itself isn't in a state that will last 'forever' anyway." She has the childish audacity to air quote the word forever. "So, at least for a time, certain people can live lavishly."

"Lavishly?!" I yell-scoff. "You, woman, are out of your ever-loving mind! And what's the next step of this 'lavish' plan of yours?" I air quote *lavish*.

"My involvement is done," she says.

"If your involvement is done, then why are you… here?"

Unfortunately she doesn't have time to answer when the stairwell door battle finally comes to a climax. My heart jumps into my throat when Jax, Julian, and Bram have to close in toward me due to the number of guards piling in.

There aren't just two or three; there are probably closer to ten. However, I can't count to verify that assessment, because I find myself retreating toward the opposite side of the room, hoping to find a different exit.

Not to leave entirely, but to somehow find a way for the guys and I to gain ground. Guess this time when it comes to fight or flight, my flight instinct wins.

Inconveniently, too, since Zinna has no intention of running. Instead, in an unexpectedly bold move, she darts her hand out, grabs my hair, and tugs me toward her before wrapping her other arm around my chest.

I have quickly determined that this woman does not scare me though. The things she oversees, the decisions she makes, absolutely. But her... in the flesh?... not at all. "This isn't a movie, Zinna," I gasp through the tightening of her arm over my chest. Having learned how to get out of this basic hold in Combat, I feel confident I can counter her.

Full of bold moves and smart-ass comments, though, she once again uses her words to strike before I can follow through. "Oh I'm not holding you to keep you down, Thessaly. I'm holding you so you can watch what my bodyguards are about to do to your friends."

I'd been wiggling a bit in her grip, but at that mention, I freeze, and her hand tightens into my hair, forcing my head still. Bram, Jax, and Julian are indeed squabbling with her bodyguards. Considering the difference in numbers, they're doing pretty damn well. However, they're already bloodied up.

I send a rush of emotional energy to Julian and Bram, and repeat the word 'surrender,' hoping with all hope that Jax will get the message. This fighting? Will end in death. A gruesome one. Of course I don't want to watch it — I don't want it to happen period. Maybe if they surrender, it'll bide us some time. Maybe if they simply hold us hostage, she'll gain entry and... we'll swoop in and get our task done.

In unison, my three guys back up, hands up in a show of surrender. Jax spits out a glob of blood onto one of the guard's boots with a sneer.

Oh Jax. I said "surrender" not "rile the bear."

Zinna's brutish men all turn their heads toward her as if they're robots and not men at all, which would be fitting considering this outlandish world we're now immersed in. However, they *are* mere men — stupid ones at that — who can't make their own decisions. Or don't dare to, I suppose.

What's in it for them? A promise to be relieved from a radioactive bath? Amnesty from a one-way trip in a rolling coffin? I mean to continue the monologue in my head, but it comes out of my mouth instead: "If you think you're exempt from the same murderous fate the bulk of the country is experiencing right now just because you're being her fists, you're just as stupid as she pegged you when she 'hired' you. Why do you think she needs access to this room? You think once she gets whatever the hell it is she wants, she's going to *spare* you?! To her... you're part of the problem. The infestation this world suffers from. She won't let you live. Not once she's completed her task here."

It's easy to picture Roux, Fen, and Warrick in this lineup. Easy to envision the three of them — Roux now excluded — being in here, brainwashed into thinking the end result is anything more or less than what we all know the truth is.

In a moment of enlightenment, the very thought of Roux previously being under Zinna's rule, reminds me that I have a weapon. One Zinna may not have created, but one that she most certainly fired up. I open my empath sensors and brush the guards' minds while they stand there considering my advice.

It isn't until I, all too easily, gain access, that I piece two and two together.

It isn't until too late that I realize, just like the subjects in the facilities, these men are being pulled by medicinal puppet strings.

"Kill them," Zinna says, tightening her grip on my hair.

CHAPTER TWENTY-SEVEN

"**N**o!" I yell at the top of my lungs, turning to a limp noodle in her grasp. Not expecting the sudden change in my body, she loses her grip as I fall to my hands and knees and crawl toward Julian, who is the closest to me at this point. He bends down to reach for my hand, but one of the men takes him from me. The men take all of them from me. Zinna doesn't bother to pull me away this time. I push through the barrage of muscle, flailing my arms, punching and wailing on any and every thing I come into contact with. All my training with Roark, all the movies I've watched… it's all for naught in this moment as my panic-induced adrenaline rush takes control of my actions.

This goes on and on — the men not touching me since I'm not their target, and me unable to see anything around the ever-enclosing circle the group of them has created.

There comes a time when I convince myself the manic punching and kicking is helping… that I'm making a dent. I begin to wonder if maybe Zinna had somehow drugged me when she had me detained. Maybe a small needle prick I didn't feel?

I don't know; there's so much adrenaline, so much surrealness to what's going on around me, that it's hard to tell. Eventually I'm alone in the center of the circle where my men are getting beaten to a pulp. Everyone around me is fighting… each other. I pivot over and over again, until I've made my own complete circle. Once my head clears a bit, I begin a head count.

Bram... check.

Julian... check.

Jax... check.

Tob— "Tobias?!" That part most definitely comes out aloud. Tobias turns his head toward me and gets the immediate consequence of said action when a fist lands into his temple. He's back in the game immediately, though, defending himself.

Zinna... where's Zinna?

I push my way through the fighting people until I'm near the door Zinna was so desperate to get through. One of her men stands before her, holding someone hostage. Zinna pulls the guard's puppet strings, and he presses a weapon against the victim's neck.

Under the bodyguard's grip, a stout man shakes, excrement staining his khakis. Instead of approaching, I listen. However, I'm once again too late. The bodyguard slices the man's neck and he drops to the ground, not quite lifeless... but approaching that state fast. Zinna's focus finds me. "Hold her," she says.

The man does so instantly.

Zinna then smears some of the dying man's blood onto her fingers.

Guess I was wrong about her getting her hands bloody after all.

From there, she swipes the blood over the door's security sensor, and the door swings open.

When the man holding me starts to move inside, she steps forward, cleans her hand off on my white cargos, and instructs the man to do everything in his ability to make sure I don't follow her into the room. He grunts, his hot breath hitting me hard against the cheek, and she turns and walks away.

Writhing in his grip is useless — every move Roark taught me is no match for our size and weight difference. At least not with the short-term training I received.

The harder I try, the stronger his grip becomes. All the while, he remains mute — too consumed by drugs to do anything more than be muscle. With the direction he has me facing I am unable to see the brawling, nor can I see what Zinna is up to. All that's in my sightline is an open door, a wall, and a dead body at my feet.

Tighter and tighter the man squeezes until breathing becomes increasingly difficult. My vision starts to form a tunnel of blackness. Even though I know my empath abilities are of no use right now, I still reach out, prodding in the crevices of the man's mind, creeping through him much like the blackness that slithers over me.

As a last minute remembrance, a number of memories flit through my thoughts, every one of them revolving around my guys. Then a rush of endorphin-induced energy fills my mind, body, and soul. A final push for survival? With clear-as-day recollection I remember Tobias's "pain" rules should I need any help. Thankfully, my hands are free, even if my arms are bound to my sides. At first, I try digging my fingernails into the sensitive pads, but when I am unsure if that is resulting in enough pain to trigger the bond with Tobias, I lift my hand up as though I'm going to wrap my fingers around the guard's forearm. Instead, I bend my head down and bite the soft flesh of my thumbs. At this point I don't care how hard too hard might be. There's nothing to lose… except for, of course, the pad of my thumb… and my consciousness. For good measure, I do it to the other thumb too.

A *"What the fuck,"* rumbles in my ear just as my head falls back against the man's chest, and the blackness closes in completely. The obscureness is immediately countered by a rush of air entering my lungs and the impact of my fall.

Vision bleary but my purpose for being here still clear, I crawl into the room Zinna entered, my mind focused on one thing. Moving forward is a challenge as I cough and gasp to recoup the air my lungs lost, but I hone in on her high heels and shuffle forward. When I'm close enough, she kicks out her foot as though trying to shoo away an unruly pet, but I dart my hand out quick enough to catch her ankle with one hand, quickly get to my knees, grab her other ankle, and yank.

Zinna lands on the ground belly down, arms spread, and I quickly let go of her ankles to throw myself on top of her. She's fast enough to flip over before I can do anything. Instead of hindering me, though, the action gives my mind just enough time needed to cycle through the few basic restraint techniques we'd learned in Combat.

As soon as she is fully on her back, and before she can attempt to get away, I situate my knee in the center of her torso in the general area of her diaphragm, focusing most of my weight there. Her arms and legs are free to flail, but otherwise, she is restrained. As an added safety precaution, I grab her closest forearm with one hand and hold down her shoulder with the other.

She does her best to defend herself, kicking her legs and using her only free arm and hand in an attempt to swat at my face and grab the arm that's keeping her held down. But every time she reaches for my face, I lengthen my body, which in turn causes more pressure on her diaphragm from my knee.

This isn't a fighting stance; it's a move designed to simply control an opponent in a way that will keep them still without killing them. I've learned a lot about myself throughout this entire experience, one important detail is that I am not a fighter. The same can be said of Zinna. Fighting is just not in our wheelhouse. So instead of fighting, I hold her down until help comes.

Help comes…

…just not for me.

CHAPTER TWENTY-EIGHT

"Thes-sal-ee," Julian's accented voice floats into my mind. A careful, yet insistent, pat of a hand stings my cheek. My eyes flutter open, and Julian's bright-green gaze is boring right into my soul. His eyebrows lift, disappearing into his curls — the ones that have gotten significantly longer since I first met him and now almost hide those amazing green eyes. I reach my fingers up and brush the curls over. His hand meets mine, and he presses his cheek into my palm.

"*Cuore mio... My heart...* you scared the shit out of us."

His words bring everything back in a rush. I shoot up into a sitting position, but thankfully Julian is fast enough to get out of my way or we would have butted heads. "Wh-what happened?!"

"One of Zinna's guards yanked you off her, and your head hit that pillar in the center of the room. You blacked out."

"Zinna! She—" As soon as the memories return to the forefront of my thoughts, I push off the ground to stand. However, the sudden movement does nothing to lessen the increasing rush of blood thumping in my head from the impact, and I stop short, blinking rapidly to clear my vision.

"Sit, sit." Julian insists on guiding me back down. "Zinna is restrained; she's not going anywhere."

"Holy shit; how long was I out for?" I ask, taking in a couple deep breaths and attempting to shake the confusion.

"We took the guard out right away, but you kept fading in and out for a good ten minutes."

"Who tied her up?"

A broad, pleased grin spreads across Julian's face. "Tobias did."

"Tobias. He... he was here? I-I didn't imagine him?"

"No, you didn't imagine him. The connection with Auden... helped." I am only partially listening, though. On hearing verification that Tobias is here, I begin to scan the room. Several men are down and out for the count. Several more — men *and* women — are standing around, taking stock of their wounds, digging through pockets of those on the floor in order to check for some form of identification of the... dead?... guards. Tobias has his back toward me and is in a deep discussion about something that must be important.

"Who are these people?" I side-whisper.

Julian shrugs. "Good guys, I guess. Not the UR though."

"Oh? Those exist? Other good guys, I mean?"

"Apparently."

My traveling focus finds Bram and Jax next, and both their gazes meet mine. A swollen-eyed Jax tips an invisible cowboy hat. Bram just gives me one of his friendly smiles... the one I fell in love with before I knew what this kind of love even meant.

A new determination fills me, and despite the pounding in my head, I slowly work my way up to standing. "We're not done," I state, straightening my back.

Julian doesn't stop me from moving forward, stepping over the guy Zinna had killed, and entering the room. He does, however, follow closely behind, his hand at the small of my back, steadying me.

Zinna is in the far corner of the room, gagged and tied, exactly how I remember my mom being when Zinna gave her back to me. I step forward and crouch in front of her, arms resting between my thighs.

"So… Zinna… what now? Hm?"

She doesn't scream through the gag or try to fight; she just glares at me.

When I move to step away, dragging my hands up the outsides of my thighs to press them into my upper thighs for support, I push up to standing from a squat, and my hands brush against something hard.

The vial from Roux.

My hand pauses there for a moment, but I'm not ready to make any final decisions regarding Zinna just yet. I'm not ready to give her the same fate she'd forced on so many — not until I get some answers of my own.

When I turn to speak with Julian, all four of my guys are standing nearby, waiting for me to choose what'll happen next.

I take stock of the room…

There's…

…nothing.

Well, there's *one* thing: in the very center of the room is the single raised pedestal that Zinna was standing in front of when I had taken her down. Like something out of a museum, there's a glass-type box on the top, and the entire thing is rimmed in… a blue glow. The word ExaIntel is engraved into the glass.

"What the fuck is this?" I ask, my eyebrows drawing inward.

Jax groans playfully. "Mmm… I really like this pissed-off, no-filter Thessaly."

Fuck could most certainly never be Jax's safe word. "You... need to get laid. How can my language possibly turn you on when you're hurt" — my eyes dart to his swollen eye — "and there are dead bodies everywhere?"

It's not a question, not really, but he answers all the same. "Well yer a fairy or some shit, remember? With those magical healing powers and mind reading. Maybe I'm an... incubus... who is also driven by blood and death." Jax shrugs nonchalantly.

I open my mouth but am so confused by this response that nothing comes out.

Shock. He's in shock. This is the way he's coping.

"Anyway... what the hell am I looking at?" I ask again.

"The host system," Tobias answers simply.

"The host system... This?"

"Mm hmm." A side grin lights up Tobias's face in the blue glow. "What were you expecting?"

"Uh... not this. Maybe like a room full of tech, wall-to-wall, ceiling-to-ceiling... you know..."

"Like in the movies..." Bram and I say at the same time.

"Right! I mean name a computer-related movie where the all-powerful tech is this small. The thing that controls the lives of millions... the size of a... box of chocolates."

Tobias chuckles, and I'm momentarily distracted by the familiar — comfortable — sound.

Maybe I'm in shock too.

I rush up to him and wrap my arms around his waist.

"It's smaller than the box," he whispers against the top of my head.

"Shut. Up." I slap him on the chest, and he laughs again.

Hug time over... for now... I turn back to the "host system," place my hand on the glass, and try to lift it open. When it doesn't budge, I look around the perimeter of the box and pillar with the hope of finding an opening... or something to help unlock the cover. What I find instead is a small, oval-shaped hole. Not a keyhole though.

I place my finger on the surrounding platform and move it over to trace the shape, but Tobias's hand wraps around my wrist, stopping me. "When we came in here, Zinna was trying to get this bad boy open. It requires a finger prick," he explains.

"Oh... ohhhh." I shudder. "Yeah... I don't plan on blood-sharing with her today. Or any other day for that matter. She couldn't get in?" I ask. Tobias shakes his head. "And... she's supposed to be able to?"

Tobias shrugs. "She killed the guy who knew. Well... not her, but she—"

"Ordered the kill. Yeah, got it... I was there." I walk back over to Zinna and pull the gag down. "What's the story here?" I ask. You know... leader to leader. If either of us can be called such.

For some strange reason, she actually responds. "The board members are supposed to be the only ones with permissions above administration access. A blood sample is compared to the one in the system. The box will only open if there's a match."

"Oh, why thank you for obliging me with an answer. And where might I — say — find one of these elusive board members?" Zinna raises an eyebrow, suddenly all out of answers. "That man bloodying up the floor over there?" I jab my thumb over my shoulder near the door. "Did he happen to fit that requirement?"

Apparently she finds no harm in nodding in response to this inquiry.

However, I saw her collect his blood with my own eyes. My guess is she already tried using it to open the box, but that failed.

Done with her for the time being, I stand and return to my guys. "We have access to the entire system right there. The admins upstairs were wearing optical-screen com-devices. What are the odds we can snag one of those, get a good visual of this machine, and send the details to—"

—to Robbie.

That's what I was going to say, until I remember they'd been compromised. A pang squeezes my heart, but I swallow hard and brush the distracting emotions away. "Scratch that. How about popping up to the top level, weaseling our way into their computers, hacking into her account again, and finding those details ourselves?"

Tobias rubs his chin — clearly having been around Robbie too much. "Possibly. Wouldn't know where to find it though... and I'm not sure we have that sort of time on our hands either."

"Speaking of time... did the attacks ever start?" I ask.

Bram is the one to answer. "They did... I'm not sure when. My guess is they went off while we were all... otherwise occupied."

My hand naturally moves to the pagers in my cargos, once again grazing against the bulge made by the buried vial. I slip my hand under the waistband of my cargos, dig deep into the stretchy fabric of my spandex,

300

and pull it out. "Roux left this for us," I explain, holding it up. I bite at the inside of my bottom lip, questioning the new person these events have turned me into that I'm actually considering drugging someone.

The guys can see the battle waging in my mind. Bram wraps his arm around me, and Jax nods and says, "We're supportin' ya no matter what."

I look up at Bram. "This will make her lose her short-term memory and answer my questions but won't kill her, right?"

"Usually that's the result, yes."

"Usually?"

"Well, there are a number of factors that go into it, like for exam—"

"Annnnd, time! Whoa. Simple is good, thanks." Man it's been a long time since I've chosen to stop him mid-lecture. "There's still a risk," I summarize, separating from his hug-hold. Bram smiles, missing those days as much as I do no doubt.

I drop the level of my voice, wanting to be sure the conversation stays between just our small group. "As far as the original plan is concerned, I see you've brought backup — thank you for that by the way — but aren't we supposed to 'keep' the data unbeknownst to anyone outside of our group and the technician performing the transfer? How's that going to pan out with all your new friends?"

Tobias had slowly stepped closer and closer to me during my short monologue and now stands almost touching in proximity. "Have I ever mentioned how much I love it when you go into problem-solving mode?" he asks, his voice deeper than it was a moment ago.

What is with these guys today? We're dealing with the pinnacle moment of our plans, and they're acting…

strange. Even so, I slip my arms around his lower back and lay my head on his chest, taking just a short moment to listen to his heartbeat and appreciate every thump. His finger touches beneath my chin, directing my head back, and his mouth gets closer and closer. Just as I begin to close my eyes, instead of kissing me, his lips brush against my ear: "They plan on killing Zinna and taking some kind of document that can apparently only be found in her personal profile." He drags his lips along the delicate portion of my neck that runs from behind my ear to my collarbone.

"What are you—" He places a kiss in the dip at the center of my collarbone, and the words catch in my throat. Apparently in problem-solving mode, my brain isn't cut out for sexy distractions, because Jax leans over with a chuckle and whispers in my other ear. "He's simply tryin' ta give you some information on the down-low, Darlin'. In the infamous words of Julian, *calma*... before you make him bust a nut in his pants because of your breathy responses and squeaks."

My eyebrows shoot upward, and, clearing the squeak from my throat, I give a nod of understanding. The sexual tension buzzes between our group, thanks in part to my reception of Tobias laying it on thick. He grins down at me, then crashes his mouth against mine — the playfulness gone, and him now caught up in reuniting for a quick moment. But then he pulls away and comes to my ear again. "Otherwise, we have the same end goal where the host system is concerned. Save the data on the down low. Shut it down. Destroy the tech."

When Tobias straightens some, I stand on my tiptoes, take his bottom lip between my teeth, and give him a gentle nip before asking, "Who are they?" on a whispery breath. Time for Tobias to reveal who these people are that he showed up with.

The side of Tobias's mouth quirks up, enjoying this back and forth even more so now that I know what's going on.

Before responding, he glances over his shoulder to check on Zinna, then looks toward the door to make sure no one is standing there either. The other guys have our backs, though, so he doesn't linger on the added security measure. His hand slips under my shirt and jacket to the small of my back, all skin-on-skin. My body immediately responds, hips curving forward toward his thighs. He places his cheek on my temple and says, "Apparently the CDC was not at all on board with murder. They bowed out soon after things went haywire according to what I've been told. However, I'm sure whatever document it is that they're wanting for themselves likely has something to do with their involvement before they made the opt-out official. These men and women are all CDC employees posed as guards.

"Auden kept sensing waves of distress from you. After the CDC took me in, S&R kept in touch with Robbie until it was safe for them to leave. Auden had also notified the Eastern UR Tech team, and they started tracking the pager they assigned you. I already knew you were headed to New York, but the Eastern UR Techs were able to tell me exactly where to find you."

Mention of Auden and the Central UR makes my anxiousness spike, but knowing worry won't fix anything, I once again brush the thought aside, choosing to speak on the topic of the CDC instead. "Techs who can fight? What are the odds."

"They did their best. Thankfully, there were more of us than Zinna's men. A few of them will need some extra medical attention as soon as it's available though."

I nod, and he drops his voice lower again. "Our plan is the same, but now you'll need to distract them while I extract the data under the ruse of wiping it. If we can do so without them knowing we've copied the data first, then all the better. From there, the technician is on standby at the Eastern UR."

"Okay. So far, we still don't know how to gain access to the host system. Zinna's blood doesn't do the trick, nor does that guy's apparently." I dart a glance at the body just on the other side of the door.

"Which is strange because the two of them were on the board," Tobias follows.

I clasp the vial harder in my hand and look down at it. "I have an idea," I state, looking back up into Tobias's silver-blue eyes. He nods, encouraging me to continue. "We give Zinna the drug. Get her talking. It'll double to wipe her memory of this host system adventure — of placing us here with her. When she comes to and the drug wears off, no telling where she'll be — in a cold alleyway on the last inches of her life; roaming New York looking for a no-longer-existing database; left in the hands of these CDC rebels. Whatever, I really don't care. Plus, we can figure out what she's after and make sure we take care of that too."

Tobias's eyes unfocus as he visualizes all the details. After a short moment, he nods and we break apart so he can address Jax, Julian, and Bram.

"What we doin', Boss?" Jax asks.

"Well, Tough Guy, I think it's time to give Zinna here a taste of her own medicine," Tobias responds.

Bram speaks up then, addressing the one part we hadn't yet considered: "It'll take about forty-five minutes for the Dub to process, then she'll turn feral before being of any use to us."

"That's… a long time of just sitting around." Julian shrugs, "*È così. It is what it is.*"

CHAPTER TWENTY-NINE

I squat in front of Zinna again, this time brandishing the vial in front of her pert, cakey nose. "I wonder if that makeup will help any when you're wailing like a banshee and behaving like a monkey on meth." I smile at her, honestly quite shocked at my lack of humanity with the comment. Guess that's what too many terrible run-ins will do to a person.

She kicks and screams now, terrified of the end result for the first time. *Her* end result. Not that of anyone else, that's for sure. Due to her bindings, she falls onto her belly, her head wrenched to the side. She tries to writhe like an inchworm, alternating with attempting to flip over.

Doing us both a favor, I slip my hand around her shoulder and roll her over since I'll need her either on her back or upright to administer the Dub.

"Julian and Bram? Care to help keep her still for me?"

"*Cazzo*, yes. *Felice di farlo. Happy to oblige.*" I figure if anyone deserves a bit of revenge, it's Julian.

Zinna's eyes open wide. Clearly she doesn't like being on the receiving end of what she so easily dishes out to others. But she's not getting out of this. Not this time.

I grab her cheeks between my thumb and fingers, causing her lips to pop open. As expected, she thrashes her head side to side, her spiky-heeled feet clacking wildly against the floor. I dart a glance at Julian and he takes my subtle hint, placing his hand over her forehead to keep her still.

"Don't do this," Zinna mumbles through her puckered lips.

"There's no changing my mind, Zinna," I respond with ease. "Now, you can either choke on it, and risk me giving you too much. Or, you can relax, and I can place just a small amount under your tongue. What's it going to be?"

Her eyes squint, and I swear if looks could kill, I'd be dead on the spot. I loosen her cheeks just enough to let her answer me. "Millions," that's what comes out of her mouth, and I make the stupid mistake of letting it catch me off guard. "Nothing you do is going to bring their lives back," she says, having the audacity to look at me as though she feels sorry for my plight.

While it does catch me off guard, it only serves to anger me more. Instead of fish-facing her, this time I pop the vial open with one thumb, and shove my opposite pointer between her lips, wrenching her jaw open. Red consumes me and all my fingers jump into the fun. Dipping behind her bottom teeth and opening her mouth wide. I bring the vial to her lips, my vision blackening at the edge. Someone's hand wraps around my wrist. Long, caramel-colored fingers. Bram doesn't pull my hand away; he just holds tight so I can't move it.

"Thess," he says, "you'll beat yourself up for the rest of your life if you give her too much." Chest heaving, vision pulsating, I attempt to focus on my breathing.

Teeth clenched, I look into the insipid woman's eyes and say, "Lift your damn tongue or you'll definitely die. At least by me allowing you this last bit of control, you'll have a better chance to see another day."

This seems to resonate with her; however, a single tear trickles out of her eye.

Ah, so she is human after all. With real feelings.

That lone tear seems to be what does it for me. I wiggle my hand free from Bram's grip and distance the vial away from her mouth. "Before I seal this fate of yours, I just have one question. Why?" I mean, I'm fairly certain I know why, but I want to hear it from her.

Zinna stops her thrashing — either from giving in, intrigue or a false assurance that she still has a chance of getting out of this mess; it doesn't matter. But when she opens her mouth to answer, I hold up a finger. "Do not loosen your holds, guys. This isn't going to turn into a mistake, no matter how much of an opportunity it gives her."

"You've seen the nation," she begins. "The overpopulation, the filth. The bulk of citizens can't even afford to live due to inflation and lacking medical care and services. More money than we can put a tag on is being spent trying to figure out how to counteract where the government falls short. People are dying. Slowly. Miserably. You can't walk down the streets of any town and not see a homeless person. There are too many children for all of them to get a proper education and health services. Those children? They're supposed to be our future. Not the result of advanced technology or research findings. Killing people with high DMIS scores is a kindness that only a select few have the brazenness to carry out.

"This overpopulation has a butterfly effect that not only directly impacts us, but other nations and the world too. There isn't a leader in office anywhere willing to do such a thing on such a grand scale. But to turn a supposedly blind eye while someone else does? That's how they'll sleep at night. I am that someone. So kill me. Enough high scorers have already been eliminated to help bring balance. There truly was no other way. You, my dear, are young and naive, but one day, when you have children of your own…" Her gaze flits to my stomach before returning to lock on my eyes again. "Maybe that's the day you'll appreciate the bold move I made. Because he or she will grow up with a good education, a nice, clean home, and the science to keep it that way. The leaders of our past fucked it up for us… and there was no hope for the leaders of our future. But now… now maybe we have a chance."

An unadulterated, raw rage shakes through me from head to toe. "Spoiler alert, Zinna…" — I bend close to her ear — "I had a miscarriage." The words come out of me as a hiss through my clenched teeth. "Your efforts… fruitless. Because you're screwing with the natural design of the world. The natural balance. This… this plan of yours will backfire. You think I'm going to kill you? No-fucking-way. You're going to live the rest of your miserable life watching and being personally affected by the shitstorm you created as it unfolds." The room becomes so silent the only sound that can be heard is the quiet whir of electronics coming from that single box in the center. Zinna's eyes widen and her head shakes from side to side in disbelief. "Besides, what would you know about having children?" I get the inclination to ask, creating distance between us again.

Zinna turns her head to the side, and the real tears come. They don't last long though. She sniffles, blinks a few times, then turns her attention back toward me, juts her chin out and says, "When you start to question me, my only request is that you don't ask that question." She then opens her mouth and points the tip of her tongue toward the roof. I lift my vial hand, and tap in a bit of the Dub. With all the braveness a woman of her stature tends to display, she closes her mouth and inhales deeply through her nose, relaxing.

"Need to swap out?" I ask the guys. When she's feral, I'm guessing her strength will intensify, so giving Julian and Bram a break might be a good idea.

Tobias and Jax take over, holding her down.

"Care to talk to me before the Dub sets in?" I ask, sitting across from her and bringing my knees to my chest, resting back on my hands.

Zinna shrugs.

"Who can access the host system?" I try.

"The board," she answers.

"Clearly not if you and your friend out there were unable to."

"Clearly one of the members changed the permissions."

"Why would they do that?"

Zinna glowers at me. "If I knew, we wouldn't be here in this predicament right now."

"Is there a way we can find out who can now access it?"

"Everything is in the data storage," she answers nonchalantly.

"What are you trying to get off there?"

"That one will have to wait until the drug sets in. I still have high hopes I won't divulge that bit of information."

"Good luck with that," Julian chuckles.

Zinna turns a question on us. "Was Roux working with you?"

I don't want to answer this question carelessly, so I look to my guys for help. Unfortunately, that small action proves enough of an answer. Zinna scoffs. "I've always been a terrible judge of character."

"Roux's character is... good." Loyal to a fault. Smart as hell. I cycle through reasons why Roux is one of the better people even in spite of the tailspin of an adventure knowing him has been. I also let my mind drift in this way to avoid how she had so confidently said 'was' — past tense.

"Exactly," she responds. "Did you even know about his daughter? Or was he playing games with you too?" Again, there goes that casual reference of Roux in the past tense.

My eyes widen obnoxiously large and I make an added effort to look angry and betrayed. I even pretend like my breathing is increasing by letting my chest rise and fall in an exaggerated way. Too much? *Maybe.*

"Did any of you know this?" I alternate glances between each of my companions. They all take turns shaking their heads.

Zinna grins and huffs out an amused laugh. "The mom was a prostitute. Bet he didn't go into detail about his past relationships either, did he?"

This part really does surprise me. There's no acting involved here which certainly helps the believability aspect. "A... prostitute..."

"Apparently he kept going back to her, trying to help her get clean. Got her pregnant. She didn't survive the birth." Zinna says all this as though there's nothing to it; as though no one's heart was broken in the process.

"That's horrible."

"Is it?" she asks.

I don't bother to humor her with a response. Clearly we don't see eye-to-eye on moral dilemmas.

Worked up, brokenhearted on Roux's behalf, mind reeling with possibilities I refuse to entertain, and tired of the small talk, I stand and start walking around the room. Lost in my own thoughts, when she does finally start reacting to the effects, it takes one of the guys approaching with an update to bring my mind back to the present.

"*Cuore mio*, we all think you should step out. Let us take care of this."

Having been through it myself, and not at all wanting to witness the transitional phase, I step out of the room, lean against the wall, and rest my head back to stare up at the ceiling.

"That bad, huh?" A woman's voice has me standing up straighter and looking in the direction of the lounging CDC crew.

"Heh, yeah... that bad." I let out a raspberry between my lips.

She smiles and steps in front of me, holding a first aid kit. "We had no idea there was a Resistance." She starts a casual conversation while digging into the kit and removing some items.

"We had no idea there was another large group of people against The Program." I give her a half-smile.

"Good." She laughs. "Let me take care of your thumbs."

My thumbs? Oh... the ones I bit.

"Well, for both of our groups, at least it means we were doing a good enough job at the secrecy part." I hold my hands out, palms up.

She nods in agreement and begins doctoring my wounds. "The CDC has centers in every state, and we have over eleven thousand employees." She takes a deep breath, contemplating, but ultimately chooses to continue. "Most of them chose the good side. The ones who didn't..."

I don't make her finish; the knowledge is enough without having to verbalize. "I get it. Can't risk it otherwise, right?"

"Exactly."

Inside the host system room, Zinna screams, and the guys' panicked voices quickly follow as shuffling noises back up those screams. I give my new acquaintance a grimace. "Won't last long."

"Oh, I'm familiar with the drug. Done plenty of studies on it. Not proud to say we're part of the reason it was able to be formulated in such large quantities."

"Oh… right…"

Bunch of Tobias's running around here, I suppose.

She bites on the inside of her lip and darts her attention to the side for a moment. I can't help but smile, being quite familiar with that particular habit. Having learned a bit of patience through this ordeal, I wait, but she doesn't keep me waiting for long. "So… I was tasked to spy on your conversation with Zinna a moment ago." She sighs, and I shrug, hoping she didn't hear the conversations with Jax and Tobias too. "We… know how to get into the host system. If that's what you're needing to know next."

"It is. We're drugging her mainly so she doesn't remember us — nor you guys — being here. While under the influence, we'd intended on asking her a few questions to get the rest of the information we need, but based on our chat with her before we gave her the Dub, she doesn't have that particular bit of information."

"No… you're right. She doesn't. But… um… We may have captured the head of the board. A man by the name of Gerald Schafer." The name doesn't ring a bell… not to me… so I just blink at her, waiting for her to continue. "It appears most — if not all — of the board

313

members weren't 100 percent on board with every step. But, Zinna is smart and accomplished things quickly and efficiently. It started with the concept of creating these facilities for research purposes, but she turned it into what it is today."

Proof right here one person can, indeed, make a difference.

A nation-changing difference.

"Anyway" — the woman waves her hand — "apparently they had a meeting after that whole debacle where her team was caught working off the books in a lab down in Alabama. Once Schafer got details on *your* name, he and the other board members went behind Zinna's back to change the permissions for accessing the host system. All of them. To make this happen, Schafer snagged your DNA sample off the evidence collected from the lab in combination with the information she had stored in her personal tablet."

While she explains this, the pieces start to click into place one by one.

"In short, *you* are the one who can access it."

This part of the puzzle didn't come together until she says it outright though. I'm caught off guard yet again. I dart a glance over her shoulder, only to find that the lounging CDC members have stopped talking amongst each other and are now watching the exchange between us.

"The *only* person?"

"Well, now, I didn't say *only*. There's one more, but Schafer refused to divulge that information. He gave us a name though. A woman that was on Zinna's team — Becky Westley. He said if push came to shove, she'd be able to figure out the name of the person given those permissions.

And the last puzzle piece slides into place.

Leta... Leta is the only other person who has permissions assigned.

The question is... does Roux know?

Probably not.

Doesn't matter, anyway, seeing as there will no longer be a host system after today. Well-played on their part though. "So... to open that fancy clear box in there, I need to put my finger over the prick thing, and it'll just... open?"

"I'm assuming so, yes," she answers.

CHAPTER THIRTY

The next hour-plus is excruciatingly long. During the wait, however, I learn that the only reason why the CDC didn't hurt or keep Tobias prisoner was because he'd had the sense to say my name which, for him, would have otherwise been unusual. Guess he was willing to take a chance based on the information he gathered under their "care."

The guys take turns coming out of the room, while the other three deal with Zinna's transition from "normal" to zombie. In between each visit, I pass the time explaining the information about Gerald Schafer to each guy and how my blood will apparently open this magical box. However, I make it quite clear that I don't like the idea of putting my finger onto a prick thingy that Zinna — and whoever else — has tried in recent hours.

As a result, and after some deliberation on the matter, we decide to have one of the CDC members help Tobias take apart the outer portion of the box as soon as Zinna is under control, with the hope that we'll be able to clean the device first.

Julian is the one who comes out to deliver news of Zinna's acquiescence. Funny how a couple hours of just the right type of activity can make a person look so worn down. Poor Julian has dark circles under his olive-green eyes. Even so, they sparkle every time it's his turn to come out with an update. Especially this time, now that they're not having to hold her down any longer. "Ready, *cuore mio*?" he says, wrapping his arms around me and squeezing hard. Just because.

"As ready as I'll ever be."

When we enter, Zinna is still sitting in the corner, eyes glazed as she stares blankly at the glowing box in the center of the room. Right away, Tobias and the chosen CDC guy begin the task of cleaning the host system's equipment.

No one in here has any desire to linger or draw out the process, so as soon as the equipment is clean and passes Tobias's final safety inspection, it's time to get on with the next step. The much-anticipated finger prick.

The event is relatively anticlimactic: I place my finger over the scanner, it pricks me, and the box opens instantaneously. The guys gape, impressed, to which I respond with a shrug.

"I'll go let the others know it worked," the CDC guy states.

Tobias nods, waiting until the guy exits the room before pulling a small case out of his pocket. "Keep them out there a while," he says, opening the case to reveal a microchip which I assume is what he intends to transfer the data onto.

I nod and make my way out of the room, rejoining the CDC crew and gathering them up to deliver any and all remaining updates on the box and Zinna's condition. "Tobias says he's going to question her once more and asked you to give him about fifteen minutes before going in there to get what you need. After that, we'll wipe it and demolish the equipment."

I'd found it a little curious that they were okay with being out here while we were in there doing whatever, as though we're the most trustworthy people. But as I watch them, I realize that they're all just like us. Well, more like Tobias on the smartness level... possibly even more so. But, still... regular people, way out of their element.

After a few minutes, I sneak back into the room. Julian is squatting in front of Zinna, antagonizing her in his own way. When I approach, he peers up at me over his shoulder.

"Getting anything good?" I ask

"*Sì...* finally got information on what she wants. Apparently, the CDC and Zinna are both in the running for the same file. A meeting report of some sort."

"Oh... right. Becky mentioned something along those lines. But... why?"

"Haven't gotten that far."

"Stand up," I say to Zinna, testing the drug's influence. She stands, albeit slowly. Julian joins her. "So, this meeting report... Why is it so important to you and the CDC?"

She blinks at me a few times. "It's proof that it was my straw proposal they accepted, of course. Without that, they could take control of what's rightfully mine and ruin everything. Plus, it contains details on each Phase — valuable information should anyone need it at a later date to carry through additional preventative measures."

Now it's my turn to blink several times at her. "What happens if this meeting report disappears?"

Zinna shrugs. Seems she doesn't have the answer to everything after all. "There's the potential they'd alter the report to remove my name — and, thus, involvement — entirely."

Sounds good to me. "And what's so bad about that?"

She gasps and her eyes widen so animatedly that I swear for a split second the drug isn't working after all, but then I remember Roux had said at one point I was a "damn comedian" while the Dub was in my system. "Not

318

be credited for what I've accomplished?" Zinna's eyebrows crease inward, knocking me right back into the present.

I roll my eyes. "You're worried about your name being omitted from the history books? Is being credited really why you want to make sure you keep a copy of this meeting document?"

She gives me a simple, yet profound, nod.

"C—" I shoot a look at Julian. "Can you believe this woman!? Recognition! She's worried about recognition!"

Jax chuckles, coming up behind me to join in on the fun.

"I... I can't *even* with you right now." I narrow a glare right into her eyes. Again, she shrugs. "If ever there was a reward for the stupidest antagonist ever, it would surely go to you. Then... then you'd get your recognition. Stupid... cow."

After a few choppy, impatient breaths, I remember what she'd said right before I administered the drug. Her request that I don't ask about her having children. I give her one hard look, biting at the inside of my bottom lip.

But then my shoulders deflate.

I'm still a nicer person than she is.

I move to walk away, but Jax's arms wrap around me, keeping me still. His smoky tone breathes in my ear. "Fuck that, Darlin'. Those impressions ya send me don't happen often, but I heard ya loud 'n' clear just now. Maybe you won't ask her, but I have no trouble doin' it." He then lifts his head from my shoulder and addresses Zinna himself. "Did ya have any children?"

Zinna immediately bursts into tears and drops to her knees.

319

Jax lets go of me and bends to her level. "What happened?" he asks, all grit and determination in his tone.

"Jax..." I might hate the woman, but that's real pain. Real memories surfacing. Well-buried ones at that.

Julian grabs my hand, tugging me toward him. "*Cuore mio*... We deserve to know."

"They killed him. My son. All that research..." she explains between sobs. "...it was supposed to help. To cure. To heal." Zinna falls onto her butt and scoots backward until she has the only support she'll receive in the entire room — the wall.

"He had a new strain of a disease. He was suffering. The doctors touted this trial program would work. Instead, it did the opposite. In an instant he was just... gone. No... no parent should ever have to experience that. Even if it means thousands of parents would lose their children in the process of getting to a world where they wouldn't have to again."

Her heartbreak made her absolutely delusional. What I want to make her realize is that if her plan had worked exactly as she'd hoped it would, the cycle would start anew no matter what. That eventually — a long time from now — we'd be right back to where we are now.

But then I remember what Roark had said about my connection with the guys — and how that same connection between other opposite pairs was the dawning of a new age. A new cycle. Children with higher resistances — unique to the present-day world. Everything the scientists hoped gene editing could achieve, was achieved organically by the way of life's natural cycle. In a moment of revelation, I turn and rush up to Tobias. "The Reverse Genus lists... we... we need to somehow make sure those go public. Make sure the population finds their matches to help counteract the steps The Program took to bring Lows together with other Lows. To counteract the loss."

Tobias looks at me, blinks a couple times, then a big smile spreads across his face. "Not sure how we're going to do that, but it's definitely something we can look into once everyone has recovered from this devastation."

With a prickle of tears in my eyes, I nod. Bram reaches across the box, and I give him my hand. "Soon, you'll be hiding all the information inside your DNA. What we do — or don't do — after that is up to you. We can walk away from the data transfer and never look back. Or we can use the data in a way of your choosing. Whatever you decide to do beyond all this, we're behind you all the way."

I return the squeeze with one of my own and smile my thanks.

"Data is collected," Tobias says, placing the small, delicate chip back inside its case. I watch closer this time and notice that the case reverberates a low hum. When Tobias clicks the case shut with a wink, I raise an eyebrow. "Later," he whispers.

Julian and Jax are keeping a watchful eye on Zinna. Beside me, Bram slips away, disappears out of the room, and soon returns with a few of the CDC crew.

They get to work right away, connecting their own electronics to the mainframe, and searching through the contents therein. Tobias steps away and casually leans back against the wall, watchful, but with the smallest of smiles on his face.

I give him a sideways glance, eyeing him closely. Since he's throwing so much shade, I'm surprised we can even see in here with how dim it already is. His gaze meets mine for only a brief moment, though, before returning to the CDC techs that are hacking the host system.

"Fuck!" one of the techs grinds out. Again my eyes dart to Tobias, and his shoulder lifts ever so minutely... along with that smile... before dropping entirely when the same man that had released the expletive turns around. Tobias puts on a show raising his eyebrows in surprise, pushing off the wall, and approaching the man. "The meeting report isn't in here."

Everyone around the host system — Tobias included — turns toward Zinna. Jax and Julian bracket her, arms crossed. When all attention is on the three of them, Jax lifts an eyebrow and turns toward her too. In his country drawl he says, "Tha fuck did ya do with the meeting report?"

She blinks a few times, looks at Jax like he's the most confusing person she's ever met, then says, "I deleted it."

Julian's eyebrows disappear underneath his curls and he now turns his head toward her. "We thought you couldn't get into the database. How'd you manage to delete the report?"

"Safeguard," she says. "Back when I flagged Lena and Harris's account, I set a stipulation that if Thessaly's blood was ever properly put into the host system, it would wipe the report and any digital trail leading to my involvement. Up until about twenty minutes ago, the details of her blood results were merely manually entered — not officially. But when she submitted her blood sample in order to access the host system, it sent the details of the sample to the nearest exacentrifuge, processed it, and entered her into the system... creating

322

a string of events that ultimately led to the report being deleted."

What in the actual hell...

Wait a minute...

The nearest exacentrifuge... is... demolished.

"B—" I start.

Jax clears his throat loudly, swallows hard, and says "Well damn... I don't understand a fuckin' thing you just said..." He then turns his attention toward the group of CDC crew and my guys still standing around the host system. "Can we get the fuck outta here yet?"

The CDC crew stands there for what feels like an eternity, wordless, staring at Zinna. One of the guys brings his hand to his chin and cups it before dragging it down and over his neck as he appears to contemplate this.

"Sooo..." he starts, "this here device..." — he indicates the box surrounding the host system — "is able to deliver blood-sample information to an exacentrifuge, and... process it?" He doesn't sound very convinced.

Tobias is the one to speak up next. "Separate and read the mutations... highly unlikely. But pull details to get enough information about her DNA to enter it into the catalog, absolutely. I worked for a State DNA Database office and saw this done a number of times in most cases to simply open a new file."

Clearly this is an AB and CDC conversation, so I step back, leaving them all to it while my mind reels. Bram leaves the group and joins my side, wrapping his arms around my shoulders, letting Tobias take over. He squeezes me against him, dropping his mouth toward my ear. "If you're wondering why we all keep finding ways to touch you, it's because you're projecting very strongly. Everything. Ever since you passed out, you

323

haven't put up your barricades. And…" He hesitates for a moment, "I think you're acting as an intermediary for… I don't know… other people. Maybe Auden? It's hard to tell."

I spin in his hold and face him. Breaths increasing, I close my eyes and try to sort — probe — anything. I'm so filled with adrenaline, so distracted by the situation at hand, so concerned about my guys and everyone I care about… the UR included. Bram is right: I'd somehow naturally tapped into all of them. But the problem is I can't compartmentalize. They are a part of me, and I'm a part of them. "What do you feel?" I ask, hoping he can bring some clarity.

He jerks his head toward the door, and I nod in understanding. The two of us make our way out of the room, and I check over my shoulder just in time to see Tobias taking the box apart while still explaining the data retrieval process from the finger prick.

Once we've entered the hallway area, we move to the opposite side, keeping away from the remaining CDC crew. Bram jumps right into the conversation, voice low. "Pretty sure I felt Auden… that's the impression I got. There was a lot of… fear interwoven into that signature. That's why they tried to redirect your thoughts earlier. Just in case it was *your* panic or fear that was setting off his."

"Has anyone been able to get into contact with them?" I inquire, their dangerous situation slamming back into me, bringing along with it a new wave of that same fear Bram mentioned.

He grabs my hand. "We haven't had a chance to try yet."

Well… that's better than them trying and not being able to. My mind continues to spin. In a moment of realization, I yank my hand out of Bram's and rush back into the room, rushing right up to Zinna.

"Did you call the attack on Robbie's Motel and Bar?" Even in my flustered state, I still don't want to reveal the UR… just in case.

"Yes," she answers.

"What… happened?"

"After removing all the hiding occupants, they completely demolished the place." She holds her hands up and spreads her fingers out in a starburst motion, puffing her cheeks out to mimic the motion while making an explosion sound.

My stomach lurches, but I swallow hard and straighten my shoulders.

Then I turn around and approach the CDC crew and Tobias just in time to watch as Tobias takes over the screen they'd attached to the mainframe when looking for the report.

"We need to go," I state as a demand, no longer caring if these people figure out how this box works. "We've been here long enough. Time to do some damage of our own and get out of here."

"On it," Tobias responds with a chuckle. "We're wiping the system now, then we'll fry, break, and burn the equipment."

I let out a sigh of relief.

But letting out that sigh isn't enough. The walls around me suddenly feel too confining. Every muscle in my body tightens, and the need to escape becomes all consuming. "I need to get out of here," I announce.

Bram darts a glance at Jax, Julian, and Tobias as if trying to make a decision. Decision made, he places his hand on Tobias's shoulder, whispers something in his ear, and Tobias's whole body turns rigid. He then steps back from the portable screen and moves to my side. I dart confused glances between Bram and Tobias.

"I'm clocking out," Tobias says. "You all have the rest taken care of?"

Everyone in the room nods, Jax and Julian included.

Tobias takes my hand, leads me over to Zinna, and takes her hand too. "Make sure they follow through," he says to Jax and Julian. "Thessaly and I will take the other ones with us to get the vehicles ready. Then we'll dump Zinna in an alleyway somewhere."

Even despite the confusion swirling around me, I still chuckle at the visual of an equally confused Zinna coming to mental consciousness in an alleyway.

Or maybe I'm going a little mad... all the best of us do.

"Wait. I... have an idea. Don't burn it without me, okay?"

After several nods of agreement, Tobias directs both me and Zinna out of the room, and she walks along easy enough. He then leads us to the door to the stairwell, turns to the rest of the crew, and with the jerk of his head, they all fall in line.

The door opens right up, thanks to Jax's earlier safeguard.

CHAPTER THIRTY-ONE

Everything Tobias said is exactly what we do. Step by step we wrap up. First, the CDC crew separates to prep their vehicles which are conveniently parked at the admin building. Several vehicles to our one Betty.

Bless her little heart — er, engine.

Before leaving the direct area, though, he makes a pit stop at one of the CDC vehicles, opens the back, and transfers several items — the equipment he'd gathered from the CDC, I surmise, and his weekend bag — to the sidewalk near the building's entrance.

From there, Tobias, Zinna, and I trudge through the snowy sidewalk a little ways until we reach a sizable alleyway between buildings. Once situated, the three of us just stand staring at each other for a time, while I consider all the things I'd like to do and words I'd like to say to this woman. Empathically sharing with her the massive amount of panic, fear, and heartbreak coming from the nearby pulse point certainly crosses my mind. But I selfishly choose to keep that talent locked up. One, because in order to push it into her, I'd need to experience it myself, and I... I just can't handle that right now. Or ever. Secondly, with Dub in her system, she'd never remember the horror.

Instead, I choose to take the high road, tapping into the last bit of empathy I have remaining where she's concerned. Hoping to soften her heart and reroute her actions once the Dub does eventually wear out of her system, I state, "Your son... is happy and healthy," trying to make the lie as believable as possible. Tobias squeezes my hand, grounding and supporting me.

Zinna looks at me and says, "He's dead."

To which I reply, "Your son is happy and healthy," again with a nod, encouraging her to absorb what I'm saying and agree. She blinks a couple of times as the information soaks in. False information, but a lie I hope her mind and soul will choose to believe no matter how untrue it might be.

When she doesn't argue back a second time, I change the subject. "Repeat after me: I have absolutely no idea what happened to the host system."

"I have absolutely no idea what happened to the host system."

Starting to feel a bit uncertain about the effectiveness of this course of action, I side-whisper to Tobias: "Are we 100 percent certain she's drugged and not putting on the act of her life?"

"Oh, I'm 100 percent certain," he answers. "The strength she had during the transition takes the influence of drugs to make happen. She could have faked the rest of it but definitely not that."

Trusting his judgement, I let it go. "Zinna?" She looks at me, tilting her head to the side. "Stay here for an hour." I bend down and tap on the watch at her wrist. "Do not leave this spot until after that duration. Understand?" The sky once again a shade of blue that indicates a new day is nigh should give us just enough cover to get out of here before full daylight takes over.

Zinna nods.

"Are we done?" I ask Tobias.

Tobias gives me a confident, "Yep," and we turn around and leave the alleyway.

* * *

THE WALK BACK to Betty seems to take longer than the journey here. But, I am thankful for the opportunity to burn off this lingering adrenaline.

Hands, toes, and nose frozen solid from the trek, I clamber inside while Tobias gets in the driver seat. With him being far more versed in driving through snow than I am, we decided on the walk that he'd be the one to take the wheel. He wastes no time getting out of there and heading back to the admin building, ready to get the heck outta Dodge. Or, New York, rather.

When we arrive, the CDC crew is gone and all my guys are waiting just outside the building, hands shoved into their white cargos, looking quite camouflage if it weren't for the black doors of the building behind them.

"Just like that, huh?" I mumble, watching as my breath fogs the window.

"Just like that," Tobias responds.

Jax approaches the car and dips his head down to speak with us while Bram and Julian pick up the items Tobias had left on the curb and put them in Betty's trunk. "The CDC people had ta get outta here, but we didn't burn it yet per yer request," he explains, opening the door for me. "They banged it up pretty good before leavin' though."

With a deep breath, the scent of crisp snow fills my lungs, and I step out of the car and gesture over my shoulder for Tobias to join us. Betty's locks disengage, and the clang of her doors closing soon follows. Jax leads everyone back into the building, and the five of us walk to the room where the host system lies in shards and pieces. We pass the admins Zinna's men had slaughtered, her equally as lifeless guards, and the dead board member en route. Lives for lives.

Looking down at the pile of wreckage, my hand slips into my pocket, and I drag my fingers over the smooth buttons of the pager inside before unclipping and removing it. As always, I have two: the one directly associated with our small group and the one assigned by the UR.

For what I have in mind, I choose the group pager. Holding it up so everyone can see, I wiggle it a bit and raise one of my eyebrows. Their faces light up with grins and they all immediately reach into their pockets and pluck out their own. "Group pagers?" I verify. "Because I don't intend on us ever separating again after this." They all nod in unison.

It has been a long long while since my chest expanded and fluttered in a way indicative of true pride and happiness — even though I know this happiness is unordinary and will soon be followed with a slew of new challenges. But, in this moment, my heart is full. My determination on point.

In sync, we all hold them up in the air, one hand supporting the device while the other pinches the clip at an opened angle. "Ready?" I ask, grinning from ear to ear.

Four variants of *yes* resound throughout the otherwise empty room. "On three. One... two... three!"

All five of us break off the pagers' clips concurrently and toss them on top of the host system's rubble, rushing out of the room as fast as possible. We each attempt to peek our heads around the doorframe at the same time to watch as the remnants of the hardware that has made our lives a living hell burns.

* * *

BRAM AND JAX get in the back with me, leaving the two guys who have experience driving in the snow up front.

Tobias doesn't stick around, nearly driving away while everyone is still loading up.

When we finally do drive away, I wipe a circle in the foggy window and peek into the alleyway where we left Zinna. As hoped, she's still there, now visible in the early morning light, standing just as we'd left her. As much as I dislike the woman, I hope the first thing she does is go somewhere to get warm.

The ride is silent for the first hour or so as we all thaw out and let the details of the incident that just took place settle. Funny how, after spending so much time building up, events seem to come to a peak and start descending awfully quick at the end.

"So," I finally break the silence, "how'd everything go in there?" I ask.

"Pretty cut 'n' dry," Jax replies. "Quite anticlimactic. The CDC wasn't happy that tha meetin' report wasn't there. But in the big scheme of things, they quickly remembered that we needed ta get the thing demolished and move on. After talkin' about it for a time, I got the impression they'd intended on vaultin' that file anyway… with hopes of it never seein' the light of day."

"But then why keep it at all?"

"Probably for the same reason Zinna wanted to keep it — a mark in history," Bram answers, a slight smile on his face.

I squint my eyes at him, and, now that it has had time to percolate in my mind, the whole scene from the room comes rushing back. "I... have questions."

"We wondered when those would come up," Julian says, an equally amused grin on his face.

I work through the scene, figuring I'd start at the part where Tobias showed up with the CDC. Tobias explains that he'd arrived at the CDC with S&R, and the place was swarming with Unis. So, he did the only thing he could think to do... and that, apparently, was walk right up to them. Not knowing who he was, they apprehended him immediately. It didn't take long once they dragged him inside for him to explain that he was a Database Tech and he was there to get some equipment. This vague response was enough to put him on the fence of both sides — good and bad.

From there, it took a while for him to get a feel for who these people were and what exactly it was they were doing, but as soon as he'd pieced together that they were merely sheep in wolves clothing, he changed his approach entirely, bringing up the topic of the database, sweeps, and sharing what he'd discovered about the facilities.

He — singular. At that point he was still not sharing the involvement of others. When they questioned him as to what equipment he was on the hunt for... well... that part he had to get creative with. He chose to be vague though — simply stating he wanted to gather up anything and everything he possibly could. Just in case. Because eventually people were going to need help, and he wasn't sure there were any groups or resources anywhere with the equipment, meds, or anything else necessary to be useful.

That's about the time when something one of the supposed guards said made him realize that they were their own resistance of sorts. He took a deep breath and said, "Does the name Thessaly Allifair ring a bell?" According to him, that got the attention of the entire room. Beyond that, they weren't very forthcoming with answers regarding how and why they knew my name, but he'd said that I was important to him — *and many others*, hinting there being a much bigger entity involved.

The conversation soon led to what their plans were. And, funny enough, they had all been gathered because it was their intention to travel to the host system and do exactly what we'd been planning to do all along. Apparently, they'd been tracking the pulses, too, and there was a budding sense of urgency, considering, you know, people were being killed in gargantuan amounts at this point.

Tobias learned how widespread the CDC resistance was but it seemed none of them had a plan beyond eliminating the database from the picture. That's when Tobias took the biggest chance of all and explained about the multipronged attack.

"At that point, the attack was so close to going into effect, even if they were blowing smoke about being on the good side of all this, they wouldn't have had time to warn anyone to stop the impending results. So, the risk was smaller than it would have been otherwise."

Piecing things together, I realize the reason my name rang a bell was because they'd been in communication with Gerald Schafer and had learned that I'd been the key to accessing the host system. Before heading to New York, they were going to have to intercept me. So, like us, knowing Zinna's involvement — according to Schafer — they'd touched base with the

CDC closest to the lab there in the Central Region and sent out an S&R crew of their own to look for yours truly.

Just as soon as I piece that little part together, a *dread* presses in on me, coming from one of my guys. I clasp my hands over my chest with a gasp. *Julian.* I reach over the front seat, placing my hand on his shoulder and squeeze.

"*Cazzo,*" he whispers, "those… Those Unis we killed during the sweep?" Eyes going vacant, he no doubt replays the scene in his mind. His head falls back against the headrest and he closes his eyes. "I knew it didn't feel right."

The world had turned into a place where it was kill or be killed — shoot first, ask questions later. Every stalled move, every stalled decision became a potential risk. Right now, though, I can't comfort him by saying, "You did what you had to do," because I know that will only leave a bad taste in both our mouths. Can't candy-coat the weight of the truth. Instead, I squeeze his shoulder harder.

The "Unis" they'd taken out were part of the CDC crew. Innocents. People who, we know now, will be a significant help to the reformation of our nation. And we need as many of those as we can get.

A blanket of silence covers us as we all absorb the brutal truth. When we can't handle it any longer, Tobias wraps up his story, explaining that he knew exactly where I was and that there was a Search and Rescue crew outside gearing up to do an extraction of sorts if he didn't hurry up and show his face again.

Still keeping him bound, they brought Tobias back outside, and untied him so that Aubrey, Harvey, or one of the other crew members watching would see their show of surrender. The rest just sorta fell into place. S&R

needed to get back to the UR because something was wonky with the communications.

The attack on the UR maybe.

Pushing it to the back of my mind once more, I cycle through the order of events yet again, still eager to make sense of everything that has happened. Next topic… Tobias's fancy container. Well, *our* fancy container. We'd brought it with us, and apparently Jax, Julian, or Bram had been hanging onto it in the event Tobias wasn't around to get the job done. But he was… and for that I'm extremely grateful. "So, the container holding the chip — or whatever — that you put the data on? I saw it glow…"

Tobias's eyes meet mine in the rearview mirror. "It kind of acts like a mini computer. The biotech guy the Eastern UR brought in is going to start prepping the data for the transfer."

"So the information is going from that box directly to the Eastern UR?"

"Yeah, he brings smart to a whole new level. What he does is not at all in my wheelhouse." This coming from Tobias does, indeed, surprise me. "He said he can tap into the satellites and use those to help him translate the bits to letters. Some of the equipment we picked up will help him synthesize it. Then, once Bram gives him the bacteria, he'll mesh the two."

My mind goes a little hazy and my eyes unfocus. Bram laughs. I swat him on the shoulder. "And… so this bacteria is then placed inside my body?"

Tobias nods. "Again, not my wheelhouse, but from what little info he tried to explain, if I'm understanding it correctly, he'll use a nanobot to trap the data-bacteria in a non-invasive part of your body. A part that, hopefully, won't resist or fight against the bacterium."

"And… it'll just stay there… forever?"

Tobias shrugs. "That's the idea."

I don't bother to ask if it's safe or not; I already know the guys wouldn't be on board if it weren't.

Brain full and heavy with all this building information, I'm eager for a much-needed break. However, there's still at least one bit left hanging that I can't make sense of — that whole ordeal with Zinna and the missing meeting report.

Again my eyes meet Tobias's in the rearview mirror as though he's expecting my next question.

"What… happened… in there?" I ask, not really sure what I'm asking after all. Doesn't matter, though, because all four of them know exactly what I'm referring to.

Jax is the one who speaks up. "That was my genius, Darlin'." He gives me a wink. The entire situation was so… very Jax-like looking back at it, this revelation doesn't come as a surprise now that he says something. "We were playin' around with testin' out the effects of tha drug on Zinna, so we — I — decided ta weave a wee tale. Fuck with her mind. I actually didn't know it'd end up helpin' tha entire situation. But, hey, whatever works." He shrugs.

Julian speaks up next. "Took me a minute to fall in line, but once I realized what he was doing, I helped. Bram and Tobias pieced things together shortly thereafter, and all of a sudden it was a group thing. Well, minus you, of course, since you weren't in the room."

Bram laughs. "Yeah, that was the trickiest part… What with your facial expressions and confusion."

"I convinced Zinna she'd deleted the report — and how she did it. Just usin' some of the stuff I've heard y'all talkin' about here and there."

"To help with the believability, Bram and I chose to not have Jax and Julian tell us what story they'd given her. Unfortunately, that backfired a bit when she said the damn box delivered your blood sample. So I had to do some quick thinking."

Jax grimaces, but it turns into a smile and a shrug. The smile is contagious... that and how proud he is of himself regardless of the mistake.

"Okay, so the box didn't deliver my blood sample. That's the part that confused me the most. I almost called her out on the spot, seeing as the exacentrifuge in question had already been demolished."

"Right," Tobias agrees. "And, let's just say, convincing other science nerds is no easy feat."

"But you did it."

"Yeah, I managed."

Tapping my finger against my chin, I ask, "But she... didn't delete it?"

"No. I did," Tobias says. "Well, I deleted it from the host system before the CDC started poking in there. It's on our chip, though."

For a minute, I entertain the thought of this entire hot mess from the day these guys abducted me to this very moment, and I give myself a mental pat on the shoulder for making that one life-changing decision in the beginning stages of everything — when I'd escaped my captors but ultimately decided to turn right back around and give these guys a chance.

There's no way — none at all — that I would have come out on the winning end without them.

CHAPTER THIRTY-TWO

Due to the tremendous amount of traveling we've done over time, the trip from New York to Rhode Island feels relatively short in comparison. The five of us take turns cat-napping, but when the Eastern UR gets close, we all straighten in our seats, eyes scanning the areas as we pass through.

When we're within a mile, I dig into one of my many cargo pockets and pull out the Eastern UR pager, typing a quick code in there to let someone know they have visitors incoming. It doesn't take long for a "10-4" to come through in response.

On arrival, the entire place is crawling with members. There is no hiding and lots of chaos. Many of these people — the ones out in the open — must be Combat, if the blood and morose looks in their eyes are any indicator. I quickly surmise this is the group assigned to hit up the closest facility — the one we'd heard was not too far from here. It's well-hidden, much like the Florida facility was. In the big, nationwide picture, this group would be the only one close enough to a battle spot to make it back to their UR with such a quick turnaround.

It takes quite an effort to refrain from rushing up to one of them and asking how everything went and whether or not they have news from any other regions. But I sidle closer to Bram instead, letting him lead me through everyone and into the UR. He dips his head down, and whispers, "Try to shut down, Thess; otherwise the rest of us might struggle to communicate with anyone."

Blinking several times, I cave inside my own mind, trying to bypass all the emotions rushing in. I push them aside in large quantities, much like walking in a field of wheat, making a path just big enough for me to focus — and, in turn, allowing the guys to focus as well.

As we enter, a piercing squeal meets my ears about two seconds before something — someone — collides with my body. It isn't until I see my dad beside me, hugging Bram, that I realize the person suffocating me is my mother. Instead of remaining rigid from surprise, I engage in the hug, wrapping my arms around her and squeezing tight.

It's hard to pull away. Neither of us want to, but Dad eventually whispers in Mom's ear and she steps back, giving him room to hug me too. I bury my face in his chest and inhale, letting nostalgia whisk me away for a moment. Dad doesn't hug me for as long, but the impact is just the same.

There's so much activity around us, so much going on, it's a bit overwhelming. And it becomes even more so when a hand tugs on mine, pulling me aside for a brief moment. Tobias squeezes my fingers and looks down at me. After a single blink and deep breath, he says, "My parents are here... Amber is, too."

The look in his eyes tells me he's just letting me know before anyone else does. Namely *her*. Amber. Otherwise, he doesn't look concerned, doesn't appear guilty, nothing like that. Just one adult telling another adult an adult thing. I nod at him and squeeze his hand back.

Tobias's attention trains on a spot in the distance, and I dare a glance at the area, following his sightline until it reaches a man, quite unmistakably his father. The older man is similar in height to Tobias, his mother closer to my meager height, looking like an itty bitty thing next to his dad. That's when I realize what the two of us must look like next to each other. An amused grin pops up before I can contain it.

Beside them, a younger woman's brown eyes find mine immediately. She seems very much my opposite in every way, and I give her a nervous smile before breaking the eye contact, patting Tobias on the arm, and leaving him to do his thing while I do mine.

If he wants me to meet his parents, I'll let him initiate that step. For now, we both turn back to the crowd just in time for me to notice that Bram's mom and dad are here too. I give Tobias a quick kiss on the cheek before breaking off to make sure Bram's long-overdue reunion with his parents is going okay, seeing as they haven't spoken much since he was old enough to start spending most of his time away from the house.

When I approach Bram's side, he's attempting to make awkward conversation with them.

"Thessaly," Cheryl coos, scooping me up in her arms like she actually cares. Then again, maybe she does after the mess going on around us. A new beginning for just about everyone, perhaps. "See you two stuck together after all." She smiles and holds me out to get a good look.

"Yes." I smile back at her. "Couldn't live without him."

Her smile widens and pride just oozes out of her. They may have been a bit detached in his teen years, but there was once a time when she was an excellent mother, according to Bram. Before the divorce. This thought brings my attention to Russel. The fact he's near

Cheryl's side is damn near surprising. Then again, once you have children, they tend to do that to couples — bring them together. Sometimes, at least.

The conversation ends there, and I ditch Bram with a supportive rub of his back before seeking out my two remaining guys.

Jax and Julian are tucked away in a corner, away from everyone. No family in sight. My heart breaks on the spot for Julian because I know he's been chompin' at the bit to hear news from his family.

Jax's situation, on the other hand, was a bit more precarious, so the absence of his parents doesn't come as much of a surprise.

What does make me happy, though, is that Julian and Jax both have each other. Another design of fate I don't think any of us expected, but one in which all of us appreciate.

I approach the two of them, trying hard not to give Julian a look of sympathy. But he feels it inside me, no doubt, and gives me one of his own, with the upward tick of a shoulder.

"This is just one UR, Julian. Not everyone can be here. And with your family living between the Central and Mountain Region URs—"

He pulls me toward him and wraps me up tightly, burying his face into my hair. "I know, *il mio cuore* is here though," he says. "*My heart* is here though. That's what matters most."

My heart. That's the second time today he has translated *cuore mio*. To think he's been calling me that since the beginning, even before we were bound by our empath bond, makes my heart swell. From the moment we'd lain eyes on each other, we knew whatever this was, was meant to be. I squeeze him a little tighter. A little longer. Trying to give him all the love I know his family would be giving him if they were here.

When we finally break away, Jax's lips quirk up at the side. "Let's figure out *what the fuck*."

I let out a big sigh. "Fuck, yes."

Jax groans at my cursing and throws me a wink. "You're a terrible influence, you know?"

He twines our fingers together and the three of us walk away from the crowd of reuniting families and just-returned Combat teams. "Yes, I do," he says.

* * *

UNFAMILIAR WITH THIS UR, we begin by just moseying about. When we stumble upon an elevator, the three of us shrug and step inside, choosing to head into their below-ground bunker, since that seems the most fitting for a group of people who intend to hide. Of course, we don't assume it'll be that easy to find, taking the hiding part into consideration.

However, there are people everywhere; they're no longer in hiding due to the latest course of action. When the first seemingly important person is spotted, I step up to her and introduce myself. "If we were to, say, need to speak to someone important in here, where might we go?"

"Ah, yes… welcome." She doesn't bother to give her name, though, because she's in quite the hurry. In fact, she continues walking away, turning around to walk backward for long enough to answer our question. "Tech room, just ahead, down the stairs, and to the right."

"Thanks!" I holler as she turns back around. She waves over her shoulder and starts jogging to get to her destination.

"Tech room, of course." I chuckle as we take the course she'd suggested.

Sure enough, when we arrive at the Tech room, it's bustling. Wishing Tobias was with us to add his commanding, techy presence in the room, I just stand there looking around awkwardly for a moment.

Julian steps forward, though, having done so a time or two on Tobias's behalf.

"Who here is the Tech leader?" he asks, voice raised, Italian accent thick.

Only one person's head turns to face us, everyone else is busy taking care of… things.

"Here!" A woman yells, sticking her hand up as she weaves her way through the group of Tech people instead of making us come to her.

At first she has that "all business" look about her, but after a scan of the three of us… lingering on me a bit longer than on Julian and Jax, her brows lift. "Thessaly?" she asks.

Not sure strangers knowing who I am will ever be something I grow accustomed to, I smile and nod, holding out my hand. "Nice to meet you."

She shakes my hand enthusiastically. Then… she hugs me and spins me in a circle. "Congratulations," she squeals. Quite unleaderish really; however, I can't help but…. like it. Instead of being appalled at the accosting, I find myself laughing and patting her on the back.

"Thanks… I guess? Not sure what I'm being congratulated for though."

She lets go of me and gasps. "The attack? We won! Every UR."

All of a sudden I no longer have knees. I dart my hand out, finding Jax as support, and manage to stay upright with just a minor wobble. "Oh… what a relief,"

343

I breathe. "But I hardly deserve any congratulations. I was probably... I don't know... riding in a vehicle while everyone else was doing all the hard work."

"Behind-the-scenes influencers still count. We're the Tech people... we know that better than anyone."

"Well... that's fair enough," I stutter a bit, tripping over my tongue. "The... what about the Central UR? We were told they got attacked directly and... took a hard hit."

"Oh! Yes. But it was just the motel that took the hit. They never made it into the actual underground."

Again, the illusion of having no knees tricks my mind. "Our source said they removed people and blew the place up?"

The Tech leader scoffs. "Your source probably assumed there were people inside the cottages. They came in, guns blazing. Or, rather, explosives. Didn't do much of a search. In and out. The UR just powered down and laid low until it was safe for someone to go up and check the damage and put out the lingering fires. It did fuck up some of their tech though. Part of the attack was on the solar panels out there. They took several of those down. They've been working around the clock since to get back up and running so that their Medical wing has the power needed to help any returning injured."

Knees working this time, I straighten and swallow hard. "Did we—how many casualties did we have?"

"Only a handful," she answers.

Air leaves my lungs in a rush and bile bubbles inside my belly. While five is a small number, every loss is heartbreaking. "How about the other URs?"

"No... that's nationwide so far."

"W-what? H-how?"

"Well, for one, most of the facility guards switched sides. It's not hard to realize when lives are dropping in the thousands right under your nose, that you'd prefer to take the high road. I can't give you a casualty count on those who didn't convert though. Common consensus was that it was convert or… die. No prisoners."

"Ruthless," I whisper.

She shrugs. "Yeah… well… you do what you gotta do. NAB can't handle the coup. And they're not in a position to increase their numbers to fight back. Though, honestly, I don't think they'd have reason to. This is a battle of science, not munitions or power. NAB were collectors, simple as that. A single representative from each UR went with each of the Combat teams, and planted a device that fries electronics at the power source of each pulse building. As soon as the subjects were moved to a safe distance, they fried the systems.

"More than half of the Combat teams," she continues explaining, "along with the medics that were on the field with them, stayed at the facilities. They'll set up shop there, increase security should any other enemy outfits decide to try taking over again, and help rebuild. There are already food provisions at each thanks to their onsite cafeterias. Medical provisions. Places to sleep. Things of that sort. More than what we've been rationing in the URs. The main trick is keeping people who were close enough to the pulses contained for a time until the danger of further radiation exposure wanes to manageable levels."

The facilities were somewhat designed to accommodate that, too, I recall, thinking back on my time there. What with the separation of Highs and Lows.

"Time," she says in conclusion. "That's all we need now. Time."

And a lot of it, no doubt. This is certainly not something that's going away overnight.

I let out a raspberry from pursed lips and widen my eyes.

She chuckles. "Yeah, that about describes how we all feel, I think."

"Thank you for the update," Julian states, speaking for all of us.

"Welcome. Robbie made contact about an hour ago. Next time he calls in, we'll let him know you made it here safely."

"We'd really appreciate that. Let him know we hope to head back that way tomorrow." I dart quick glances at Jax and Julian to see if they're of a like mind. The two of them nod their approval. Of course, we'll need to make sure Bram and Tobias are agreeable first, but I'm feeling overly eager to get back to our "home base" and see everyone we'd been living with for the past while in the flesh. Witness that everyone is safe and well with our own eyes.

CHAPTER THIRTY-THREE

The family reunions piled on top of the excitement from the last couple days' events are enough to wear us out even more. As soon as we're done being pulled in one direction or another, and the five of us have a reunion of our own, we're quick to find someone who can assign us a place to sleep.

However, even then, there's still one more thing to accomplish. We all agree that we'd rest better knowing everything has been taken care of rather than delaying yet another important task for us to check off.

The data... transfer.

Or whatever we're calling it.

We settle in our temporary quarters, and with the equipment from the CDC in hand, we then make our way to the lab area and seek out the biotechnologist who would help seal the deal for us.

During the hours of time spent in a vehicle these past couple days, I had plenty of opportunity to think and had formed an idea that I hadn't yet explained to the guys simply because... well... if I'm being honest, I have been uncertain about the idea myself. Just before we enter the room, I stop short and pull everyone to a quiet area nearby — wishing, at this point, I would have already brought it up. Considering all the circumstances, I give myself grace and spit it out without further worrying about the poor timing. "The Dub Roux gave me," I start. The guys listen intently which warms me and further feeds my confidence. "I was thinking...

347

maybe the tech wouldn't be opposed to... a bit of memory tweaking?"

Tobias's eyebrows rise higher than anyone else's. Actually, they're all donning quite similar reactions. "You do realize asking a scientist to forget about something major like this is pretty much asking them to throw all their education and time out the window? He's not only doing this just to help.'' Tobias continues, "This is big science here. World changing. They've been able to store data inside people for a while now, but that doesn't mean they've actually done it on any significant level. This is a big deal."

I take a deep breath. "Okay... so... no, then?" The rest of the guys let Tobias take this conversation, but the look on Bram's face verifies he, too, finds the idea somewhat appalling. I've never really considered Bram as a scientist up until this point which I realize is stupid... because he's very much a scientist. "You know... you're right." I wave away the idea. "I... wasn't thinking."

Jax speaks up. "Hell yes ya were." Leave it to my Southern charmer to try to lessen the blow. "I mean... is this guy a straight shooter?" The comment makes me smile, because Jax might be country, but he's not *that* type of country. Still, I love the way he says things sometimes. Okay... all the time.

Using Jax's bravado, I continue, "Yeah... the idea here is that we're the only ones who know about this transfer. Otherwise, it becomes a potential new problem. Maybe not now but definitely in the future. Maybe not even while I'm still alive... but eventually. He could do something as simple as logging it in a journal or record of some sort. Then, years down the road, someone stumbles on the information, and we've got scientists digging up my grave."

Bram starts to laugh. When I narrow a glare at him, he says, "Pretty sure we watched that movie once."

"Hey! A lot can be gleaned from movies and books," I defend.

"I'm not disagreeing," he says with a grin.

Julian had been quiet but chooses this moment to add his two cents. "We can... suggest it. See what he says? If he isn't *accommodating*, we can force a dose on him after the transfer, kinda like we did for Zinna."

Tobias swipes his hand through his hair, then drops it to his side and throws his head back to have a silent conversation with the metal ceiling. After a moment of silence, he takes a deep breath, lets it out, then looks me square in the eyes. "It would be stupid of us to mess up this entire plan for the sake of one man's pride. Even if it hurts... on his behalf... thinking about doing such a thing."

I let out a heavy breath... the result of several short ones I hadn't realized I'd accumulated in anticipation of his response. "Thanks," I offer.

Tobias gives me an exasperated but genuine smile, and I return one of my own.

With the group in agreement, we move from our temporary hiding space and enter the lab. This particular room is a hybrid between a Medical room and the Tech room. The biotech — at least I presume the man in the room is the guy we want — is sitting in front of a monitor, inputting data into different fields and such, I also presume. Certainly out of my realm of expertise, that's for sure.

At first, the man doesn't notice our presence — so engrossed in whatever is on the screen. When Tobias clears his throat, the tech nearly falls out of his rolling stool. He then stands and adjusts his lab coat — very much the stereotypical sci-genius type. Or at least, the stereotype I've formed in my mind.

Then again, there's always Tobias, who is not awkward at all yet is equally as smart. Bram too.

Okay, clearly I'm nervous and my mind is coming up with nonsensical things to muse over.

During said musings, it's evident that Tobias had introduced me. The man now stands there, hand outstretched, and suddenly I'm the awkward one who fumbles in an attempt to make up for my delayed response.

"Hello, Thessaly," he says with a gentle shake. "My name is Bradley; it's very nice to meet you." His smile is kind and patient, for which I am thankful.

"Pleasure to meet you as well."

"The guys here have mentioned that you'd like to take an added security measure — by having me consume a hybrid version of the street drug Dub?"

I dart a sideways glance at the guys, then back to the biotech and give him an anxious nod and grimace. I suddenly feel horrible for the suggestion, considering what it does to the body while its effects take place. "Unless, of course, you know of a better alternative?"

"So glad you brought that up, because I was going to do just that. Suggest an alternative, that is. I don't want to do this, but I understand how important the precautionary step is."

All the tautness in my shoulders and back loosens. Clearly, I'd been more worried about this Dub plan than I had realized, though I did second-guess myself right away. Perhaps my intuition was trying to tell me something but I wasn't fully paying attention. "Oh, that's great!" I squeak.

"Glad you approve. We will get on with the data storage, then Tobias will assist me in performing a quick memory alteration."

He slings out the words as though it's the most natural thing in the world. When I look at Tobias, his eyes spark with that unmistakable child-like excitement. His excitement, in turn, assuages my lack thereof since every other emotion seems to be overridden by nerves.

With little more to talk about, Bradley gestures to a nearby chair — one that looks similar to an old school desk, minus the desk part. A panel is raised prior to me sitting in the chair, but after I am seated, the panel is placed down and becomes a resting spot for my arm.

"Bram..." I say, a tremor in my voice.

Bram is at my side right away, taking my hand in his.

Jax chuckles and says, "Don't pass out this time."

The biotech looks up at me. "Do you usually pass out during things having to do with needles?"

"Well... I have, yes."

"Oh, Darlin' I wasn't talkin' about you." Jax tilts his head toward Bram. "New Guy nearly passed out during that draw. Took some quick reflexes on my part to make sure he didn't topple on you, while Julian made sure you didn't hurt yourself in the process of you fallin'."

"Not making any promises," Bram says.

And this is why he works with plants... not people.

The visual instantly lightens my mood, and I chuckle. Despite the laugh, tears still fill my eyes. Tobias recognizes the unstable emotions just a beat after Bram and Julian feel them internally. He drops to a squat in front of me and cups my face in his hands, rubbing his thumb over my cheek. "Bunny ear fingers?" he asks.

I blink away the fog and nod my head, holding out two fingers against the cool arm-platform while the biotech swipes an area of my upper arm clean. With my other hand, I squeeze Bram's fingers.

"The RNA strand was made to mimic and bind to a certain sequence in the DNA. The data was stored into plasmids that were then mixed inside the bacterial cells your friend Bram, provided. Using this method traps the data into a safe location. Since DNA holds such a high-capacity of information and is quite stable, it makes for the perfect database of its own." While the biotech uses the equipment and bacteria Tobias and Bram provided to prep the needle and other supplies, he explains the science behind it all.

All the details are very intriguing. I've always known the human body was a pretty amazing thing especially as in tune as I am with the mind-body connection. But... to be a storage device that goes beyond the storage of what the body already does — to hold the personal, DNA information of millions of people inside a single individual — is miraculous.

Bradley goes on to explain the process is actually quite simple and only takes a few seconds. It's an injection, and the body takes care of the rest. If it doesn't take, the only risk is that the information is lost. The guys and I decide if that should be the case, we'd simply let bygones be bygones.

Despite my nerves, I can appreciate how amazing this science is. Advancements in technology have gotten us in the predicament we're in now — the nationwide mass devastation — but it is further advancements that will fix everything too. Just like the treatment of a snake bite, for instance: like treats like, after all... right?

Bram lets go of my hand, and I assume it's because the transfer is complete. When I see the needle in my arm, I realize that is not the case.

"Bram?" I ask, watching as he leaves the room.

Julian steps in, taking my hand, but it's too late. At the sight of the needle, and the way Bram stumbled away, sweat coats my forehead, my throat goes dry, and everything turns completely black.

* * *

"YOU TWO MAKE QUITE THE PAIR, you know that?" Tobias says, exasperated, as I float back into consciousness.

"Hmm?" I mumble.

"Seems you and Bram play off each other. When one of you doesn't feel well, the other is affected. Not sure how much weight that holds in other scenarios, but when it comes to needles, it's definitely an issue."

Needles...

Oh!

I try to sit up, my memory and consciousness returning full-force, but Tobias's strength keeps me held in place. "Be still," he whispers, "or else you'll pass out again."

I relax under him and take a couple calming breaths.

"The transfer is done, and the tech and I performed the memory alteration, stunning certain neutrons in his brain that stored the main elements of this short-term memory. When we were through, I cleaned out all the files and translated codes from his computer. Once the procedure was done, we told him the database had been

353

wiped before we were able to retrieve it and no longer needed his services."

If the smile on his mouth and squint in his eyes are any indicator, I'd say he enjoyed being part of such a thing. As I lie here, my brain turns over this information. "Wow, imagine how helpful something like that could be for trauma patients."

"That's the idea behind it, apparently," Tobias explains. "Our brains are complex though. Just because the short term memory is wiped, doesn't mean the brain hasn't processed the details elsewhere. It's a work in progress. However, since it wasn't a traumatic experience, there should be no regressing or PTSD involved that could cause symptoms of the memory resurfacing in that way."

"So, it's official, then? I am a human database?"

Tobias grins ear to ear. "Yep."

"This pleases you, hm?" I ask with a smile of my own.

"A little." He winks. "Feeling better now?"

"Well, you're holding me down, and I generally feel pretty good no matter what when that happens."

With a waggle of his eyebrows, he lets me go, and I attempt sitting again.

We're no longer in the Medical room; instead, we are in the bedroom we'd been assigned for the night. All the guys are in the room, having been waiting patiently — and quietly — for me to recover. The four of them looking as though keeping their eyes open is an exceedingly difficult task. My own feel heavy as well, despite the short nap I just had — proof that passing out doesn't quite qualify as rest.

They all liven up a bit once I'm mobile again, though, and we immediately move around the room and decide the sleeping arrangements, seldom more ready to go to bed than at this very moment.

As I lie down in an awkward, yet oddly comfortable, pile with all four of my guys, I feel light and trouble-free for the first time in what seems like ages.

CHAPTER THIRTY-FOUR

Everyone is on board with heading back to Robbie's Motel and Bar. By everyone I mean not only Bram, Tobias, Jax, Julian, and me but a caravan of others as well. Primarily the Eastern UR members who had at some point gotten word that they have friends or family in the Central UR.

My direct circle is no exception. After the long overdue reunions, none of us are eager to part from our families — my and Bram's parents as well as Tobias's parents... and Amber.

Tobias approaches me, just prior to everyone gathering up to figure out the vehicle assignments. "I..." — he swipes his hand through his hair and drops his gaze — "would like you to meet my parents before we leave here. I know they're coming with the caravan, but I think once we get to the Central UR everyone will probably be busy doing their own things for a while."

I dip my head down to meet his eyes. "I'd love to meet your parents. And... if it's Amber you're worried about... I can take her." His gaze rises to mine, and I give him a wink, holding my fists up toward my face like a boxer. "Haven't you heard that I have a pretty mean boob-punch?" I strike my fist out and punch him in the chest.

He clasps his hand over the impact area and doubles over. "Oh, ouch," he groans dramatically before laughing and leaning forward to give me a kiss. He then slips his hand inside mine and brings me to his awaiting family and ex almost-wife.

As soon as we're standing in front of them, his free hand immediately goes to his hair, and the eyes of all three women standing in the circle follow the movement — every one of us recognizing the habit intimately. The middle-aged woman's eyes twinkle in amusement — a trait Tobias is apparently accustomed to if the narrowing of his eyes is any indicator. "Mom... behave." She gasps and clasps her hand over her chest. Tobias then introduces us. "Thessaly, this is Mom. Mom, this is Thessaly." Despite the playful nagging between the two of them, Tobias throws his arms around her shoulders and tucks her into his side.

Mom grins, turning her attention to me. Although Tobias has all his dad's height, he definitely has his mother's smile. She reaches her hand out in greeting, and I accept. "It's nice to meet you, Thessaly. You can call me Mom or Tonya." She then reaches for my left hand and looks down at... my knuckles? Whatever she's looking for, she doesn't find, and she shoots a glare up at Tobias. Tobias throws his head back, mumbling something toward the ceiling.

Tonya then pats my hand, wiggles her way out of Tobias's side-hug, and steps forward to pull me into a hug of her own. "Thank you for making my son happy," she whispers in my ear. I wrap my arms around her and whisper back, "Thank you for raising such an amazing man."

She steps away, beaming proudly.

Tobias's dad steps forward and takes my hand, leaning down and placing a kiss on my knuckles. "Nice to meet you, Thessaly. I'm Frank."

Tonya says, "That's where Tobias learned how to properly treat women. My husband definitely gets credit there."

I nearly choke in an attempt not to laugh at the turn my mind took regarding how Tobias "properly treats women." I very seriously doubt Tonya and Frank have any idea…

Tobias presses his lips together to hide the smile forming on his own face at my almost reaction.

"Very nice to meet you, Sir." I give him a nod of respect. When I look back up, both he and Tobias have a single eyebrow raised.

What—

Ohhh…

"Um… it's a Southern thing. Ma'am… Sir… you know, things of that sort." My cheeks blaze hot. The smile Tobias had been trying to cover up appears after all.

Frank lets go of my hand and steps back.

My eyes land on Amber whose face is blanched, her expression not nearly as amused as Tobias's and mine. The smiles on both Tobias and my faces drop in an instant.

Amber had been with Tobias much longer than me; I assume she, too, is well aware of Tobias's preferences, a thought that makes my belly flutter nervously.

Well… this is certainly not the best approach to an introduction. Tobias swallows hard, but follows through nonetheless. Instead of introducing her to me, he takes the opposite approach, introducing me to her. "Thessaly, I would love for you to meet Amber." In my mind I pretend to fill in what he might say next were she not listening: *She's crazy as hell, but I care about her.*

I extend my hand, but Amber chooses not to accept the greeting. She does respond though. "Thank you for everything you've done for the Underground

358

Resistances," she says. "I've heard a lot about you and your... harem... of guys."

Tobias's eyebrows flatten, and those flutters in my stomach drop like lead.

When Tobias opens his mouth and raises a finger to respond to her, Tonya speaks up instead. "Everyone in the UR knows about your Reverse Genus," she explains, shooting Amber a side-glare. "Quite an intriguing scientific discovery." Tobias blinks down at his mother, a smile of thanks relaxing his features. She flashes him a grin. "He might've gotten his manners from Frank, but he most definitely got his love of science from me."

Amber doesn't say another word, and I don't bother to offer any extended greeting measures. She played out the scenario the way she saw fitting, and I quite honestly don't have the energy to counter.

"Well, I know we all have a bit of situating to do before we can leave," Tonya states. "Again, it was nice meeting you, and I hope we'll all be able to get together on occasion." She gives me one more hug and pats Tobias on the bicep. Frank gives me a friendly smile and hugs his son.

From there, Tobias wraps his arms around me and we break away without another glance back.

"You should've boob-punched her after all," he states, rolling his eyes. "Sorry about that. I really had higher expectations. Should've known better."

"You know... I can't say I would've acted any better if I were in her shoes. She lost a damn good catch."

Tobias answers with a kiss to the top of my head as we approach the guys. Thankfully, we still have Betty to bring back to the Central UR, so there won't be any random caravan passengers for us.

For safety's sake, we leave as soon as possible and plan to travel straight through. With the number of people joining the caravan, there are enough drivers to alternate sleeping and driving. But considering there's a possibility that danger may still lurk on the roads, and the fact that the trip is roughly twenty hours long, we're quite careful to stay on the safe routes from the map Roux had provided.

Of course, in the end, it takes closer to a full twenty-four hours with stops and the occasional need to reroute. However, we don't run into any problems and that speaks volumes about the progress the URs must've made during the attacks. Either that or the remaining opposition is too busy recovering to be worried about the roads.

Whichever the case may be, we'll gladly take it.

Rather than being exhausted upon arrival, the lot of us are wired with excitement. Everyone piles out of the vehicles, several looking around the motel's parking lot in confusion. It doesn't help that at least a quarter of the cottages are burnt to a crisp.

When we were about ten minutes away, I paged the Central UR with the pager I had again exchanged with Eastern Tech. Because of the head's up, not too long after we arrive Robbie and Kait open the office door to greet everyone. The "open" sign clangs against the glass, and the faint sound of the dinging bell brings with it a flood of memories.

With a deep, cleansing inhale and exhale, I rush up to Kait and wrap her in a tight hug. After several seconds, she leans back and her bright-blue eyes meet mine. "Girl! I fucked up one of those cats in the facility. You shoulda seen me slingin' and slayin'! Think I found my callin'!" There's a nasty red gouge across the side of her face, threatening to reopen with the lifting of her cheeks as she gives me a huge, dimpled smile.

My hand comes to my mouth, and I cover the mix between a gasp and a giggle. Maybe even a choke and a wail too. It's hard to tell with so many reactions competing at once.

Robbie's exasperated voice breaks the buzz between Kait and me. "Ya've created a damn monster," he says. Poor guy was probably borderline stroke or heart attack the entire time she was gone. "She didn't kill anybody," he sighs. "Don't let her trick you into believing that."

"Kicked him in the jewels though!" Kait exclaims. "Then he conceded, all hunched over, bowin' at my feet, as he should."

This time I don't try to hide my laughter. "Way to go, Sweets!"

"Hell yes!" she responds.

Robbie presses his lips together, unamused. "Thank goodness you're back." Robbie rolls his eyes, but throws me a wink to counter his apathy.

"Aww, ya like it." She nudges him in the gut.

Robbie groans. "There are a couple people here, eager to see you safe and well," he says, trying hard to ignore this keyed-up version of Kait. However, he fails as Kait whispers, likely something raunchy, in his ear. His lips lift, once more betraying his indifference to her behavior, and he ends the conversation with a distracted, "I've got something to take care of…"

With that, he and Kait step behind the desk to let everyone pass through the door in the back of his office that leads to the safety room which, in turn, leads to the UR's entrance.

As soon as we're all past the moving wall, the rest of the caravan moves into the Underground in search of their friends and family. A couple leaders intercept the family members that had joined us and offer to show them around and assign them a place to stay, which they gladly accept.

Two familiar faces are waiting near the entrance, leaning up against the stone wall. Celeste and Auden. Hair still in a high ponytail and still wearing the UR-issued top, Celeste gives me a tentative smile. "Hey," she says... to no one in particular.

"Hey," Jax and I say at the same time.

"I... uh... just wanted ta tell Thessaly thank ya for trusting me ta head a team. We weren't tha best out there, and we were tha first ta be sent back, but we still helped, and that's what matters. Learned a bit about myself... in tha process." She then tilts her head at me in acknowledgment, her long ponytail moving forward over her shoulder.

Her eyes focus on Jax this time. "How... how are ya feelin'?" she asks.

Jax had been a bit tense, his hand finding mine as soon as she had addressed me. But at the question, he loosens up a bit. "Never better," he responds. Her eyes flicker with acknowledgment, then she gives him a genuine smile. A smile that, for once, isn't filled with want, longing, or jealousy.

She doesn't linger, doesn't make it weird. She smiles again and looks at Auden, figuratively passing the mic to him before heading off to do... whatever it — or who — she does down here.

"Wow... you look..." Auden starts. "You look great, considering everything I'm sure you've been through since we spoke last." Leave it to him to make things awkward.

Beside me, Julian lets out a low chuckle, amused with how Auden is clearly not a natural at... compliments? If that can be considered one.

Auden darts glances among the five of us. "So," he says, "that practicing we did? Worked. But it was always a strange mix of emotions the entire time. Both things." He exaggerates the word *both*. Meaning sexually driven emotions and fear.

With the guys trying to calm my haywire empath pot while we were dealing with the host system, it's no wonder he felt those emotions. "Well, I know you had to go a roundabout way to send help, but your efforts worked. Tobias was able to get to us just in time to help diffuse a scary situation." I give Auden a reassuring smile. "With more time and practice, I'm sure you'll refine the ability."

"Does that mean you're sticking around?" he responds quickly, almost before I can finish the statement.

"Right now, we're going to collect more of our things, and then we're leaving for a while. Just long enough to recover a bit — a vacation, I guess you could say. We don't plan to stay gone indefinitely though. Before long, we'll want to help at one of the URs or facilities."

Auden gives me an understanding — albeit disappointed — smile. "Oh!" he adds, changing the subject, "Ruby is elbow-deep in feeding all the returned Combat teams and new members, but she wants Tobias to know she's safe and well because 'he'd be worried about her.' That, and he still owes her a dinner date, apparently."

363

Tobias laughs. "Update received. I'll go pop my head in there and say hey. Not sure we'll be able to swing the dinner date before leaving though."

"I'm sure she'll at least appreciate seeing you," Auden responds. And with that he takes a deep breath and slightly widens his eyes. "Welp," he says, popping his lips together with the P. "Glad you all are safe and everything seems to be in or—"

Before he can finish the statement, I sling my arms around him and hug him tight. "Thank you… seriously. If… if Tobias hadn't gotten there, I… I'm not sure the outcome would have been good."

At first, he opens his arms and awkwardly pats my upper back, but when I don't let him go right away, he engages in the hug, wrapping me up in his arms and squeezing back equally as tight. Then… his nose comes to the hair that's bunched over my shoulder. I loosen my hold a bit and whisper, "Are you… smelling me?"

Auden clears his throat and quickly steps away, eyes falling to the ground and cheeks blossoming a healthy shade of pink. "I… uh… mmm."

Tobias laughs and claps him on the shoulder. "Yeah, she makes us stupid too… Don't take it personally."

I press my lips together and leer at him.

"Anyway, *ahem*," Auden clears the squeak in his throat. "You're welcome, and… I guess I'll see you when you're back from… vacation," he says, backing away slowly before turning around completely.

"Yep! See you later." I wave at his now retreating back.

When my attention returns to the guys, they give me a combination of head shakes and chuckles.

"Thirsty," Jax whispers, giving my butt a good swat.

The five of us finally attempt to progress deeper into the Underground, but the crowds are thick — even more so than usual. Similar to the Eastern UR, many of the Combat teams must've arrived not too long before we did. Several still walk in and out of the Oracle Room, dressed in their UR-issued uniforms. Based on the traffic, I would guess that they opened up the Oracle Room for overflow Medical care.

To take stock of the damage, we all head there first. Ahead, I spot Dr. Hughes near the bar area, doctoring up a wounded member. My eyes scan the room, my mind and heart intuitively looking for the one vital member of the Resistance that wasn't at the entrance to greet us. Instead of finding my mark, however, my eyes land on the next best things — or, rather, people. Both Bauer and Becky approach.

I throw my arm around Bauer's shoulder and squeeze him against me, stepping beside Becky who is holding Leta, per the usual as of late. "Rumor has it, some kid converted a crap ton of guards prior to the Central UR showing up at their facility." News had spread like wildfire, going as far as reaching the Eastern UR before we'd left.

"Yeah, a lot of guards don't want to be there; most were just putting up a good front," he explains. "After I talked to a few, news of an internal coup started to spread, though, and before long most of the guards were on our side."

Bauer grew up fast throughout the experience, that much is evident. Environment has a way of doing that sometimes. "We never got a transmission from your lens after the interrogation. I… I'm just glad you're okay. All the rest is an added bonus."

Leta coos, drawing everyone's attention. Her round doe-like eyes — golden brown, very much like Roux's in so many ways — take in everything around her.

Thankfully, when she sees my face, she doesn't immediately break into tears. Instead, she simply scrutinizes the group of us, fist in her mouth, until her gaze falls on Tobias, and her little legs and feet rev up like she's in the running to win a race. Tobias chuckles and bends down to her level, bopping her on the nose.

Smiling from ear to ear, my eyes leave Leta and drift up to Becky. Just under those cute barrel-curled bangs, her tired and aging eyes are red and glossy. As soon as our gazes meet, her lips quiver and those red and glossy eyes well with tears.

The smile on my face drops in an instant.

Words get stuck in my throat like a boulder blocking the maw of a cave.

My head shakes side to side in a disbelief of its own.

With every heartbeat, a piece shatters and crumbles into a fine, sand-like consistency.

"No one could find him," Becky's voice trembles. "They looked everywhere."

Several warm and steady hands and arms encase me as I collapse to the cool stone floor.

"They brought Search and Rescue in… They… they did everything they could," Bauer explains, but I scarcely make out the words as all the din around me morphs into hums of vibration.

When Roux had shut off his empath connection from me after that brief allowance during the last feed, I hadn't felt him since. Not an inkling.

I knew this would be the outcome… we all did. But it didn't stop us from hoping. Didn't stop me from envisioning an end to this madness that included Roux celebrating by our side.

The sensation of someone picking me up and holding me against them only slightly warms and stills the unbearable chill shaking my body.

Through the blur and burn of salty tears, I catch one last glance at his legacy as I'm carried out of the Oracle Room.

But he's not there.

Roux's not there with his daughter, holding her in his arms like he should be.

He's not here at all.

CHAPTER THIRTY-FIVE

When they ask if I want ta drive through my hometown on the way back ta Florida, I do give it some serious consideration. But, everythin' I could ever want or need is already in this car.

Family. There had been so many times durin' my childhood when I'd wondered what it would be like ta have one. While I may not have blood relations to Thessaly and the guys — thank god, because that'd be weird as fuck — they have since become all the family I'd ever need. They're so much more than the definition of what I'd always imagined family should be too. The five of us together have, in a way, taken tha concept of family and made it our own. Better. Stronger. More dependable.

Everythin' worth fightin' for. I'm damn happy as fuck to have 'em in my life, and proud as hell that I made the cut. "Nah, just keep on drivin'. My home is wherever we're together — even if we end up havin' ta set up shop here in Betty." Thessaly smiles and leans her head on my shoulder.

"Good thing we won't have to do that," Bram states.

After discussing our options, Bram's place seemed tha most fittin'. Mine was just a small, rented out apartment in a questionable area. Julian lived with his parents. Tobias had signed the deed of his house over to Amber. Bram's was the only place 100 percent owned by him. From what I remember, it was much too small for a family of five ta live in, but like hell if I'm gonna complain. The fact it doesn't even have a bedroom, though, should be entertainin'.

"I've always loved Bram's studio. Definitely marks one of my — if not *the* — most favorite places." Her and Bram's eyes meet in the rearview mirror, and they share a smile. Thessaly's smile drops a bit, and that bottom lip snags behind her teeth. Bram raises an eyebrow at her and her lip pops free. "I was just trying to picture how we're all going to fit in there. The idea I had... well... I'm thinking you won't like it."

She'd hardly spoken a word since receivin' news about Roux. Every time one of us tried ta speak with her, a new set of tears would spill. Her heartbreak was raw, and we all felt it in one way or another through our bonds.

Ta hear her finally speak instantly lightens tha mood, and Bram is more than willin' to keep her talkin' no matter the topic. "Try me." He shrugs.

She takes in a deep breath and lets it out first. "Your conservatory? I was thinking maybe we could enclose the top... turn it into a bedroom?" She grimaces and I dart a glance at the rearview mirror. I'd be surprised as shit if Bram had it in him ta turn her idea down. I don't know much about this 'conservatory' though. In fact, I don't even remember seein' what she's talkin' about. Then again, when I was there it was just long enough to drug her and get her out.

Bram takes his time ta answer. A character trait that he's always had... and that has always seemed to set Thessaly on edge. She waits as patiently as possible though. "We'll see," is his eventual response. She gives him a nod of understandin' but decides to end the conversation there for now.

We'd been in long-travel situations enough times now that tha time passes quicker than it seemed ta in the beginnin'. Sleep is the number one way we prefer ta pass the time. And, thankfully, after Robbie's last upgrade, we no longer have to manually charge the car. With the built-in panels and generator, it takes us from point A to point B — even if it's across the nation — with little ta no trouble. The upgrades save us loads of time.

Screwin' with Thessaly is another one of our favorite ways ta pass tha time. Especially when she's in desperate need of a distraction. Tha most ideal situation is usually when Julian and I are sittin' in the back seat together with her. This time, though, Tobias and Julian had made some sort of bet and Tobias lost. So for the past few hours, his six-foot-plus, too-tall body has been scrunched in the back with Thessaly and me. Julian rides shotgun while Bram takes the scenic route and drones on about native versus invasive plants or some shit.

After a particularly long explanation, even Tobias throws his head back against the headrest and rolls his eyes up toward the roof.

But the motion of his head moving again out of my peripheral vision, catches my attention, and I look over Thessaly's head toward him.

Our eyes meet, and half his mouth lifts in a side smirk. A similar look that I'd expect from Julian — or myself — not usually Tobias.

Curious, I raise an eyebrow in question.

His attention casually darts to the rearview mirror, checkin' on Bram I guess, then back to me. Then, his hand slips under the blanket Thessaly's cocooned in and plants itself on her upper thigh — if the new bulge under

370

the material is any indicator. Casually at first, just resting. But bein' the type of guy I am, his intentions crash into my mind right away.

Hot damn; didn't know he had it in him.

Julian and I had managed to make a threesome happen with her, but that was in the confines of a private space. While I'm pretty confident she'd be up for explorin' things beyond that, I know for certain Bram is not down. While he has agreed to this group thing we have goin', he's made it explicitly clear that anyone doin' anythin' sexual to Thessaly, while he's around or involved with her, isn't really his kink.

Just as casually, I bring my hand to the top of her shoulder and slip the neck of her loose t-shirt down just enough to be able to drag my fingers along her soft skin.

That's enough of an answer for Tobias, and the two of us go ta work, seein' just how much we can get away with under tha watchful — yet presently distracted — eye of her best-friend-turned-lover.

I'd been cursin' tha damn cold weather since we had to leave the comfort of the south, but… gotta admit the fact she's covered in a blanket because of that same weather — no matter if the heat is cranked high in Betty — is goin' ta take Tobias and me much farther on our journey.

And the way Thessaly's body changes from relaxed to tense tells me Tobias is already takin' that route.

I tilt my head down toward her face and watch as she lifts a bit and her gaze travels to the rearview mirror.

Tobias bends down toward her ear and whispers, "Be still, and he'll never know."

She swallows hard and rests her head on my shoulder again.

Tobias's head falls back against the headrest again, all nonchalant like… as if his fingers aren't deep in her sweatpants right now, strummin' her slowly no doubt.

My own fingers trail over her shoulder and up the side of her neck. She melts into our touches, scootin' her ass over a little, unable to stay completely still as Tobias had suggested. He clears his throat, and her impatient movements stop.

Since Tobias and I hadn't worked together like this before, I'm not quick ta figure out what's goin' on. But when she scoots back over toward me, I figure he's reprimandin' her for not being still… by removin' his hand entirely.

My assumption is verified when his hand reveals itself, and his index finger comes to his mouth.

I can't help the quiet chuckle. Thessaly's hair moves from the breath, and she tilts her head back to narrow a glare at me. I bring my nose to hers and smile, wrappin' my fingers around the back of her neck and givin' her that head-slightly-tilted look she seems ta love.

Once her head returns ta my shoulder, Tobias's hand returns beneath the blanket.

In a moment, her body turns soft again.

But it's not for long, though, since both Tobias and I are determined to make her tense so tightly it'll be a miracle if she can stay still through to the end.

Tobias has prime positionin' ta work under the radar. And since I'm tha one directly behind Bram, if we stay to our corners, there will be a bit I can do that falls outside of his rearview-mirror vision.

The blanket moves near her lower belly as Tobias works her pants down past her knees. Little time passes before his fingers move back up to their target.

Knowin' he's touchin' her again — in just tha right spot — I adjust a little so that I'm somewhat on my right hip with my back against the corner between the window and the seat. In this position, she can no longer use me as support, so she has ta adjust and sit up a little straighter. Tobias doesn't stop this time, though, knowin' that it was my fault for her movements.

I slide my hand under the blanket, wrap my fingers over her thigh and spread her open, encouragin' her ta rest her bent knee at an angle toward me. This, in turn, scrunches her pants all the way down to her ankles. Since Tobias made tha first play, and since we'd never tag-teamed together before, I make the decision ta let him follow through with takin' her all the way. As much as I want to coat my own fingers with her juices, guess I'll have ta make good on that desire another time.

Oh, but that doesn't mean I can't make what Tobias does to her even better… in other ways. My hand trails up her thigh until I'm near the crease and I squeeze her inner thigh at about the time Tobias must be dippin' in a finger. Based on her slight jump, I'd wager a guess that we'd timed the activities just right.

However, this is just enough ta draw Julian's attention through their bond, and his ability to feel her when she's turned on.

He's smart enough, though, to not jerk around in surprise. Instead, his head turns to casually check on us. I give him a wink, and he mumbles some Italian under his breath, readjustin' his attention to the road ahead. It makes Thessaly giggle, which in turn, has Bram adjustin' the rearview mirror so that he can see her face. *Dammit.*

She does good, though, keepin' a stoic expression, considerin' she's usually pretty terrible at that. Probably because all movement under the blanket had stopped ta help her out a little. Bram darts a look at Julian, just as he adjusts in his seat, tiltin' to the side a bit ta get more comfortable on account of the long car ride.

Or because he's gettin' a boner... which is tha most likely reason.

Bram seems satisfied enough with whatever he was lookin' for and readjusts the mirror, returnin' his attention to the drive. Since he chose to take a bunch of scenic roads, he had ta turn off the auto-drive feature entirely. The decision proves helpful: more for him ta do than worry about what's goin' on in the backseat.

The fact that Tobias has to keep startin' and stoppin' and startin' and stoppin' has my girl pretty sexually frustrated already... but Tobias is patient. That much I do know about him, which is hilarious because Thessaly is most certainly not patient.

Before Tobias continues again, I am quick to slip my hand under the blanket and steal a quick thrust of my own. Fuck all that toyin' around, though, if I only get one chance.

My fingers push from her knee up the inside of her thigh and I dip my middle finger in, give her a little twist, then slip it back out, draggin' it along her clit on exit.

Her chest rises and falls at the motion as a gasp catches there and her body tenses. I'm out fast enough that my hand is clear when Tobias's takes its place. He's not as eager though, knowin' this is a long-ass car ride, and he doesn't intend on lettin' her finish anytime soon.

Gettin' inside her, though, was enough ta make me lose a bit more patience than I'd like to admit. Tobias's hand meets the heat and wetness between her thighs, and mine escapes the blanket. With one hand, I grasp her chin, direct her face toward mine, and brush my lips against hers. It's just enough of a motion that has her lips partin', beggin' ta be kissed right. But I have somethin' else in mind. First, I give her a little test of what she wants, usin' my tongue to tease hers. When she leans in, closin' her eyes, I lift the middle finger I had used and drag it along her bottom lip before fingerin' her mouth with one slow thrust and twist, just exactly as I had done moments ago to her pussy.

As much as I want ta watch, I do have tha sense to dart a glance ahead first. But then she closes her lips around my finger and sucks, wrappin' her tongue around me. Any effort I'd attempted to make sure our activities are still under Bram's radar are thwarted by the suctionin' of her mouth and then the light drag of her teeth.

My eyes dart to hers but hers are still closed, completely lost to the dual pleasure of Tobias's fingers… and mine. I ease my finger from between her lips, slip my hand around the back of her neck, and bring our mouths together. She might be lost, but I'm tryin' hard ta hang on to this thread of sanity. We'd managed the short mouth-fingerin' goin' unnoticed. But intense, hard, and fast kissing will most certainly not go unnoticed. Every time I see the bulge of Tobias's hand under the blanket dip and thrust between her legs, I slip my tongue inside her mouth just enough ta tease.

Assumin' we're in this for the long haul — assumin' we're gonna leave our girl achin' in tha worst way — when I hear her signature thought float into my mind, I realize this is comin' to an end much sooner than expected. She fuckin' loves this. Question is… does Tobias know?

Because right now, Thessaly is throwin' the mental f-bomb like she's about ta explode any second. The only time I get her word-impressions are when the short

375

thought or phrase is repetitive and all-consuming. Like right now as her mental voice pants "Oh fuck" over and over again. I can't drop the smile that creeps up as I kiss her this next time. For as proper as she is with her vocabulary, the fact that I now know her go-to orgasm inner monologue is "Oh fuck" abso-fuckin'-lutely makes my day.

Mind racin', tryin' ta figure out what move ta make ta bring her over tha edge entirely, I run through several different choices before optin' ta move my hand from the back of her neck to the front, wrappin' lightly around her throat and pressin' upward toward her chin. To pair with tha motion, I bring my tongue to her ear and trace the lobe before whisperin' low, "I fuckin' love seein' ya shatter."

While my hand tightens and I dip my tongue back inside her mouth, the "Oh fucks" pile on top of each other in such copious amounts they blend into somethin' more along tha lines of "Omnhhhhhfunncchhhh." Then, in the next moment, the projection is gone. Silent. Her eyes pop open, breaths choppy and hard, as she sinks back into the seat before Tobias removes his hand from the blanket.

CHAPTER THIRTY-SIX

Thessaly

It isn't until Bram turns Betty into a marshy wooded area a few hours later that I stop thinking about what Tobias, Jax, and Julian just did to me. Especially since I was impressed with the way Julian projected all these hot emotions toward me while sitting seemingly innocent in the front seat. I could almost hear him saying something along the lines of "Like hell am I getting left out of this," but in Italian, of course.

Needless to say, it didn't take them long to reach the desired end result.

What's more, it gave my heart a small reprieve from the dull ache that hasn't left me since news of Roux's disappearance. After an entire restless night in the UR agonizing over all the possibilities, I decided to stop dwelling on the worst-case scenarios and start hoping for the best-case ones.

Even if hoping is all it would ever be.

I straighten and peer out of the window. "Where are we?"

"Picking up my truck... if it'll start," Bram explains.

"Oh! I completely forgot we ditched it here when all this started."

"If it doesn't start," Tobias speaks up, "we can move the generator from Betty and connect it to your truck. Then tow Betty behind, and she'll collect the energy with the panels."

We quickly learn that's the case. With a bit of tweaking, it all works out in the end. Everyone piles into Bram's truck, Tobias the most appreciative of the added space.

"Based on that groan and stretch of approval, I'd say you didn't much like being in the backseat with me."

Tobias's side-smirk proves he knows I'm joking, to an extent.

Julian slides into Tobias's past spot, leaving me with the Country-Italian duo.

After a bit of brow waggling and teasing, the excitement is far too high for us to concentrate on anything other than the mile markers as they pass one by one. A different problem we faced written in invisible pen on each, left behind the more forward progress we make.

"You know... I can't help but worry there's something waiting for us right around the next curve," I say. "That's how it's been since this all started. One unexpected twist after another. Just when we think we have a break, we're hit with another problem."

The truck becomes weighted with silence as we all feel every bit of that statement. But then Jax shakes his head. "Nah, Darlin'. Not this time. This time tha only problem around that next corner is who's gonna sleep on Bram's futon with ya tonight."

"Me. Problem solved," Bram says. "In fact, I think a supply run will be in order shortly after arriving too. I've got three friends I know for a fact are up for the task." Bram's attention moves around the cab, meeting the eyes of said three friends.

Julian grins. "See, *cuore mio*? No problems. I've got dinner covered tonight. Not sure where we're going to find supplies, but such is life right now, hm?"

Bram's gaze meets mine in the rearview mirror and he smiles — a real, relaxed smile filled with a calm reassurance for the near future. The smile also swims with something just on the other side of friendly — a hop, skip, and jump over that fine line between friends and lovers.

I've seen this in movies and books, old and new... this is our happily ever after. All five of us. Flip the page, and in big, bold letters it'll say "The End."

But it's so far from the end.

We all share glances, feeling the significance of what's yet to come — the rebuilding and the restructuring of life in the wake of what's left of the nation.

But for now, it's time to embrace the calm before the next storm. To hold on tight to each other and appreciate everything we've accomplished as a unit. But, most importantly, to work together and with everyone we've met along the way in order to ensure life as we want it is preserved for future generations.

THE END

ABOUT THE AUTHOR

Adell Ryan is a hubby/wife pseudonym. Adell writes unconventional love stories about fierce women and their numerous male suitors. Because let's be honest, we need more than one to satisfy our multi-dimensional needs. Right? Ryan simply puts up with Adell's crazy fantasies and toots her horn regularly. Occasionally he'll add in a shoulder pat, and a deep, sexy "Damn that's good stuff."

That southern boy (bless him) stole this northern girl's heart and they live together in the deep south, raising their three boys. When Adell isn't writing she's homeschooling — primarily working on dictation, making sure they say 'creek' instead of 'crick' and 'fire' instead of 'fer.' She also dabbles in photography and graphic design. Oh yeah, and reading. Every. Night. Much to Ryan's dismay. Sometimes she puts the steamy stuff down and gives him a quick kiss on the forehead though.

To be the *first* to know about new releases and exclusive behind-the-scenes stuff, join the fun in her FB Group: facebook.com/groups/authoradellryan/

You can also check out her website at https://www.adellryan.com and sign-up for her newsletter.

Still not enough? Find her at the listed social media platforms as well!:

| Goodreads | Instagram | Pinterest |
| BookBub | Twitter | Tumblr |

Made in the USA
Monee, IL
04 November 2020

46641563R00213